Dragon Noir

Underhill

Cedar Sanderson

DEDICATED TO:

My children, the kintsugi of my life.

Chapter 1

The End in the Beginning

I blew open the doors of the Great Hall with a resounding crash. It matched my mood, hearing the splintering wood. My hands were too full to have gestured a more subtle spell of opening, and my brain was too full of anger to think through the education I was giving to the gathered High Court. This was one way to announce I'd recovered my magic. At that moment, the audience didn't exist for me, fading into the background as I marched toward the two people I was there to see. My burden made my arms ache, but pain was good, purifying my resolve and anger.

Physical pain kept me from dwelling on the mental pain, from thinking about what I was carrying. I kept walking, on foot in front of the other. This morning had been the bright start of a new life, and now I was about to make an ending.

An ending had already been made for what I carried, and a mere hour ago I had learned of this. It had begun innocuously enough. Bella was going to be in Court for the day, meeting with the Council in part to report what had happened when we visited Eastern Court, and in part to begin the preparations for her coronation. Corwin was anxious to get that over with, and her officially working. I was left at home, anticipating a day in the armory, but first I needed to see a few people. Being able to travel on my own was only one of many things I was enjoying for the first time, but damn, it felt good.

Ever since I'd lost most of my magic to the elf shot, I'd operated carefully, never using much, or paying for it later. Underhill, this made me a cripple, an object of pity, and in the human world it made me slightly more than human. With the carelessness for my own life I'd operated under for most of two centuries, this had formed me into what I was when I went to collect Bella. She'd softened me, and ultimately, healed me.

She'd also addled my brain. I was standing in my library, hands on hips, laughing a little to myself as I gathered a bubble to go see Devon in Elleria when there was a ringing knock at the door. I didn't even open my Sight to see who was there, I just went and opened it. Dangerous, stupid thing to do. Sure, I have warts around the place, and in theory ill-wishers would trip it, while those who have been given pass-keys can pass through. It's still a good idea to look first before you swing open that last barrier of the door between you and your potential foe.

There was no one there. I stood looking out over the tangled gardens of my lodge, the home I'd carved from a forgotten pocket of wilderness Underhill, and where for so many years I'd lived virtually alone. Absently, It crossed my mind that Bella might like to clean up the garden. This all happened in a second, looking out, a fleeting thought... and then I looked down.

My sister lay at my feet. Pale, composed, and I knew even before I dropped to my knees that she was dead. I didn't touch her, I closed my eyes and wrenched open my Sight as wide as it would go. Nothing. Other than the green glow of Ellie, somewhere over my left shoulder in the vicinity of the kitchen, there was no other living being anywhere around. I focused that internal blind sight on my sister's body. Traces of magic still lingered, like the last sparks rising from a dying campfire. The aura she'd had in life was gone, extinguished as surely as a bucket of water hitting that campfire. What remained visible was not Margot, it was remnants of whatever had killed her. Inhuman, magical, and of this world, not the one above. Which meant nothing. I had no enemies in the human realm. All my enemies were here in the enchanted world of Faerie, which I had indulgently managed to forget how lethal it could be, in my distraction with my new bride and elevation in social status.

I opened my eyes reluctantly. Using the Sight came with a price, and my renewed power was not enough to escape that. But if my head hurt, my heart hurt more. Margot and I had not been close as children. She was older than I, old enough to be considered an adult when I was old enough to be aware of her. And for years I had held a grudge against her, and my mother, because of how my apprenticeship had begun and ended.

That didn't matter, now. We'd made up, as adults, discovering the shared likenesses that might have been blood relationship, or simply the ways we were molded by the world around us and our shared mother. My father had died while I was still a boy. Margot, I'd discovered, had hidden a keen mind under the airy ways of Court and hedonistic whirl that society kept.

That mind had most likely led her to this. If she were to have been killed as a direct message to me that would have happened long ago. Her delivery to my doorstep, when all of Court still believed me a non-magical, pitiable cripple, meant something else entirely. I turned my head and pitched my voice low, with a ripple of magic to carry it beyond the limits of sound.

"Ellie. I need you."

It did me no good to see the wood elf lose her composure as she neared the door and saw Margot at my feet. She pushed a fisted hand to her mouth, turning a little green in the complexion.

"What happened?" She managed after a moment, keeping her gorge down with a visible effort.

"I don't know. I am going to find out, but I need you to call Ash, and any others you think necessary, to protect the house. Alert my mother, and Devon, to come here, but don't tell them..." I looked down at my sister's body, at the gaping, bloodless wounds. Someone had cleaned her carefully.

I went on talking, urgency kept me from dwelling on the details. "Tell them I will be back soon."

"Where are you going?" She was wide-eyed, and as pale as I'd ever seen her.

"To find out who did this."

I dropped into a squat, pushing my hands under Margot's limp body, then with an involuntary grunt, I stood up, trying not to notice how her head fell to one side loosely. As soon as I was braced, I snapped a bubble around us and transported my macabre burden to Court.

I had landed just outside the Great Hall, and had gone through the massive wood doors as though they were paper without even a passing thought for the mess. The objects of my attention were in front of me, standing with their eyes on my sister's pale corpse. Around me, I was dimly aware that there was shouting and a shrill scream. But I only had eyes for my wife.

"Bella."

She was pale, but composed, her eyes locked onto mine as she started toward me. In my peripheral vision, I could see that I had picked up an honor guard, of sorts. Men in uniform were moving quickly into position around me, not looking at me, but the crowd which seemed to be having a collective breakdown. I could see King Trytion standing on the dais behind Bella, making hand motions, no doubt giving them silent guidance. I was no threat to him, that he knew of.

"Lom... what happened?" She held out her hands and I felt Margot's weight lift. Bella was supporting her, magically, and I wondered why it hadn't occurred to me to do that. Some errant sense of duty, I thought dully, looking at my sister's cloudy eyes.

"I don't know. I came to you to see if you could tell me. Or," I looked over her shoulder at the king, who was coming nearer. "If he could tell us, since this is likely related to the work she was doing for the Crown."

He flinched a little at my words, but his blue eyes were unwavering. "Yes, it is. Lom..."

Bella closed her eyes, and drew herself very upright. I knew what she was doing. My wife was far stronger than I was, and I was probably the strongest man, magically, in this room. I couldn't hold a candle to her, and she had a tool beyond her full understanding at her disposal, Alger's Library. I stopped talking. Margot hovered between us, flickers of visible energy tracing over her, licking at the edges of her wounds. I could see details I hadn't seen before, like how clean her clothing was, and how unlike Margot that long archaic dress was. From the way the magical light was acting, there were unseen wounds under it, too.

I could feel my rage building, and I clenched my fists, not wanting to disturb Bella. If there were others in the room besides the King, Bella, and I, I was beyond being aware of them. I trusted Joe, the majordomo and my friend, to keep them away from us. I met Corwin's eyes. As King Trytion, he had to remain objective, above the emotions that he could feel as the man named Corwin. But now, I could see the sorrow in his eyes, the tears that would not fall. He could no more cry for her than I could.

I would avenge her. He would have to remain here, in safety. For that, I could almost pity him. Bella opened her eyes, and the fey light died away.

"I don't know where she died, Lom, but I would know her killer if I saw it."

"It?" I parroted, a little disappointed that I wouldn't have a location to begin with. She nodded, and swayed a little, raising a hand... not to her forehead, but her belly.

"I don't feel well." She gasped. Corwin caught her from behind as she sagged. "It's ok... I'm not going to faint."

He must not have believed her, as he didn't let go. He looked at me. "Lom." His voice was gentle. "Will you allow Joe to take over with Margot? I think we need privacy, and a healer."

Which meant Melcar, and he would want to examine Margot's body, and there were some things even I could not stomach. I nodded, feeling everything drain out of me at once. Bella regained her footing and came around the floating body. I felt her arms around me, and held her close, burying my face in her hair. I'd like to think this was a bad dream and I'd open my eyes to our dark bedroom and warm sheets, but I knew better. Margot had been savagely murdered, and I still had to tell my mother.

Bella was shaking. I opened my eyes, reluctantly, to see Joe draping a white silk shroud over my sister's body. I was shocked when he looked up, and I could see the tears streaming down his cheeks.

"Joe?" I didn't know what to say.

He shook his head, unspeaking, and made a gesture. I looked toward the ruined doors – I had made a mess – and saw Melcar hurrying toward us, the leaves in his hair rustling audibly. Wood elves wear their tree's leaves to remind them when they must return to the tree for renewal, and Melcar's time was coming soon. He was, however, the most powerful healer in the kingdom, and the only one who had ever added human medical training to his repertoire. I trusted him with my life. Literally, and several times over. He looked from me, to Margot's shrouded body, and then to Bella, who was leaning heavily on me.

"Bella." He'd made a decision that quickly, which one of us needed him most. "Can you walk, my dear?"

She nodded, and tried to stand upright. I supported her, feeling a sudden pang of alarm. Bella was the independent type, and had seen death – had dealt death at my side, with a laugh – many times. What was wrong? Well, yes, her new sister-in-law was dead, but she had faced down an angry goddess and stolen away her pet dragon. Bella was no shrinking violet. Something else was going on.

We followed Melcar toward the smaller room behind the Great Hall, where I had so often met the king for mission briefings in the century I'd been working for him. I didn't look back at Margot's body. Joe, who had never let on how he'd felt about her, was standing guard now. Melcar got Bella settled on the couch, and cupped his hands over her belly.

"Nothing is badly wrong," he told her. "It is simply your body reacting to the sudden stress." Melcar twisted around and glared at me. "Would it be too much to ask you to control your temper? There was no need for this."

I looked down at him, tamping down my sudden wave of anger. I really hadn't lost my temper. This had been very much in aid of something, whether he understood it yet, or not. The appearance of rage in their midst had been a message to the Court. I would find whoever had done this, and they would pay.

"There was need." I told him simply. "What is wrong with Bella?"

"There's nothing *wrong* with her. She's pregnant."

I felt my mouth drop open as it hit me like a punch in the gut. "Bella?"

She looked like I felt. "I'm *what*?"

Melcar looked faintly smug. "I'd call it about two months gone, m'lady. Oh, and..."

He took my hand and dragged me toward my wife, bringing my palm gently down over her belly. "Look. Look with *an dan shealladh* and see."

I dropped to my knees and closed my eyes. Below the shimmering veil of Bella's magic, I could see two... two? Tiny pearls of light. I opened my eyes and looked into hers.

"Dear one," she said, her lower lip trembling a little. I folded her into my arms and held on tight. Death, into life, and the cycle unending was bittersweet today.

Chapter 2

Leavetaking

I left Bella with Melcar, reluctantly. But I needed to get home to Mother and Devon, it was my solemn duty to tell them the news, not to leave that to others. Melcar insisted that Bella was fine, just overstressed, and she should rest if she could, while Corwin cleaned up after me. I didn't give a damn about the mess. I'd sent my message, and the Court would remember it.

There was also a sense of urgency, folded up around that paper Bella had given me as I kissed her before bubbling out of the receiving room. She'd magically created an image, a *sense* of the thing that had killed my sister, and imprinted it on the sheet like some kind of macabre magical police sketch. I now knew what she meant about *it*, not he nor she, this wasn't a human or Fae. As the moment of time in transit passed, I looked at the picture, then folded it back into my pocket. Mother didn't need to see this. I'd be happier if she didn't see Margot's body, in the condition it was, but I knew she'd insist. She was a tough old broad.

"Lom..." She came to greet me, her deep purple skirts rustling, her face pale. She knew it was bad.

"Mother, I'm sorry." I kissed her cheek, feeling the papery skin that reminded me how old she was. Even Fae grow old, and die. It just takes us a hell of a lot longer than humans. Usually. Unless someone cuts us off short.

I turned to my nephew and put a hand on his shoulder. "Devon."

He paled, looking in my eyes. "Is it Bella? Dorothy?"

We had left his girlfriend Above, learning to fly tiny airplanes without the support of magic. She was fine, so far as I knew, enjoying the hell out of it, and it was a good thing for her. I shook my head.

"I'm sorry, kid. Your mother..."

I felt a lump in my throat. I'd never had any children of my own. Never even had the chance, before Bella, and Devon was the closest thing before those two pearls I had just seen. "Margot is gone."

It was a pale euphemism, but I wanted to shield them a little. I know I can be a rough man, and these two were products of a society I'd spurned long ago. Soft. Not that that's all bad. I didn't see the need to roughen their edges any more than I was forced to.

Lucia sat down, hard, in the nearest chair. I felt Devon's knees buckle through my grip on his shoulder, but he didn't go down. Blindly, he groped for a chair.

"Gone?" my mother's voice was thready, almost inaudible. "What do you mean?"

"She's dead. Someone delivered her to my doorstep this morning, but I'd say it happened at least yesterday." I didn't add that I knew of preserving spells that could keep a corpse fresh as a lily for... a very long time. The human tale of Snow White had a sick basis in reality.

Lucia leaned back, closing her eyes. She had no color at all in her face except the pale rose of blush powder on her cheekbones. I knelt at my mother's feet and took her hands in mine.

"I will find who did this, and why."

Devon gasped a little. "I want to come with you." He was crying, silently, the tears rolling from beautiful eyes that were so much like his mother's had been.

I shook my head at him. "I need you here." I wasn't going to tell him that he'd be useless to me in this state. "I need you to look after your grandmother, and Bella."

"Bella?" Lucia opened her eyes and looked at me, her worry plainly visible over the shock. She was not crying, and I didn't expect to ever see her do so, not in public.

"Bella is not coming with me. Bella is expecting our children, and must be protected."

Lucia nodded. She was still in shock, but that wouldn't stop her. I had vague memories of her after my father's death, moving around the vast mansion like a martinet, making sure everything was as it should be. It had been left to the weird Banshee to comfort me, the wee child who climbed into that fearsome creature's lap and begged her not to wail so. I'd tried with all my toddler might to make that sad creature smile, and mother had been like ice while the Banshee coddled me that strange night.

Now, I needed that icy calm. I had to trust her with Bella, and our children, while I went out after those who would do my family harm. Margot's death had been a warning, a message, and that was all I knew, so far. I didn't know what the full text of that message was, and I had to find out, quickly, before the unseen enemy resorted to more artistic media of passing a warning along.

Lucia drew herself up. I watched as she shoved her pain into some little mental box, and pushed it onto a shelf alongside the one labeled with my father's name in some cobwebby part of her mind. It was an almost visible process, one I had used myself to keep going under great duress.

"She is at Court?" my mother asked about my wife, now.

"She was being watched by Melcar, but told me she would come home as soon as she could."

Lucia nodded. "I will return here, then, but I must go to Elleria and make arrangements, inform the staff..." She took a deep breath.

"No banshee, mother. Not here."

She looked at me oddly. I wondered if she knew about that night so long ago. Family tradition dictated that the death of a Mulvaney was always accompanied by the dree wailing of the Bane...

"Lom, there are no more banshee."

I stood up, tucking that bit of information away. Why had she sounded as though I should know this?

"People will be arriving here soon. Devon..." I turned to him. He was leaning back in the deep armchair, tears drying on his cheeks. Now he opened his eyes and looked at me.

"Do I have to do anything? I don't know what to do." He looked and sounded much younger, suddenly, sliding backward from the young man he'd been only an hour before, to a child bereft.

"Come with me, and we'll talk."

He stood up, and followed me wordlessly. I knew him well enough to know that the best thing right now was to keep him busy, and not let him have time to brood on his loss. He followed me down the narrow steps to my armory, buried deep beneath the house, and stayed cautiously behind me as I unlocked the door. The layers of defenses on my private place were well known to be unpleasant, or if tried too far, lethal. Never mind that it had been decades since anything had tried hard enough to actually get themselves fried, all it took was one smoking goblin corpse to persuade certain factions to leave me the hell alone.

Devon had likely never tried any of the protections. He was a most obedient child, and one who had from an early age held me in some awe. I hadn't dissuaded him of that, being the black sheep uncle held much attraction, and I didn't need Margot killing me should Dev follow me into trouble. I swallowed at the memory of my sister's temper and swung open the heavy door.

12

"You know how to use a pistol, I taught you that much." I walked toward the workbench, seeing in my peripheral vision that he was rubbernecking at the shelves of weapons all around us. Good. He was going to be distractible from his grief.

"Yeah." He stood and looked around while I took my time finding his weapon. I knew exactly what I was going to hand him, but I had to admit the armory was worth looking at. More than a century of trophies here, weaponry both mundane and magical. It wasn't laid out fancy, very few people had ever been down here. But what had started as a handful of things had grown to be near enough kit for a small invading force.

I piled things on the bench. "Come here. Holster, semi-auto 9mm, ammo, more ammo, magazines..."

He was awkward with the shoulder rig I was giving him, and I made him put it on, take it off, and repeat until he was comfortable with that process. Only then did I hand him the pistol. He started to holster it, and I raised a finger.

"Ah!"

Devon froze and looked at me. "What?"

"Did you check?"

"Oh... sorry." He pulled it carefully and checked that it was unloaded and only then did I hand him a magazine, which was full.

"Look, I know I'm being a hardass." He started to shake his head, and I stopped him. "Yeah, I am, you just lost your mother and I'm treating you like a green recruit. I have good reason. Whatever got your mother is likely to come after your grandmother, and possibly Bella."

He gulped, and lost some of the color he'd regained in his face during my lesson. "That's why I have a gun."

"Yeah. And I hope you don't have to use it. But this is Underhill, and guns are not common. That doesn't mean they don't exist. I know

I'm considered uncouth for using them, that it's a sign of weakness because I didn't have a lot of magic."

He considered that. I could see on his face that this was something either he'd heard, or had been told to his face. Most likely at some social function. Kids are cruel, and although Underhill handles education differently than Above, in human realms, they still act like little packs of wild animals given the chance.

I continued, "so I'm giving you a gun. And I'm telling you something your mother never wanted you to know. She was a spy, of sorts. Your grandmother was her spymistress, is King Trytion's spymistress with more underlings than you or I will likely ever know about. That's why she died."

The boy's face was transparent as glass. I could see his thoughts chasing themselves around in his mind, like puppies with tails to catch. "Mother?"

"She was a brilliant woman, with a façade of a..." I trailed off. Dumb blonde didn't translate well into Faery, where it just wasn't the epithet it was Above. "Parents are usually more than their children give them credit for." I told him gently. "I don't know what she was doing that got her killed, but you should know she likely died a hero. Which also means this family is in danger, and possibly the whole kingdom. That's what I have to go find out."

He nodded, speechless. I'd given him a lot to think about. I handed him a canvas rucksack with the boxes of ammo and spare magazines tucked into it. "Keep this somewhere discreet, but nearby. You know your grandmother's trick for luggage?"

His face cleared a little, and something that was almost a smile crossed it. "You mean the nospace?"

I hadn't heard that name for it, but it fit. I nodded, and he picked up the bag and tucked it into thin air, where it slid through a slit in reality and disappeared. It would follow him until he wanted it and pulled it back out, but as it didn't intersect with the real world, it wouldn't bump into things. Very handy trick, and one I had long wondered where my mother had learned that one. Likely from Alger, and that brought me back to my next unpleasant task.

I squeezed Dev's shoulder. "Now git, kid. I have people coming, and when Ash shows up, send him down here, please. He'll be the one running security for the Lodge, you will be staying at Elleria."

He nodded solemnly, understanding that he would be in charge there, at the manor. He'd been in charge for months, since my assumption of the Dukedom and long illness coincided to make me unable to execute those duties. Until the changes in life that had landed Bella in our family, he'd been my heir. It occurred to me now, listening to his footsteps going up the stairs, that my children would supplant that inheritance. I wondered if he'd mind.

I had left the doors wide open, and sent a brief message to Ellie that those who arrived were to be sent down to me. I didn't care how out of character it might seem, I knew they would come, and there was no point in playing games. I'd made a splash with my noisy arrival at court, it was time to see what the ripples brought back to me.

Dean walked through the door, silent as always. I looked up from the pistol I was assembling, and he nodded, reached out and squeezed my shoulder, then turned to the shotgun rack. We didn't need to talk. There was enough water under that bridge to know where the course would take us. Violence, and shadows.

We'd worked together off and on since we'd both been apprenticed to Alger at the same age. It had ended in tragedy for me, and to this day I didn't know how it had ended for Dean. I didn't ask any questions, and he told me no lies. He was an outcast, never showed his face in Fae high society, and had spent years living Above as a human, which he could pass for better than I could. That, too, had ended badly. But he was a good man in a fight.

I'd moved on to a bigger gun, and Dean was assembling an impressively heavy load out even for him, when we heard the pipes. I felt my eyebrow go up on its own, and exchanged glances with Dean. They were coming closer, the mad skirl of the music crawling up and down my spine like a live thing. Without a word, we both headed for the stairs.

Ellie and Ash were standing in the open doorway, and when Ellie realized I was behind her, she stepped aside so I could fully see what it was. The garden was full of sprites. I'd never seen this many in one place before.

"What the hell?"

The pipes screamed to an ending, a cacophony of shrill wails, and fell silent. I'd known about the pipes, but had never seen this many assembled in one place, either. They were ranked, like... like a military battalion ready for review. Sprites, like most of the wilding Fae, were not known for organization or regimentation, so this was beyond strange.

A familiar sprite popped into the space a mere foot from my face and snapped off a sloppy salute without waiting for me to return it.

"Reportin' for dooty, sor!"

"Ewan? What is the meaning of this?"

"We haird y'had big troubles, mon, and t'Queen might need us."

"The Queen. You mean Bella?" Ewan McGregor nodded with a wide grin. "Since when do your people have loyalty to a Queen?"

"Sinc't she's a bonnie warrior lass who will gi'us glory and freedom!" He practically quivered in midair, his wings a shimmering blur.

"I... I don't know what to say." I had a garden full of a Sprite army, and I had no idea what to do with it.

He nodded, a sage look on his face. "Dinna fash yerself. M'captins will take their troops to assigned posts."

"Where. Wait.."

But it was too late. Like a firecracker, he popped sharply out of my personal space, and into the ranked masses in front of me, setting off a chain reaction as the group broke into roughly four sections. With a ripple of popping, they transported out to who-knew where. One remained in the garden, and then there was another sprite in my space, saluting again.

"Ian..." I started. Then I stopped myself. I was going to say something I'd regret later. "Report to Ellie and Ash."

I turned on my heel and headed for the Armory. I needed a little space, and time to think. Then I needed to get out of here before it turned into a three-ring circus with more clowns. The thing about making waves, it wasn't a very controlled way of getting results.

Chapter 3

Past Intersects Present

Alger came late, as I knew he would, in the evening. I'd sent him a message urgently that morning, before my Court entrance, but I hadn't known where he and his apprentice were, so there was no way of telling how long it would take them to get back. He could have been anywhere Above, or Underhill. I was still in the Armory, alone, having billeted Dean to a room here in the Lodge, while most who came in during the day were given brief instructions and dispatched elsewhere. I wasn't gathering an army. Not yet. Now, it was time to prepare, and train. I didn't foresee action for a considerable time, if ever. This could all be some small, petty thing. But I didn't think so. There was too much pressure built up in my Court, and at the Low Court with the death of the Low King by my hands.

Something was coming, and it was ugly. When Alger walked into my armory I greeted him silently, unsmiling, with a grip of forearms and then handed him Bella's sketch. He and I had history, some good, most bad. But he was family. And he was arguably the most powerful magic user living. If anyone would know what that thing was, it was him.

As he looked at it, I turned to Mark and greeted Bella's cousin with a more conventional human handshake. The man hadn't even known his special skills were magic until he'd been part of a party of humans led Underhill by Bella in an attempt to rescue me that had gone spectacularly well. I didn't remember any of it, having been rather badly damaged.

"I'm sorry to hear about your sister," He told me, then looked around with a low whistle. "This is impressive."

"Feel free to look around, just don't touch... some of it is dangerous in ways that aren't visible."

He nodded his understanding, and as his gaze flickered back and forth between the tall, stooped Alger and I, I knew he got the subtext. I needed to talk to his teacher alone. Mark was no child, but his training was progressing. I wondered if Alger was learning anything in return.

"He's a good kid." Alger spoke softly as Mark disappeared into the shelves.

"Not really a kid." I looked at him, but he was still staring at the paper, his bushy gray brows furrowed in thought.

"Look, boy," He said without looking up, "From my point of view you're all kids."

"Bella created that after she'd scanned Margot's body," I explained. "I don't know what she did, or how, but she was pretty certain that thing is responsible for Margot's death."

He looked at me directly, his eyes penetrating, his brows still drawn down. With the long beard obscuring the lower half of his face, it was difficult to read his expression as anything but glowering. I stood still and returned his stare.

"Do you know what it is?"

"No. I don't, and I'm less and less able to access my library these days. Something is keeping me out of it, and I would have come back even before your message to compare notes with Bella about this lack of access. It's important, and the answer is eluding me."

He tossed the paper at me and I caught it. "The library is more important to you than Margot's death?"

"Not more important. But without it, I fear I can be of little use to you in hunting for answers." His shoulders dipped a little. "I can only keep so much in mind, m'boy. The library has been the repository for all the things I needed to know, or knew and have forgotten. So while that..." he pointed at the paper I held half-crumpled in my hand, "is important, and I think I've seen something about it, without access to the library, I am unable to give you a direct answer."

"You told me once the library was a physical place. Is that where you were?"

"No. It's not... accessible easily from Underhill. And before you ask, it's not Above, either. It's on another plane entirely. I discovered it by accident, and I won't return in corporeal unless I need to."

He pounded his staff on the floor, glaring at me. I held up both my hands in a gesture of mock surrender. "Don't get angry with me. I'm just looking for the easy way out. If you don't know, I can only think of one other I can go ask, and he's not exactly fond of me."

Alger huffed, fluttering his mustache. "That fool. If he won't give you an answer, take him to the nearest doorway and dump him Above."

"I need Conrad alive and talking, not decaying in a heap. He may be impetuous, but he's not, that I know of, linked with Low Court."

Mark had come back to us, no doubt drawn by Alger's staff pounding. I nodded at him, letting him know silently that he could stay and listen. Nothing I had to say was a secret.

"Low Court is behind this." Alger muttered.

"Normally I'd blow that off, you say Low Court is behind everything. But this time I think you're right."

"We've been asking about Low Court on our travels," Mark said. Both Alger and I looked at him, and he shrugged. "What? I know I wasn't supposed to know, but after a while there was a pattern, and I'm not deaf or stupid."

He glared at the old man, and I stifled a chuckle. Alger really had been treating him like a kid, but then again, the old man had never been discreet, either.

"So what have you learned?" I asked Alger. Mark might not have gathered the significance of everything he'd overheard or deduced.

"With the death of the Low King..." He began.

Mentally, I filled in the picture they wouldn't know about, the shotgun jerking at my hands as I fired from the hip, the look of surprise on the Low King's face as the shot took him in the belly, opening a huge red blossom of flesh and blood. I'd known I'd only get one shot, and I'd known I'd die right after it... why I hadn't, I still didn't know. Alger, oblivious to my wool-gathering, kept going, his voice falling into a familiar pedantic rhythm.

"There was a power vacuum in the Court. None who could have challenged him had been allowed to live, or have any power themselves. It took many months before another emerged from the shadows who the Court bowed to. They accepted her for two reasons. One, they needed a leader, craven as they are, they were like weasels in a henhouse, unable to stop killing even when they were sated."

I hadn't known this. During my long illness, I'd lost touch with many of my informants. I wondered what had become of them, and shook my head. I needed to get back in the game. If I'd been more aware of this level of chaos, I might have been able to prevent Margot's death. Alger was still talking.

"Second, and probably most important, they accepted her because of her connections. Like it or not," I knew he was directing that at me, "fairies are considered by many to be the true ruling Elite of Underhill."

I really didn't give a damn. Pixies had intermingled with fairy blood until it was more a label than an actual difference any longer, if there had ever been a difference. High Court might be mostly fairy, but that was a reflection of where it had come from, not where it was going.

"The newly crowned Queen is connected to fairy, and to High Court. In fact, she claimed from her coronation throne that she is entitled to rule all of Underhill. By blood and..." He paused, and I knew what was coming with a cold chill that sank to my bones. "By marriage."

"Dionaea is no longer my wife, and House Mulvaney long ago renounced any pretensions to the throne of High Court." I could feel the rage, wrapping around me like an old familiar lover.

Alger shook his head slowly. "You and I know that. But to a woman who is taking the reins of power, and who you know has had no other thoughts since she grew to womanhood, truth has no significance."

"Whoa... you were married to the Blood Queen?" Mark broke in.

"*What* are they calling her?" I wasn't sure I'd heard that correctly, and I know it came out more harshly than I intended.

"Hey!" He threw up a hand and stepped back. "It's not me, it's what every underling who mentioned her said. I didn't even know her real name until just now."

Alger, his voice brittle, "They are calling her that because rumor has it she bathes in her enemies' blood."

I felt my nose wrinkle in revulsion. "Not unless she's changed rather a lot, she couldn't even stand to be in the room with raw meat before."

I ran both my hands through my hair, feeling the headache that had been building since Alger's arrival.

"Is she behind Margot's killing?" I asked him.

"I don't know. I heard much, but nothing related to Margot... or to Lucia."

Mother's voice came from behind me, "It is unlikely." I spun around to see her standing in the doorway of the armory.

"Mother! I thought you were at Elleria."

"I was. I had a message from Alger to meet him here, to plan."

I shot a look at Alger, who was back to being stone faced.

"Learoyd," I winced at her use of my full name, and she glided into the room, closing the door behind her with a slight gesture. "Mark, dear boy, would you rather not stay?"

She was looking full at him, and I watched him brace as though standing in a stiff wind. "I'd rather stay and hear. Knowing what's coming makes it less likely to leave me open to unpleasant surprises."

She nodded with an approving expression.

"Mother, I think we should have Bella in on this."

"I agree. Also, held somewhere with more comfortable... indeed, any, chairs. As well as tea and refreshments." There was an audible sniff in there somewhere as she looked around. To the best of my knowledge, my mother had never before been in the Armory, and she looked as out of place as a china doll on a battlefield.

I closed my eyes and counted to ten. Few people could affect me the way she could. I love my mother, but she is very domineering. In some ways, she had been the cause of my life being a living hell for longer than I cared to remember, and there was a reason I had not consulted with her before reclaiming House Mulvaney, or proposing to Bella.

I opened my eyes. They were all still there, staring at me. I'd rather face an oncoming goblin horde than my family.

"Shall we adjourn to the kitchen?" I suggested. It was, in this house, the only room with enough chairs for everyone I could imagine joining in this meeting.

Chapter 4

War Council in the Kitchen

I picked up my coffee cup and inhaled. The black ichor of the gods was all that was going to get me through this. Night had fallen, the council had gathered, and it was time to reap the whirlwind I'd kicked into action that morning. Bella's hand on my thigh and her chair scooted as close to mine as possible told me my new bride was nervous, for which I did not blame her. Everyone was looking at me.

I looked back at them, savoring the coffee and deciding how to begin. Bella and Dean had joined us, Ellie was doing something quietly in the kitchen behind me, but I knew she was listening, and would not hesitate to add something if she felt like it. Ash was leaning against the doorframe, a compromise between being left out and on guard. There were sprites flickering in and out, most of them were out in the dark garden, I could hear them riotously cheering at something.

Daffyd, my old companion and the best archer in the kingdom, had joined us at some point that day. Ash had appointed him to external security, meaning that I had wood elves inside and out. Something very few people knew about my lodge is that it was built partly around a massive oak, Ellie's home tree, and was thus partly living itself. There were special magics involved there, and the wood elves were best able to take advantage of it.

I was killing time, now. Bella shifted restlessly in her chair. She preferred being in action to waiting, and I didn't blame her. Finally, with a soft pop, the final member of my ad hoc council materialized in front of the fireplace. Covered head to toe in a deep brown cowled cloak, he spoke with a deep voice.

"Lom, introduce me."

I inclined my head to him. "Corwin, my friend, joins us."

There was a reason for that bit of byplay, as Corwin shook back the concealing hood and took a seat by my mother, who had known who it was at once. I didn't think he was fooling anyone in this room, but technically as Corwin he could do things impossible for King Trytion.

Now, I could begin. "Margot's death was the final step in something that has been building for some time, and due to my illness, then the trip to the Eastern Court, I haven't been aware of this. Lucia, and then Alger, have been keeping their thumbs on it."

I nodded to my mother, who was sitting very straight, her pale face composed. She took up the narrative with a steady voice.

"Margot and I were aware that a new queen had been crowned to Low Court's throne. We were unable to ascertain for some time the identity of the woman, who was calling herself the Blood Queen, and who wore red veils to conceal herself in open areas where we were able to scry, or bird-ride."

I knew she meant not physically, but like Raven had done with me so long ago, to look through the bird's eyes at what lay below it. With the lesser birds, some amount of control to their flight path was also possible.

"We did know that she did not mean for us to discover her, not only from her furtive movements, but..." Lucia looked at me. "Margot's was not the first death. One after another, our informants in the Low Court fell silent. Some we knew their fate, others," She spread out her hands and fingers. "Just vanished. Finally, Margot went to visit an old friend, to ask a very dangerous favor. I had expected to hear from her tomorrow."

"Could her friend have been turned, and done this?"

She shook her head. "This person is not connected to Low Court. We were asking for the loan of an artifact, which might have gained us entrance to it in secret."

I raised an eyebrow, but she only shook her head a fraction. I looked at Alger, who cleared his throat.

"Mark and I have been traveling on the fringes of the Low territory. We ascertained through inquiries..."

Mark interrupted. "He means through getting schnockered in a lot of greasy dives where the barmaids look like they were exhumed, or in the nicer ones, like Harpies."

Alger glared at him, and I suppressed my chuckle. Mark had just gotten his own back for the 'kid' earlier.

His train of thought shaken off course, Alger continued more conversationally. "We discovered the true identity, and the goals, of the Blood Queen. She is Dionaea, formerly wife of Lom, and she wants to rule all of Underhill."

Bella's hand gripped my leg tightly. I patted it out of sight. We would talk later in private, and I would assure her again that the whole marriage had never been my idea in the first place...

Alger went on. "What we didn't hear anything about was a planned killing of anyone from High Court. Egged on by their queen, the Low Court grows contemptuous, saying that we are weak, soft, and lack the will to resist. However, to my knowledge there are no firm plans for how they intend to take over. I suspect this is largely a ploy by the new queen to gather support."

I nodded. "Perhaps. But while she likes to talk a big game, and play for big stakes, she's also impatient. Which is why we aren't married any longer."

They all looked at me, and I sighed. I'd opened my big mouth and inserted a foot up to my ankle. I'd forgotten that none of them knew what had led up to my kicking Dion out, and divorcing her quietly. She'd gone without much fuss...

"She wanted me to maneuver a coup, and overthrow Trytion. I told her I'd see her in hell, first, and when she mocked me for not having enough magic to prevent her, I pulled my pistol on her." I didn't want to talk about the attempts at mental manipulation that had gotten me carrying the weapon every moment of the day, not knowing if I would use it on myself when I finally felt her break through my mental shields, or her. It had come very close to being her, I'd pulled the trigger a fraction of a second after her panicked bubble had burst in midair. I'd never seen her again, and there was a book in the library with a bullet embedded in it.

I shrugged, dismissing the memories, and seeing the looks on everyone's face. I looked at Bella, whose eyes were full of horror for me. "You don't have to worry about her, my dear. It's not a mistake I'd make again."

My mother twitched a little and caught my eye. I looked at her, my face smooth. I would not betray my feelings again. She looked away, and I relented and looked at the others to give her time to compose herself.

"Dionaea means to have all of Underhill. But she lacks the skills to take it. Or she did, a century ago." I corrected myself. I knew how much I had learned in that passage of time, and my ex-wife might be evil, but she wasn't stupid.

"Did she have Margot killed?" Bella asked. "I don't know what I saw in the magic remaining on the body, but it wasn't... female. I don't think." She looked at Alger. "Did you know what that thing was?"

He shook his head. "I suspect she is behind Margot's death, but we cannot simply storm into Low Court demanding her head for it."

And for the second time that night, jaws dropped around the table. He smirked, almost hidden under the voluminous beard. "I'm not always a hothead. Sometimes I leave that for the boy, here." He gestured at me. "First, we must establish the connections. And then..." he hesitated and met my eyes squarely. This was more eye contact today than we had had in years. "Then we talk to the Huntsman."

I nodded. Killing one Low Court royal had been enough for me. I knew he was expecting me to object, given my history with the Hunt, but this was, after all, their role Underhill. And if Dionaea had grown cunning enough to claim a throne, making those connections would be tricky enough. I looked around the table.

"We have the inkling of a plan, then. To find the thing that killed Margot, and then discover who was pulling the strings."

They all nodded. I went on. "It is a slim possibility that her death was unconnected to High or Low Court, but the ritualistic manner of her return makes that unlikely in my mind. That was a message, to me, and through me to you." I ended, looking at Corwin, who nodded. I made a mental note to talk to him alone, soon. He couldn't go on blaming himself for her death. His subjects died, and if he took it this hard every time... he had never taken it this hard before. Something was going on, but I trusted that if it related to this discussion he would have spoken.

"I will go, soon, but not rushing, to speak with a source who may know what manner of creature it is that killed her. I'm not raising an army and going in with drums and pipes like the bad old days of the wars between Courts. This is going to be my way, one stubborn fool with a gun."

Bella looked sharply at me, opening her mouth, and then closing it with a lost expression. We would talk tonight. I might wind up sleeping on the couch. But I wouldn't risk our children, even if I were willing to risk her. And from the way she had just cut herself off, she had thought of that, too.

I squeezed her hand under the table, a silent promise. And I looked around, meeting everyone's eyes in turn. "Suggestions, thoughts?"

My mother looked smaller, somehow, than when we'd sat down to the council. She was silent. I knew she'd want to talk to me soon, and I didn't know that I owed her that. Corwin shook his head at me. I'd have his backing, he just didn't want to give any input yet. No one else had anything to say, although I suspected that was partly because there was a lot of new information and everyone was still digesting it. We would talk again in the morning.

Suddenly I wanted nothing more than to be alone with Bella. We hadn't had the chance to talk about a lot of things, and this had been a hell of a day. I stood up.

"Get some sleep, everyone. Mother, Corwin..." I nodded to them, and headed for the door.

If I stood there doing the social thing, it would be midnight before I had the chance... Bella was right on my heels. Behind us, I could hear the soft popping of transportation bubbles. There were places and times for niceties, and this wasn't one of them. We all needed to deal with the pain before we could deal with one another in a civilized manner again.

Bella closed the bedroom door behind us, and threw herself into my arms. I'd been holding them out to her, so it wasn't a knock-me-over throw like it could have been. She was crying. I didn't say anything. There was nothing I could say, when the tempest breaks like this all you can do is hold on tight.

I did maneuver us to the loveseat. My bedroom, with the long illness I'd been going through when it was built, was more of a self-contained suite than just a place to sleep. There were times I really appreciated that. It didn't take her long to get to the sniffing and hiccupping stage.

"Sorry." She whispered into my slightly damp shoulder, hiding her face. We'd been together less than a year, but I knew this wasn't typical of her, and she wasn't happy about it.

"Been a rough day, darling. Had I known…? I wouldn't have brought Margot to you. I would have waited for Alger." I hugged her more tightly, and then let her move so we were both more comfortable.

She looked up at me. "No, I know what you were doing. That wasn't anger, that was theatre. And you were right, the magic was fading already when you came to me. Waiting for Alger would have meant losing it."

She put a hand on her belly, and I covered it with one of mine. There was nothing to feel, yet, but just knowing they were there made it all strange and wondrous. Bella hiccupped, then sighed. "We have so much to talk about. And you're going to leave me alone while you go into danger."

"I have to. I know we're partners, but…"

She stretched up a little and kissed me, silencing what I was about to say. "I'm pregnant, not sick."

"You're no less capable than you were a day ago." I agreed. "But the risks just tripled, and I'm no gambler. Not anymore."

"What are you going to do?"

"Going to go visit someone who knows as much about Underhill flora and fauna as Alger does. Alger would never admit it, but Conrad has made a lifetime's study of it. He's a specialist, not a generalist."

Bella frowned. "I need to talk to Alger about the library. I don't understand what's going on, there."

"He should be in council… when do you meet in full council again?"

"Later this week. Today was a preliminary meeting to set the agenda."

I grinned at her. "So I broke up a boring meeting. No loss."

She made a face at me, then sobered. "Oh, Lom... poor Margot. Catch whoever did that to her. She was always so sweet and nice to me."

"I will, dear one. I have to... even if she weren't my sister, and thus a family obligation, I think this is the pointy edge of an attack on the kingdom."

She nodded, and I could see the fear in her eyes. "This is... about me, isn't it. Oh, that sounds so narcissistic."

"Only if you weren't Consort-Elect, and coming into your full powers with a coronation in three months. They have to move before that, or face a united Court. So it's not about you, but it is."

"And Dionaea." She didn't need to say anything more. There was a lot hanging in the air just from that name, things I hadn't talked to her about, had hoped to never need to talk about. I'd fostered the impression most people had, if they knew I'd been married before, that I was genteelly widowed, and to bring up the idea of marriage was painful to me. Which it was, just not in the way they thought.

"I was married young, for Fae, and not for the right reasons." I began, bending my head so I was resting my cheek on her hair. She cuddled up, and didn't talk.

"Dionaea was my mother's idea." I closed my eyes and remembered the whole scene.

Chapter 5

First Marriage

"I'd been told I'd die, after the elfshot. But hours turned into days turned into months... Mother was concerned about me, I'm sure. But she seemed more concerned that I would die and there would be no one left to carry on the Mulvaney line. Our House might have fallen into disgrace, but even among society it was assumed that after the third generation, the Crown would be petitioned and Mulvaney would rise again. And I was the fourth generation from Alonzo."

Bella murmured quietly, "I'm going to hang that portrait of him."

I squeezed her gently and kept talking. I only wanted to do this once. "Dionaea y Eudicott is from a dying family line. She was very proud of her heritage, and that she was the last of her line. I'm not sure what she promised Mother... You know about the Fae, and conception, yes?"

Bella looked up at me, her eyes wide. The room had been growing darker as the lamp someone had lit was dying slowly, but I didn't get up to relight it. All I could see was the pale oval of her face and the bright whites of her eyes. "Pixies, fairies - and the only difference between us is name, and custom, if you hadn't already picked up on that – we don't have a child unless it's by mutual arrangement. Accidental pregnancy is unheard of, Underhill."

"I'd known the population was much lower here than above. But I haven't had time to consider it, and that's a delicate subject. No one talked to me about it. But Lom, how?"

Our hands were still interlinked on her stomach. "We both wanted. Maybe not consciously, at that moment, but we did."

I couldn't see her blush in the gathering dark. Her skin, darker than mine, made a nice contrast where our hands were twined together.

"Why did you and Dionaea never have children? Especially since that's what your mother wanted?" Bella asked.

"Never had a chance." I laughed harshly, remembering the pain and confusion of a much younger man. I hadn't unpacked these memories in a long time. "You have to have sex to have babies."

"When I married her, I was too sick to care. I don't remember much of the wedding, other than being in excruciating pain, nearly blind with a headache. After... not sure when, it was probably at what mother had gotten up for a reception, I vomited. All over Dionaea, because they were making me dance. I passed out, and woke up about a day later."

"Not an auspicious beginning." Bella said.

"Dionaea was unhappy from the beginning, even without that public humiliation. I would not live at Elleria. It made me ill to be in it. We didn't know then that any level of magic use poisoned me slowly, and when I'm there, something triggers me to shield. Always has, I suspect. One day maybe I'll go and spend enough time to find out what."

"That's why it was shut up." Bella filled in a gap in her knowledge. I shrugged.

"That, and the family couldn't afford to keep it open. Another bitter pill for Dionaea. She had a dowry, but it wasn't enough to maintain that monstrous expense."

"And you didn't want to be Duke."

I kissed my bride on the forehead. She was a smart cookie. "Not then, not now."

"But why?" Bella started to sit up and I held on.

"Stay there... because I wanted you. And I thought I was dying. Seemed the decent thing to do, to take care of you and greedy me, have you too."

Bella subsided. "So she wound up here, with you?"

"This house was built for us. Proceeds of one of my first jobs. She hated it. The only thing she got that she wanted was incorporating Ellie's tree into it. Dionaea assumed that by having the tree in the house, Ellie would be bound to her." I chuckled, bitter still after all these years. "Ellie was a servant of the House Eudicott, as wood elves everywhere were servants. But Dionaea forgot that servant doesn't mean mindless drone."

"Ellie stayed with you. Not because of the tree..."

"Not because of the tree. Because when Dion discovered that it was Ellie providing the mental shield spells for me, she almost killed her with a beating. Then she came for me, while I was sick from protecting my mind with magic, and I almost killed her." I shrugged again, feeling a chill like a worm crawling up my spine. "She's irrational, and she's dropped out of sight for a century. Fae are patient, Bella-mine, and Dion is..."

"Mad. Oh, Lom..."She shifted around so she could hug me. "This is why you're so cool with your mother."

"Yes."

"Is she still...?" Bella sounded concerned. I knew she liked Lucia.

"No, she's mellowed. Still likes to be in charge, but after a century she knows better than to try and push me around." I kissed her soft lips. "You're the only one who gets to push me around."

"Mmm-hhmmm..." she couldn't make words, but I got the meaning of that approving noise. And a minute later she had the clearance to say, "I'm pushing us to bed, mister."

Which I understood perfectly even if it didn't make sense, and was perfectly willing to obey my queen. We both needed what she wanted. Death makes life that much sweeter.

———

Morning came far too early, after that late of a night. Ellie didn't come in with the coffeepot as she often did, and not for the first time I wondered just how connected she was to the house, to know when entering our bedroom would be indiscreet. I decided, as I opened the door and found the tray on folding legs set up there, and the coffee smell hit me, that I didn't want or need to know.

Bella whimpered a little when I pulled back the curtain and the light fell on her face. She rolled over and burrowed under a pillow, until all I could see was a heap of tousled, silky black hair. I poured a cup of coffee and sat at my desk. I was in no hurry to waken her.

Peaceful, but under the surface my mind was racing. I knew why Dionaea was acting now, to precipitate matters before the coronation. But why me? Especially since everyone Underhill had known until yesterday morning that I had no magic at all, not even the traces I'd had after the elfshot. I should have been out of the equation altogether as far as she was concerned. I didn't believe she was obsessed with me as a person. Not after a century of silence.

Bella. Margot's body was to have been a message to Bella, not me.

I looked over at my wife's slim body, barely a lump under the down comforter, still sleeping. I was contemplating joining her, when there was a pounding on the door. Bella sat bolt upright, her hair spilling over her bare breasts.

"Wha?" She started to ask, but I was already at the door. I looked over my shoulder.

"Stay here."

She might have argued, but I was following Ash down the stairs at a dead run. Others, disturbed by the noise, were coming out of doors. Dean was right behind me, fully dressed already. Ash led me straight for the front door, which stood wide open. As we reached it, the cloud of sprites parted and revealed what laid on the ground.

"Oh, shit..."

This was not how I wanted to wake up. I knelt next to the wretched body. I knew who it was, even in this ruined state. The stench was truly horrible, but then, he'd never smelled much better while alive. Ghouls are alive, and some of them are decent folks, even if you can't walk downwind of them. I pounded the ground with my fist.

"Dammit!"

The last time I'd seen him, in Seattle, he'd sold us weaponry. And he'd warned me bad things were coming. Looked like Georgio had met them before me. I got to my feet, feeling weary, old, and useless. Bella slipped under Dean's arm at the door, why he was trying to keep her from seeing this I didn't know, and looked down.

"Oh..." was all she said, one hand pressed to her mouth. That would be from the smell.

"I have to go. Now. Do you understand what this means?" I pointed downward, at the mangled remains of Georgio, the ghoulish arms dealer I'd made a deal with. He got me what I needed, when I needed it, Above where weapons are hard to come by, and he got to stay up there and live where his beloved neon lights glowed.

She nodded. "They are working Above and Underhill. This is bad, yes?"

"It means they are escalating. And if they draw attention to us, Above..."

She shivered. "You have to go. Do you want me to look – like I did for Margot?"

I didn't. She didn't need to be out here in the chilly damp morning wearing only a silk robe and her feet bare. Ellie pushed a pair of slippers into Bella's hands just then. There was a small mob of people around us.

"Yes. Please... I'm sorry. But I need as much intel as you can give me."

She bent to put the slippers on, and held her hands out, not touching Georgio, just being close to him. I turned to look at the others. I kept my voice down, but time was of the essence now.

"I'm going. Dean, you know where, as does Alger. I won't say it out loud, we don't know who's listening or watching. Ash, Daffyd, Ellie..." I pointed at Bella, kneeling at my feet and ignoring all of us.

They nodded in concert. The wood elves as a community had flocked to me after Dionaea's actions toward Ellie had become known, and I had personally paid off indenturements for dozens of them out of my bounties. They had, in a century, transitioned from virtual slaves to respected craftsmen, and they credited me for it. I didn't think it was me, I was just a catalyst, they'd have done it for themselves anyway. But their loyalty was unquestionable and I was leaving them to guard my most precious lives.

"This may keep happening again, them throwing bodies into our garden. Be on guard. Alger may come to see if he can indict and intercept a bubble, it takes a lot of skill or power. Bella can..."

"And Bella will." She held up a hand and I gave her a steadying arm to get up from the cold ground. "The same, I think. It's... veiled, somehow. Like maybe I'm seeing the inner reality and it's wearing a glamour."

I pulled her close. She murmured. "You will be here for the coronation. I'm not doing that alone."

"Yes, my queen." I whispered for her ears alone.

Bella pushed me away gently. Her eyes were dry, and I knew she was holding it together for the benefit of everyone watching us. "Keep your powder dry."

"I'll be home soon."

I turned and walked toward the gate, my hands empty, but I bubbled and traveled before I reached it. Everything I needed was with me, just not visible to the prying eye. If someone was watching, I wanted them to think I was blindly rushing off in a rage. I'd built that impression with my reaction to Margot, and I'd use it, now.

In the bubble, I pulled clothing from the rucksack I'd had stashed in nospace – useful word, that – and dressed. Even I was never so reckless as to run into battle in flannel pajama bottoms and nothing else. I'd only had those on because it was cool in our bedroom, and I was in the habit of slipping them on as soon as I got out of bed. The house slippers were replaced with wool socks and heavy boots. Then, I focused my mind and started the bubble toward my real destination, strapping on a holster before sliding a dirk into the top of my boot.

By the time I'd reached my destination, I was ready for anything. With a shield in place, I dropped the bubble and braced. The shotgun blast rocked me hard, even so.

Chapter 6

Great White Hunter

I wheezed for air, and managed to hold up my hands so he could see them empty.

"Conrad, dammit..." I had to stop and suck wind.

"Hellifino who you are." He boomed, from close range. I was bent over trying not to throw up, and could only see the big boots as he walked up and stopped, boots wide, in front of me. "Do I know you?"

"Lom." I got out. "I'm Lom."

"Dammit, Boy!" I felt a big warm hand under my elbow, lifting me straight. The pain was starting to ease. I made a mental note to make the shield thicker next time. I really didn't need broken, or even cracked, ribs right now.

Conrad Ray looked just as he had the first time I'd met him, a century or so before. I'd been trying to identify a weird creature, and rumor had it the peculiar human was the man to see. Rumor, in a rare twist, was perfectly right. The Boer man had somehow stumbled through a gate to Underhill while out hunting, and he'd immediately cottoned on to being somewhere not-Earth. Rumor, which I trusted about as far as I could throw it, had that he'd traveled back and forth at first, until he feared that he'd age and die Above, having been told by Fae of the time differences.

So here he stayed. His monomania with animals of every description extended to the peoples of Underhill, which he'd learned quickly might look like animals to him, but weren't. Somehow, I'd never learned how, he'd made allies of a Brownie sept, which was probably what made his independent existence Underhill possible.

He might know what it was that had killed Margot, then Georgio. It was a thin lead, and probably not worth getting shot in the chest over, but I'd had to try. It was a good thing I'd known to shield.

"So just how many people have you killed recently with that thing?" I asked, taking a slow, deep breath to test for broken ribs. No sharp twinges, just overall ache. Good.

He looked offended, his round face topped with a thin fringe of wispy gray hairs. "No one has been to visit me in so long..."

"Because they know you'll shoot them!"

"Hey! My friends know to put up a shield. You did." He pointed out, correctly.

I grunted. He was leading us toward his shack, hand still wrapped firmly around my arm. I let him think he could hold me, and went along with it. The interior was the same as it had been last time I'd been privileged to enjoy his hospitality. He hadn't shot me back then, though. Conrad was getting more trigger happy and paranoid in his old age.

He pushed me down onto a bench at the long table, which was strewn with papers and books. With a grunt, I sat and watched him bustling in his kitchen area. The shack was pretty big, and although it looked a shambles outside, inside was all warm wood, gleaming white plaster, and rows of books covering two walls of the building. The Brownies were still with him, I could see, as only the table was a pool of chaos in the otherwise tidy dwelling.

In the corner, his curtained bed caught my eye with a slight movement, and I guessed where the house brownies were hiding. They wouldn't come out while I was here. Conrad set a big mug of steaming coffee in front of me with a thud.

I sipped gratefully while he stacked some drawings off to the side where they weren't in danger of a spill. He was a gifted watercolorist, and I could see he'd been doing a study of puça. The ghostly creatures were depicted nicely in their several forms, I could see a horse and a rabbit on top of the stack.

"You came for a reason, I'm thinking." He sat heavily, and I looked more closely at him. He looked tired, and the lines around his eyes were much deeper than I recalled them.

"I need your help identifying, and maybe finding, a monster." I pulled the folded sheet out of my shirt pocket and pushed it across the table to him.

He nodded silently and took it, then looked up at me before he unfolded it. "I have a price, this time."

We locked gazes. He'd never asked anything of me before, and had reacted with boyish glee when I brought him some oddity I'd found on my travels. It had been an even exchange, over the years, but one we'd never verbalized or formalized. I'd known something was wrong with him, and this confirmed it.

"I might not be able to pay it." I answered, feeling a chill of concern. I was vulnerable at the moment, and maybe that movement hadn't been the shy Brownies. I let one hand fall off the table into my lap, inches from my holster. The other held the heavy mug of hot coffee. It would make a good distraction if thrown.

It's not paranoid when they really are out to get you.

"I, um, hear you're pretty connected at High Court." He ducked his head like a shy little girl, and I watched this unexpected display with amazement.

"Might be. Depends." I wanted to stay noncommittal, I had no idea what he knew, but I wanted him to talk more.

He rubbed the back of his neck with a meathook of a hand. I'd felt the power of it just a few minutes earlier. "Well, I was wondering. I mean, I know it's a lot to ask. But..."

Now I just wanted him to spit it out instead of this slow searching for each word. "Yeah?"

"I'd like to get a pardon." He blurted.

"Huh?" I blinked at him. "You want a what?"

"A pardon." He repeated slowly, now looking up at me. I could see his eyes were full of unshed tears, reflecting the gray of his iris. The red rims told me he was seriously upset.

"You need a pardon?" I leaned back and took a swig of the coffee. I'd never heard of him doing anything that would run him afoul of the Hunt. There were very few laws Underhill, and justice was usually swift, and inexorable. Pardons were possible, but they came from the Huntsman, who might or might not listen to the King of High Court. Conrad had ahold of the wrong end of the stick.

"Not me. Someone... someone I care about." And now I caught it. Just the faintest twitch of his eyes, toward the bed.

"Unh. This someone female? What'd she do?" I was watching the curtains with my peripheral vision, and there was a twitch, all right. I'd hit the mark, because the twitch was mirrored on Conrad's fleshy face.

I didn't look toward the bed. Wait and see what this was. Watching Conrad's face, I could see his thoughts as his face fell, then brightened again.

"Yeah, Lom, is a girl. She's good girl." His voice was reverting to the accented English of his youth. "Yust needs a helping hand. Can you help?"

"I don't know. I need to talk to her," I wanted her out in plain sight. Angry females are more deadly than the males, Kipling wasn't wrong about that. He'd not been wrong about many things, and I missed his cutting wit.

Conrad turned his head. "Mbwasho, coom forth."

A lovely girl slid out from between the curtains, dressed in a simple shift, her feet bare. She had a sulky expression on her face, and she wagged her finger at Conrad as she walked toward us. Very tall, her regal bearing was borne out by her autocratic tone.

"You are too easy to sway!" She scolded him. "Now he has seen me, and can testify I am here." She stopped and looked down her nose at me. "You do not look like a Duke."

"You do not look like a fairy." She was, in point of fact, lacking one very visible attribute shared by all Fae women that I had ever met. It wasn't her dark skin and hair, or that she looked like she'd stepped out of a Masai thorn *enkang* into the room. It was the smooth shoulders and unbroken cloth over them. Mbwasho had no wings.

She sniffed and turned around, proving her wingless state. "I am no fairy. I am Masai, I have come to Conrad's *kraal* to keep house for him."

I looked at Conrad, who just shrugged. With the voluble young woman in sight, he seemed to have lost his ability for speech. Mbwasho, emboldened by my silence, rattled on. "This is a most marvelous place, but they say I must have a pardon to stay, and that I can never go home again." She tossed her head. "I would rather stay here, and not share my husband, nor have to be an emorata."

I wasn't sure what she was talking about, but it was clear she was human, very young, and probably didn't know where she really was.

"Conrad, what were you thinking?"

"I'm lonely." He mumbled, looking at the table top, and my folded paper in his hand. I thought of what Bella would say.

"How in hell did you get her here?"

Mbwasho answered me that. "The little spirits of the earth, they carried me here while I was sleeping. I awakened and saw the stars streaming by over my head, and I thought I was dreaming, even though I could feel their little feet running," She mimicked a rapid scissoring with her hands, "Under me, and I was moving like lying on running water. But I thought it must be a dream, so I closed my eyes, tight, tight, and then I opened them and it was all green, and a man stood there."

"You kidnapped a child bride?" I asked him in astonishment. It seemed the least likely thing I could have thought of from Conrad, who had never been unhappy to have company, but just as glad to see me leave so he could go back to his life's work.

She sniffed, but stayed silent. I could see she didn't like being called a child. Conrad shook his head violently. "I didn't kidnap her. The Brownies did." He looked around, guiltily.

"The Brownies brought her to you." I had gathered that from Mbwasho's account of her night crossing of the gate to Underhill.

He nodded. "I didn't ask them to find her." He said firmly. "Didn't even say I wanted a woman. But," he shrugged fatalistically, "Now she's here, I want her to stay."

A sept of Brownies had crossed the veil between worlds, kidnapped a girl I was fairly sure wasn't old enough to drive in the United States, although probably long in the tooth for marriage in the Masai culture, and given her like a gift to their favorite pet. I rubbed my face with both hands, looking with the Sight while I did so. There were Brownies everywhere, I was surrounded. I dropped my hands.

"Mbwasho, do you want to be here?"

"Yes, I do. It is so *easy*." She nodded eagerly, her necklaces and earrings flashing.

I could imagine it was, to a girl who'd had a life of hard physical labor. Masai culture dictated men not marry until they were elders, so the age difference – which wasn't obviously as great as it was in human years – wouldn't bother her. I'd had very little to do with Africa, the magic there was eldritch, weird, and didn't bother the locals the way it did in more civilized-in-name areas. But the Masai as a group interested me, and I had spent some time with them at one point, learning their legends and hunting enough to impress them. That was long before this child was a twinkle in her mother's eye.

There was another factor. Like the sprites, the tiny Brownies were a race to be cautious around. One at a time, they were insignificant. But they would swarm you, and six would die willingly so that one could slash your hamstring. I couldn't see them with my eyes, but I'd seen their lifeglows, and there were more than enough of them to take me out. I had other things to do, and better ways to die.

"I will talk to the Queen. I think your pardon will be granted."

Mbwasho squealed and jumped up and down, clapping her hands. I raised an eyebrow at Conrad, who blushed, a trick with his ruddy complexion. "Thank you," he said simply.

"Can you look at the paper now, please?"

He unfolded it carefully, then turned it right side up. Mbwasho leaned over his shoulder and pursed her lips. "Ugh. This thing is..." She shivered and crossed herself.

Conrad got up, leaving the paper on the table. Mbwasho slipped around the corner of the table and looked in my cup, which was mostly empty.

"Do you want more?" She asked sweetly. Conrad was mumbling under his breath and running a finger over the spines of books. This could take a while.

"Sure." I watched as she got it. She knew where everything was. I wondered just how long she'd been there, and why the Brownies were importing breeding stock. A smile quirked my lips. They liked their pet, evidently. She came back with the mug.

"Thank you." I wondered if Conrad would relax with the shotgun now that he wasn't being so protective. I'd like to bring Bella to meet Mbwasho. They would have even less in common than Bella had with the Fae women at first, but I thought Bella would like the girl. And it might give Conrad some relief to not have his little hen pecking at him all the time.

Conrad stumped back over to the table, his arms full of books. I helped him get them stacked up neatly, and Mbwasho retreated. I didn't think she was illiterate, the crossing motion spoke of a missionary education, but she wasn't sure of me, as hard as she was trying to be polite.

"I have an idea," he told me. "I am a cryptozoologist, you know this."

I did, but let him think out loud at me without breaking into his stream of thoughts. This was part of his process, I'd learned, talking it all out.

"I can believe the unbelievable, study the impossible. It is my gift. Is why God sent me here."

He flipped open a book, then closed it with a grunt of disgust. Without pausing he went on to the next one in the stack. "I have all the records, even of the things they say cannot be. This one..." He stabbed a thick finger in the direction of Bella's sketch. "This one is physiologically improbable. But so are centaurs, and minotaurs."

I blinked at that bland assertion, and opened my mouth to ask if they were real, then closed it again. I didn't need to know, right now, I had other fish to fry. Maybe another time.

Conrad rolled on, not paying me any attention while he flipped through the stacks of books. "So, I say to myself, must be magical. Like fairies, who can fly, along with bumblebees, when science says no, is not possible."

I blinked away the mental picture of Bella as a bumblebee, and the memory of her reaction to her wings. She had not been a happy lady, and had let me know that in no uncertain terms. Besides, we already knew it was magic, it had left traces of that on the bodies. Conrad picked up a book, flipped a few pages, stopped talking, and flipped a few more.

He set the book down flat, rotated it so I could see, and folded his hands one over the other, flat on the table. I knew that look. It meant he thought he knew the answer. I leaned over to see the pages he was showing me. There were no illustrations on them, just crabbed, ancient handwriting in a language I couldn't read. Or maybe that was really bad handwriting, in bleached-out oak gall ink, it looked like.

I looked up at him. "What does it say?"

"Doppelganger to the Germans. Ka to the Egyptians. Vardoger to the Norse. Etianen to the Finns. Ankou to the Cornish and Normans. My research shows they have been around for a long, long time. And only ever spotted by those most alert. Do you ever know what a shapechanger's natural form is? Or what happens to those they replace?"

Chapter 7

Shapechanger

I had been hoping for something definitive when I left Conrad's shack, not a will'o the wisp chase. Instead of having a direction to look in, I had the idea that he'd either slipped off the deep end entirely, or I couldn't trust anyone. If a true shapechanger existed, how would I know? The Sight might tell me, but I could hardly walk around Underhill with my eyes closed until I spotted something strange.

I weighed my options. It had been months since I'd contacted any of my friends in Low places. With the death rate Alger and Lucia had reported, it seemed likely that many would be gone, and if I did find one, it would put them at a higher risk. My lack of magic hadn't been a vulnerability in the past, as I'd had enough to trigger premade spells supplied by others, and an itchy trigger finger to back them up. If I walked into a dive now, with the rumor I'd lost all magic... people would die. I wouldn't be one of them, but it could cause ripples that would interfere with the patterns I was looking for.

Which meant I could return to High Court, and take the subtle path of watching and waiting. I knew at least one of the members of the High Council was corrupt, and connected to the Low Court. A promise of more power with the consolidation, or revenge, or... the possibilities were endless. Everyone has a price.

I went to find Sean, instead. This was no time for subtle waiting. Passively standing there watching the tide roll in was not my style, and it seemed like a good way to lose everything. Given time, and warning, we could channel the tide, harness the power, and divert it off harmlessly.

Sean's favorite drinking hole was a real oddity, Underhill. A century ago when the gates were more open between worlds than they were now, humans had unknowingly exploited one. Thinking it was just an inconspicuous location that kept the police from raiding their speakeasy, they'd built not only a nightclub, but an entire warehouse to hide the hooch. The industrial chic styles in some parts of the club contrasted starkly with the decadent art nouveau of the central barroom.

The veil had rippled, as it did every so often, the gate vanished in an instant, and some of the guys and gals bellied up to the bar had never quite clicked that their world was gone. The neon sign, which had to be powered by magic now, although I'd never asked, blinked slowly in the neverending darkness of this pocket of Underhill. Eat – At it said in small letters, and then in a flash of glory, JOE's lit up the sky.

Joe's was neutral ground, and I nodded at the bouncer as I walked through the double doors. He grunted an unintelligible greeting, and the gold rings around his tusks glinted as he looked down at me. The only ogre I'd ever not killed on sight, Terrence was the height of civilized Fae. What the stranded humans thought of him, I had no idea, although I'd seen one stagger up to him one night and politely address him as Mister Howard. Ten feet of muscle covered in olive drab skin, I'd seen him throw a misbehaving dwarf through a wall, and it was no mock-up Hollywood wall.

Past the door ogre, I looked around, squinting a little. Joe, wherever he was, rest his soul, had evidently believed that light was a tool of the angels, so forbade it from being flung profligately around in his place lest it attract too much good. It was quiet, but not empty. Joe's was never empty.

I strolled toward the bar, contemplating a quiet beverage whilst I waited for my quarry. The barmaid intercepted me as I slid onto a stool. Rubbing a soft cloth unnecessarily over the shining zebra wood of the bar counter, she asked in her charming accent, "What'll you have, Lom?"

That accent... might be Russian, might be European... I'd made the mistake of asking her, once, and Terrance had come and loomed over me while she shouted that she 'vas Amerikan, by Bob!' at me. I'd apologized profusely with a weather eye on the frowning troll and the other one watching her hands fiddle with the hilts of various... several... more than I could keep track of... knives. I'd bought her a few shots of Devil's Cut bourbon and promised to never bring it up again.

"Black ichor of the gods," I told her, and she smiled. She knew what I meant. There was a contraption in the corner that made ominous noises and glows when it was in operation, but the liquid it produced was divinely coffee. She added the measure of Irish I hadn't asked for, and slid it to me.

I sipped, slowly, and sighed. "Hits the spot." I looked around the nearly empty place. "I haven't been in here for too long. Who's around?"

She shrugged and went back to polishing the wood. That wasn't a good sign. If she were happy, she'd pull up a stool on her side, pour a shot, and plunk both her elbows down for a good gossip fest. I took another slug.

"Do me a favor," She was talking to the bar, not me, but I got the message. "Have your coffee, and go down the road. I don'need no troubles."

Oh, hell. Not here. "Yah, I hear you," was all I said aloud. I looked sadly into my cup. Joe's was supposed to be the one place where your affiliations were left outside, and no one talked politics or religion.

I took another swallow. No point in looking like I'd been run off. I turned away from the bar, and saw Sean walk through the door. There was no missing the big wolfman. He stood upright, for one thing, a head taller than me, and for another, the *were* had the worst taste in suits I'd ever seen. His chartreuse zoot suit was from the wrong period entirely for Joe's, but no one seemed to care or even notice. Terrence was beautifully attired in white tie and tails, red cummerbund. The barmaid favored flapper dresses in red with nets of jet beading. But Sean strutted in the zoot, cuffs tight to ankles, black and white shoes custom fit to long wolf toes... and the hat. The hat with the holes for his furry ears.

I gave him a look, and twitched my head toward the outside as I stood up. I went on out, and waited. The alley was appropriately atmospheric, dark, and filled with fog. The effect of the neon colors flashing overhead was nice to look at, without providing actual illumination. I leaned up against the wall, feeling the chill of the bricks soaking through the leather and sheepswool of the bomber I was wearing. Sean was a smart wolf, he'd give it some time, and a drink at least, before he followed me.

It was several minutes before he came out, and he walked toward me without looking at me, like he was just happening to head in this direction. I pushed off the wall and melted in a few steps behind him, knowing how long it would take for the mist to obscure us from the side entrance... and then I bubbled us both.

An instant later we were standing in a sunny meadow. Well, I was standing. Sean, who'd still been walking, stumbled badly. He whipped around and growled at me. "You could have warned me!"

I grinned disarmingly – I hoped – at him. "More fun this way."

"You and your sense of humor. Going to get us both killed." His tail wasn't wagging. This was one very unhappy wolf below his flippant façade.

I shook my head. "I didn't want to involve you. But I need answers."

He pulled the hat off and scratched one ear. "I get you. I got answers. But they might not be the ones you want."

I shrugged my jacket off, out here in the sun it was making me sweat. "Margot Mulvaney."

"The pixie chick?" He cocked his head at me. "You have the same last name."

"She was my sister." I didn't believe he hadn't already known that. He was stalling.

"The Blood Queen ordered it." His ears flattened as he said that, and he looked around nervously, then again, with one eye closed. He was looking for a magical signature near us, but I already knew we were alone. Even a hijacked animal would still have a tell-tale trace. Besides, no-one could have known where we would wind up talking. We were as safe as it was possible to be.

"A source told me it might be a shapechanger working for her."

Now his ears were back flat to his skull "Damn, man, that's scary shit. You wouldn't see one of them coming, could be your best friend and skkkzzt..." He drew one long claw across his throat fur.

I stepped closer and reached up, grabbing that throat. "Tell me straight, or I really will make good about that promise to turn you into a fur rug."

He gargled a little. I wasn't holding tight, but his efforts to get free were bouncing right off me. A nice magical shield was handy. Would have been nice to have in years past. Oh, well, you use what you got.

I mused out loud. "Your mangy hide might actually look good, all flat in front of my fireplace. Firelight'd bring out your highlights, way it flickers."

He coughed as I let go and stepped back. "Talk, wolf."

"Would..." he gasped and rubbed his throat "Would you at least have sex with that hot wife of yours on me?"

I burst out laughing. He was irrepressible. Sean's ears perked back up, a tell-tale sign he was feeling better about the situation.

"Look, man. No hard feelings. But there's some bad shit going on down at Low. I can't go back in there, my hackles go up, I can't get 'em to lie down, and I get funny looks." He shrugged. "If it makes you feel better, I didn't hear anything about a shapechanger." He shuddered. "That's scary..."

"Shit, I know." I finished it for him. "I'm not asking you to go to Low."

He looked relieved.

"I just want you to hang around Joe's, keep your ears open. Not your mouth, you mangy mutt, just ears."

He nodded, and I fished a small leather bag from my pocket. It clinked, and his eyes brightened and the ears were all the way up. I held it out to him. "You send me a message, you hear anything. Kapish?"

He took the bag and made it disappear somewhere into that voluminous suit. One thing I'd say about his style, plenty of room for pockets.

"I got it, boss." His eyes narrowed and he looked me up and down. "Something different about you."

"Yeah. There is." I bubbled him and sent him back to the alley, still standing in the meadow alone. I finished my thought after he was gone. "I'm back, and this time I'm all here."

I stood there alone in the sunlight, thinking, for a long time. Out here it all seemed so far away, and my day had been frustratingly empty of productive answers. Time was trickling faster toward another death, and I couldn't stop it. Time to do some legwork.

Chapter 8

A Darker Side

They say violence answers nothing. I'd say a man with a gun is a great leveler, and a gun in the kidney gets a result. Magic makes that a bit more reliable than it does Above, of course. It's not without pitfalls, even so. When you want someone to say something bad enough, they can and will say anything, doesn't make it true.

Except I know that. And I know how to tell if they mean it. I dug the gun into his hide a little harder. I didn't need to see his eyes to know that he was scared, or that he was lying. I could hear that in his voice.

"Where's the Blood Queen's enforcer?" I asked him again.

He gobbled, a curiously high-pitched noise from a ghoul. I waited. He was breaking, I could smell it now. Came close to gagging me, that flush of sweat driving his fear out through his pores along with his diet of rotting flesh. The ghouls were always on the fringes. No one could stand to be around them for long, to begin with, and you always felt like they were just waiting for you to die so they could chow down.

"She's gonna kills me." He moaned, finally, sagging. I pulled back a little.

"Kills?" I wanted to know if that was just his bad education, or if it had meaning.

"You know. Kill me. Then kill me again. Maybe kill me again after that." He shivered, I could feel it. "Ghoul's gotta live, y'know."

"And you can't do that if you keep getting killed."

He nodded so hard I had fears for his scrawny neck. "Prezackly. Ain't gonna be no zombie, not when her... her thing gets to you."

"So what will you be?" I felt like we were getting somewhere, now. He didn't turn around, even though I'd mostly stopped jabbing him with the long barrel of the revolver I'd chosen for this task. Mentally I promised myself, and it, a good cleaning afterward.

He moaned wordlessly, shaking outright, now. I promised a clean death, and this thing... "You be hunger, be eating and eating and never get full. No thinking, no nothing. Just dead and hungry."

"What is it?"

He shrugged. "Dunno. I don'wanna know. It isn't from 'round here, an I wish it'd go back to where it came from. You gonna put me down?"

I was half tempted. He'd never know anything more, and what she promised sounded like it would be long and painful. I holstered the weapon. "Nah, man. You get on, now. We never talked."

He gobbled again, this time in relief. "We din't talk." He repeated as he scuttled down the alley, not looking back, carefully. He didn't want to see me, to remember me.

I bubbled and went away. I didn't know how much of this traveling I could do before I started to strain my resources. So far, other than being tired, hungry, and sick to my stomach from inhaling ghoul sweat, I couldn't feel it. Having magic was good. But it wasn't a cure-all, as I well knew. Back in the meadow I was sort of using as a pivot, I shucked out of my jacket and shirt, stuffing them into a nylon sack. I didn't want to smell that while I was eating. I sat cross-legged and had my pasty while thinking some more. For the first time, I had solid information. Clues, as to what it was, and the biggest indicator, that it wasn't from Underhill.

Even had it been from another area Underhill, like Dreamstime, the ghastly ruins of what had been Mayan Court or Eastern Court, the ghoul would have known. They might not have second Sight, but they seemed to have a sense for magic. Georgio had talked to me about it one time, when he was gut-full of a bottle of Retsina I'd brought him, and he was feeling maudlin. Which was why I'd laid for the ghoul outside the bar. Conrad was human, not a trace of magic in him. Alger would have known if the thing were a common Underhill race. But what the ghoul said... this was from somewhere else.

I finished Ellie's meat pasty, and pulled a cold beer from nospace. I stared at the beads of condensation forming on it. Alger had said his library was somewhere else, not Above or Underhill. I'd always thought of the two worlds as mirrors of one another, with a shifting veil between them. But what if there were other worlds? Parallel universes, like the human writers were so enamored of in recent years? Could this thing have come from one of them?

If so, how was I going to find it, what did it want, and how could it be killed. Those were the questions. Dionaea, now the Blood Queen, had ridden to power in its bloody tracks. But dealing with her would come after it, because I wasn't willing to pay the price of ignoring her monster, or taking her on directly. War was not inevitable, if you were willing to walk on the darker side and nip the buds before they bloomed in fire and death.

I didn't want to play this game. I wanted to go home, cuddle my wife, and grow some beautiful babies. I pulled a shirt out of my rucksack and shrugged it on. Then a shoulder holster with a semi-auto, this time, and a magazine in each pocket. Finally the rank leather bomber, because I hadn't packed more than one. Short-sighted.

I needed more answers before I could end this. And I needed to keep moving, before Dion sensed me circling her, closing in on her. Because when that happened, it was going to get ugly, and I had no desire to meet the thing the ghouls feared.

Walking in spraying and praying was the attack of a rank beginner, one who had a deathwish, or worse, didn't care one way or another. I'd no intention of bringing a massed magical attack on myself. The gun was insurance, that was all. I probably wouldn't show it, but it was there if I needed it.

Low wasn't a city, they said. It was just there. It had grown around the castle Low Court called home, picked up the name from the Court, and wore it with a perverse pride. The Courts had been divided by rank, once. Low peoples, and High. The aristocrats, and the middle class, as it were. But that had been centuries ago, and I wasn't sure it was true. Myths were made by those who had stories to push. What was real, and here, in Low, was that Low court was the nexus of the bad in my world.

Not everyone that lived in this place was evil. Some were simply weak, lost, and broken. Others liked it here, and that was a good description of the woman I was going to see. Not the Blood Queen, but someone who was proud of her heritage of blood and tears, and who did her best to continue that legacy. Somehow, although I was wary of her, I couldn't blame her. A kelpie is born to it.

I had circled the Low until I was upstream, and now I settled the little paper boat onto the gently rippling water of the stream and set it on its way. She'd have my message once the swift stream reached the river, and it was safer for me to summon her here, far from that home advantage. I looked around.

Magic can be used Underhill to warp the forces of nature, and produce the landscape desired. I'd done it with my own home, having windows that opened into each of the four seasons in a slow rotation. Although that was more illusion than reality, my garden only had one season at a time. The Eastern Court gardens had entirely enchanted Bella with their beauty and serene perfection, created by powerful gardeners over the centuries.

The forest around Low had only one purpose. To repel visitors. I didn't know if it had been deliberate, at first. By now, it certainly was, things lived in there and drew magic around them like a giant spider web, warping the land for miles around. Someone like myself who could use transport bubbles only found it inconvenient. Those with less power found it a formidable obstacle.

I'd chosen this place for two reasons. One, to get some distance between myself and the kelpie's source of power, and second, to stay outside the interdiction shield around the Low Court castle. Breaking that took a lot of power, even though Alger had told me with no little astonishment that Bella had done it without batting an eye. And breaking it meant alerting the Court.

I didn't want to turn my back on the forest, on the trees with their tentacled limbs and watchful eyes. But I really didn't want to put my back to the water. The whole thing had me more than a little jittery.

The beautiful white horse didn't surprise me. I'd been expecting her. I settled into stillness, my hands on hips, only inches from the butt of my gun.

"Hello, Peg." I greeted her, and the ears flickered back and forth. She stamped a forehoof, her fetlocks floating with the movement. But when she neared me and stretched out her nose toward me, nostrils wide, I could see her eyes. Black and empty, they were the product of a thousand nightmares before me.

She whickered and tossed her head. I bared my teeth in what might have been a smile. "I know, I never call, I never write. I walked out one morning and never looked back, and *now* I want a favor?"

This time the whicker was very close to a laugh. I kept going. "Peg o' Dee, have you had your dead this year?"

The horse reared, striking out with both forehooves. I stood still.

She wasn't aiming for me, but she might hit me if I flinched. "How long has it been, Peg, since the blood you crave was given?"

The horse dissolved into a girl. "Are ye offerin'?" She asked, reaching out taloned hands to me.

"Not my blood, no. But I hear there is one who calls herself Blood Queen..." I pointed toward the smokes of Low, visible down the river. "Ruling there, where your waters flow."

"She gives me no blood." Peg sniffed and spat in the waters. "Only she gets the blood."

I wondered how much truth there was to the rumor Dion was bathing in the stuff. Elizabeth of Bathory had, but she was using it as a complexion-enhancer, powered by a fairy spell. I hadn't been around for that, but Alger had told me stories when I was younger and relished a shivery tale by firelight. Come to think of it, that probably explained some things about my later career.

Peg absently ran her long nails, sharpened to points, through her tangled green hair. "Will you give me blood?"

"I intend to." It might take a little while, but that was what I meant to do, find Dion's enforcer and open its veins, if it had any, into Peg's river. Making a bargain with her would give me a lot of access to Low I wouldn't get any other way. The waterways riddled the city which had grown around them and the moat around the castle, which was flushed with Peg's river.

Peg nodded. "You hae kept your bargains."

If I hadn't, I'd have been dead. Peg o' Dee was inexorable in her wrath, and her waters ran deep and far. She tilted her head to one side, running her fingertips down the line of her cheek and jaw. "You would bring chaos again."

"Yeah." Here, anyway. Chaos here meant peace elsewhere. It was the balance of things.

She looked toward the forest, her black eyes showing no white.

Pits into nightmares. She had a dreamy expression on her face. "You are in a hurry."

I wasn't sure what she was thinking. "There have been deaths."

"Not mine." She shrugged.

"No, mine. Those close to me. I prefer life, Peg."

"You do." She pouted, bizarrely childlike for a moment, her hands fluttering at the ends of her dangling arms. "You like life, and you cling to it, and poor Peg is cold, so cold."

"Peg could be blood-warm, if she will help me."

She settled into stillness. "Turn away."

"What?" She was mumbling, and I wasn't sure I'd heard her.

"Turn away," She snapped, showing her sharp teeth. "I don't like to change in front of prying eyes."

"Oh," Dutifully I turned to look at the forest, wondering how she categorized those eyes, watching her behind me. I could tell from their movement when she walked around me.

The tall white horse tossed her head and knelt.

"I'm supposed to what, just climb on? Peg..."

She looked at me with a great sigh.

"All right. You did say I liked life."

She nodded slightly, and I got on her back. Clumsy with lack of tack, but once I was astride and had a double handful of soft white mane, she surged to her feet and turned back toward the water. She walked, and I wondered what was coming, as she picked her way delicately around storm wrack, following the stream bed closely, sometimes walking in it. We neared the river, and she broke smoothly into a canter, water flying from her hooves. She leaped onto a bank, and ran across the smooth grass toward another bank, cutting the chord of the waterway's intersection. I expected her to follow the riverbank, as she had with the stream.

The muscles bunching under my legs was the only warning I got, and when she jumped, I tried to throw myself off, to land hopefully on solid ground – instead, I discovered that I was stuck. I couldn't loosen my legs, or even let go of her mane. We hit the water with a monstrous splash. I tried to gulp a big breath of air, but as we sank into the green water, I watched the silvery bubbles spiral far over my head, and then they disappeared into grayness, and I knew I was out of air. Finally, there was only the black.

Chapter 9

Underwater

I woke up with a drip of water falling on my face. It took me a while to focus properly on the ceiling, because it wasn't really there. I didn't know what it was made of, but it looked like flowing water. Greenish light filtered weakly through it, and it dripped constantly. I sat up and looked around. My head ached.

I was sitting in a boat. I'd been stretched out on the rowing bench, and my head likely hurt because the boat canted at an odd angle, so my head had been lower than my feet. I stood up, looking down the length of the ancient craft. There hadn't been something like this on the oceans or rivers in millennia. This boat was empty, besides me, but I caught a flicker of motion in the porthole of the closest wreck. A much newer boat, with an enclosed cabin. Peg's home, at a guess.

I shuffled more than walked across the slick wet surface of the deck. Water flowed eerily away from my feet, leaving me walking through ankle-deep water with none of it touching my boots. I paused at the edge of the ship, gauging the distance between it and the other, more level, surface. Both were wet. Jumping would be a bad idea. I didn't like the idea of using a bubble, not knowing where I was. If I broke the interdiction, the Low Court would be able to track me.

Perhaps there was a gangplank. Peg had to get around somehow. I could see now that there were other boats and ships all jumbled up together, with a dome of water over the whole mess. Her prey, bones picked over and bleached with age. I walked toward the stern of the galley, picking my way carefully around the jumbles of broken benches, oars, and other debris. I wondered why she'd left me here, and why she'd brought me to her home in the first place. I'd never visited it before.

Kelpies were a strange breed. They were never male, to begin with. I supposed life began by the impregnation of a mother with the seduction of a sailor, and likely followed by his death once he'd served his purpose. Some kelpies could be satisfied with a sacrifice of lesser animals, others demanded people, and on a regular schedule.

Finally, a rickety bridge over the water between the boats, merely two planks placed one atop the other, presumably for strength, as they were very thin. I stepped onto it cautiously and felt it bow under my weight. A quick couple of steps later and I was on the deck of the other boat, the planks clattering in my wake.

Peg came out of the cabin, a wriggling fish in one hand. "You are awake."

She was back in girl form, dressed in a ragged white dress, and her hair looped back with a coil of waterweeds round it.

"I am, and wondering why I'm here, wherever here is."

"The home of my mother, and my mother's mother, and..."

I held up a hand to cut off her flow. I got the idea, the family had been here a long time. "Why," I repeated, "am I here?"

"I was lonely." She scuffed one bare foot across the deck, which was covered with a thick coat of algae but otherwise almost dry. "I wanted company, and surely a day, perhaps two, will not hurt?"

I blinked at her. She brandished the fish. "I will prepare dinner." She announced in a grand tone before ducking back inside the cabin.

I stood on the deck for a moment longer, thinking about this and hoping there was going to be heat involved in that preparation. My stomach grumbled, and I was reminded it had been a long time since the pasty in the meadow. Then I followed her into the cabin.

It was warmer in there, something I hadn't noticed outside, the gathering chill. Peg was standing by a stove, where a skillet was sizzling merrily, and there was a table, and chairs, and it all seemed to be dry and lacking the fuzz of algae everything outside grew. I sat when she waved at the table, while looking intently into the pan.

"I don't cook often," she said.

"I appreciate the effort." I really did. Sushi might be a recent fad Above, but in my opinion it was good for bait, and not much else.

"I apologize for not warning you, but I was afraid if I asked, you would say no." She flipped the fish in the pan, awkwardly. "I used to have friends. But since the Low Court came under *her* spell, no one visits me. And there is no blood." She sighed.

"When did she arrive?" If Peg was going to be talkative, maybe I could get some answers.

"She was here for visits while the Low King still reigned. She would have been his queen, I think, had he not died." She carefully slid the crispy fish onto a china plate and brought it to me.

"Is it good?" Peg was curling strands of her hair around one finger with an anxious expression.

"It smells wonderful." I assured her. There was a napkin, and silverware, all of it very nice, and no doubt looted from shipwrecks. Maybe not the napkin.

She sat down opposite me. I was just as glad she wasn't eating. With a mouthful of needle-like teeth, her dining habits were unlikely to be attractive.

"She brought a creature from Above with her, when the King was dead. Any who resisted her, she gave to it." Peg didn't seem to mind I was letting the fish cool a touch before I took a bite. "She doesn't share the blood. Her creature was allowed to roam the streets of Low, once, and I thought..."Peg licked her lips, which turned my stomach. "But it doesn't share, either. It both kills and drains, or it doesn't kill, and the one who isn't dead..."

"Is hungry." I filled in from what I'd learned before. "Peg, it came from Above? There is very little magic up there. How is it this thing can roam untouched?"

I knew she would have killed it already, could she have. And while I once would have said there was no magic, Above, that was before I'd met Raven. The presence of the trickster spirit – he emphatically denied being a god, although he was the first immortal I'd met for sure – had altered my belief on that topic.

"It came from Above, and intends to go back." Peg leaned her elbows on the table, and her eyes were far away. "I went Above, once. In the time when men foolishly rode horses into rivers, ah, then I could choose a handsome one when I liked, as my mother had, and my mother's mother, and..."

I picked up the fork. The fish smelled really good, and my stomach was asking if my throat had been cut. "The Blood Queen intends to conquer Above, after Underhill?"

That sounded like Dionaea. Overweening ambition. Only now she had the power to do it. I would give Peg her company, but I needed to leave soon. The fish had been gutted, but not scaled and I peeled the skin back carefully and extracted a flaky bit of white flesh from the underlying bones.

"The thing, it was once a god, Above. It has promised her powers beyond magic."

I lifted the forkful of fish, thinking this was why I didn't eat much of it. Too much work for so little reward. The bite never made it into my mouth. There was a splintering crash that shook the boat, and sent both of us sprawling to the floor. With a shrill scream, Peg darted out the door, me on her heels.

She stopped dead on the now-tilted deck, and shrieked like a million teakettles. I clapped my hands to my ears, my eyes watering under the aural assault. Shaking my head to try and clear it, I looked in the direction of the noises, which were smaller, but no less alarming considering that I was underwater. Under water, and no idea how deep. Pressure kills, I knew, but Peg's home seemed to have left me unaffected.

I did not expect to see the creator of the noise. Shaking his head after the piercing kelpie scream, but heading toward me with a determined look in his eye, was Beaker. The red Chinese dragon was as long as the galley he'd just smashed, able to breathe fire, I knew from the first time we'd met... and bonded very firmly to Bella, who he seemed to consider family.

"Beaker!" I scrambled past Peg, who seemed to be rooted in place. I didn't blame her. The dragon was a fearsome sight if you didn't know he was amiably dim-witted. "Beaker, bad boy. You don't break things, haven't we had this discussion?"

He reared his head back, his massive eyes glinting at me, and his golden whiskers which formed a sort of mustache over that mouth full of very sharp teeth twitching. Then he swooped his head down and grabbed me. I yelled.

It's not that it hurt. But when you're that full of adrenaline and shock, you don't feel injury right away. No, it was pure surprise. The last time I'd seen Beaker we had left him in the care of my friend David, the firebird, who lived Underhill in the wilderness where Russia was Above. A half a world away, and with instructions to stay there.

Had he hurt David? I realized he was holding me with a soft mouth, like a retrieving dog, and that we were rising through the water. None of it touched me, he was magically keeping me in a bubble. Peg was nowhere in sight. How had Beaker found me, and why?

Beaker swam as well as he flew, with a sinuous back and forth motion. I lay crosswise in his mouth, and fumed silently. Now Peg would be angry, and I had still been working on her for her help against the Low Court. Beaker couldn't, or wouldn't, talk, even if his mouth hadn't been full of me. Bella's theory is that at one time he could shift to human form, like her grandfather could. Bob was a Western Dragon, the last one of his kind, according to him. Bella was a quarter dragon, but couldn't take dragon form. Beaker, Bella thought, had been injured or abused to the point where he could no longer shift, or think very well any longer. He was certainly doglike in his actions and devotion.

"Take me to Bella!" I yelled at him. Beaker made a garbled noise deep in his throat. That was no help. His vocalizations could be expressive, but not with me in the way.

We broke the surface of the water and I took a deep breath. I could breathe in the bubble of air he'd created, but it had reeked of fishy dragon breath. Now I sucked in lungfuls of cool... ocean?

We were in the sea? I craned my neck to see what was around and could only see water. Beaker was still swimming, and I could feel the breeze on my face as he moved rapidly through the water. I wondered where she'd taken me, and just how long I'd been out while she was carrying me on her back. Questions and more questions, and just when I'd been getting answers.

Chapter 10

Search and Rescue Dragon

Beaker rose out of the water and into the air before too long, but he didn't relent and let me out of his mouth. I was beginning to hurt, now. Not that he'd bitten me, but the cold air on my unprotected face and the awkward position. I dearly hoped he wasn't taking me into danger. I was going to be useless for a while until I got feeling back into my limbs.

I had to close my eyes, the wind whipping my face made them sting and tear uncontrollably. I debated bubbling and going elsewhere, as we were clearly nowhere near Low Court any longer, but I wanted to know what Beaker was up to. I'd hang on, or let myself be hung onto, a while longer.

When I felt his flight path alter, I opened my eyes again, blinking rapidly to try and clear them. It didn't work. All I could see was a blur. There might have been some changes of color from the gray surface of the sea, but I wasn't sure. I closed my eyes again, swearing.

Beaker made a confused noise and I realized I'd been swearing loudly, and at length. Well, if he hadn't known the words before, there were times they were useful. We landed with a bump. Every time I'd seen him before, he'd been graceful in every movement. The cursing must have thrown me off... just like Beaker did, now. I hit the ground rolling, feeling like a thrown rag doll, and just as helpless to stop myself.

Beaker nosed me, "Meep? Meek meek."

I groaned. "I'm jus'gonna lie here a minute..." I still couldn't see, although presumably I was face up now. I could breathe, anyway. Both legs and the one arm that had been pinched in his jaw tingled painfully.

"Lom?" Now, that was a voice I knew. I rolled to my side, then sat up. My legs were still useless.

"Bella?" I rubbed my eyes with my hands and got them mostly clear. I was looking at Beaker's nose. He was looking worried. "Move, you big brute. I forgive you. Come on. Shoo."

He turned his head, and I saw Bella hug his snout. "You found him."

That explained a lot. She'd sent him after me. "Honey, I had planned to send you a message before I dossed down for the night. What couldn't wai..."

The words died in my throat as she turned fully toward me. I scrambled to my feet, swaying slightly. "Bella!"

She came to me, her face solemn. I stood still. I was in no shape to move, and she was... She was very pregnant, now.

"What happened?" She asked me, stopping a pace away from me. Her nose wrinkled. "Phew, you smell like fish."

"Beaker had me in his mouth. Bella, how..." I gestured at her belly. "I've been gone a day."

She shook her head, and I could see the tears fly out of her eyes. "It's been more than two months. We've been frantic, looking for you, and dealing with... Oh, Lom."

I stepped forward and pulled her into my arms. She stiffened, and then melted into me, sobbing. I looked over her head at Beaker, who was crying too, big drops that splashed when they hit the sand. He coiled his body around the two of us, giving us shelter. Beaker seemed to sense her moods and react to them, I'd noticed before. Maybe it was the dragon connection.

"I can't have been out that long. I didn't even grow a beard."

She looked up at me. "You have a little stubble. But no more than your usual. A day? Where *were* you?"

Her voice kept going back and forth between angry and upset. She started to push me away, and then clung tight. I didn't blame her at all. She hadn't needed my disappearance, and with the babies, and the coronation...

"Did I miss the coronation?"

She hiccupped. "You would think of that first. There were nights I wondered if that's why you weren't coming home. No, it's next week. I called Beaker out of desperation and sent him looking for you."

"Good. I really didn't want to miss that, no matter how much I complained."

She looked up at me. "Are you going to tell me where you were?"

"I was in the kelpie's house. I passed out from lack of air on the way down... I was riding her..."

Now Bella did push me away. "You were what!"

"Now," I started to laugh. "That sounded really bad. She isn't human, my dear lady, she was a horse, at the time."

"Really." She got that absent-minded look I knew well. She was accessing the library. Which reminded me to ask her about Alger's lack of access. It had been two months and surely they'd had that conversation.

"Oh." She refocused on me, a look of surprise on her face. "A beautiful white horse, right?"

I nodded. She went on, like she was reading bits of a book to me. "But they have a female form as well."

I broke into her narrative. "Very unattractive. Wears seaweed in her hair, and the talons, not to mention the teeth... Bella..."

She kept going. "Usually found in rivers and streams, demand tribute in the form of lives every seven years, oh, wait, some of them want more like two lives a year, it seems to depend on where they are found. Different individuals, then, not one as the Greeks seemed to think. They had a legend that all the water in the world was one linked system, and the naiads would know anything that happened in water anywhere in the world..."

"Not quite, but Peg would be a powerful ally for information of Low Court which is why..."

"You were visiting her? You know what legend says about men who are invited home with them?"

I didn't know, but I could guess based on what I'd known before, and the way Peg had been acting. "Dammit, Bella, you know I wouldn't..."

I held out my hands to her. She shook her head at me. "Why would you go off with a strange woman, Lom?"

"This is Underhill. There are a lot of strange women. And my job means I have to talk to some of them. Even, yes, go off with them. Bella."

I wasn't going to beg, and I was wondering what had gotten into her. This was not my level-headed princess.

"You didn't come home! It's been months!"

"Bella!" I stepped toward her and grabbed her arms. "Bella, this isn't like you. What's wrong?"

She burst into tears, again. I wrapped her in my arms. I wasn't going to let go again. "Mine. You're mine, and I'm yours. Remember that?"

She buried her face in my shoulder. "I keep crying. I hate this. I just... I thought you were dead. We couldn't reach you. Messages just... wouldn't go. They'd sit in my hand when I tried to reach you. Alger sent Mark above, and Raven..."

I groaned and laughed at the same time. She'd dragged the trickster into it. I was never going to hear the end of this.

"I don't know why, Bella. You know I wouldn't have left you like this of my own free will."

"The kelpie kidnapped you." Bella looked up at me again. "Do you think she was trying to keep you prisoner?"

"Um, no idea. I thought we were going to have dinner and talk." My stomach, on cue, growled.

"Did you eat anything?" She not only looked alarmed, she hugged me tighter.

"No, Beaker broke in just as I was about to have a fish dinner. So I haven't eaten in... months?"

That didn't feel right. I was hungry, sure, but that would have killed me.

"I think if you had eaten that fish, you would never have been able to leave. She really did want you for herself."

I had completely missed that cue. Peg had acted like she was willing to work with me, not like a black widow. Then again, no one knew what became of the men the kelpies took for themselves.

"Bella, I'm here now, and I have no idea what happened to the time. Will you forgive me? And maybe feed me?"

She chuckled. "Gladly. To both. Ready to go home?"

"Oh, yes..." She had us in a bubble before I could finish. "What about Beaker?"

"He always finds his way to me. He's a good search dragon." She was still holding onto me. I bent and kissed her.

We were still working on that, catching up for lost time, when we arrived at home. She'd brought us right into our bedroom, and we had privacy... so she sent me to take a long bath, and scrub hard. It took a while to get the fish and old ghoul off my skin and hair.

Evidently I'd transferred some to her, because Bella joined me after a while. The big tub and shower I'd taken the trouble to install came in handy, since she was no longer as slender as she'd been the day before for me. I got reacquainted with her, and the glows of our children, nestled in the new shape of my bride. I was not happy that so much had been stolen from me.

There were things I needed to know, and people I needed to talk to, to assure I was still alive, and that I knew more about Dion's enforcer... all that could wait. I needed to make sure Bella was all right, first. It involved food, bed, and sleep wrapped up in one another's arms before either of us was willing to let the outside world know I was back.

We hadn't talked much about anything of import during those few hours. She'd sent messages to King Trytion and Alger, merely letting them know I'd been found. So when I walked down the stairs, it didn't surprise me to find them waiting in the kitchen. I sensed Bella's hand in this. She'd been the one who asked me to go find coffee, and tea for her. Coffee, it seemed, was no longer agreeing with her pregnant system.

Alger wordlessly greeted me with a bearhug, lifting me off my feet. I was taken by surprise. He, at least, didn't seem to have thought I was hiding out and shirking my duties. He sat me back on my feet and scrutinized me closely.

"So. Where were you?"

"Kelpie's house. For less than a day."

He nodded and let go of me, satisfied. "Time runs differently in the underwater kingdom. It's how they live for so long."

"And why some of them only eat once every seven years?" I had a small epiphany. He nodded. "Damn. Glad I didn't stay for dinner, then." I turned to Trytion.

"Sir..." I wasn't sure what to tell him.

"That was cryptic, and yet I understood some of it." He stood and clasped hands with me, then returned to his breakfast. When had my place become the guesthouse for royalty?

He waved a forkful of eggs in my direction. "It worries me, you know, that I got any of it at all. Some of the worst parts of kingship are having to know everything, and I try to avoid it."

"Um..." I needed to take Bella her tea. And I needed more coffee in me before I had this conversation.

"Sit, Lom." Bella walked into the kitchen. "We have a lot of catching up to do."

"That sounds ominous." I sat as ordered, and Ellie put a plate in front of me. She squeezed my shoulder before she went away again, which was an outpouring of emotion from her.

Bella started to tell me everything, with Alger and Corwin filling in a little.

Chapter 11

Bella Alone

Bella hadn't expected me back anytime soon, certainly not that night. She wasn't looking forward to the next morning, though, after two bodies in as many mornings. When dawn broke, and I wasn't home, but there wasn't a body, all she felt was relief, and then she had calmly left for work at the Court.

Court was always hard for her. Raised American, with a strong dose of Alaskan independence and resourcefulness, she'd intended to spend most of her career alone, out in the woods. She had a big, loving family to socialize with when work was done. Now, she was virtually alone, surrounded by people whom she couldn't trust. Joe was grieving, Corwin would only make brief appearances in between being King Trytion. Bella had given him an apologetic glance as she was telling this part, and he'd just waved a hand. Don't trust him fully myself, he told her, and she went on.

Tensions were running high. This was the first full Council session since I had so rudely interrupted with Margot's body in my arms. Alger and Lucia were the only faces she could count as friendly, and both wore masks over their pain. Bella sat next to the king, and waited to see what would happen.

Wait and see had become her motto. Corwin had warned her this would be the case. Do too much, too soon... or in some cases, do anything at all, and bad things would come of it. Benign negligence was the best way, he told her, to keep a kingdom on an even keel. So, Bella asked him, we take over the world and leave it ruthlessly alone? He'd laughed, told her she had it in one... and now, she serenely faced the people who wanted to make things happen.

Each one, she was learning, had some motivation. Buckingham was half-mad for family, and pure blood fairy rule. He had sent her on a mission where she could have been killed, with malice aforethought. Lucia told her that as malevolent as the man was, he wasn't smart enough to have come up with it on his own. The true one to watch for, she'd been warned, was the Duchess Laenven. Of the Willow clan, she was the aunt of one of the spurned princesses, who after Bella's selection had mostly retired to their estates to sulk for a season. Only Dill and Lady Herbale remained at court, becoming friends with Bella. Only Lady Herbale wasn't on the Council.

Bella kept her face a smooth mask as the meeting began with formalities, but behind it she was day dreaming of molding the council membership to have more friendly faces. It would be very nice to have a congenial workplace. It would be positively invigorating to know none of the faces in the room were looking at them all as enemies. She was very aware that someone here was a traitor, and likely the reason Margot died and Lom was off running dangerous errands.

But there was no danger here. No one was shooting her, or hunting her to grind her bones for bread... at least, that's how she remembered the stories about ogres going. This was all highly civilized, and cold, and how are you today very well and you. No one talked about death, except when Buckingham stood and cleared his throat.

He wanted to propose a measure of censure against the newly reinstated Dukedom of Elleria, for the behavior of their titular head, and to reluctantly remind their majesties that if the Dukedom was found to be incapable of ruling peaceably and productively, the blood-line would be stricken from the rolls entirely.

Bella didn't know what that meant, but it sounded ominous, and provoked a dangerous glitter in the king's eyes. Buckingham, his chest puffed out like a male ptarmigan in full display, stood waiting for something.

"We will take that under consideration." Trytion's voice came out like a granite block moving slowly under pressure. Buckingham, with a slight smirk, started to sit down. "We will remind you. Indeed, all of the council that the Lady Margot was on our business when she was cut down so cruelly. If the bonds of blood drove our trusted friend to rash action, it is no more nor less than could be expected of a loving brother."

Buckingham looked as though Trytion had hauled back and punched him in the gut. His eyes flickered back and forth between Bella and the king before, tellingly, sliding to the Duchess who sat with her hawk-like face still, and her wings at rest. She didn't even twitch as he fell back into his chair like a sack of potatoes.

Bella had decided then she never wanted to see that face again. Buckingham might piss her off, but the Duchess scared her. The rest of the council was much more proceed-as-expected deathly boring, but at least no one was trying to eat her, that was what she kept telling herself. Afterwards, in chambers, she tried to explain what her thoughts had been to the king.

Trytion stroked his beard and heard her out patiently while she paced and tried to formulate her argument for ridding themselves of the troublesome Duchess. It's a bad idea, he told her later, to try and manipulate friends into power and those we don't like out. Doing that led to having a cadre of yes-men, and greater men than me, he'd pointed out gently, have been led astray doing that.

Bella had felt like crying, but let it go. How could he endure having a traitor sitting there calmly learning all the inner plans every time they met?

Trytion, leaning one elbow on my kitchen table listening to her talk, his eyes dark with sorrow, reached across it to take her hand.

"I can endure it because I know it will not last long. As soon as we have enough evidence."

"You couldn't have told me this before?" Bella glared at him.

"You have been distracted. I'm sorry, Bella. But..." He looked at me. "I needed your mind on him, to be honest, not on her. I could take care of her and the Council. I've been doing it for more than a century. But you're the only one who could find him. I know Lom well enough to know he wouldn't just vanish with a pregnant wife, and his sister's death unsolved."

I nodded and Bella took a deep, shaky breath. "The pregnancy hormones aren't helping. I can't tell you how many times I've come close to bursting into tears at the worst possible time."

"That explains a lot." I commented. She hit me. Gently. Then she started talking again.

"I knew something was wrong when I tried to send a message to you the next night. I'd been waiting to hear, and then the body turned up..."

"What?" She hadn't said anything about that. "Where?"

"At Court, not your home, which is why we thought they might be unconnected." Corwin broke in.

"Well, that, and this one had not been brutalized." Alger spoke for the first time. "We initially thought the man had starved to death."

"At Court?" I was perplexed, but had an inkling...

"His stomach was full. Of... everything. Dirt, rocks, plants... he was found in the garden, emaciated, but he'd been eating literally everything in sight."

"While I was making inquiries... before the kelpie, sorry, Bella."

She squeezed my hand. "I know that wasn't your fault."

I kept going, reassured. "The general consensus seems to have been that the thing Dion is using as her enforcer causes hunger. One told me it kills, but the victim isn't really dead, it's just hunger, until it dies again. He wasn't real clear on how long this would take, or if it could happen more than once. And then I learned that it came from Above. Bella..." I looked at her. "I know you grew up not really knowing about magic, but could there be other spirits like Raven, remnants of legends lingering on?"

Alger stroked his beard, looking at the ceiling. "I think there's something..."

Bella got that far away look. "I'm looking."

I glanced back and forth between the two of them. "I take it the library situation hasn't been cleared up?"

Alger shook his head. "I haven't wanted to add to her burden. I can only access a little, on the fringes..."

"Aha." Bella spoke, her eyes still dreamy. "Native American spirits causing hunger and... ugh. Self-cannibalism? Um. Could this be a Wendigo?"

"She had no trouble getting in." I looked at Alger, who was a trifle peaked around the edges. "You ok?"

"I think I'm losing my mind." His shoulders slumped. "I'm sorry, boy, but I'm of no use to you any longer."

He had all our attention, and for once, I didn't see the old familiar drama on his face. The puckish sense of humor was gone, and what was left was a shell.

Alger reached for his staff to lever himself to his feet. I'd never seen him do this before. "I held out until you were home, but I'm going. Better I not..." He waved his free hand dismissively. "It's not a pretty way to go. I'd rather die in combat, but that's a way to take others with me."

I remembered Martin, and how he'd fought to the end. The old man had died with dignity. Alger was right, but...

Bella went around the table and caught his hand in both of hers. "Uncle. Why didn't you speak to me before?"

He looked down at her and his eyes went gentle. "I never meant to give you the library, only the outer shell, and in my haste I didn't try to unwrap it. That you would have the power you do... It's been a joy to see that bloom."

"Lom told me when you had given the library you asked for no price. He said you would ask later, and that I might not want to pay it. At the time, I had no idea the gravity of the possible prices. But Alger, I would pay that now."

He drew back a little, startled. "M'dear girl. Any debts owed were waived when you came into the family."

I couldn't help myself. "And all the fees I've paid over the years?"

He broke into a smile. "It was the only way I could continue teaching you those tasks."

I laughed. "You old fool, you benefited from all of that."

"Well, yes, or you would have caught on." He looked back down at Bella. "I am old. It is my time."

"No. No, there is something else that is going on, and we are going to get to the bottom of this. I need you. Your damn library is so out of order I can't possibly learn all of it on my own." She poked him in the chest.

"Bella..." He sounded oddly helpless.

"Better give in, Alger." Corwin offered. "I'm learning not to oppose her already. Woman is going to rule with an iron fist."

"We are going to the library, right after the coronation. End of that argument."

"But your condition!" He protested. She looked at me. I raised both hands.

"Alger, is the library dangerous?" I asked.

He snorted. "The library itself? Only if a stack of books falls on her."

"Which it might." Bella came back to her seat, smiling. "Now, I want to talk to my husband. Shoo."

They went, not without a little leering. We still had things to talk about, but all of us were going to cater to her. In the light of day and with clear eyes, I could see that despite the swollen belly, her face was thin and there were blue shadows under her eyes.

"Only one body?" I asked her, and she nodded. "That's good. I was wondering if there would be a daily body until we..."

"Did what? She hasn't contacted us directly. There have been no overt threats, or demands, or..." she fluttered her hands. "Anything."

"Which is more nerve-wracking than something."

"Yes..." She picked up her tea and frowned into her mug. "I don't like just waiting for something to happen. And I don't like the idea of a spirit as powerful as Raven running around acting as the Low Court's hitman."

"I wonder what they are up to. Oh, shit."

"What?" She looked up, confused, as I jumped up.

"When you couldn't reach me, what happened?"

"I'd form a message spell, and then when I tried to send it it would spiral up into the air slowly, then settle back into my hand, glow for a second, and..." her lower lip trembled. "Go out."

"Damn. I have to go do something." I leaned forward to kiss her. "I promise I will be right back."

"No. Oh, no, you don't." She got to her feet. The pregnancy had not yet slowed her down. I remembered Margot, with a lump in my throat, waddling around carrying Devon. It didn't seem possible she was gone. Bella whisked a bubble around us. "Where are we going? If you think I'm letting you out of my sight for one second, Learoyd Otheris...."

I stopped her with a kiss, and gave the spell a nudge in the right direction. We'd find out what Terrence thought about a woman in jeans and a sweater wanting to waltz into Joe's.

Chapter 12

The Crowning Day

As it turned out, we never found out what the ogre would say about casual dress. Sean was waiting for us in the alley. He'd gotten my message while we were on our way, and wanted to jump right back out.

"Where to?"

"I don't care, man, just fast." He was looking everywhere at once, the whites of his eyes showing all the way around. The big wolf was scared half out of his mind. I took us to the sunny meadow, which wasn't that sunny today, but it was the first place I could think of. He took a deep breath, and let it out slowly, turning to see in all directions.

"We're alone." Bella spoke for the first time, and Sean really looked at her.

"You're real." He swiveled his head back to me. "You're alive."

"Yes, and yes. What did you think, that was my ghost back there?"

"You were gone a long time, and my messages..."

"I know, they didn't go through. Long story. What has you ready to bolt?" I looked around the meadow, hoping it wouldn't start to rain. I figured it was time I created a place to take people and talk that wasn't my house. I needed a bolthole.

Sean took a minute to get his equilibrium. Bella helped. She stuck her hand out. "Hi, I'm Bella. Mr. Rudepants here forgot to mention that."

I raised an eyebrow. Sean got a look on his furry face I'll never forget. He held out a paw to Bella, all misshapen fingers and a thumb with long nails and short brown fur. I didn't think I'd ever touched him. Sean considered himself a freak, and was touchy about his appearance. Bella took his hand and smiled widely at him.

"I'm Sean. Er... Sean the wolf." He gave me a wild-eyed look that wasn't fear, or at least not fear like it had been before.

"I really like that suit. I must get the name of your tailor."

Now she had both our attention. Sean looked like he might fall to his knees in front of her, and I had a sheer moment of horror that she meant to outfit me like the wolf, who was sporting a shade of crimson that just escaped being pink by a dark hair.

"Sh... Sure thing, Lady Bella." He told her with a little stammer.

"Just Bella. Now, talk to me. What's wrong, and how can we help you?"

He slumped, and I wondered if we could bottle her essence. She had a gift for leveling with people, and they opened up to her like a cork coming out of a champagne bottle.

"I'm in big trouble. That thing... the enforcer, they're sending it after me."

"What?" I had told him not to open his mouth. He shrugged, palms up in apology.

"I wasn't getting nowhere. Joe's was drying up. Everyone was antsy, but nobody blabbed. If they did come in, they was like a clam, drinking the ocean but never a word."

"And you thought you'd ask questions." I would have, had I been in his shoes. Not that I'd be caught dead in today's puce and maroon two-tones.

"Seemed like the right thing to do. Buy a drink or three, I felt guilty not using that money you gave me for results, real info. I thought I'd get the straight dope and instead..." He shivered.

"What happened?" Bella prompted.

"My guy, the one I'd been leading on. Third night I'd intercepted him in this real dive bar, not Joe's, and he came in with a funny look on his face. Like he wasn't all there, you know? I stood up and he went for me. Growling, and gnashing his teeth, like, and I jumped back so fast I tripped over a chair and went down, wound up under the next table which I figure saved my life."

He pulled a maroon silk handkerchief out of his pocket and wiped his eyes, which were welling up. "The bouncer, he was just a dwarf, he tried to bounce the guy, and got bitten. The next thing I know, they are tryin' to eat each other. The guy, he even got to gnawing on his own arm. They were so wrapped up in each other, I got out of there. But Lom, that was meant for me."

I nodded, feeling grim. "I know. That's the Blood Queen's ticket to power, a thing that creates an insatiable hunger in a person, it eats and eats and starves to death."

He nodded, his eyes haunted. "I heard they were both dead in two days, looking like they'd been without food for weeks, but chewing on anything in reach. I went into hiding. I didn't know what I was going to do, I'd used my last favor and the money up, and then I got your message."

"We'll get you someplace safe." Bella reached out and took his paw again. He gave her puppy dog eyes in return. It was faintly revolting.

"I've got some ideas. Did you get anything at all?"

He nodded. "She's raising an army. Rumor has it they mean to hit High Court at the coronation."

"When they figure we'll all be so distracted we won't be ready."

We wouldn't be, either. That wasn't very much time. We had no proof to sway the Wild Hunt in our direction, just lots of supposition and innuendos. Bella put a hand to her belly. Sean followed her motion.

"When are the pups coming?"

Bella choked back a little laugh. "The babies are due in about four months."

He wiggled his ears. "Hope they take after you and not that ugly sonofa..."

Now she did laugh as he bit off the end of what he'd been saying. I didn't care. Teasing meant he was back on track, and I did not need an insanely worried werewolf on my hands.

"Bella, we have to get back and tell the King what's coming. Sean, you're coming with us."

His ears laid back. "I'd rather not."

"I need you to tell him. I'm in his black books right now," I fibbed a little. Truth was, I wanted him at Court. We needed every set of hands and paws on deck for this one. I'd dealt with a goblin incursion with only a dozen men, it was going to be a little trickier this time.

He sighed deeply. "If you need me."

"Please come." Bella laid a hand on his arm and looked up into his furry face. She may have batted her lashes, I couldn't see from where I was standing.

"Yeah. I'll come."

I bubbled the three of us before he could change his mind, and we were on our way.

"Where to, m'lady?" I asked Bella. We were going to Court, but where?

She pursed her lips in thought. "I think the small receiving room. It ought to be empty at this time."

I saw her flick message spells as quickly as she could. I had a feeling that room wouldn't be empty long. I was right, it was pretty crowded when we got in there, and it took a while to clear it out again until there were only three of us standing in it, looking at each other, and thinking.

Not for the first time, I thought about why this room had no windows. So you couldn't tell what time of day it was outside Court, and you couldn't tell how long you'd been waiting – there wasn't a clock in it, either. There were books, and usually refreshments, and a necessary room. But you could be left in here for an undetermined time and never know how long you'd been waiting, unless you had a watch, and that wasn't common among the Fae.

I had a watch. And I wasn't waiting, the king was standing here looking at me, like I was the man with the answers.

"We haven't got time," I told him. In this room, all warm and mellow, my voice sounded flat and cold to my own ears. "We might have had time before Peg pulled her trick on me, but now?" I shrugged. "Raising an army takes time we just don't have."

"I know it." He ran a hand over his beard and looked back and forth between the two of us.

"Leave her out of it. Bad enough you're putting that crown around her neck, without dragging her into a battle in her condition."

"I'm not sick, I'm pregnant." She kept her voice low, and then turned away to go sit down.

"Can you find out the size of this army? Or even if there is one?"

I nodded. "And then what?"

"Joe is already summoning men."

"Beaker." Bella spoke again and the look on Trytion's face told me he thought the pregnancy had gone straight to his brain.

"I take it you haven't met Beaker yet." I said to him. He shook his head.

"Another like your wolf friend?"

"Not exactly. He's a little more intimidating to look at. Bella, can you get him to play door dragon?"

She chuckled. "He'd rather be in the throne room with me, but I think I can show him he won't fit, and he'll do what I ask."

I walked over to her and put a hand on her hair. She twisted around and took it, kissing my fingers. "You will be here?"

"I promised."

"What are you going to do?"

"I'm going to see how far I can push a bubble, and how fast." I nodded at Trytion and walked out of the room. Court was under an interdiction, and although I knew I could break it, it took more effort and I was saving myself, now.

I wasn't going to Low Court, she didn't have room to gather any kind of force there, and it was too far. Underhill, an army had to travel more or less like one above, on their feet, or paws, or scaled bellies... Transport by bubbles worked for a small group, but it took a lot of power, and when you got where you were going, you might need that power in a fight.

Which helped me, as there were few places you could approach High Court, and fewer that would allow an army passage. All I needed to do was figure how far they could travel in the time before the coronation, and look there.

I was going to try a trick Alger had taught me, taking a bubble in, thinning it enough to see, and then going again. Hopefully without being seen myself. The first few hops were nothing, all quiet. I stopped to think and take a breath. Just travel wasn't as wearing as this stop and go, and the strain of expecting something to shoot at me wasn't helping.

"What if I don't find them?" I asked the air. I didn't think the wolf had been lying, but I didn't trust whoever had told him near that much. It was possible this was all a ruse to get us up in arms. And then what?

It was the old story of the boy and the wolf again. Keep getting ready, then nothing... when the real threat came, you were too worn out to care any longer. Dionaea might have the patience for that. Her ally did, from what we'd been learning, and I wasn't sure who was really in charge over there.

The Wendigo had come Underhill for some reason. When, I wasn't sure, but it couldn't have been too long, or we would have heard of the sickening deaths it wrought before this. Dion had taken a century to get where she wanted to be. No... halfway to where she wanted to be. What she really wanted was what Bella was going to accept in little more than a day, now.

Night was falling, and I was glad of it. Dark was better for sneaking and peeking. Some of the things in Low Court were nocturnal, sure, but I was a shadow in the shadows with my bubble. I kept hopping. One thing about this errand, it was telling me where my limits might lie. In some ways it was good to know I had limits. I didn't want to be super-powered, and I didn't think I was. If you know where your limits are, you can avoid hitting them when it comes to the sticky end of things.

I found them out much further than I'd expected. If they were traveling by ground it would take them a week to get to High Court. Their camp was chaos, fires blazing and a madhouse of creatures having a party, it looked like, around them. I circled the perimeter and looked again, then went away. I was sure I hadn't been seen. No one was looking.

I sent message spells, and then sat on a rock and thought some more. I'd have bet money Dionaea wasn't traveling with this lot. There was no red tent or grand caparisoned contrivance for her. Which didn't mean much, as she could always come in later, to give them a pep talk or instill fear, whichever worked for her. I also didn't think the Wendigo was down there with them. The atmosphere was too happy. Everything I'd spoken to before this had been in abject fear of the spirit.

I felt a hand on my shoulder, and then Daffyd was crouching

beside me, looking down into the dimly lit hollow where the camp was. I didn't mind him sneaking up on me, that was his job.

"What do you think?" I asked him, not bothering to keep my voice down. We could barely hear them, and they were screaming and cavorting.

"I think this is a diversion." The slender archer looked at me, and I could see the flickering light reflected on his eyes. "This is not serious."

I nodded. It was good to hear what I'd been thinking. "What are we going to do about it, spank it and send it home to mommy?"

His teeth flashed white in the night. "Not tonight, perhaps."

I shook my head. "No. Tomorrow night. After the coronation, which they are in no danger of disrupting. Can you and a few of your boys keep track of them? I'd hate to be wrong."

"Yah. No problem watching this lot, like a wounded bear in brush. Dangerous, but noisy."

I clapped his shoulder. "I'm off to report in, then. Thanks, Daff."

"My pleasure. You do find the best fights." He settled on the rock I'd just vacated, and I wearily wrapped a bubble around me and went home.

Chapter 13

Queen of Fairies

Home was surprisingly empty. There was no one in the kitchen, although I found my plate of dinner in the usual enchanted cupboard, fragrant and warm like it had just been served. I sat at the table, and had a serious moment of dissonance. Here I was peaceably masticating, while relatively near, there was a blood-mad army out for death and destruction. I'd been working myself to the bone, escaping death and worse. But here I am having a workingman's meal, with the hope of a warm bed with a warmer woman in it.

I went up the stairs to that promise, and didn't come down until morning. The house was considerably fuller.

"Morning, Alger." I sat down at the table with my coffee in my mitt. Ellie was conspicuously absent. We'd fetch our own breakfast, the women were up to their necks in clothing and doo-dads.

"You found the army?"

"Daffy's keeping an eye on it. I don't think it can possibly make it to Court within a week. We've already started calling up troops."

"Why did she even bother?" He was wearing a thunderous frown and gazing so hard at his plate I expected his food to shortly become cinders.

"I think it's a diversion."

"Diversion from what?" He chased his egg around the plate with a bite of toast.

"I don't know, and it worries me."

He looked at me. "You lost a lot of time."

I nodded. "I have to be here today. After... she knows I'll be back at it. I have a bad feeling, and she agrees with me. She's mad as a wet hen she can't go with me."

He nodded. "I promised I'd take her to the library, but it will have to wait until this fracas with Low Court is settled."

"I don't think this little playground tiff is going to settle it." I really had a bad feeling growing in the pit of my stomach like poison.

Devon walked into the room, and I got up to clasp forearms with him. I squeezed his shoulder and looked at him for a long minute. He was thin, but brown as a nut.

"Been working hard?" I asked him. I hadn't seen him since I'd set out after his mother's killer.

"Work keeps me from thinking." He smiled. "Glad to see you back."

"Glad to be back, even if I didn't know I was gone."

"Any news?" His voice was diffident, but his eyes were intense. It had to be rough on him to have been held at the manor, with me missing and no work being done on his mother's murder.

"I know what did it. I know more or less where it is. But we still need to tie it to Dionaea, and lay it before the Hunt. It will take time." I kept my tone serious and held his eyes with mine. I didn't need him taking off on a wild hair and getting himself in trouble.

He nodded. I let go of him, and he made a beeline for the food. Teenagers, if you could harness that energy you'd go broke feeding it. Alger got up from the table and followed me out of the kitchen.

"I'll be in the audience with the Council today." He told me.

"I'll be in the anteroom. I'll watch without being watched."

He nodded. "I'd rather, myself. See you later."

Alger vanished, and I stopped at the foot of the stairs and looked up the gentle spiral. I didn't know that I wanted to go up there. Bella was trying to choose a color, last I'd seen, and my eyes were beginning to threaten to bleed as she magically kaleidoscoped her dress fabric. She hadn't been this nervous on our wedding day. It had probably helped when we'd been married more than once, of course. I turned and retreated to the armory.

I wound up going to court without Bella. When I'd come up from the armory Ellie had been waiting for me.

"She's gone ahead." The tiny elf was all but tapping her toe in impatience on the floor.

"I got distracted, sorry." I did feel bad, I knew how wound up she'd been.

"She said to meet her in the usual place."

I nodded, and got there quick. She was pacing, her dress rustling. I stopped to watch her for a second, and then whistled low and long. Bella's face lit up.

"You look ravishing." I took her into my arms and could feel her trembling with tension.

"I look fat. But thank you, dear." She relaxed into me.

"You only look more beautiful than ever, with our children there." I cupped one hand around the curve of her belly, which was covered in green silk. She'd gone with a dark, sedate shade, a more modern cut of dress than most women in Court favored. Underhill lagged more than a century behind Above, and like my mother, seemed to think Queen Victoria (the younger version) was the arbiter of fashion.

"You'll knock 'em dead. Just smile and look regal. That's all you need to do."

"Lom, this is... I never wanted this."

"You never wanted what?" I knew, but I also knew she needed to talk.

"Never wanted to be a queen. Or even a princess."

"I know. I'd say I'm sorry, but I'm not."

She chuckled, a little gurgle of amusement. "There is so much responsibility, Lom. I'm supposed to be taking care of, somehow, all these people. I can't possibly..."

"No one expects you to watch over every sparrow. You're just supposed to be wise and good..."

She pushed at me, but I kept one arm firmly around her. "You're not making it any better!"

"Bella my love, you already are those things. No, you're not perfect, but you're not alone, either. Stop being so afraid of screwing it all up."

"I am very afraid."

"I'll always be in the shadows. And you have many who love you for you. Already, my egalitarian American girl, you have a salutary effect on Underhill, which you might not see. The ripples you started began with your arrival. They are becoming waves with your coronation."

"You are being quite poetic." She kissed me gently and we parted. "I have to go."

"I will be watching through the screen in the anteroom."

She walked out the door, and I wondered if she had any inkling yet what it meant that she was about to assume the Queen's Crown. She was not a pureblood fairy, being part human and part dragon, although that last wasn't something the Court knew about. Speaking of dragons...

I went out the back halls, which were full of bustling servants, and made my way to the main gates, where Beaker was resting his massive head on the ground and eyeing everyone who passed through them with suspicion. I slapped his jaw, and he greeted me in return with a toss of his head which nearly knocked me over.

"Mreep." He remarked, almost conversational.

"Good to hear it." I thought he meant that no one had gone by him with ill intent. Being able to almost understand him was a bit disconcerting. I dealt with it. He was an asset.

"Meep, meep... memeep?"

"Sorry, old man, there's just no room in there." I pulled a mustache whisker. "I'll tell her you asked, and tonight we'll see you in the garden, eh?"

He nodded, and went back to watching all and sundry. He was making people nervous. I didn't care. He was making me feel much better about the people who would be streaming before the new Queen at her presentation. And it was time for me to take my place in that.

Like actors in a play, they were all taking their places. The Council, standing in a semi-circle around Trytion. Bella, standing outside the chord of their arc, facing him, her face serene. She didn't show the nerves I knew she was feeling. I couldn't see the faces of the Council, but Alger, leaning on his staff near the end of the line, was in profile to me, and I could see his bright gray eyes darting from face to face. He would see much, as the ceremony preceded.

Trytion was wearing his crown, and holding the one he would place on Bella's head in both hands. I'd never seen this ceremony, but I had read along with Bella as she was prepared for it. He turned, took three steps, and handed the crown to the councilor on the far end from Alger. A dumpy little Duke whom I knew only by his title, Newington, took it gravely.

"We approve the King's choice of queen," he intoned, "and grant her the power of High Court." He passed the crown to the next person.

Lady Waecra, who was a friend of my mothers, said simply, "I approve."

The crown proceeded slowly along the Council. It came to Buckingham, and I know I wasn't the only person who could see and feel the tension in the room. His head had been bowed, but as he took the crown he raised his head up and spoke ringingly. "I challenge the right of Belladonna Traycroft Mulvaney to claim this crown."

Bella paled a little, but stood still. This was something we had known might happen.

Trytion spoke, his voice calm, "Do any second this motion?"

Lady Laenven spoke up, "I stand with Buckingham."

She stepped forward, one pace, breaking the rank of the Council. Alger was glaring at her, but stayed still. Buckingham, with a sideways glance at her, followed her lead. I hadn't thought he was the brains behind this, and their movement had just confirmed that.

"Are there any others who would challenge the consort-elect?" Trytion still sounded placid. I knew him better than that. This was rage, icy and deep.

"I join them." The voice almost squeaked with nervous tension, and the flutters of her movement as she stepped forward told me that Lady Willington was not as sure as she wanted to sound.

Three, against the other twelve of the Council, and Trytion. Not an overwhelming majority, or even minority. I wondered why they had chosen to reveal themselves, here and now. Drama? That seemed unlikely, as I knew Buckingham had been resistant to Bella from the beginning. No, something else was going on, and I felt the hackles on my neck begin to rise as I scanned the audience.

The huge room was by no means full, we simply hadn't the populace to fill it any longer. Perhaps, in the distant past, before Low and High Courts split, that had not been the case. All those present were riveted on the small group standing on the dais, and at Bella, who had her back to the audience for the moment. The script said she would turn to face them as part of the formal presentation by Trytion after the crown was placed on her head. All very symbolic and as choreographed as a ballet.

Now, the choreography had stopped cold. The entire room seemed to be holding their breath. Trytion spoke into this deep silence, his voice booming by contrast.

"What grounds do you challenge the consort elect from?"

"We challenge from the original Charter. The Queen and King are to be unblemished, of pure descent, and held worthy of high office by their peers. We claim the right to inspect the person of the consort-elect, and to see her lineage laid out. Finally, we put to you that she is not held in respect by her peers." Lady Laenven had been stolidly expressionless during this speech, but at the last sentence I could see the sneer on her aristocratic profile. I was sure that I'd be able to see more emotion were I face-to-face, but I was not going to leave my place just yet. Disruption was going to cause more harm than good.

Challenging from the Charter was an interesting approach. The original document had disappeared a thousand years before, it was said, and all that remained were copies of portions of it. Some of those were dubious. I was slowly getting pissed at the idea they wanted to inspect Bella like she was a prize heifer, and that her mixed descent was even a concern. The Court didn't know about her dragon blood, yet, and I wasn't sure how they'd react. Human blood was bad enough. Respect by those three... it was just as well she didn't have that.

Trytion raised one eyebrow slightly. "Are you sure you wish to do this, Lady Laenven?"

She lifted her chin a little, making her wattles wobble faintly. "I challenge..."

A sardonic voice from the audience broke in. "Aye, woman, dinna fash yerself aboot bluid. Fairies, pixies, hoomans... all alike. But whoe'er haird o'a half sprite?"

The blood climbed up to her cheekbones, giving her a mottled appearance under her cosmetics. She ignored the sprite. I wondered about her own descent. Humans and fairies have a long history, and pixies were merely another clan of fairy, no more different than one brother to the next. Underhill, genetics were unknown. Lines, kept carefully in ancient, cracking books, were all that mattered. Unlike the human's technology, the lineage could be distorted very easily. A bribe, a lie, an impotent husband willingly cuckolded...

Maybe Bella should get some equipment installed at home and start a certain project... no, she wouldn't have time. I wondered if importing a technician would go over. Mapping the fairy genome would be very interesting, and have repercussions over more than one kingdom. I brushed the thought aside and waited for Laenven to finish making a fool of herself.

"As we cannot consult the original Charter..." She started again.

Alger – twitched. All eyes turned to the old mage. He opened his mouth, closed it, and then with a pained expression, he spoke.

"The Charter still exists."

Lady Laenven lost that blush the sprite had given her. She looked positively ghoulish, she was so pale. "How can this be?"

Alger regarded her calmly, leaning on his staff. A moment ago it had been incongruous, now it blended into his persona like it was one of his legs. I realized I'd never seen him without it at arm's length away, at most. "I was never stricken from my appointment as Court Librarian, Esme."

She rocked back slightly, whether from anger at his use of her first name, or the realization that he had the upper hand, I wasn't sure.

"You can produce the Charter?" Trytion broke into this exchange.

Alger frowned. "Once I would have snapped my fingers and had it in a trice. Now, the library is drifting, out of our plane and more inaccessible to me than ever before. I am not sure how long it will take."

Bella spoke for the first time. "Where in the library is it, Alger?"

He looked at her. "Early history, Court, law documents..."

She held up her hand. "Wait. You can't... Alger, this place is *such* a mess!" Her voice went up slightly at the end as she closed her eyes in concentration.

"This is a travesty." Lady Laenven snapped. "These two can claim whatever they want, but until the Charter is verified and physically present, I will not accept their biased reports, and neither should anyone else!"

Bella opened her eyes. "Alger, you need to take me to the library."

I stepped out from the alcove. There was a little wave of whispering in the audience. I ignored it. Last time many of them had seen me, I'd been carrying a brutalized body. Then I'd disappeared for two months. Now...

"I am going as well."

Laenven sniffed loudly. "You will take an expert with you, who can be objective."

"You have one ready? I plan to leave now."

She looked wildly into the audience, then over to Buckingham, who took a hasty step backward. I looked at my mother for the first time and was surprised to see a faint smile on her face. She was... Something was going her way.

"You!" Laenven pointed out into the audience. "I command you to come here at once!"

An elderly fairy stood slowly. I didn't recognize him. "Milady..."

She stamped her foot. "Coward. You would betray our cause? We stand on the brink of reclaiming Court for the fairy people, and you would not give of your time and security for this?"

Reclaiming Court? This woman was a moonbat. Court was still the same stuck-in-the-mud system it had been since before my birth, and Bella actually promised to reform some of the injustices placed on the 'people' by the former queen. That one had been more fond of her own comfort than any concern for the populace she did her best to ignore.

The fairy sat down, and looked pointedly away. An older fairy, his face plump under a white fringe beard, bald head, and round belly, stood up. I recognized him as a historian, although I had never met him outside a few court functions.

"King Trytion," he began, not looking at the raging Lady Laenven. This was a good sign. "I would be honored to be appointed observer."

Trytion nodded. "Thank you, Lord Byrne. This will not be forgotten. Duke Mulvaney," he turned to look straight at me, his brows drawn together. "Can you be ready to depart immediately?"

I nodded. "I can, but the consort-elect, and the Librarian may need to change and gather supplies."

Alger snorted audibly. Bella smiled slightly, and her voice when she spoke was pitched loud and clear as a bell. "I stand ready, my lord!"

"Then go quickly, and return without delay, the Charter in hand. I will speak with the council in your absence." Our king commanded, his face as hard as stone, but his eyes fixed on Lady Laenven.

That sounded suitably ominous. I walked to the edge of the dais, meeting Lord Byrne, Alger, and Bella there.

"Alger, lead the way." I asked, and he pulled a bubble up around us instantly.

Chapter 14

The Library Path

He debubbled us in my own library. Lord Byrne looked around, his eyes wide in surprise. "I pictured it as being... larger."

I laughed. "This is my home, not the Library. I think we are here for?"

Alger harrumphed. "Clothes, supplies, weapons..."

"Here and I thought you were all prepared." I teased him, smiling. "You said the library was only dangerous if a stack of books fell."

He shook his head, looking gloomy. "This isn't going to be a walk in the park. The Library is in a hostile place, and even inside it, there are dangers. For one thing, it's... changing. Becoming less open with every passing day. I am afraid we might be too late."

I stared at him, trying to wrap my brain around this development, and to squash the rage building up inside me. He'd downplayed it, when we were planning the initial expedition. Why had he lied? But yelling at him wasn't going to help right now.

Bella patted his arm. "I still have access to much of it, I think.

More than you do, as we already know, even if we don't know *why* that is. Besides, if I'm not crowned Queen, it's not the end of the world."

I caught the shock on Lord Byrne's face. He hadn't realized she was a reluctant appointee, obviously.

I growled at my former mentor. "We need information, Alger, as much as you can give us, about this place, and what we need to have with us."

Bella nodded. "I already know from the ogre mission how difficult it is to pull equipment from one dimension to another, I don't know even if I can do that from the library. I've only ever accessed the books and material virtually, not physically removed them from the library."

"I thought I'd seen you?" I remembered some nights with her reading by my bed while I was ill and she thought I was asleep. Watching her peaceful face, wisps of hair curving alongside her cheek and pearly ear; that had been balm for my soul. Bella shook her head.

"From your own library, or, like this..." She held out her two hands, palm up, and focused. A large tome appeared in them, glowing slightly, but otherwise looking solid. I reached out, and my fingers passed through it with a tingle. She carefully balanced it on her swelling stomach and one hand, turning a page with her now-free hand. "I can manipulate it as though it were a physical object. As you can see, it even seems to have mass."

"Can you hand it to me?" Lord Byrne reached out.

"I don't know," Bella closed it and extended the big book toward him. But as she let go of it, the energy faded away and the book disappeared. "Huh, not that easy, I guess."

"Lord Byrne," I started to speak, as his face fell when the book faded out. He turned to look at me.

"Please, call me Forrest if we are going to be adventuring together." He grinned puckishly.

I hesitated. "Forrest, then. Adventuring is one word for it. Have you... ah, adventured before?"

He shook his head. "My life has been dull, I'm afraid. I applied myself early to my passion for history, but my time is much consumed with my estate. This is an opportunity to not only see the legendary library Alger has compiled, but to *do* things."

"I see." I did, too. I could easily have wound up in his position, had pivotal moments not happened. But they had, and with Alger muttering under his breath about dimensional planes, and nightmares, I was beginning to feel very uneasy about dragging a civilian into this particular adventure. I was past feeling uneasy about taking Bella along. I didn't want to take her... On the other hand, it was by royal decree. I had to take him, and I had to keep him alive, and at least mostly intact. "Follow me, please."

This was getting to be almost routine, inviting people into my sanctum. Forrest looked wide-eyed around the armory.

"Have you ever done any hunting? Handled a weapon?" I asked him.

He shook his head. "Mother didn't approve of blood sports."

I raised an eyebrow and he looked sheepish and rubbed the back of his neck. "I know, but, well, you have a mother."

"I do. And she can be demanding. But since you don't know how to protect yourself, that becomes a problem here and now. Blood sports aren't any fun on the receiving end, trust me."

I took a Mossberg off the wall rack and handed it to him. He took it awkwardly. "Well, I know that end is where the bullet comes out, but..."

I took it back, and walked along the racks for a minute. He stood in place and watched me curiously. I paused, my hand hovering over a bow, and then dismissed it. He didn't look like he had the upper-body strength for that. Underhill, firearms were rare. Archery was more likely to be taught to youth here. Finally, empty-handed, I came back to him.

"I have an idea."

He looked puzzled. "Do I need to be armed? I am not sure I can be any help, but I don't want to be a hindrance, either."

"We're going to arrange a bodyguard for you."

"That sounds reasonable. But do we have time?" He was still distracted by all the shiny sharp stuff on display. He wasn't really paying attention to the firearms, I noted. A fairy downfall, that. If they armed their armies like humans did, Underhill would be a very different place. I didn't mean to make that suggestion, ever.

"We will make time. Let's go."

He followed me up the stairs again. I flicked message spells off my fingertips as we went. Alger was in the library, looking at a book. His staff leaned against the shelves. He didn't look up as I took Forrest into the kitchen.

"First order of business, eat."

He sat in the chair I'd pointed at, looking puzzled. "Well, I appreciate this, I am hungry, but..."

"We have time. I don't know what you thought, that we'd just jaunt off in a bubble to the library and be back in an hour? The coronation was recessed until, say, dinnertime?"

I wasn't being nice. I wasn't trying to be nice. He looked like I'd hit him across the face with a dead fish. I kept going. "You think I meant to go away for two months? Sometimes these things don't go according to plan, and this time, we don't even have a plan. I don't have enough intel to plan."

I didn't see Ellie, which was odd, so I looked in the chiller cupboard and found the ingredients for an omelet. That would work well, lots of protein. I would need to make enough for all of us.

"You understand that the human realm, Above, and Underhill are two separate planes, yes?" I was cracking eggs into a bowl while I lectured him. Either Bella or Alger knew more about this, but I was the one with the experience when it came to crossing between them.

"Yes, I do, and the theory is that they are only loosely connected, which is why there are sometimes great time differences between them." His answer had me nod as I dumped cream in the eggs. I can do omelets with water, milk, even that nasty blue watery stuff some humans favor, but cream was what Ellie stocked my kitchen with.

"It's been a long time since we had a shift, which means they are currently stable. But the Library is in a third plane. One I have never visited. I'm not sure anyone has besides Alger."

"Oh." He looked thoughtful. "I wonder if a small monograph after we return will be in order."

I found myself laughing as I gently folded the omelet in the pan. "*If* we return, m'Lord. Alger doesn't seem to think it's going to be easy, and I'll let you in on something. He's been worried about the Library for months now, but he hasn't gone there to look into it, and it's possibly the most important thing in his life..."

Alger's voice broke into my soliloquy. "Not quite. But it is the most important tool I had. Losing it has been like losing a hand."

He sounded tired and sad. I waved him to a chair while I plated Lord Byrne's omelet. "I was just telling our amanuensis here how dangerous this is likely to be. Care to elaborate for us?"

"Amanuensis?" Alger sounded amused.

"I was thinking perhaps a monograph..." Byrne offered hesitantly. Alger still had a reputation, I could see.

"Ah, certainly, although I will want to review it before publication. Some details are best kept close to the vest, my good fellow."

I could guess that meant things like the exact location of the Library. "And this is predicated on us getting back here. Which you implied might be a problem."

I started Alger's omelet, wondering where Bella was.

"Well, it isn't that there are specific dangers I can warn you against." Alger looked at Byrne, who was tucking into the food with a hearty appetite. "Am I correct in assuming you have never visited Above?"

Byrne shook his head. "I have, once, to see a castle mentioned as being the dwelling of an ancestor."

I wondered if this meant he had human blood, as well, or if he meant a Fairy who had chosen life Above for a time. It happened far more often than history had recorded. But I let Alger continue, curiosity about Byrne's family was irrelevant.

"Then you are aware that Above is more rigidly physical than Underhill is. You will not have had time to see, but Lom's home here is an example of the manipulation possible on this plane. He can have a window open to every season of the year, rather than being limited to the weather and vicissitudes of the climate surrounding his dwelling. Humans cannot manipulate their weather, not even to keep a storm from destruction on a scale Underhill cannot conceive."

I slid Alger's omelet onto his plate and started Bella's.

"Thank you, Lom. As I was saying, the planes become more plastic the further, er, down you go. It's not a direction, but it will do as a metaphor for understanding."

"So the third plane, where the library is, that is most plastic?"

"Practically unformed, Byrne." Alger waved his fork with no regard for the molten cheese quivering from his bite of omelet. "Exciting, really, if it weren't so demmed dangerous to stay there long. Magic, or the force we call magic, flows freely."

"Oh, rather." Byrne looked fascinated.

"What can we expect, Alger?" I wanted to keep this discussion on practical, rather than academic interests. "Other than a lot of change and magic?"

"Hm, well, it's hard to say. Last time I was there, I had to move very cautiously. Too much noise and you attract... things."

"Things?" I wasn't happy in his vague definitions.

"Very big things, or swarms of little ones." He nodded, like he'd told me something useful.

"Can I shoot them?"

And that was Bella, looking lovely in jeans, sweater with an edge of t-shirt hanging below it, and a pack slung over her shoulder. She wore her pistol holstered at her waist and strapped to her thigh in the approved manner. I realized what had taken her so long... and Ellie, who walked around her where Bella was standing in the kitchen doorway and headed in my direction. They had been modifying her gear to fit around her pregnant belly. She wasn't huge, yet, or I would have forbidden... Oh, hell, who was I kidding? I couldn't stop her if she wanted something.

I let Ellie take over the cooking and went to embrace Bella, ignoring the identical smirks on the other men's faces. I could just imagine what they were thinking, young love and cute as puppies. I didn't care.

"Ah, well, I don't know." Alger finally got around to answering her question.

"You don't know?" Bella sat down. I gestured at Ellie to give her that omelet I'd been cooking. "What did you do?"

"I mostly hid." He admitted. "I was alone, and it was no time to find out just what it would take to defeat them."

I grunted. Not unwise, alone in a strange place. But not terribly helpful.

"We can leave when Lord Byrne's bodyguard shows up, then. Better to get it over with, unless you think a reconnaissance trip would be helpful." I will admit it pained me to say that. I just wanted it over, this waiting thing was painful.

"No," Alger shook his head. "As it is, this is going to be difficult to keep even a small party stealthy. Penetrating the veil alerts them and they would be waiting when the rest of us arrived. Division invites defeat in detail, as you know."

Speaking of defeat, I wondered how Dionaea's bumbling army was doing. This little detour in the coronation was only playing into that timetable. Just how closely was Lady Laenven in contact with the Low Queen?

I'd sent messages earlier, while looking like I was browsing my armory for a weapon for Byrne. Now, I was waiting for responses. But I had one more question for Alger.

"How did you learn about the Library, and how did it come to be on the third plane if so few know about it? You keep implying you're the only one who's been there."

He nodded. "Of all the written records, there are only allusions to the other plane, and those couched in terms that make it seem as though it were only a myth, a place of dreams. However, I became convinced that the Library was a real place, when I was taken into it as a lad."

That meant it was something that had been there for a very long time. I had only ever known Alger as old. I'd never stopped to think about his boyhood. "Who took you there?"

"My teacher, as I was your teacher."

Ouch. I was all too familiar with Alger's teaching methods, which often enough involved invading my inmost thoughts and dreams and manipulating them to his own ends. He was telling me that he'd been taken on a dream journey to the Library, then. And this had to have happened a thousand years or more ago. Great-Uncle meant he was my great-grandfather's brother, in this family. All the others were gone, he was the oldest pixie that I knew of.

"How did you find it again?" Bella was acutely interested in this, since she'd been the inadvertent second librarian after Alger gave her access. I knew she would be looking forward to seeing it in reality.

"It took a long time, searching, dead ends... I thought for a long time it was in the Human lands. I finally succeeded in opening a gate to the other plane, only to have it collapse on me."

He looked positively glum, an odd expression for the normally confident and sarcastic mage. "Not sure how close I was to dying, but I don't think I've been closer any time before or since."

"You fill us with confidence." I told him, my tone dry. I heard a knock at the door, and Ellie went to answer it.

"I can open a stable gate. I think I can hold it open long enough to get us all through." He looked at Bella "My dear, will you be up to helping me?"

She grinned. "I'm pregnant, not ill. Of course."

Ellie returned, with three sprites flying close behind her. I nodded at them. "Ewan, Ian, Mac. I have a mission if you choose to accept."

"Och, coom on naow. Y'know we allus say yus." Ian's accent was, if anything, thicker than his brother's were. If they were brothers. I had trouble keeping track of the complex clan relations.

"This isn't either Underhill, or Above. It's another place entirely. We don't know what the dangers are, but we do know that it will be dangerous. It's a place where stealth is more important than killing everything in our path, and finally, I need the three of you to stick to him," I pointed at Lord Byrne, who was looking like his internal meter was swinging back and forth between academic interest in the elusive sprites, and revolt at their table manners. Ewan was currently gnawing at a chunk of ham almost the size of his head. He hadn't grabbed it off Bella's plate, at least, she'd skewered it on her fork and handed it to him. The fork was as long as he was. "Like cockleburs to a collie. He's a scholar, not a warrior, and it is crucial he returns to Court alive."

Ewan nodded, taking up a position near Byrne's left shoulder. "E'en in one paice, shore."

"Yes, we want to keep him intact."

Byrne was looking alarmed, and I threw that last comment at him just to reinforce the gravity of the situation. I didn't need him wandering off to check some oddity out, and putting the rest of us in danger.

"Now that you are here, let's go. Alger?"

"Hmph, boy, you have no sense of theater. Follow me."

He led us out to the garden, which was in winter. It had been fall when I found Margot, and the ghoul, lying here. I tucked that away. It wasn't time to deal with that yet, revenge really was a dish best served cold, and having Bella crowned was just a twist of the knife before I delivered the coup de grace.

Chapter 15

Attack of the Things

I had expected Alger to take us somewhere else. Gates between Above and Underhill are location specific, after all. Some were easier to use than others, with less space between them. Or at least I presumed it was space that meant some transits took longer, and more effort, than others. I wasn't a physicist, and I doubted that one of those would even know. Underhill wasn't exactly open to having that sort of scientific scrutiny, yet.

I didn't know if we ever would be able to accept that. The society here was old, rigid, and it worked. Letting some human tramp all over it might be a bad thing. I wasn't going to worry about that just now, though. I watched Alger as he closed his eyes and moved his hands into a position like he was holding an invisible beach ball. I had shut away my earlier anger at him. I'd let it out later, when it wouldn't compromise the mission. Bella stood beside him, eyes also closed. I surmised that she was using her Sight to keep an eye on what he was doing, so she could help at need. Byrne and I stood behind them, the sprites quietly hovering around his head and shoulders.

They had been warned about the need for stealth, and I knew

their silent language of hand gestures well from previous missions with them. Now, I flickered another caution, to watch Byrne. We'd told him a lot, but I still wasn't ready to trust him fully. He could say he didn't know how to use a weapon, that didn't make him harmless.

I would take my cue from Alger, and the sprites would take theirs from me. I tensed as Alger's invisible ball began to shimmer, and he spun it hard away from him. Like a whirlpool, it opened up into a vortex of... nothingness. I could see the garden through the shimmer, but in the center, my eyes slid away from the twisting motion, with a sickening lurch of my stomach. Alger, staff in hand, stepped toward it, and then walked into it, fading out slowly with each step. Bella opened her eyes.

"Go. I will come last, to keep it open for all of us. Hurry, this bugger is taking..." I didn't hear the rest of it, I had already poked Forrest Byrne through ahead of me. He didn't seem to be afraid, which was a relief, I didn't want to carry him.

I wasn't sure what I had expected. Passing through a gate between the other planes was attenuating, a sort of stretched-out vertigo that was accompanied by some visual effects, often sparkles, and a flavor, or smell, that seemed to vary for each person talking about it. This was much more intense.

Had I thought that leaving Bella behind would have worked, I would have happily done so. I felt like I was being turned inside out, even as I took step after plodding step. What this was doing to our unborn children, who had no context nor awareness, I wasn't happy thinking about. I felt a hand on my shoulder, and put my own up to clasp hers, briefly. I couldn't walk out the other side without both hands ready, but it was good to have that contact. Whatever lay ahead, we were together on this one. At least nothing could follow us.

The other side was confusing. It was like a foggy day, but lit up, as though a rising sun were hitting the water droplets in the air. The cumulative effect was a golden suffused glow. I could see Byrne, but not Alger. Bella walked to my side, and we all stood still for a minute. There was a far off sound like water dripping. Slowly, I could see shadows and shapes resolve in the mist. One of them was Alger, his floppy hat already wet, and an irritated look on his face.

"Don't just stand there." He snapped. "Follow me."

"How far is it?" I asked, gesturing for Byrne and Bella to precede me. I wanted to make sure nothing was following us.

"I got us fairly close. Only a few minutes out in..." He waved an arm at the mist vaguely. "This mess."

I thought we were walking through an open parkland of sorts. The heavy mist stayed the same glowing lightness, but tree-shaped shadows loomed as we neared them, then faded out again. I became aware of a high-pitched buzzing noise coming from somewhere past my right shoulder. I gestured at Ewan, and he nodded, then banked silently off into the mist. I wondered how he could navigate in that stuff. I'd never asked sprites if they used sonar or radar. They wouldn't know what I was talking about.

He reappeared and landed on my shoulder, talking into my ear with low tones. A whisper will carry further than a conversational murmur. "Sommat like a bee-hive, only bigger."

"Let's not disturb it, then. Thanks."

He returned to his place in the formation, and we kept walking. The hum died away behind us after a few minutes of walking. Alger held up one hand, and stopped, the rest of us gathering around him. I could see it once I was abreast of his position. A wall loomed in front of us, the same color as the mist, it looked like.

"Here it is." He kept his voice low.

"This is the library?" Byrne spoke for the first time since we had crossed over. I could see his head swivel back and forth, then upward. All we could see was wall, stretching into mist. The ground we walked on was short, evenly cut... I knelt and pulled a few blades. No, this grass grew this high. Interesting.

"That wasn't so bad." Byrne sounded pleased. "How do we get in?"

"We find the gates. There's only one way in. And be quiet, because things use this wall as shelter."

I made another mental note to have a long, firm talk with Alger about endangering others when we returned to Underhill. It was one thing with me, either as a monster hunter or the boy apprentice. It was altogether unacceptable with my pregnant wife and children.

"Which way?" Was all I said aloud. I was going to resist the shouting for now.

"It's round. We'll get to it eventually." He started forward, walking along the wall.

I gritted my teeth and fell back to the end of the line again. He didn't know where we were, not really. And now I was seeing shadowy movement out of the corner of my eye, as though something were walking parallel to the wall with us. I checked my holster to make sure my pistol was loose and ready. I wasn't going to count on this spooky place staying quiet.

I was ready, then, when they came out of the mist. I saw immediately what Alger meant when he called them things. They were almost formless, it was like being attacked by a stampeding herd of protoplasm. One had long cilia, which struck the ground with enough force to sound like a herd of galloping horses. I put my back to the wall and pulled a shotgun from the nospace where I'd stored it. Out of the corner of my eye, I could see Bella doing the same. Alger was far enough I couldn't see him clearly, although I knew it would involve his staff and fireballs of magic. Byrne was just trying to make himself one with the seamless wall, while the sprites hovered in front of him.

I fired first. Once an attacker gets within a certain range, you can't stop him even if he's dead. Dead doesn't always know it's dead, that catches up later when the body starts talking to the brain again. During a charge, everything is on autopilot, and these things were charging. They were also big. Elephant sized, even if they didn't have legs.

My shotgun blast whipped one around, and I could see a gout of clear liquid squirt out. It writhed on the short grass, and I turned my attention to the other two. There were only three? Maybe. I couldn't see any others, but the mist was heavy.

Bella and I fired at the same time, and the second one folded in on itself and sort of slid toward us. The third one hesitated, like maybe it was talking to whatever it had for a brain. Then it came to a stop, and poked its fallen buddy with a pseudopod. I held my fire. Maybe they would realize we weren't easy food, and would go away. The first one I had shot weaved back into an upright position. Liquid still gushed out of it.

The eerie thing was that there was no noise. Maybe they didn't have lungs or mouths, but other than the thudding while they ran at us, nothing. The mist swallowed up any sound, although I could hear Byrne panting in fear next to me.

"Run." Hissed Alger.

"What?" I really didn't want to put my back – or side, since we couldn't retreat – to these big baddies.

"Run! More will be on their way. They may stop to finish these, if we hurry." He was already starting to edge along the wall, into the mist. I could see what he meant. Something was moving out there, and the three in the first wave seemed to have stopped. The mist would cover us.

Bella nodded at me and clipped her weapon to a combat sling so she could shoot from the hip if needed. I gently took Byrne's upper arm and all but hauled him along with me. We weren't fully running, just hustling with intent. Once I got the older man started, I let go, and kept scanning behind us as we got far enough from the beasts to lose sight of them. I could feel the ground shaking as something showed up to feed back there.

One thing for sure, we'd picked a direction and couldn't change our minds. I kept moving at a steady lope, wondering how long Bella and Byrne could keep this up. Alger was tougher than cape buffalo hide, I wasn't worried about him.

Alger held up a hand and stopped so abruptly that Bella almost ran into him. Byrne did bump into her, and I found myself growling wordlessly at him under my breath.

"What is it now?"

I kept my back to the wall, and edged closer. It looked like a ramshackle hut, leaning up against the wall. Like someone had used the big wall rather than build a fourth one of their own. There was a fence between us and the shack, a woven willow wattle. I recognized it as an old Briton design. The end of the fence was... glued, sort of, to the smooth wall with gobs of glowing magic. I closed one eye.

The whole thing, fence, house, all of it, was closed in a glowing purple dome that started at the wall and extended out further than I could see with regular eyesight. Someone had strong wards. I was looking at this when a loud sound nearby sounded.

"Maa!" and I opened both eyes to look down. A small goat with bright golden eyes looked at me from across the fence. There was another one standing a few paces behind it, eying us suspiciously. Bella held out her hand to it.

"Bella!" I saw her push right through the warding as though it weren't even there, and the goat nibbled at her fingers, making her smile.

That was very odd. I held out my hand, and then jerked it back. Ever grabbed an electric fence? That's pretty much what this felt like.

"Alger?" I asked him. He'd moved away from the wall, and had one eye closed so he could stay away from the shielding. "What is this?"

"I have no idea." He looked back at Bella, who was caressing the goat. "Warded, but keyed to her?"

"Shocked me." I told him. Byrne was looking wild-eyed, and I guessed that meant he'd felt it, too. The sprites were watching our backtrail so we didn't get caught unawares here. Good men.

"We could go around." Alger closed an eye again. "It doesn't go out too much further. Only about an acre under the dome."

"I see a garden, and dwarf trees?" I made sure I wasn't too close to the ward. "I thought you said no-one lived here."

"I'm the only one that knows about it," he protested.

I pointed. "Then who is that?"

Chapter 16

Lavendar

The figure that was walking quickly toward us was distinctly humanoid, and as she grew more clear, obviously female. A long coat flapped around her legs, making her look like she was wearing skirts, but she was dressed very practically for someone who kept a little farm out in the middle of a howling wilderness.

Bella cried out, and tried to get over the fence as the woman got near. "Grandmother!"

I looked at her, scrambling over the twigs, and shouted. "Bella! Watch out!"

I knew what a strong glamour could do. And Bella was the only one of us who could pass through the wards. All my internal alarms were jangling, but Bella, over the fence, was running into the arms of the white-haired fairy. Both of their wings were sparkling brilliantly. I sighed and ran my hands through my hair.

"Dammit, woman..." I touched the ward again, and danced a little as the pain passed through me. "Bella!" I shouted again.

She looked toward me over the woman's shoulder. I could see the smile on her face. They let go of their embrace, but the older woman took Bella's forearms in hers and was talking to her. They were too far away from us for me to hear her.

"Bella! Don't make me break this thing down!"

Alger grabbed my arm. "Lom, stop. Look..."

He pointed into the mist, his back to the warded dome. I looked away from the women.

There were a lot of them. More than I could count, as they kept moving in and out of the mist and changing places. Some looked sort of like real animals, this time, although they mostly had too many legs, and mouths. They weren't charging, but rather creeping toward us, with the occasional flinch backwards. I had to assume they had tangled with the woman in the dome before, and it had gone badly. But we were not in the dome.

I looked at Byrne, who was trembling slightly. "Can you use the sight? See the dome?"

He shook his head.

"Holy Mother..." I swore. This was not going to work well. "Ewan?"

"Aye, sar, passin' well."

That was good, at least. "One of you stay on him. Get him worked around the dome, I don't want any of us trapped in this niche by the big wall."

Ewan nodded. I looked at Alger. "do you think that gate is close?"

"Doesn't matter without her." He didn't take his eyes off the slowly approaching mob of things. "I don't think it will let me in."

"Is it sentient... nevermind. Not now. We don't have a lot of choices if Bella doesn't come out of there."

"Do you think that's her grandmother? I thought she was dead?" Alger started to side-step, keeping his eyes on the monsters.

"Damned if I know. I thought it was odd, we would have known had protocol been followed, but Lavendar was a rogue to begin with, and Bella's family is..."

"Powerful." Alger offered absently. I had been going to say crazy, but I left it. They were on my side, even if they were odder than anything I'd seen Underhill. Raven was a little god, if he was everything I'd seen and been told. Although he'd thumped me painfully when I expressed that to him.

I risked a look behind us. Bella was walking toward the shack, still talking to the other woman. What was going on? She wouldn't leave us if she realized we were in danger. I wondered if she could see outside the dome. Was she telling Lavendar to let us in?

Alger's fireball caught my attention and I had to put my wife's strange behavior out of my mind. One of the things had decided that we looked tasty enough to overcome any conditioning, and Alger had obviously decided that a reminder was in order. Unlike the first things we'd met, these chimeras made noise. The injured one was currently shrieking like the kettle on the boil.

"Look!" Byrne pointed a trembling finger at the massed creatures. Several of them, ranging in size from elephantine to dog – albeit a big dog – were falling on their injured companion. They really did cannibalize, as Alger had suggested earlier. I grimaced.

"Put your fingers in your ears." I told him, slinging the shotgun and pulling another weapon out. Maybe if I fed them enough, it would buy us more time. It wasn't that the RPG was loud, it was just awfully close to him, and I didn't need him panicking. The weapon was one that you shoved a warhead into the muzzle, then fired from your shoulder. I didn't have a lot of reloads. The ragged man I'd taken it from somewhere in a dusty desert Above hadn't planned on living long enough after his attack on an American squad to need many. I'd taken it before he could use it, and he was right. He hadn't lived long.

I braced, and fired. Before I even saw the rocket hit, I was jamming another into the barrel. The backblast had passed right through the dome. I'd assumed it would, otherwise the old lady would need an air supply. Wards were usually set to react to living matter, not inanimate.

In theory, I could throw rocks through it to get Bella's attention. But not now. One thing about this weapon, it was pretty foolproof. Which was why the dusty fools liked it so much, I supposed. I'd seen too much of that toxic brand of ideology over the centuries to have any respect for it. None of them could shoot worth a damn, anyway.

I fired again. I was losing track of Alger and Byrne as I went into the fighting fugue state I knew all too well. Oh, sure, they were there. I was able to know precisely where, and how we were moving, step, step, fire... step, step sideways.

The rockets were beginning to cause dissension in the ranks. I was aiming for the biggest ones, in the idea that a sheer volume of available meat, or whatever the hell these things used for flesh, would be irresistible to the hungry others.

I got to see the results of one blast. The thing had translucent skin, and the rocket penetrated deep, the percussion of the blast a visible bubble in front of the warhead... and then it blew, showering the ranks with globs of slime and near blinding me with the flash. I stopped looking back, then, just shoot and scoot.

We had made it around the belly of the dome, and I ran out of rockets. I tossed the weapon into nospace, hoping I'd be able to retrieve it later, but I couldn't take the time to push it in carefully right now. I swung the shotgun back up and hesitated. Something had changed.

Alger, during all this, had been steadily firing fireballs into them. His didn't explode, but they stuck. The only time I saw one of them extinguished was when I blew up the clear one. Byrne was quiet as a mouse, and the sprites were staying out of it. With only three of them, their advantages of massed attack were nullified.

Now the two of us held fire. The things were no longer pressing their attack. Many were falling on their injured or dead, ravenously tearing them to pieces. The noise had risen to a crescendo. But they weren't coming at us, and a few were actually backing away. As I held fire, I kept moving, sidling around the dome. The sprites were helping guide us since it wasn't visible to eyesight.

Maybe my plan had worked. I risked another look over my shoulder, and felt my heart jump when I saw Bella there, just on the other side of the woven fence. She pointed in the direction we were already going, and then started running in that direction.

"Ok, I think we're going to be let into the dome. Move faster."

Alger broke into a lumbering trot, his staff held high. With one hand, he held his ridiculous hat on his head. Byrne just followed doggedly. I tried to keep an eye on the monsters, but they seemed to have gotten the idea that we'd taste bad.

Bella and the old lady were waiting at a gate. When we got there, she opened it, and I trusted my wife, running through it even while Alger and Byrne held back a little. They came in on my heels and she closed the gate. I stopped and looked around.

You couldn't see outside of the dome. Also, inside it was sunny, warm, and as peaceful as a balmy summer day. Birds sang, and there was a little breeze. I stepped close to the fence. You could sort of see out, like looking through a two-way mirror. Bella wouldn't have known we were in trouble until she came looking.

Bella was leading the older woman toward me, holding her hand and beaming in joy.

"Lom, this is my grandmother, Lavendar."

"Pleased to meet you, ma'am." I wasn't sure if I was supposed to put out a hand to shake, or... I took her hand and kissed the back of it. What the hell, I was covered in soot and gunpowder, I must look a fright. Might as well not scare the old lady.

"And I am delighted to meet you, young man. Bella is going to have to tell me more, but she has already conveyed that you are something special."

I ran a hand through my hair, with a raised eyebrow directed at my wife, who was grinning like a loon. "There are a lot of, um, things out there."

She nodded. "I know. I'm so sorry we didn't let you in sooner, I was so surprised to see Bella..."

Alger cleared his throat. Bella gestured. "Grandmother, this is Alger. And this is Lord Byrne, and then Ewan... what are your names, men?"

She was addressing the other sprites.

"Och, aye... He's Ian, and ah'm Mac." One of them bobbed an abbreviated air bow to the smiling Lavendar. I was rather pleased Bella had included them in the introduction. That alone would show the long-exiled Lavendar how much had changed. A properly-raised fairy lady would have considered the sprites servants, and would sooner have introduced the furniture.

"So nice to see all of you, if somewhat mystifying how you found me." She turned to Bella. "I had presumed you were told I was dead, but how did you learn....?"

Bella shook her head. "Grandpa Bob was told you were killed in a plane crash. That's what he told me. I left school for a semester..." her lip wobbled as she remembered.

"Bob told me you were dead, as well, and I thought it was odd."

She nodded. She knew what I meant.

"I never meant to return to Underhill, so when it became obvious that I must move on, I started to look for this place."

"Why did you leave us?" Bella asked.

"Um, I hate to break up the family reunion and recriminations, but there are a whole load of angry things just outside." I pointed out.

"Oh, don't worry about them. They cannot breach my wards. I leave them alone, and they have learned to ignore me." Lavendar dismissed that worry and took Bella's hands in hers, looking my bride in the eyes. "I couldn't stay with your grandfather, my dear. We had never been on the same page, and..." she bit her lip. "It was just not working."

"But me?" Bella sounded like the little girl she'd been when her parents died, and Bob and Lavendar took up the task of raising her. I made a mental note to talk to her about that, sometime. My little hellion would not have been easy, and we were about to welcome two just like her into the world.

"You were in college, dear, starting a new life and could manage without me. I know it hurt, but I had to go." Lavendar pulled Bella into a hug. "And here you are!"

"We weren't looking for you." I pointed out, bluntly. My nerves were still jangled from combat, we were effectively cut off from our objective, and as nice as it was to see Bella rediscover her grandmother, a family reunion really needed to wait. Or happen on home ground, by my preference. It seemed unlikely that this woman wasn't who she said she was, as Bella would know different, but that didn't mean she was trustworthy, either. My lovely bride thought the best of everyone. I didn't want to spoil that, but I wasn't letting it take my edge off.

Alger spoke for the first time since we had entered the dome. "You were not dwelling here the last time I was at the Library. I would have visited you for old times' sake."

"You know grandma?" Bella looked between them. Both had their chilly social masks on – at least I presumed that was what Lavendar's expression was. It was certainly many degrees cooler than her look at her granddaughter.

"We were acquainted, before I left." Lavendar told her now.

"Before you ran away." Alger looked down his nose at her. "I had not taken you for a coward, before. Now I see you make a habit of it."

"Alger!" Bella's eyes flashed with anger.

"I'm afraid it is the truth." Lord Byrne spoke very quietly, but firmly. "And she cannot return Underhill with us, as I'm sure she knows."

"What?" Bella turned to her grandmother, who was standing with head bowed under this onslaught.

"If I were to return, it would be the Hunt who would take me." Lavendar sounded very far away. "Bella, I did not run away from you. But I did flee my home when I left Underhill."

"Leaving a certain notorious red cloak in a very inauspicious place." Alger growled. My ears perked. Lavendar had something to do with the fall of House Mulvaney?

"I was sorry for that, but I didn't know what happened until far too late."

Now Bella just looked confused and upset. She came and wrapped her arms around me. I hugged her back and held her close to my side. We faced Lavendar. Alger pointed at us. "You heard your granddaughter call him Lom. He was not born until long after you left Underhill, and his given name is Learoyd Otheris..." He leaned closer to Lavendar. "Mulvaney."

She let out a startled little cry. "Bella is..." She looked at us. I was probably glowering, and Bella was all but hiding her face in my shirt. Lavendar took a step back and straightened out. Her short white hair fluttered a little in the sudden breeze. I could see the power crackling off her. Between Bob, the dragon blood, and this for a grandmother, my wife suddenly made a lot more sense.

"I think we need to talk. But a little social lubrication is in order, and you all must be tired after that fight. Please, come with me."

I looked down at Bella, who gave me a little nod. I followed her grandmother, who had already begun to walk back to the shack. Post-combat shakes had been postponed, for a different, quieter sort of combat.

Chapter 17

Grandmother's House

When Lavendar reached the door, she reached out for the carved wooden handle, then looked over her shoulder and winked. "It's bigger inside than it looks on the outside!"

She pulled open the handle and stepped into a spacious foyer. It seemed to double as her pantry. Bundles of dry herbs and flowers hung from the high, exposed rafters. From the outside, the shack seemed as though it would fit into this room alone, but I could see that there was a hall further in. I remembered what Alger had said about this plane being more plastic than Underhill. Stretching space to create this place was possible, then.

We walked past the shelves and cupboards, into a great room that held her living quarters. Kitchen, sitting area, even a small library, all centered around a massive stove. Bella walked up to it.

"Grandma, this is like the one you had..."

She nodded. "In Tok, yes. I do like a masonry stove. When the old bones get cold, I can curl up on it like a cat."

I'd seen them before, mostly Russian, but this one was decorated in blue and white Dutch tiles, it looked like. Or something close enough to resemble them. I saw familiar windmills, ducks, weeping willows, and as I got closer, I could see sprites and fairies in the street scenes. So, not human-made.

"I have tea, no coffee, I'm afraid, gentlemen." She had a kettle on the stove, and with a hand gesture, made her table grow longer, to accommodate all of us. It had only one chair, and she frowned, then made a pair of benches appear. "Sorry, I haven't the time for more complex."

I was a little taken aback at this casual magic. Fae conserved their power. Unless she was showing off? But that seemed unlikely, given the rustic furniture she was toying with. Perhaps it was just this place. Bella was wandering around, looking at everything. The other men and I sat, and Lavendar sat with us.

"You have landed on your feet." Alger still sounded sour. "As always. More cat than pixie, I always said."

Lavendar laughed, although it sounded a little forced to me. "You also used to say I purred when petted."

Bella came back over to the table and sat by her grandmother. "You wanted to tell us how you came to be here? It feels like far too much of a coincidence to have found you when we weren't looking for you."

"You were coming to the Library, weren't you?" Lavendar asked. "If so, that is also why I am here."

Bella blinked and waved a hand at the comfortable house. "With all this? And if you were in the Library, why hadn't I met you there?"

Lavendar's jaw dropped a little. "You have been in the Library already?"

"For months, even if it has been virtually, I've touched enough shelves and books and scrolls to know it was just like being there in person."

"And it's my Library." Alger growled. He was mad again. "So, you would steal this as well?"

"What?" Bella exclaimed.

"No! I was not trying to steal anything, not before, and not now." Lavendar cried out, putting her hand on Bella's. "Please believe me."

"You'd better explain. The way I remember it, a certain objet d'art went missing, and the only clues led to you, and Alonzo. I know he didn't have it, so that leaves you." Alger subsided, glaring at her. I had always known he was angry over the events that had led to the fall of our House, but not the depths of it. Nor did I know details, other than it was considered treason.

"Art? That's not what it was, and you know very well..." Lavendar snapped back. Then she looked around at us, and deflated a little. "Lord Byrne, do you know what it was? You were very young..."

"I was, but not too young that I would forget you. I carried a little flame," He got some color in his face. I hadn't noticed how pale he'd grown until the blush rose. "You were accused of being part of a conspiracy to assassinate, or at least dethrone, the Queen."

Bella gasped. I contemplated the irony of it. "Lavendar, have you any idea why we came to the Library in person? What did you and Bella talk about when we were outside the dome?"

Bella flushed a little and answered for the older woman. "Babies, and... well, you, my dear. I was reassuring her that I was safe and happy."

"For values of that..." I muttered. Lavendar had been deciding, then, if she would let us in. I had no doubt that had I been found wanting, we would have been locked out. I spoke loud enough to be heard. "We are looking for the original Charter, thought to be in the Library, in order to confirm that Bella is worthy to be crowned Queen. There is some doubt, given her mixed descent. No doubt that being related to you is considered into this, which I wasn't aware of before."

Byrne shrugged. "It came up during the nomination process, but enough of us had seen her in action to know for sure it was not her motivation, and indeed, that she knew little or nothing of Fae history."

Bella looked thoughtfully at him. "So that is what that conversation was about."

He nodded. "Finding Lavendar here is, um, a bit reassuring on that front as well. You would hardly have run risks in your condition had you merely been able to reach out and ask her for help."

"Oh, you can't message out from here." Lavendar stated casually. Alger nodded.

"Messages in don't work, either." He confirmed. "We are on our own until we're ready to go home."

Lavendar got up and brought the kettle back to the table on a tray with mugs in assorted sizes and colors. "There is honey, no sugar. Some things I simply cannot get, and I have been unwilling or unable to travel away from home. When I ran out..." she shrugged. "You make do, and I don't mind. Just never expected company."

"Why did you stay here?"

"When I couldn't get into the library, and I didn't have any place else to go, it seemed fitting." Lavendar poured tea for all of us. I appreciated the warmth of the cup. It had been an overwhelming day. "I was not part of a plot to assassinate anyone, let me begin there. I was trying to help those who wanted her removed from the throne. She was... not a good influence. Alonzo was my contact, that night. I don't know who all was involved in the plot, he kept us compartmentalized."

I'd had no idea how organized and sophisticated this had been. And Alger? Had he been part of it? It seemed to fit how he operated. He was sipping tea, the steam hiding his eyes and expression from me. Lavendar kept talking.

"We were trying to gather proof that she was conniving with Low Court to undermine the Council and seize the complete power of the throne..." she turned to Byrne. "Is she... did she finish young Corwin?"

And again, my world rocked a little. Young Corwin? And the old Queen meant to kill him?

Byrne shook his head, and his face softened in the light of her obvious distress at the idea. "The former Queen is long dead, she succumbed to a cancer. They are not unknown, even if vanishingly rare among the Fae. Corwin is a beloved ruler under his royal name, King Trytion."

"Ah." Lavendar leaned back. "I thought she must be gone, when you said Bella was... but then again, she ascended to the throne when Mab stepped down of her own will to spend her twilight years in meditation."

"She wasn't the kind who would relinquish power." Alger said.

"No, she wasn't. I always wondered why you were not with us, against her." Lavendar looked at him, her eyes shiny with unshed tears. I wondered what their history was. He was older than her, had been older than Alonzo, but... Fae didn't count such things like humans did.

"I preferred to do it my way. Out in the open, none of this sneaking around, which brought the Hunt down on you."

"The Hunt! Grandma..." Bella reached for me, not her grandmother. I took her hand and squeezed. Bella didn't like the Hunt for good reason.

"If we had been able to..." Lavendar sighed. "It's all history now. She's dead, and I will never return Underhill."

"Why were you trying to break into the Library?" Alger asked. "And what did you do with the Crown?"

"The Crown?" Bella asked. "Trytion has it."

"No, girl," Alger shook his head. "That's a new one, a replica made when the original Queen's Crown was stolen, by your grandmother."

"I did not!" Lavendar's eyes flashed in anger. "I will admit I was there that night, with Alonzo, and we were looking for documentation of her link to the Low Court, but neither of us took the Crown."

"Why didn't anyone tell me about this?" Bella asked plaintively.

"I didn't know, either." I told her.

Alger answered. "It was a closely guarded secret. No one, outside of a handful of people, ever knew about it. Corwin and I are perhaps the only two alive... Or so I thought until today."

"So... if Grandma didn't take it?" Bella looked dubious. "I believe you." She told her grandmother, taking her hand away from me, and holding on to both of the other woman's hands. "Is there any way to clear your name? Our name?"

"No, dear, not after all these years. It has been hundreds of years, in human reckoning. And sweet girl, I am happy here. I washed up here like driftwood, but remember when I used to take you to the ocean? Sometimes great beauty comes from the raging sea."

"Oh..."

Alger cleared his throat. "All very pretty, but why the Library?"

"Like you, I wanted the Charter." She looked at him levelly, her eyes dry now. "I wanted to repudiate the Hunt."

He leaned back. "And you think you would invalidate them with that document? I think the Huntsman would have something to say about that."

"He lives still?"

"If you call that living. But the Hunt still holds sway over the evil that would wash civilization from the face of Underhill."

"How can you say that?" Bella protested. She had never forgiven him for nearly letting the Hunt have me, when I lay unconscious and dying in Tower Baelfire. "What did Lom do to deserve becoming a living automon for them? And now? With Dionaea threatening to conquer High Court, when is the Hunt going to ride in? What purpose do they serve any longer?"

"Lom had broken the law." Alger's voice was soft, and he was looking at me. "But it wasn't that I was thinking of when I told the

Huntsman to take him. He was dying. The laws of our land are not so corrupted as to be thrown away with ease."

"Why does the Hunt leave him alone now?" Bella looked confused.

"I can explain that." I broke in. "For the same reason they left me alone for decades before. I am the Hunter Above. I serve the Hunt, Bella my love. I am not of the Hunt, but bound to them nonetheless." I finished in a very quiet tone. "I told you I was a monster, did I not?"

"You did. I didn't think... I still don't think you're being fair to yourself."

I hooked a thumb at her grandmother. "If she appeared at our house, I would have to turn her in."

Bella looked stubborn. "You didn't with Georgio."

I'd forgotten she would catch onto that about the ghoul, and others I had in my – our - network. "No, he was useful. So are the others like him. Might happen with Lavendar like that, but might not. I'd advise her to stay here."

Alger interrupted. "With my Library?"

I looked at him. "Why are you still het up about that? Might want to figure out what really happened with the Crown, old man. She's not *in* the Library, as you can see."

He subsided. Byrne spoke up. "This is all... fascinating. And perhaps Lavendar is the one who could tell us what happened with the Crown. No..." He held up a hand to forestall her protest. "Not that I think you, or Alonzo," he nodded at me, "took it. But perhaps you remember who else was there that night? And why did you leave that cloak behind?"

She nodded. "There was someone. But I didn't see a face. They grabbed my cloak, and I broke the clasp to escape. I was terribly bruised around the throat for weeks." She shivered in remembered fear. "They were trying to kill me. Alonzo was ahead of me, but I couldn't even cry out for him, the cloak was too tight around my neck."

"Did you see anything?" Bella asked.

Lavendar hesitated, then answered slowly. "I remember a strong smell, and... the hand that clawed at my face was covered in hair, like a beast."

"A 'smell?' like what?"

"Like a wet dog." She said simply. "It was raining that night, which was why I wore my cardinal."

"Cardinal, like the bird?" Bella looked confused again.

Lavendar laughed. "No, it was a red wool cloak with a hood. The bird, and the human religious leaders both were named for the cloak, not the other way 'round."

"So you were attacked by a wolf." I mused, my mind busy. "I wonder..."

"Oh, surely not Sean." Bella protested. "I liked him."

"No, not Sean. He's a mere puppy. But there is a line of werewolves connected with Low Court."

"Does it really matter? It has been a long while, and I am merely a tired old woman." Lavendar looked it, too.

"We must finish this quest, first." I told her.

She shook her head. "You will not be able to leave the dome for some hours, until they give up. Spending the night here will allow you more safety in the morning, and you must be exhausted."

I looked around the room. "I hate to inconvenience you, but this seems better than out there for a doss."

"It's no inconvenience. This realm offers... much in the way of possibilities." She got up slowly and walked across the room. I could see her age, now. She was very old, even for a Fae, and it was showing after the conversation we'd just had.

She opened a door. Beyond it I could see another hall. "You will find all you need in the rooms, and if you need anything, simply say my name."

"No." That was Bella, leaning on my arm, one hand on her belly.

"I can see how tired you are grandmother, and I am almost fresh, since the men did most of the fighting. I can supply any needs."

"But..."

Bella shook her head. "Grandmother. I have learned much since I came Underhill, and had excellent teachers even before I arrived here. But that's a tale for another visit. I can see what you are doing, to manipulate the magic here, and I can recreate that."

Lavendar reached for her granddaughter and gave her a hug. "You have grown up far surpassing my wildest dreams. Good night, Bella."

"Good night, Grandmother."

We walked down the hall. I kept opening doors to see what lay behind them. A trio of bedrooms and a well-appointed bathroom. The rooms smelled fresh, like hay that had been drying in the sun. The furniture was like the benches, rustic and simple. I pointed into one room. "We'll take this one. Good night, gentlemen."

I shut the door in their face and pulled Bella into my arms. She was crying. She'd held it together, as I'd known she would, until we were alone.

"Oh, Lom..." Her wings were still and drooping.

"She was your hero when you were a child. So was Bob. Then you grew up, and found feet of clay."

She nodded, hiccupping a little. She wasn't given to gusts and sobs, just quiet dissolution in tears, and even that happened rarely. I would have said, if she asked, that this was mostly pregnancy hormones.

"Besides, there's something you may not know. Your predecessor was cordially loathed."

"She was? I have to step into those shoes?" She made a face. "Still my grandmother fled. She didn't stay and try to depose the Queen, if she was that bad? For that matter, why didn't Alger?"

"Alger, and a couple of others, put a leash on her, from what I know. He had to step down after the trial of Alonzo. But the work went on, and she was relegated to bedroom games..." I stopped. "Er, that didn't sound right. It's a term that means she was only able to have limited power, not sex per se although..."

Bella chuckled. "You're cute when you get tongue-tied. I'm not that innocent. So, they muzzled the bitch."

I felt the laugh bubble up involuntarily. "Yeah, pretty much. Ok, I'll stop self-censoring. Trytion has been the ruling power for a long time, but it's meant to be a balance, you know. He was really looking forward to having you as his right-hand woman. And as you learned from Byrne today, you have earned respect in your own right."

She frowned. "If my mixed blood... and Lom, they still don't know about the dragon. Oh, Lom, why did she marry him?"

The tears came back. Definitely pregnancy and fatigue. I scooped her up, and she squeaked in surprise. I didn't drop her on the bed, but it bounced under her as I put her down. She was laughing through her tears. "Stop talking?"

I suppressed whatever she was going to say. It was time to stop talking, yes, and I distracted her from unanswerable questions.

Chapter 18

Unicorns Rampant

The next morning, Lavendar insisted on feeding us before letting us leave her home. I didn't resist. Home-cooked meals were far and away better than trail food eaten cold while moving. She didn't bring up the conversational thread of the night before, and by unspoken assent, neither did any of us. What was to be done about her was a matter for the future.

Bella looked queasy at the sight of food, and didn't eat much. I didn't like that, but let her pick and choose, knowing that having her vomit after we left the dome could be fatal. There might not be any intelligence in the things outside, but they were unendingly hungry. I was hoping we could find the door into the Library quickly and take refuge inside. Lavendar had confirmed that it was no more than an hour's walk – or sneak, in this case – in the direction we had been traveling.

At the little gate, Bella hugged her grandmother. "We will stop on our way back. And I will be back for a visit when I can."

"If you can... Bella, you have your wings now." Lavendar caressed the tip of one. "You can fly without me holding you on the ground."

"I will be back." I recognized that stubborn tone, and so too did Lavendar, because she just opened the gate with a faint smile, and a nod for the rest of us. I noted as they passed her, each sprite gave her a salute, which she acknowledged with a bent head.

Then we were back out in the misty plane, less golden than it had been, and even thicker. I put one hand on Byrne's shoulder.

"Keep in touch with Bella... and Bella, with Alger."

Linked like this, we walked slowly along the wall. On the short grasses that were the only things growing by it, our progress was almost silent. Once when I heard a snuffling breathing approach, I squeezed Byrne's shoulder and stopped our forward momentum. We stood in silence, listening, for several minutes until the only thing I could hear was the dripping of water off the distant trees. How anything grew here, with no sunlight, was beyond me. Then again, I'd never seen one of those trees clearly, they might be giant mushrooms for all I knew. Satisfied we were alone, I gave the signal to go again.

The sprites were riding on shoulders, Ewan on mine. I felt him give a little shiver. The poor guys were out of their element, and I almost regretted bringing them along. I wouldn't tell them that, though. No point in rubbing salt in an open wound. We kept creeping along the wall. It was getting darker, I realized.

It had been happening gradually, but I could barely see past Bryne, who was only at arm's length in front of me, his shoulder warm under my grip. He was shivering, too. I had to give it to the elderly scholar, he hadn't complained at all. He just kept going.

Until he stopped so suddenly I almost walked into him.

"What?"

I couldn't see anything.

"We're here." Alger's voice was low, but carrying. "Look."

As Byrne and I edged forward, I could see it. A niche in the wall. Alger and Bella were standing in it. Ian, who had been riding with Alger, flew up with a shielded elf-globe in his hands. The light from it only fell on the gates, keeping us from being obvious to anything in the forest.

"So beautiful," Bella breathed.

The gates were towering, set three paces into the wall, which made me revise upward the thickness of the Library walls considerably. They consisted of two panels, and on them were two unicorns, rampant. They looked as though they were carved of ivory, with jade insets for mane and tails. The hooves and horns were covered in gold.

At their feet, in heaps, were carved scrolls and books, in such detail I could see the words on them. I couldn't read them, it wasn't a language I had seen before. It was striking, and looked heavy.

"How the hell are we supposed to open these?" I asked Alger.

"We aren't..." He was pointing to one side, and I looked, seeing a more human-sized door set into the wall near the gates.

"Are you coming?" Bella sounded amused, and I looked away from the access door.

She had the gates open. It looked like a crack when you saw the scale of the thing, but she was standing with one hand on the open gate, looking back at us with a big grin on her face. Light streamed out from the interior, making her look like she was glowing, and her wings were doing their happy sparkly thing.

Alger muttered a curse into his beard and started forward, Byrne following. I looked up at Ian and shrugged as he extinguished the now-unneeded elf globe. "That's my girl."

He laughed and zipped ahead to catch up with Byrne. I followed quickly, not wanting to wait and see what appeared out of the mist. This was going more smoothly than I had anticipated.

Inside, we stood in what looked like a museum. The vast room, with vaulting roof overhead, held a myriad of statues. Most of them were wonderfully lifelike, and I looked around, trying not to be distracted while I assessed the situation. Alger had said that gaining entrance to the library was only the beginning. The floor underfoot was slightly dusty over the parquetry. I scanned for movement, but only saw Alger vanishing behind a griffin, with Byrne in tow. Bella must be ahead of them.

I looked up at the snarling beak of the griffin as I walked under one outstretched wing. The whole thing looked like it had been carved from one block of marble, and it easily rivaled any statue I'd seen Above or Underhill. I dragged my attention back to the room. Other than the muted murmur of voices ahead of me, the Library was almost oppressively still. I hurried up my steps a little, wanting to ask the mad academics to shut up for a minute so I could listen... I assumed Bella would know enough to be quiet.

Something in the dust caught my eye. Swirling, sinuous curves tracked off to one side, behind another rearing unicorn statue. The plinth under this one was massive, to allow for the statue of a man, Fae or not I couldn't tell from here, who had fallen to the ground and was desperately holding a pike upright to keep the beast from tearing him to pieces with hooves and wicked teeth revealed in an equine scream. Whatever had made the tracks had gone this way, and I could see other footprints at right angles, headed in the direction Alger's voice was coming from.

Those would be our party. What had left this other mark? I broke into a trot. Time to get everyone together, and on alert rather than art appreciation. I went around a hideous Medusa head, lying on its side with filmy brass eyes, and dying snakes flailing. There wasn't any rest of her, just the gruesomely detailed in brass anatomy of a violently severed neck. On the other side, Byrne and Alger stood, in animated conversation. Alger was pointing upward at something, and Bryne was gesturing as he spoke.

"But the records indicate..."

I never found out what. "Shush! Where is Bella?"

They turned to me, startled. "She was just ahead of us..." Alger peered vaguely around.

"No, she wasn't, look." I pointed at the ground. Their footsteps had milled around a bit, here, but there were none leading off any way but how the three of us had come in. I looked up at Ewan.

"Get up high enough to see the whole room if you can. Beware, there's something else in here with us, I saw tracks back there." I pointed back toward the rampant unicorn with his prey, and the sprite nodded, shooting upward in a humming blur of wings along with his compatriots. I looked at Alger. "What lives in the Library?"

"Nothing lives here. What did you see?"

"I don't know what made them. Not us, come and look."

I led them back to the unicorn. Both men looked surprised and bewildered at the tracks. I let out my breath. Shouting for Bella was more likely to warn this thing, if she hadn't already encountered it. But she would have made a noise if she had, a shot if not a scream. The sprites were circling overhead. One swooped in to report.

"Nothing moving in here. But there are doors all around."

I pointed at the track. "Find where this goes. Don't be seen." I wasn't going to comment on how much better his English was under stress. I'd known for years the thick brogue was put on for outsiders to be confused by. Nor was I going to comment on how big the thing that had made these marks would have to be. They could figure that out on their own, and I wasn't in the habit of insulting my men's intelligence.

If Bella wasn't in the big room any longer, either this thing had her, or... "I'm going to backtrack, see if she split off earlier."

Alger nodded. "We'll stay here, stay out of your way."

"Thanks." I moved off, looking down, trusting them to have my back and the sprites to have the air cover. The three of us had waltzed in fat dumb and happy from the door, our footprints wandering all over and even back on themselves in a few places. How many steps had there been time to take since we'd come in the gates?

I got back to where I could see the gates, which were smooth on this side. They were tightly closed again. I could see the little access door off to one side. For defense, it sucked, but I didn't think it was defensive, not the way it was laid out. More likely easy access, and impressive access. For some unimaginable audience long gone without a trace.

Bella's smaller boot prints had veered off here, within sight of the doors. I had been looking at Alger's back, then, not prints, and hadn't even noticed. The dust wasn't as heavy here, but I could see the scuffs. They turned into full prints behind a small plinth that held up a sleeping lion pride. One looked as though it were about to roll off, a paw of golden flecked stone dangling almost to the floor. Bella had been looking at it, too, her prints at right angles to the statue, her stride as she left it relaxed.

I stopped and listened. One of the sprites was almost overhead, and I could hear the low hum from his wings. Other than that, heavy silence blanketed the room. I looked up, and he made an exaggerated shrugging gesture. Still no sign of her, then. I kept following the tracks.

Here... she had fallen, it looked like. And crawled around the base of a plinth. I walked around the corner and strangled the cry before it left my throat. There were her clothes, scattered in shreds on the floor, dusty, torn – but no blood. I turned in a tight circle, my heart in my mouth. No sign of blood, at all. Her pistol lay up against the plinth, still in the holster, which had been... unbuckled? Had the thing forced her to disarm?

I picked it up, looking at the dust and scratches that cut deep into the nylon webbing. Something had scrabbled at it. I walked in a circle around her clothing scraps. On the other side, the sinuous marks started again. So, it was carrying her. Not a snake. I found a three-clawed footprint off to one side, half-obliterated with a lighter, almost sweeping, mark. Whatever this was, it was big. Bella wasn't fat, but she was dense. And pregnant. I felt my hands clench into fists, helplessly.

Alger could see it on my face as soon as I came into view around yet another bedamned statue.

"What happened? Is that...?" He pointed. I nodded.

Ian swooped in. "Follow me, quiet-like."

I broke into a run as he zipped off again. Alger and Byrne could catch up if they liked. I needed to find Bella. Ian led me in a wild chase around statues, which I wasn't really looking at any more, to a dark doorway. I stopped there.

Listening is as much feeling as anything else. And what I felt here was a pressure. Air was coming out of the stone hall, not enough to call a breeze, but positive flow. And on the air I could smell a peculiar musty scent I associated with snakes, or lizards. My mind went back to a mission involving a particularly large lizard the locals had been calling a dragon, which it wasn't, despite having dined on several goats and possibly more than one child. I felt my skin crawl.

Look, there are reasons serpents and dragons were one of the early atavistic fears. They are quiet, deadly, and when it comes to dragons, I'd never believed in fire-breathing until I met Beaker in action, but something with wings and the jaws of a crocodile was bad enough thank you very much anyway. Whatever had taken Bella down this way, it didn't have innocent intentions.

Ian landed on the door lintel, standing easily on the raised carving of a tree branch that framed the opening at the top. One side was a trunk, the other simply the wall. I was beginning to overload on visuals in here. One thing I hadn't seen yet were books.

"Hear anything?" he asked.

I shook my head. "You?"

"Not now, earlier there was a sort of scrabbling, far off, y'ken?"

So it had come this way. The talon-marks in the dust would account for the noises. I looked over my shoulder as Alger walked up, leaning on his staff with each step. He'd aged a decade in the time since we had walked into the library.

"Are you going to follow it?"

I glared at him. "What else should I do? It has Bella."

"How can we help?" Byrne looked pale, but resolute. I appreciated his courage.

"You two can stay here, with the sprites. If I don't come back out, get yourselves back to Court and tell them we died doing what we do best." I bared my teeth in something that couldn't reasonably be called a smile. "Hunting a monster."

Chapter 19

Library Monster

I walked into the darkness, and paused when I was far enough into it, to let my eyes adjust. Pixies have excellent night vision, but I really didn't want to walk into it before I was ready. I had strapped on Bella's pistol. Shooting two-handed was possible, sort of. Not the way human movies showed, and hadn't those been fun to watch with Dean.

Being alone on a mission was nothing new. I worked with others, but this way was easier. No one to worry about, just the objective, and the adversary. I could move fast, and take time to think in silence when needed. Right now, I was thinking over this direct approach. It was possible the Library was labyrinthine. Likely, in fact. Given time, I might be able to find another way to reach the monster, one that didn't involve following it into the dark. But time was something I didn't have.

Distantly, I heard a horrible scream. All my hairs stood on end, and I started running before my brain had time to stop me. The scream died away, and I kept running. Ahead, a tiny light twinkled. I slowed as I got near enough to see that it was an opening. There hadn't been another scream.

I flattened myself against the wall, feeling the cool stone brushing my hands. It was dry, and the hall I'd taken had been flat, so this was on the same level as the statue room. The hall had a much shorter ceiling than that vast vault, but still far over my head. Alger and I could have stood in the hall with outspread arms and touched finger-tips, maybe. The scale the Library was built on seemed to be massive, solid, and inhuman.

Taking a chance, I peered around the corner into the lit area. It was filled with a soft light that seemed to be coming from several windows high up on the far wall. The room was semi-circular, and absolutely crammed with books. Shelves on the walls were full, but there were heaps of them on the floor, right up the door I was hiding in. I didn't see any movement in the room, but there were three door-ways into the hall I was in, extending down quite some ways. I could tell, because they all flooded light into the dark hall.

I sidled into the room, slipping behind a head-high stack of books. No, I revised that. There was a sort of cart, with stacks of books on it. These weren't the books most would think of in these modern times. These were all old, so old I was a bit surprised they weren't falling apart. Then again, calfskin vellum has staying power. And the Library positively exuded magic. I tried closing my eyes and looking with the Sight, but the glowing walls, hell, even the books... I opened my eyes again as I heard a rustling noise.

It had come from the center of the room, which was hidden behind a low row of bookshelves. Relatively low. This set wouldn't need the rolling ladders all the wall shelves had. I looked up. There was a balcony up there, too. I headed toward the rustle, moving as silently as I could, and not in a straight line. Even on this floor, which felt like wood rather than stone, and was inlaid in astonishing designs,

I wasn't going to walk in a rhythm. Move, pause. Move a bit more... slide from one stack to another.

The rustling sounded louder, and I could hear hoarse panting breaths. There was a sudden movement, and a low groan. I could smell blood, when the air moved. My heart sank and my throat tightened painfully.

Now, I had to decide between rushing in to try and save Bella, or staying silent and reconnoitering before I got her killed, maybe. I moved slowly again, coming to the edge of the shelves, and again, risked a look around them. There had been an open space, here. I imagined that once it had been full of tables, chairs, and a comfortable circle of couches. Oh, not human style, but still cushioned and meant for lounging and cheerfully exchanging ideas in the manner of students since time immemorial. I could imagine this because most of the furniture was still visible. It just wasn't intact. There was a vast, rough nest made up of cushions, tattered fabric, and all manner of debris. The wood, and even stone, had been used to create the rim, while the softer stuff was all piled in the center.

On this heap of destruction lay a dragon. It was curled up, nose almost tucked under its tail, and it was panting heavily. I could see the ribcage rising and falling. The almost-black wings were tucked up tight along the ridge of backbone, and as I watched, it mewled pitifully. Bella was nowhere in sight. Had she injured it? The wings and tail would have made the sinuous marks in the dust, and blotted out the actual footprints in most places. So... this had to be the monster that had taken her.

There was no way I was going to be able to take on a dragon single-handed. Even if this one was small, in comparison to the, oh, a whole two others I'd seen in real life. My ass was grass without heavy weapons. When I'd taken on Beaker it had been with no options, and without knowing what a dragon was capable of. I knew better, now.

I held still, watching. The dragon's eyes were closed, and as I watched, it arched, stretching its neck out. Light coruscated off the scales, showing it to be purple, with green highlights in places. I was reminded of a hummingbird I'd once seen, a living jewel covered in metallic feathers. Only this beast had scales.

The dragon screamed, and I fell to my knees. The volume and pitch of the sound rang me like a bell, and I found myself leaning against the bookcase, hands pressed to my ears, until it died away again. Once I had my breathing and shaking hands back under control, I peeked again. The dragon was drooped back into the heap of bedding, looking utterly worn out. The rim of debris meant I couldn't see all of the nest, and Bella could still be in there. Maybe this was a good time to charge in and challenge it, while it was obviously in distress.

I was gathering myself to spring, pistol in hand, when the dragon's head whipped up. It seemed to be looking straight at me, eyes shifting colors rapidly through a rainbow spectrum. Something about them reminded me... It got up and rushed out of the nest and before I could even react, it was gone, out of the room through the door I'd come in.

I was torn. It had to be going after Alger and Byrne, but Bella... I ran forward to the lip of the nest and jumped up to grab it, pulling myself up and in with one fluid motion. I fell onto a mess that could only be comfortable to a dragon with scales. Pieces of broken wood, cloth, wads of coarse hair that had once been inside cushions... and in the center, glowing with a light of their own, were two eggs.

Suddenly the dragon's distress was clear. Still no sign of Bella, but the poor thing had been having labor pains. I circled cautiously around them, looking for any sign that Bella had been here. Other than a few faint bloodstains and fluid on and near the eggs, which had to be from the laying process, there was nothing. I rocked back on my heels, crouched low enough to be out of sight in the nest, and stared at the eggs.

It took me long enough to cue into the solution to this puzzle.

When it hit me with a blinding flash of insight, I felt like the world's prize dummy. I closed my eyes.

The glow of the eggs was piercingly familiar. One pearly white, the other faintly lavender-hued. My children. I reached forward and touched one shell. It wasn't hard, like a hen's egg. The leathery skin gave slightly on my contact, and I could feel the pulsing motion that was the baby squirming. It was very warm.

Bella was the dragon. Somehow entering the library had triggered her to change into dragon form, and she had fled in pain to...

I looked around, with wide-open eyes. She couldn't possibly have made this in the short time since we walked into the library. It had the air of long living, the nest so neatly arranged. I noted that no books were in the nest materials. She was careful of her library. Bella had been here before. No... something had been here. Bella the woman I knew had had no time to come here in person since she had been taken Underhill for me, and she had been given access to the library on that flight.

My train of thought was interrupted by the faint scratching of talons on the floor. Bella was returning to the nest. I stood up and walked to the edge of the nest, and swung my legs over it. I was sitting on the edge when she walked in. We both froze, staring at one another.

I knew where I'd seen those eyes before. When Bob showed us his dragon form for the first and only time, his eyes had looked just like hers. The reflections of inner and outer light as her lenses moved in the big eyes made it look like they were prisms, reflecting rainbows. Her wings, like his had been, were tucked along her sides neatly, and she walked on all fours, snakelike neck held high, and long tail dragging as a counterbalance should she need to rear up.

She tilted her head to one side. I remembered that Bob was non-verbal in dragon form. Beaker could express himself, but we still weren't sure he had a human form, so there was that.

"Bella." I spoke softly. "Are you all right?"

She lowered her head and hissed softly, eyes narrowing. I didn't like the looks of that.

"It's Lom. Do you know me?"

She answered this by blurring into motion, forepaws with talons outstretched toward me. I dove off the nest and as far to one side as I could go. She hit the nest with her shoulder as she tried unsuccessfully to turn in midair. I ran.

When I hit the hall, I didn't go in the direction I had come from. I had only one hope, that in her dragon form she wasn't thinking clearly, and I could put some distance between us without having to hurt her. I'd lay my life down for her, but this wasn't what I'd had in mind. I got several bounding strides down the hall before I realized I wasn't thinking clearly, either, and I bubbled myself out of there.

Transport with a spell like this was used only if you knew where you were going. A bubble into an unknown place risked coming out intersecting with something solid. Which would be a very bad death. So when I threw up the bubble I was headed for the lions sleeping in the statues. I wanted to collect Alger and Byrne and give Bella enough space to settle down until we could figure out what was happening, and how to talk to her.

Where I came out was not where I had intended. To begin with, you try to land as close to the ground as you can without being *in* it. The more expert you are with this spell, and after all the years I'd been using it, I could call myself that, the closer you get. The margin of error is slim. It certainly isn't the four foot fall that left me sprawling on top of a heap of papyrus scrolls.

Thanks to that ancient cushion, I was only damaged in the *amor propre* and a gale of sneezes that seized me after I gasped and sucked dust. I looked around and confirmed that I had no idea where I was. After regaining control of my breathing, I listened. Nothing. Only a heavy, muffling silence. This was a long, low room absolutely chock full of bins of scrolls. The dust looked like it had been undisturbed for longer than I cared to think about.

I floundered out of the bin I'd fallen in, and got to my feet. One thing for sure, I wasn't going to risk another bubble for transport. I composed a message and sent it, wondering if even that small magic was going to work. Then I sent another, even though she probably couldn't understand it in her current state. Finally, I started looking for a way out.

Both Bella and Alger had alluded to the size and disorganization of the Library. It took me about three rooms to realize that neither of them had a hope of ever making this place make sense. It would take a whole city of librarians. Who, I wondered, looking up at the size of the doorway I was walking through, had built this place? And why here, on a plane where nothing worked right?

I sent another message spell. I was hoping that Alger would get them, that he would recognize where I was from my descriptions, and that, if nothing else, he was staying well clear of a certain mother dragon.

My stomach growled, surprising me. I had no idea how much time had passed since breakfast, or even if time meant anything here, in this place. I found a room with tables and chairs. Sitting there, facing the door while I ate and drank icy-cold water from my stash in nospace, I contemplated the whole ridiculous situation.

Bella was the least of my worries. I had a plan when it came to her. Our children, on the other hand... we were stuck here until they hatched. I didn't even want to think about returning to Underhill with them on the outside. Which meant we'd be here for a while. I needed to get an update to Corwin, and Ellie, and my mother, and Holy Mother Titania, how was this going to impact the situation with Dionaea?

I wanted to put my face into my hands and laugh hysterically at the mess, but I didn't dare let down my guard. Time to go find Alger and get the plan rolling. He wasn't going to like it. Hell, I didn't like it. Lavendar was going to absolutely hate it. I cleared up, even though I would never be able to find this room again. The Library was confusing, and laid out irregularly.

I went round a corner and frowned to myself. I was tired, dusty, itchy, and this looked a lot like somewhere I had been before. I looked down. Sure enough, there were my tracks... I'd made a full circle. Most of the rooms had windows, and those which didn't, had light sources which could only be powered by magic. I had been trying to use the windows to navigate, but what if this was...

I leaned against the wall. I was lost. I couldn't think how I was supposed to find the statue room, the lobby, I'd dubbed it. I was tired, and if Bella had already found Alger and Byrne, then all was already lost. I'd been walking for hours.

A message spell popped in the air about two inches from my nose, making me flinch backward. I slid to the floor in sheer relief, sitting against the wall while I listened to Alger's voice.

Chapter 20

Locked in the Library

"Got your message. I think you're in the Phoenician wing, m'boyo."Alger sounded gruff, but I thought I heard overtones of concern. "You ought to be able to find the central passageway from there, if you don't get sidetracked into Norse."

Who the hell had sorted the collections out in this place? That made no sense geographically or chronologically. I knew I'd seen a room with 'books' made of thin wooden slabs, not too long before. Maybe that was Norse? I certainly hadn't seen anything that looked like a central passageway.

He went on. "I understand your plan. I'm to go get help. You're going to stay where you are. Byrne and I have been playing hide and seek with the dragon, er, Bella. We'll be just as glad to get some space between us, she's not happy. Good luck, Lom."

His voice ended and the spell faded away. I stared off into midair. I'd sent him to go get the only person I thought could get through to Bella in her state. And he'd have to take Lavendar along, to prove his bonafides. In the meantime, I was stuck here, in the library, avoiding a dragon. There was only one thing I could do.

Look for the Charter. Also, learn how to navigate this rabbit warren. If only there were something sensible, like a map. Alger could have at the least...

Another message spell popped into being, this one across the hall from where I sat. I lunged forward and caught it, triggering it. Alger's voice sounded out, again, repeating the same thing I'd just heard. I let it play through, in case he'd added more content with this attempt. When it had faded away, with no new words, I got to my feet.

A clever human once proposed a certain hierarchy of needs. Food, shelter, clothing... I'd add to that a bathroom, which was something I hadn't seen this far into my explorations. I'd begun to think the Librarians were a most impractical race, whatever they had been. Human, Fae, and other materials all mingled here in a vast building, and no place to leave waste. Shelter I had. Food, a limited stock of nutritious if boring comestibles and plenty of water. Even a flask of good whisky, although I'd intended that for the sprites to begin with. Clothing, a few changes. If this went on, I was going to need a place with water, for bathing and washing up.

So I wanted a fountain. A garden would be nice, to accompany the Library. Sure the beings who'd made this place had liked such things? I knew they shared similar tastes in statues and art. I'd been largely ignoring the paintings and tapestries on the wall, but I'd seen them in passing. A place of great beauty.

I found Alger's central passageway. It was long enough to go almost to a vanishing-point in both directions. I swore to myself, loudly. My voice echoed back to me. Some needs were becoming pressing. I walked into the long corridor, and looked.

There were footprints, here. Some that looked human – Alger, I decided. – and the sweeping marks of a dragon. They went in both directions. I stood very still, and listened.

The sound didn't register, at first. I was listening for footsteps, not the continuous low murmur of running water. Look, in the real world, total silence is a rare thing. Your brain is trained to filter out the background sounds. Otherwise you'd walk around in a state of total panic all the time. You catalog and dismiss the majority of sounds as harmless and go on with your life. Add to that my level of fatigue, and it took me a minute to catch what I was hearing.

Then it took me a little while to find it. It wasn't a garden. Well, not a traditional one. This was more like a terrarium. It was enclosed in a dome of windows, set into stone shapes that made the whole overhead effect like being covered in an upside-down colander. There was a running stream passing through it, and when I opened the door to walk in, a burst of tiny, colorful birds flew overhead and into the cluster of dwarf trees on the far side of the stream.

I'd found a place to stay, if Bella didn't know about it. I jumped over the little stream and explored the grove of trees. They gave enough cover I could sleep without worrying about being immediately visible to someone coming through the door. First order of business was a cathole far from my sleeping spot, and taking care of pressing needs. After that was done, I could relax and make myself comfortable. Sleep followed almost immediately once I was curled up on the deep forest duff in a sleeping bag pulled from my stash.

The light, I discovered in what felt like morning to me, did not change. It was the same hue, the same brightness, as it had been however many hours before when I entered the terrarium. My watch, when I checked it, was not working. I ate perfunctorily, and explored my little sanctuary. Other than the birds, there were frogs, at least one newt, and brightly-colored fish in the stream. The trees were perhaps double my height, no more, and from the depth of the soil, this whole system had been functional for a considerable amount of time. It wasn't jungle-thick, simply because there wasn't that sort of environment. It reminded me of some park-like forests I had been in, pruned and maintained not by hands but growth patterns.

What I did not find was any sign of Bella-dragon having visited.

Even if she was able to fly, which I didn't doubt she could, supplemented by magic, there wasn't room. The roof tapered, the further up it went, into almost a cone. Nor were there signs of claws digging into the clay bank of the stream and grassy stretch between it and the door.

So I had found a reasonable sanctuary. I risked a tiny fire, not for warmth, but to make warm food, and something else. If I was going to venture out of here to find the hall of statues – a necessary task – and try to find the Charter, I would need a way to find it again. The day – or however long – before wandering in a circle had been discouraging.

It was possible there was more than one of these inside gardens in the Library. It was certainly large enough to hold many of them. I wasn't going to risk that. So I made charcoal sticks, for marking the walls. Before I ventured out, I slept again. I was worn thin from the excitement, and there would be time to recuperate. Always sleep when you can, because there will be times when you can't.

I left the terrarium and discovered that although the light in it was unchanging, the windows in the corridor were showing a night sky. As I had done the day before, I moved slowly, stopping to listen often. I was in no rush, and had no desire to stumble upon Bella unawares. I marked a doorway, one of many that lined the corridor, each with two tall narrow windows in between them, and went in to see what books were in this section.

The Library did not house only books, I discovered. This room was full of art. Some were wrapped in muslin bags, brittle with age, and stacked on low shelves. Others hung on the walls. I scanned the room, noting that the style was largely that of the human Renaissance period, and retreated to the main corridor again.

As I did, I casually glanced at the mark I'd made on the wall. It was gone. I checked the other side, wondering if I'd already forgotten where I'd made it, with the stress I was under. Still nothing. The light creamy stone was flawless. I took the charcoal stick I was holding and made another mark, then stood and watched.

As though it were melting backward into the stone, it dissolved and disappeared, leaving no trace of the stain. I did it again, and again, the wall cleaned itself.

I went back to the terrarium, where, comfortingly, the scrape I'd made in the duff for my bed, and the fire-ring of stones were just as I had left them. I rekindled the fire for comfort and a pot of coffee, then sat staring into the flames. I was more than a little shaken, and I needed to think.

The Library was not alive. If it were, Bella-dragon could not have created and sustained that nest. However...

I tried to think like an alien, long-dead librarian. What were features I would look for in a massive installation created for the sole purpose of collecting intellectual artifacts from at least two realms, and holding them essentially in stasis for eons?

The self-cleaning might be why the whole building was saturated with magic. Or that might simply be a pleasant by-product of preserving the collection itself. No wonder Bella had trouble with getting it organized, the Library itself was resisting that.

Now, how the heck was I going to explore without getting lost? Marks in the dusty floor, the only place the Library seemed to allow a mess. That might work, unless Bella came along and wiped them out. And that brought another thought to mind. If I were able to find the Charter, which seemed like a slimmer possibility with every accumulating event, would I be allowed to remove it?

I slept, and ate, and repeated this pattern until I was bored enough to start contemplating something, anything. I was going to go crazy if I had to sit here until help arrived. I was also still doubtful that they would be able to reach me. I'd had no fewer than three identical messages from Alger before they stopped. Which didn't mean he'd sent all of them, or that he hadn't sent more. I was going to go crazy simply from doubting anything and everything that seemed real around me.

I spent some of the endless terrarium day catching a bird. I'd never been good at this magical skill of hitching a ride in an animal mind, but it was worth a try. Perhaps the Library would enhance my abilities. It seemed to magnify magic.

I steered the tiny thing around the terrarium roof, and brought it back to land on my finger. I wasn't trying to completely control it, I didn't know how to be a bird. I was just giving it some nudges, impulses to do as I wished.

Feeling triumphant that finally, something was going according to plan, I opened the door and let it out in the Library corridor. Then I made myself comfortable on the grass, closed my eyes, and followed the bird's vision. It was rather confused, poor thing, and I helpfully sent it down to the far end of the corridor, in the other direction than I had come when I found the terrarium.

By using the bird, I hoped to either avoid Bella-dragon's notice, or if it were seen, to escape by being smaller and more agile than myself. The bird flew unerringly to the end of the corridor and then out, into another huge hall. Not, to my disappointment, the statuary hall. This one was echoing empty. It was designed similarly to the lobby we'd entered, and had parquet floors, but it was...

Ah! There, that looked like an orchestra pit. This seemed to be a ballroom, on a vast scale. Whatever the librarians had looked like, I thought I could safely say that they had been larger than any human or Fac. I could feel the little bird falter, and sent it a picture of home, then let it return. I would not be so cruel to kill it on my errands.

It had been roughly four days, perhaps five, since we had walked into the Library and Bella became her dragon self. I had not seen her since I fled that first day, and now I was about to go back to the statuary room. It seemed logical that it was on the opposite end of the corridor from the ballroom. I decided to sleep, eat, and scout with a different bird after that cycle. The constant light was messing with my sense of time, and I felt disoriented. I needed to get out of here.

In the 'morning' I did just what I'd planned, and it was anticlimactic to send the little bird swooping over the huge statues, dwarfing the feathered steed my awareness rode in. I'd gotten my bearings, finally. I had the bird land on the same tree-framed doorway where Ian had directed me to the dragon's lair, and we listened. There was a faint noise, then another, but she was not close. I hesitated.

I wanted to see her, and the eggs that were our children, but I didn't want to disturb her and frighten her with the bird. Nor could I risk her following it back to me. I sent the bird the signal to return home, and opened my eyes. Laying on the grass looking up at the endless sunshine, I felt the hope I'd been nurturing slipping a little.

It was possible that Bella's mind was forever gone. This place was stranger than anything I had encountered before, Underhill or Above. It could be possible that nothing would ever bring her back to me. And the children? I got to my feet to let the bird back in. I didn't know.

Chapter 21

The Charter

One thing I'd learned early in life was how to not think too much about things I couldn't change. Long periods of illness had oddly helped me later, when I had to stake out a suspected magic-user above. Waiting was annoying, but part of life. While I waited to find out if Bella could be restored, and our children live normal lives, I would turn my attention to something else.

Namely, retrieving the Charter. I had more than a little curiosity about what it said, with Dionaea wanting it, and Lavendar, and Lady Laenven. It had been lost for longer than my lifetime, why was it so important now? I paced on the grassy area, noting ruefully that I had worn a path already. I was impacting the delicate terrarium. I decided to spend the next day exploring.

Since marking the walls would not work, I would mark the floors. I would also recheck my first mark before getting too far, just in case. I still had no idea how, or even if, the rooms were organized, but I had decided that if I could find a room full of Fae books from the right era, then I'd be on the right track. Before I curled up for a sleep period, I

165

could hardly call it a night's sleep when there was no night here, I went out and made my mark in the dust.

The corridor was dimly lit when I exited the terrarium. Perhaps my body was right in telling me it was morning. I didn't look forward to trying to return to anything like a routine, when we got home again. I walked slowly toward the distant ballroom, past the room where I had gotten the scare of the disappearing charcoal mark, and, kneeling, checked where I had earlier made a mark in the floor only inches from the wall. It was less likely to be disturbed, there. Too close, and the wall might play its tricks again. To my relief, the mark was still clearly there.

I could safely enter the hallway. Some doors off the corridor only led to a single room, others, like this one, to many. I counted four doors, with a pretty bow window at the end of the hall. It was arranged as a place to read, with an age-brittle cushion lying on the bench formed by the window. Outside the window, only the glowing mist of the Third Plane was visible.

The presence of the cushion led me to believe that Bella-dragon had not been here, collecting for her nest. I had an irrational urge to put the cushion in the corridor, where she would find it. I stood there staring at it for a long time, then I picked it up gingerly, hoping it wouldn't just fall apart, and carried it out, laying it in the center where she couldn't miss it.

The four rooms were relatively small, but I could still tell hours had passed in my inspection, as my stomach was clear on this subject. Time had passed. I paused in the hall before emerging into the corridor. The cushion lay forlornly in the dust. I decided I would eat a handful of my diminishing stash of pemmican rather than returning to the terrarium, and continued to the next hall.

The next room I entered was far more interesting than stacks of dusty books and scrolls. It was another very large room, and full of low tables and benches. Low to me, that is, after so much time adjusting to the Library scale. On the tables were games, in mammoth scale. The chessmen were fully waist-high to me. Carved in almost abstract shapes, they disappointed me when I inspected them. I had been hoping for a clue to the librarian's identity. Nearby, a vast game of Go was laid out, with the oldest version of 17 grid squares. I ventured past it, to another table with something I didn't recognize laid out on it. I jumped up on the bench, and looked down at the arrangement of rough stone pieces. It took me a minute before I recognized the arrangement. It looked familiar because I had seen it many times.

This game board held Stonehenge, or something like enough I could tell what it was. Amused, I looked at the stack of pieces nearby, either discarded, or not yet played, who could tell? Reluctantly, I left the room, knowing that I had to keep moving if I were not to be discovered. On to the next hallway. I looked back, to the cushion. Well, at least this would give me warning if she came nearby.

The next door led to a single room. I stepped in, realized it was another art storage area, and almost walked out again. A face on the wall caught my eye. This room was dim, with no windows, and I didn't quite believe what I had seen. Carefully, I conjured an elf globe and held it up, revealing a familiar countenance.

I walked carefully around the room looking at the portraits that hung there. Several were of the first woman, the one I knew. One was her, with her family gathered around her, and I stood there longest, looking at it. I remembered this painting. I had seen it before.

I knew now I was in the right place. Portraits of Mab meant that this was where the Fae were chronicled. I had last seen this painting of the revered Queen hanging in Elleria, when I was still a very small child. I had never seen it after my father's death. I extinguished the elfglobe and stood in the twilight room, thinking. Perhaps Alger had brought it here, how else could it have gotten from my family home, abandoned not long after my father's death? Elleria had been all but vacant for a hundred years and more. This might have been his way of protecting the art and books which had been left to rot with neglect.

I wouldn't blame him if that was what he had done. I did wish he'd told me. I turned toward the corridor, still lost in thought. I was walking out when something stopped me. My subconscious, honed by days of listening carefully, pinged in alarm, and I threw myself to one side, hugging the wall by the door.

Footsteps. Soft swishing of the dragging tail, and the tick, tick, of claws on the stone floor of the corridor. Bella was out there. I was almost tempted to step out, to talk to her and see if she had regained her senses. But I had no retreat, if she was insensate. I stayed still, almost not breathing.

She kept going. I was fortunate that she was not a scent hunter. With those huge eyes, I would categorize the dragons like herself and her grandfather as sight-hunters. They would no doubt be able to catch the slightest movement from a great distance away in flight, like an eagle. So I would stay out of sight, like a mouse. I waited several minutes after all sounds had faded away, to be sure she was gone. Only then, cautiously, did I put my head out, to look.

She had taken the cushion. I felt oddly pleased by that. It was a little thing, not really providing for her and the eggs, but still. I did worry about what she was living on. Other than the little birds and fishes in the terrarium, which would hardly be a snack, I had seen no signs of life in the Library.

When I ventured back out into the corridor, I felt exhausted, as though I had just run a race. All this hiding was hard work. One more hallway, and then I could retreat for rest. I was still excited over the discovery of the Fae art. I slipped along the wall, bent and made a mark, and then went into the dark hallway.

Here, I discovered that unlike the other places, there had been activity. The hall was long, and curved gradually out of sight. Bella's tracks were visible on the floor. I would have to hurry, and be careful.

This, then, was the Fae wing of the library, and it was where she came. For what purpose, I didn't know, but it gave me a flicker of hope that she remembered. This was her place, and she might still come back to me.

I went into the first rooms and discovered that they were neatly organized. I realized after a few minutes of looking at shelves that I was smiling. This room showed all the signs of having been the recipient of my loving wife's tender care and organization. Furthermore, the Library had allowed it. However, this place held mostly volumes on magic, not history.

The next room held more recent history. I was tempted to look for volumes on my own past, just to see if they existed, but I didn't have time. I went on to the next room. Here, I thought, I would find the thing I was looking for. The problem was that I didn't know what it looked like. Was it a book? Or a single scrolled document? There were both, and this room was large. I felt my earlier euphoria draining away.

With some hesitation, I set a ward at the doorway. It was not enough to stop her, if she returned, but it would give me some time to hide in the stacks. There were enough shelves and bins in this room to keep me out of sight. She hadn't gotten this far in her quest to tidy the Library. Then I started to look at books.

If there was a pattern to the way they were shelved, it wasn't obvious to me. Volumes that were written for no other purpose than to chronicle long-forgotten Council meetings were shelved alongside scholarly treatises on the trade with Humans, and how to conceal magic in that realm. I put that book on a table, for later reading. It was very interesting, as a precursor to the troubles that created my job a millennia later. That, and it was hard to read. It would take me some time to puzzle it out.

My stomach started to accuse me of having my throat cut and not telling it. I wondered if I would have to leave and come back after a good night's sleep. If Bella knew I was here, in the library, would she

169

look for me? I didn't know. I'd taken a risk with the cushion, but it had been irrationally happy-making.

I pulled the last of my pemmican out and gnawed on it. One thing about nospace, the dried meat and fruit mixture didn't really dry out, more than it was when packaged. I washed it down with water, and kept going through the old books. Fae had developed bookmaking to a high art, using a combination of magic and more mundane methods to preserve their records far earlier than humans had picked up the same methods.

I almost didn't recognize it when I picked it up. The cover didn't look right. Most of what I'd been handling was bound with thinly slabbed wood that had been covered in intricately tooled leather. Like I said, works of art. This one had been badly broken, like someone had dropped and rolled on it. I held it up into the light, and closer to my face. It had a strange odor, and there were foul stains on it. Dried blood? Curious, I carried it over to a table, and laid it flat, carefully opening it.

There was no title or fancy heading. The first page simply stated the opening premise of the charter. I scanned the faded script. This was going to take a little time. Byrne could probably read it at a glance, I was going to have to take it back to my refuge and keep it safe while I puzzled it out.

I picked up the two books, and dropped the wards. A peek into the hall showed no motion, and I moved cautiously out. This was going to drive me crazy. No way to fight back, just wait, hide, and not sleep worth a damn. The lack of darkness was getting to me.

I reached the corridor, and slipped into it silently. Maybe tonight I would sleep somewhere outside the terrarium. Maybe not. It was safe, and I had already upset the order of things with the damn cushion. I carried the books into the ever-present light and moisture. I couldn't keep them here long. I'd developed a theory about the Library. The clean walls, the shelves and bins... it was all set up to preserve the books. The stream in here would do bad things to ancient ink and vellum, I was afraid.

I set the books aside and went through my little ritual of making a small fire. Having that bit of cooked food made life a little better. And it was one of the few things I had control over right now. It wasn't much, a bit of stew, but after a day with only pemmican it tasted good. I resisted looking at the Charter until I had done my housekeeping: put out the fire, put away leftover food (well, a little to the birds, who were becoming quite tame), and made a new cathole. I'd been keeping track of where I put them, so I wasn't overburdening the soil in one place.

Then I sat cross-legged on my bedding, the book open on my lap, and a little elf-globe hovering just at head-level for a reading light. Much of what it laid out, in remarkably clear language, I had already known. No king or queen was to be a direct descendent of the previous one. The selection process was largely the Council, but weighted by certain things.

Now, that was interesting. Of the princesses who had come to Court to be seen, three of them had never been eligible at all. It wasn't age, but experience the founding Council had wanted to see. Dill, the little girl Bella was so taken with, had nothing to show them. I wondered how altered the Charter copies were.

My eyes were tired, and my head throbbing after squinting at the faded ink. I resisted the urge to use a spell to enhance it. Anything I left a trace on, could be used against Bella. I tucked the books into nospace to protect them from the terrarium environment, and curled up to try and sleep.

I dozed, awakened, and dozed again. With the unchanging light, passage of time was impossible to calculate. I could go look out into the corridor, which did have a day cycle, but I wasn't quite awake enough. I drifted back off. The second time my sleep was interrupted, I got up and relieved myself. This time, I did go to the corridor door. I reached out to open it, and then stopped, alerted by the little birds.

They flew up into the trees, just like they had when I first started invading their space. I couldn't hear what they could, but I trusted their instincts. I risked a bubble.

I didn't go anywhere, though, I just pulled it up and thinned a window enough to see, but not be seen. The door swung open partway, then a darkly scaled foot hooked it the rest of the way open. Bella had found me. She slid awkwardly through the door, her head swinging to and fro as she paced into the terrarium. I knew she would find the bed, and signs of my habitation.

I took advantage of the trees and ornamental plants as she leapt over the stream and vanished into them. Dropping the bubble, I ran into the hall, leaving the door open. I needed to find another hidey-hole. And where was Alger, dammit! I couldn't keep this up much longer now that she was looking for me.

Chapter 22

Three Dragons

It was still night. I didn't think I was getting any more sleep, though. I sprinted up the corridor and into a hall where there had been no Bella tracks. She didn't seem interested in very early human history. Then again, I didn't think she could read runes or hieroglyphs. I was heading for the room where I'd first blundered out of my bubble. With all the bins, it would be a good place to hide. For a while.

With no hope of success, I sent a message to Alger. I may have sounded a little testy. I was beyond caring about that. Then I hunkered down and made myself think small and silent. I couldn't hear anything. After several minutes of this, I relaxed and slumped to the floor. It was cold and uncomfortable.

Well, shit. I'd gotten cocky, and it had bitten me. Whether it was the cushion, or moving the books, she was after me now. I'd lost my bedding, and that I didn't carry back-ups for. I pulled a long coat out of my stash, which was significantly smaller, and wrapped up in it. It was going to be a long time until morning.

By morning's first gray dim, I was cold, stiff, and had an idea. I got up and worked out the kinks, before munching survival rations – that was how low I'd gotten, down to the sardines packed in mustard sauce – and washing it down with cold water. Coffee was not an option. Once I was fueled up, I headed for the statuary hall, ignoring the other pressure.

I couldn't leave the Library. Bella might kill me, but the monsters outside would certainly eat me, and I didn't think I'd be able to access Lavendar's dome. But if my theory was correct, there were two more wings of the Library. Bella was in one. The other I could access through the vast entrance gallery. I was hoping for another garden.

The hall was still. I sneaked from statue to statue, keeping them between me and the doorway where Bella's nest was. I kept stopping to listen. Something was bothering me. It wasn't a noise, really. It was more of a vibration.

I made my way around a familiar Medusa head, and almost smacked into a wall. That wasn't right. I couldn't light anything to see what it was... I stretched out a hand and touched it. Warm, and covered in dinner-plate sized scales. Not Bella, her scales were smaller, more feathery.

I risked a tiny light. The wall was a metallic red, with a bit of gold just visible. Now, why hadn't I thought of this before? I got my bearings from how the scales were laid out, and started toward Beaker's head. He was fast asleep, wound around several statues delicately, like a cat on a shelf. I got to his head, feeling the soft vibration of his snores, and resisted the absurd urge to throw my arms around his muzzle in a hug like Bella did when she greeted him.

I slid to the floor in the crook of his neck, feeling his warm bulk. He grunted in his sleep and angled his head a little, wrapping me up in his jaw folds. Beaker knew me, and he was more than Bella's match. Also, if he was here, had been here for who knew how long... although not more than a couple of days, or I would have seen him with the bird. She knew he was here, and had accepted him.

I slept. I hadn't realized how badly being alone was affecting me. Having Beaker as a massive backup meant I could rest for the first time in who knew how long. I was awakened by a low rumbling growl. I rubbed my eyes and sat up, trying to interpret this noise. I froze when I saw Bella in front of me. She was crouched, her tail lashing like a cat, her wings partly spread. Beaker was growling at her.

The huge rainbow eyes shifted back and forth between us.

"Mreep. Meep. Mememe..."

That last came out like an opera singer warming up. I didn't know he could make sounds that high. She rocked back on her haunches and shrieked at him. I stayed put. Beaker's jaws were between the two of us. He stretched out his neck and...

Booped her in the belly with his nose. She batted at his face, hard, but he had closed his eyes. He snorted. She backed up.

I was torn between laughter at his tactics, and indignation that he was tickling my wife's belly. Bella dropped to all fours, glared at both of us, and then turned away. She rapidly retreated in the direction of her nest. I looked up at Beaker.

"She's thinking 'men!' so loudly I can practically hear it."

He blinked at me amiably.

"I'd stay here, but the bathroom, and something beside the floor, not to mention food..." I sighed. I was talking to a dragon. I patted him on the muzzle, and he purred. It always astonished me how catlike the giant lizard was.

"I should be more worried about you, old boy. How are you going to eat?"

He looked at the vast doors.

"I suppose that's how you got in, too. Although you do have a knack for showing up in the oddest places."

He nodded, his eyes squinched, and moved for the doorway. I backed up and gave him space. Beaker nosed open the vast doors, and swam out, a foot or two above the ground. I rarely saw him use his almost vestigial legs for locomotion, he preferred to fly. The doors closed behind him, and I beat a hasty retreat. Without him as a buffer, I'd prefer not to encounter my wife.

The message spell took me by surprise. I had just spent a couple of hours exploring oddly empty rooms. I hadn't found anything like the terrarium. The spell broke my focus, and almost my nose. I rubbed my stinging face while I listened to Alger's voice.

"Sorry for the delay, m'boy. I'd no idea how far you were sending me for help."

Of course he would complain about that. I shook my head, still listening. "We are at the gates. Wanted to see you before we entered, better hurry."

I hurried. I could only hope Beaker was back from hunting. I ran into the hall without practicing my usual caution, relying on speed to carry me through to the small door before Bella caught up with me. I didn't see her, and could only spare a quick glance upward to confirm she wasn't in the air, before I started having to watch out for statues. Weaving in and out of them slowed me down a bit, and I could hear pounding at the small door before I reached it.

I grabbed the handle and pulled, and Lavendar tumbled in, closely followed by Byrne. "Good god, man, took you long enough!" Byrne scrambled up, his face red.

I ignored him and looked through the open door. Bob, a long rifle in hand, was firing from the hip while Alger sent fire downrange from his staff. A crowd of the weird monstrosities was pressing toward the Library gates.

"This is getting old." I commented. I braced, and let out a piercing whistle. Alger glanced back at me, quickly.

I had no idea how far away Beaker was. "Get in here!" I bellowed.

Alger slid past me, and Bob fell back, firing once more before he too entered the Library. I really hoped Alger had warned him about the effect it had on dragons. I slammed the door shut and dropped the heavy bar down, just as something heavy thudded into it.

The door didn't even quiver in its frame. The Library had defenses. I turned around just in time to see Bob hand his rifle to Lavendar.

"How long do you think I have?" he asked me.

I shook my head. "A few minutes. Not more, if it works like it did on her. I don't even know if it will, she was... She'd never shifted, and you have."

He nodded. "Excuse me, then, I do prefer privacy." He looked straight at me, "Last time was for her, you understand."

I did. He walked away, his silver hair gleaming, and vanished behind a statue. I looked at the rest of the party.

"And a fine hello to all of you, as well. I'm afraid I can't offer refreshments..."

Lavendar broke into a hearty laugh. "I'm just glad to find you alive, after how these two were describing..."

She broke off, her face twisting a little. I looked over my shoulder. Bob was in his dragon form. He dipped his head to us, then glided away among the statues, his wings tucked back and out of the way.

"I have only seen him in that form once before." Lavender spoke so softly I could barely hear her.

"He is aware." I assured her.

She shivered a little, and looked at me, as though she had forgotten my presence for a moment. "Oh, yes, he is aware."

"Then this shouldn't take too long." Alger rubbed his hands together. "And I can get to work."

"I don't understand what happened to her." Lavendar ignored Alger. I wished I could accomplish that feat.

"I think it's the Library. It's saturated with magic. Spells here go awry, or work rather better than they ought." I was thinking of my flights with the little birds. Which reminded me that I could go check on them, now.

"Would you like to see something?" I asked her, and looked at Byrne. "You will like it as well."

Alger harrumphed. He knew I was irritated with him. Behind us, the doors slid silently open. Alger thrust his staff forward, and I parried it upward with my forearm.

"Beaker!" I shouted at him.

The dragon snuffled at my back and almost knocked me off my feet with a nuzzle. He sniffed a discomfited Alger at length.

"This is Bella's pet." I introduced him to Lavendar and Byrne. "Well, not sure pet is the right word. But he's to be found wherever she is. I didn't think he'd follow her here, but then..."

I thumped Beaker's cheek, hard, the way I usually did. He sighed and broke into his low rumble of a purr, then finished entering the big room. I could see past his tail that the crowd of monsters had been reduced to shreds. Some of them quivered slightly. I grinned. This was how he'd been eating, and Bella as well, most likely.

The trip home ought to be easier, for one thing. When the doors were closed, I turned back to Lavendar, who had a funny look on her face. Amused, maybe.

"Shall we?"

Walking through the statues with no stress was a great deal more enjoyable. With Beaker on guard, I could relax. I pointed out a few things I'd noted in passing. I might have gone through quickly, but I was trained to note details. Byrne and I chatted while Lavendar stood staring at the statues. She would look silently for a moment, then walk to the next one.

"I looked after the goats." Byrne told me cheerfully. "Lavendar wouldn't leave them, but I proved that I could do it..."

Lavendar broke from her reverie. "He is quite a handy milker. Surprising, really."

"It was a pleasant pastoral interlude." Byrne chuckled.

"I'm glad you enjoyed yourself." I felt a little grumpy, considering.

"Through here." I pointed. "It's a bit of a walk."

"Should we, er, watch for Bella?" Byrne asked, looking behind us nervously. He'd been a bit skittish since we left Alger with Beaker.

"No, between Bob and Beaker we will have plenty of warning."

He looked down at the two guns I was wearing. "Would you have, ah...?"

I shook my head. "I didn't have to. I might have, had it come to it. But it wouldn't have hurt her too much. I know what dragon scale is like as armor."

"Really?"

He really did want to know everything. "I shot at Beaker a few times, when we first met. Didn't bother him a bit."

"Oh, my." Lavendar shook her head. "You really are a match for my girl, aren't you?"

"I hope so, ma'am."

I opened the terrarium door, and the birds fled in a twittering mass. Good. Bella hadn't hurt them. I didn't think she would, she wasn't the person to lash out in anger when she didn't get her way.

"Oh, how lovely." Lavendar went to the stream and dabbled her fingers for the little fish to nibble.

"Now, this is interesting. Wonder how long this ecology has been developing?" Byrne was looking up at the trees and the bright light.

"I can tell you the light doesn't change. Night and day, all the same." I said dryly.

"Oh, you stayed here?"

"This was the only place where Bella didn't go, until last night." I wondered if my bed was still there, but this wasn't the time to check.

"I say, have you had a chance to look...?" He looked like an eager schoolboy.

Lavendar gave him a speaking glance. "I have to wonder how safe it really is to be roaming around until Bob has had a chance to talk to Bella."

I felt like there was an undercurrent here, between the two of them, and I lacked context to put a name to it. Alger had known her, before, had Byrne? I made a mental note to ask Alger. I might even get an answer. I owed Byrne an answer.

"Yes, I have. It's safe."

"Oh, really." He rubbed his hands together. "Might I see it?"

I shook my head. "Let's wait. It's not in the best of condition, and we are under time pressure, even though..."

"Waiting is difficult." Lavendar was looking at the flow of the water. "How quickly do you think it will be until Bella returns to herself."

Byrne shook his head. "This whole experience has been most odd."

"It's this place. This whole plane is odd." Lavendar walked briskly toward the door. "I would like to see my great-grandchildren."

I intercepted her. "That is not a good idea."

"If Bob has had a chance to talk to her..." She tilted her chin in a way I recognized. "Then I would like to, as well. I am not a delicate piece of china, young man."

"As you said, waiting is difficult. But you have just arrived."

"I'd like a comfortable chair, and tea, and rest for my old bones." She frowned. "Age is not for the weak of heart, young man."

"I haven't got a chair. I do suggest we return to the entrance room and wait on Bob and Bella."

She was distracted on the return, paying no attention to the statues. Byrne was still twitchy. I was beginning to feel that way, myself. Being alone was a lot less wear on the nerves than shepherding other people. I still hadn't grasped at the cause of my unsettled feeling. Beaker greeted us, his body twisted around the plinths as I had seen him before. He didn't seem at all uncomfortable. I thumped him on the jaw, and he sniffed at Lavendar and Byrne. Byrne shrank back a little.

"He won't eat you. Well, unless Bella tells him too."

Lavendar smiled tightly. "A pet fit for a queen, indeed."

She walked away, and I let her go. Byrne looked at Beaker, who rolled his head slightly and sighed. The dragon's sigh was enough to flutter clothes and smelled strongly of his last dinner. Not fish, as it had been when I first met him. I'd trust the beast with my life, had done so on my rescue from the kelpie.

"I think he likes you." I told Byrne.

"How could you tell?" He looked as though he were torn between retreating and holding out his hand.

"He wants to be scratched. That's why he just offered you his chin."

I showed Byrne how to reach the sensitive spot among the golden whiskers. Beaker started to purr and closed his eyes. I chuckled. "Just like a very large cat. You have made a conquest, Byrne."

He grinned, still scratching. "Call me Forrest, please. And he does rather remind me of a certain calico."

"I wonder if Bella would like a kitten. I always said that I wouldn't have one, because a kitten becomes a cat. But she had to leave her cat behind..."

I had asked much of her, leaving everything at a moment's notice. It hadn't been for me – that had come later – but I had been the one who tore her from the loving arms of her family. No wonder she had some unexpressed hostility toward me.

I turned as I heard the sound of approaching footsteps... dragon talons, in their distinctive clicking resonance.

Chapter 23

Changes

Bella walked toward me in dragon form. Bob loomed behind her, fully twice her size. I stood very still, and from the corner of my eye, saw Forrest Byrne similarly frozen. Could it have been this easy, after all? But then, it hadn't been easy. I'd had a rough few days, and so had she.

"Bella?" I took a step forward.

She kept walking toward me, the big eyes enigmatic. She finally stopped with her nose about a foot from my face. Then she put her head on my shoulder, and I wrapped my arms around the scaled neck. Bob, behind her, nodded slightly, and then veered off behind a statue.

"It's ok," I told my silent wife. I wasn't sure if she could speak in this form, but the trembling of the jeweled body told me what she was feeling.

"We'll get out of here, and you'll be back to yourself. And if we have to stay here for a while, we are at least together now."

She pulled her head back and nodded. Then she looked to the side. I followed her gaze. "Your buddy wouldn't leave you, you know that. Wherever you go, there he is. Just like me."

She looked back at me, then gently pushed her nose into my chest.

I hugged her slender neck again. "You have no idea how glad I am..." I didn't finish. There were others listening.

Byrne cleared his throat. "Does this mean we can go home now?"

I let go of Bella. "No, it does not. There are... extenuating circumstances."

"What are you talking about?"

"May I go see them?" I ignored his confusion and talked to Bella. Alger hadn't told him, but had told Lavendar. Interesting.

Bella turned and led the way back to her nest. For the second time I found myself scrambling over the lip and into the pile of soft things.

"I'm just as glad you didn't go traditional and heap up loot." I told her, reaching out to touch the nearest egg. It was warm, and taut with little dragonet growing inside. Bella curled herself around all of us - eggs and me. She nosed an egg and rolled it over. The baby wriggled, faintly visible through the leathery shell. "Don't worry." I told her. "All will be well in time. I'm not going anywhere until the babies have arrived."

Bob spoke, and I startled. I hadn't heard him coming. After the last few days, I was rather nervy.

"She said she has no idea when they will come."

Bella nodded.

I shook my head. "We won't leave until they do. It doesn't matter how long until they arrive safely."

Bella looked at me, then at Bob. She worked her throat, but I couldn't hear anything. Then it occurred to me that the dragons were speaking, just at a range I couldn't hear. I could feel the vibration of her body.

"She says that there is a place for you to stay, and that I don't need to, nor do the others."

I raised an interrogative eyebrow, and he bared his teeth. "I see no point in going so soon. Looks like an interesting place, and she needs to learn to share it."

Bella hissed, agitated. Bob kept talking to me, while she pulled her far wing over her face. "The Library is her hoard. This is what has been happening, keeping Alger from most of it, she's been unconsciously protecting it."

She was embarrassed, that was why she was hiding her face. I put a hand on her shoulder. It felt odd, to have warm scales under my palm. "I thought dragons hoarded, well..."

"Gold? Some of us did. But not all, and each individual chose something. Bella, with no manifestation of dragon nature, I didn't talk to you about this, I am sorry for that omission. We thought it was best you didn't know. The Fae side was bad enough, for a woman we thought would live out her life in the human realms."

She pulled her head out and I could feel and hear her this time, with a hiss and a snap in the statement.

"She says that this sucks, could I please go away right now, and tell grandmother to ask Alger about the scholar's lodging."

Bob shrugged, which did odd things to his wings. "I have no idea what that means. But I think I will leave you two alone."

He retreated. She might be half his size, but still. She had put her head back down, and although her eyes were closed, I could see big tears spilling out. Dragons cried, it seemed.

"You can't talk, I know. He can. Is it the magic?"

She shrugged, not opening her eyes.

"I'm glad you at least know me now. I'd hate to have become dragon chow."

Bella slitted open her eyes and glared at me. Ok, she wasn't in the mood for humor. I tried another tack. "I have the Charter."

She nodded.

"You knew? It wasn't the cushion, then."

She dropped her chin slightly, then looked back up with a dragon smile. The lips are not very flexible, I noted, and it was more menacing than the humor I guessed she was going for.

"So," I leaned back against her, the eggs cradled by my hip and her hindquarter. "The Library somehow alerted you to books being out of place?"

She nodded.

"Tagging and tracking of a magical nature. Can we remove the Charter, do you think?"

Awkwardly, she indicated herself with a foreclaw. She thought she could do it.

"I did snitch another book, but that was just to read. I was going to return it, I promise."

She purred. The motion startled me. Beaker purred, I knew, but this was... higher pitched, in a smaller body. No less powerful, at least at this range.

"I am looking forward to going home. This is... not ideal for a reunion."

She nodded and laid her head on her forepaws. I relaxed into her and closed my eyes as well. Sleep had been hard to come by, and I needed to catch up. As I drowsed off, I felt Bella shift, but I just couldn't open my eyes. I was... so... comfortable...

I was awakened by her coming back to the nest. At some point while I was passed out, she'd left, and I was curled with my arm around the eggs, sleeping on my side. I fought to open my eyes.

"Somethin's wrong." I slurred at her. I couldn't wake up, the fatigue was like a black tide sucking me under. "Ge'Alger."

When they lifted me into a sitting position I could feel them handling me, like I was a long way off. I tried to open my eyes and could see Alger a long way off. Oddly, he had one hand on my shirt-front, holding me up. I tried to make sense of this paradox and failed.

"Don'feel good." I told him, my voice echoing oddly in my own ears. "Wha?"

"Just a minute." He said. He looked over his shoulder, the change in perspective doing very bad things to my inner ears. I gulped loudly. "Bob, can you ask Bella to use the Sight on him? If she can?"

Why hadn't I thought of that? I wondered, feeling my head loll. Bella's nose came close, her eyes closed. I closed my eyes, too.

The light was different when I opened my eyes. I was stretched out next to Bella, who seemed to be sleeping. I itched like hell. Writhing, I moved away from the eggs to keep from bumping them. I couldn't seem to focus properly. Bella lifted her head in alarm.

"My back... itches." I told her, frantically trying to reach it. I pulled at my buttons, wanting the shirt off so I could reach skin... I got the shirt half off and heard her gasp.

She shouted, "Alger! Grampa!"

Then she scratched my back with her forepaw, and I was starting to sigh with relief when it hit me. "I heard you! How did...?"

Alger and Bob came into the room at a brisk walk, which was probably the equivalent of a run for them. Bob did a funny head-tilt thing and made a strange noise. Alger didn't seem to notice the dragon had stopped.

"Bob said..."

"I can hear Bella!" I told him, excited.

Alger looked at me, looked at Bella, and finally, looked back at Bob. "What in hades?"

"Alger?" I rubbed my throat. It felt sore, like I'd strained my voice. Then I pulled at my shirt sleeves, having somehow gotten tangled in my half-off shirt. "What the hell?"

I was scaly. I rubbed my throat again. Felt like skin there. But my arms... It looked like I had vambraces of green scales. Finer than Bella's, they were still indisputably dragon scales. I stood up, holding them out in front of me, panicked; "Whatthehellisgoingon?"

I didn't fall out of the nest only because Bella had me by one stubby wing and kept me on my feet. I looked over my shoulder. "Bella?"

She had her mouth clamped on my wing. It wasn't my pixie wing, it looked like a batwing, only green, and not nearly as large as it ought to be. I felt dizzy.

Alger spoke, "You had better sit down."

I nodded, and Bella let go. Her mouth free, she started to talk. "You are being cataloged. I think."

"What? That doesn't even make sense." I stared at my scales.

"It's the Library." She said. "You've been here long enough it has adjusted to your presence, and when I accepted you," she shrugged. "It did too. The eggs had both our DNA, or signature, I'm not sure which, and so the Library is classifying you as both. This place is flooded in so much magic, it can, and is, manipulating you on the cellular level. But thank goodness, I can talk to you again."

"Yes, and that's a good thing. But I'm not even a little dragon."

Bob laughed. "No, you aren't. Alger..." his voice changed in timbre, and I could somehow see the magic in what he was doing. Oh...

"Alger, he's not talking human, it's dragon. Like Bella. He's all right. No harm done, I don't think."

"I'm ok." I did the thing with my voice, and both Alger and Bob looked at me. I guessed I'd done it right. "Pissed, but not hurt. This place is really starting to get to me."

Bella flowed out of the nest and reared up. She seemed to glow, suddenly, and I felt as much as heard her voice ring out. The tone was like striking a bell, it reverberated.

"*Hear me. I am the Librarian, and you are to cease interference with any of my party. These two...*" she indicated Alger and me with sweeps of her forepaw and wings, "*Are my trusted assistants, and are to have full access.*"

Chapter 24

Hatchlings

She stopped speaking, and the reverberations took a full minute to die away. In the silence, after, I felt more alert, like a pressure had been taken off me. I glanced at my arms. No, still scaly.

"Are you...?" I asked Alger. He pushed up his sleeve, revealing a thickly hairy arm. Gray mostly, but no scales. He sighed. I couldn't tell if it was relief, or disappointment.

Bella dropped back down. "The original Librarians were dragons. When Alger gave me the library, as a safeguard..." She shot a look at him. He looked sheepish.

"As a what?" I asked.

"You remember you told me he always gets his price?" She asked.

"Wait, I can hear you now." He interjected.

"Of course, the Library is translating now. You're in, fully. You might not like it, though." She warned him. "Lom, his price for the magic instruction was for someone besides him to have a copy of the Library and keep it safe. He knew someone was trying to get in, and his own access was illicit. He didn't know... I didn't know, until we

189

found her, that the intruder was Lavendar. And none of us knew about my dragon blood, which triggered the Library to awaken and pull me in as Librarian."

"So much coincidence." I said, trying to wrap my head around it. She shook her head, her eyes flashing multicolored light reflections.

"Not a coincidence at all. How many copies of the access code had you secreted, Alger?"

"A few." He sounded grumpy. "I had been completely unsuccessful, though, until you came along. And then I couldn't figure out why you, and no-one else, had been able to open it."

"Because I'm part dragon. Not, as you thought originally, royalty. Really." She sounded revolted, and I chuckled. Bella's egalitarian streak was still alive and well.

"So... why is he going to regret it?"

She tilted her head and stared at Alger. "Because the Library asks two things of its Librarians. An avatar, and more data."

"Huh?" That sounded more like the human internet than ancient dragonish library.

"That's why the nest. Why Alger kept losing ground, and struggling with an unseen foe when he visited here. I've had a part of my subconscious sectioned off as the Librarian, and living here. Alone, confused, and doing what dragons do best in all the stories." She shrugged again. "Making a hoard. Only I hoard information. So that was the avatar, and now both of you... sorry, Lom. Both of you will share in that duty."

"And more data?" Alger asked. He sounded rather more interested than put off by it.

"The Library has been largely cut off for some time. You fed it a little, but it's hungry."

"It wants more books." I filled in.

"Yes."

"Will we be able to leave?" I looked at the eggs. I didn't want them to grow up here, as dragons.

"Yes, I think so." She looked at the eggs, too. "Lom, this is so... so strange. I feel like a monster, and they ought to be inside me."

She was close to tears. I slid off the rim and went to hug her neck. "You aren't a monster. We will go home, and they will grow up to be little pixie-fairy-dragon things. Proper children, noise with dirt on them. Don't worry so."

Bella sniffled. Bob put his head in the room. "Ok to come back? Lavendar would like..."

"Oh, yes." Bella shook her head, tears flying away. "I'm coming."

I hadn't even noticed the big dragon leave. That must have happened while I was freaking out over my scales. I checked. Still there.

"So, why not you?" I asked Alger.

"I'm not a dragon's mate." He told me, his lips quirking up.

"I am defined by my wife. Not a bad thing, really."

"They do say you are what you..."

Bella's abrupt return put a stop to our repartee. She was moving quickly, and looked agitated. "Lavendar is ill." She told me, and I translated for Alger.

"I was afraid of this. She had some difficulty while we were traveling, but didn't want me to talk about it." He looked worried. "Lom, you know that time travels at a different pace in each plane, yes?"

"You told me once it is a river, with currents and undertow. Magic is like the rocks in the water, affecting the flow of time."

Bella nodded. "I was reading a book about that, Alger recommended it."

I told him. He fidgeted with his staff, then leaned on it. "Lavendar had been here, in a place steeped with magic, for quite some time. The, we had to pass through Underhill, briefly, and spent a week traveling Above. It was... difficult on her body as the time caught her in an eddy, so to speak."

"She's aged a decade, at least." Bella sighed. "This is my fault."

"No, no... Fae are not immortal, and you did not ask her to do anything. This was her own decision." I rubbed her shoulder.

"She died once." Bella's voice was more mournful than I'd ever heard it. The dragon speech did odd things to intonation.

"Would it help to get her back to Underhill, to Melcar?" I asked Alger. The little wood elf was the best healer I knew, blending magic and human technical skills.

He shrugged. "Perhaps. Or it may accelerate it. Here at the fount of magic, she may heal on her own."

Bella paced. I jumped over her tail as it arced past my legs. My dear wife was not used to having a tail, I thought. "I don't want to be stuck here, Lom. The babies... they might not come for months. There was an army at the gates of Court when we left and I know..." She brandished her wing, the equivalent of waving an arm. In dragon form, it sent a stack of books sliding across the floor. "I know that the three of us are hardly pivotal to the defenses, but Lom."

She came back to stand in front of me, her big eyes shining with unshed tears. "I need to be there, I took on a job and part of it is being..." She ran out of words. I knew what she meant, though, I was feeling it, too. Our place was on the battlefield. Or, in her case, being a shining beacon for the men to rally round.

I looked over her head at Alger as she rested her chin on my shoulder. "Have you any ideas for getting us back?"

He scratched his beard. "Lom, there is so much I do not know. Perhaps... But no. I will not cause any harm to come to her, or the babies."

Bella whipped her head around. "What is it?"

This, he understood, without needing words. She was toothy and in his face. He backed up a step.

"It is possible, that if you were to, ah, bundle the eggs next to your skin and then pass through..." He shrugged. "But I am afraid of what would happen on the other side if it did not work."

"I will ask Grandpa. He will know if dragon eggs can survive Underhill, or Above."

"He is with Lavendar?"

She nodded.

"Where is Byrne?" I asked, suddenly aware of the elderly fairy's absence.

"I left him with Beaker." Alger looked thoughtful. "He was talking about finding a book to read, I suppose I ought to check on him."

Bella shook her head. "Tell him Byrne hasn't touched a book, at least not to take it from its room. He'd know, if that happened."

"That's interesting." I contemplated knowing everything that went on in this vast place. I was just as happy there weren't more people running around loose in it. I passed the information on to Alger.

"Lom, find me a big enough piece of fabric in all this mess to use as a sling, please." Bella fluttered her wings a little. "I really hate not having fingers."

I rummaged through the mess and found what looked like it had been a tablecloth. "You know, if the library was built for and by dragons, who did the weaving?" I wrapped it diagonally around her, between her wings. Having the forelimbs helped keep it in place if she went on hindlegs. Fortunately, they were muscular enough to let her do this. Bob couldn't, but Bella's frame was much smaller and more agile. Alger went to get Bob and Lavendar, while I cradled an egg and helped settle them into the sling one at a time.

"I know it's odd to have them on the outside," I told her. "But I rather like being able to hold them like this, and feel the little wiggles."

"Being in this form means I don't get kicks. But then again, I don't get kicked in the bladder, which my cousin assured me was the worst."

She looked up as Lavendar came into the room. Someone had

found her a stick, and she was using it as a cane. My heart sank. In the light, I could see the aging. The day before it hadn't been visible, which meant that this place was accelerating it. Alger had been optimistic about the third plane helping.

Taking Lavendar Underhill was the only option for her survival. But doing so left her to the mercy of the Hunt. Bella walked to meet her, the sling and her posture making her awkward.

"Can you tell her that I want her to come with us?" Bella asked me.

I was moved by impulse, and held out both my hands, and when Lavendar gave her hers, I folded it into mine.

"I'm terrible with words." I told her. "Bella loves you, so I must. Will you return Underhill with us? I'm afraid this place has gotten unhealthy for you."

"You are a dear, under that crust you cultivate." She squeezed my hands. "I have lived quite long enough. I would have liked to see the babies, but I will not go quietly to the Hunt."

"I don't blame you. I wouldn't myself, but there are ways..."

She shook her head. "I have nothing to offer. And my animals need me."

"But when you are gone? You cannot linger here alone, with no one to help you."

"I will not be alone. Dear Forrest has promised to come back and stay... as long as necessary."

I thought I saw. She would have a keeper, and it would be a way for him to learn history from one who had made it.

Bella spoke. "She can stay here in the Library, I will make it understand."

"No, no, my home is more comfortable. My yen for the Library has faded, now I have gained entrance." Lavendar replied to my translation. "I will go with you to see you off. Alger was able to open a gate just outside my wards, I think he could do so again."

"And we will be able to supplement his power." I commented.

"We should go. I feel... anxious." Bella headed toward the statue hall without waiting for me.

Alger and Byrne were waiting with Beaker, who was twitching the tip of his tail. He was anxious too, for some reason.

"Where is Bob?" I looked around.

"Here." He came into sight around a statue. It was a measure of the scale of that room; a dragon could hide in it.

"Then we are ready. Bella?"

She nodded, silently. It was difficult to read emotion on her face, but the way she was cradling the eggs spoke volumes.

"Beaker! Chow time!" I called to him.

He bobbed his head and nudged the doors. As they swung open for him, I realized they were on pivots. I'd missed that, before. I checked my guns. Even with the dragon on patrol, I wasn't going out there unarmed. Alger, Bob, and I walked out abreast, with the women and Byrne behind. The old man was supporting Lavendar.

The golden mist swallowed us up, and as I scanned our surroundings I shivered in the damp. I'd gotten rather accustomed to the perfectly controlled environment of the Library. A squeal in the distance made me jump a little. Beaker had struck again.

"Alger, do your thing." I ordered. "Let's get out of here."

"Working on it, my boy."

I kept an eye on the mist, watching Lavendar hug Bella out of the corner of my eye. It might be the last time they saw one another.

"Ah! Here you are..." Alger sounded triumphant.

"Bob, can you go first, to look after Bella," I started.

Bella cried out. "Oh! Lom... we can't. Back to the library!"

"What?" I'm not sure who said that.

"The babies," she reached into the sling. "One is hatching."

Alger dropped the gate. Somewhere in the mist, Beaker roared in triumph.

"Dammit. Back to the library. Bob…"

He kept pace with me easily. Between Lavendar and the anxious Bella, we weren't traveling very fast. We brought up the rear. "What do you know about hatching?" I asked him, scanning the mist. Something was moving out there.

"You know that Bella, Beaker and I are the last dragons, right?" He asked me. His voice was very dry.

"You've never seen a hatching?" I felt my panic in my voice.

The bulk in the mist was getting closer. I raised my guns. Bella and Lavendar were just opening the gates.

"Not a one, sorry, lad. I'm almost as nervous about this as you are."

As the pseudopods swung at us, uncannily accurate from a beast with no eyes, I fired with my left hand. Endless practice meant I was ambidextrous, and I had a lot of bulk to aim at. Bob reared up and belched fire at it. The thing sizzled, when his fireball struck it.

"Time to get inside!" Alger bellowed at us. I fired with the right handgun, just in case, and ran through the closing doors just behind Bob. We were all in, except Beaker, and the dragon could take care of himself.

"The women went to the nest." Byrne blurted. "Better hurry, Lom."

He clapped me on the shoulder as I hurried past him, holstering the guns. "Good luck, lad."

I would rather have been back outside the gate, with the guns. At least then I was useful. What good would I be at a birth? I knew the myths around birth involved boiling water, although I couldn't think why. I wondered what dragonets needed. Not the same thing as baby fairies, I was sure.

I was about to find out. I ran into the nest room, and saw Bella and Lavendar in it. How she'd gotten her grandmother up into it I didn't know. I doubted Lavendar was able to fly, she was visibly… crumbling. My heart fell. I hadn't known her at all, but Bella was…

I heard a peeping, and broke out of my pause to clamber into the nest with them.

"Look..." Bella was hovering over the eggs. Lavendar had her hands on one, and the other was making the noise.

"Is it... Shouldn't it be all the way out?" I looked again with the Sight, and was reassured by the steady glow around the little body. I opened my eyes.

"Chicks don't hatch all at once." Lavendar was smiling. "Your son will take some time to come into the world, and it's good for him. Gets the blood moving."

"My son?" I looked at Bella, who shrugged.

"I don't know, but she seems certain."

The egg wiggled, and the little tear lengthened. A shiny little nose peeked out. I couldn't look away. He was panting, and lying still. I put my hand out and caressed the unbroken bit of shell.

"I can't bear it. So beautiful." Bella leaned her scaled cheek against mine. "This isn't how it was supposed to be, though."

"Can you forgive me?" I asked her quietly.

"For what?" Bella asked.

"For this." Lavendar cradled the other egg. "She's coming."

"Why would this need forgiveness, Lom? They are absolutely amazing."

"It's a big thing, having children. Oh, Lom, you should take her." Lavendar pushed my peeping daughter still in her egg toward me. She leaned back on the cushions. "I'm rather tired. I'll rest."

Bella scooped a cloth up to cover her grandmother. "Don't fuss over me, dear, tend to your children. I'm quite happy."

Bella looked at the egg I was holding. "She's coming out."

I looked at the tiny nose. "Indeed she is. And her brother is about to open his eyes..."

"Oh!" Bella nuzzled the little bright blue dragon who was now half-way out of his shell. With another big wiggle he managed to stretch out, and took another rest, still panting.

In my arms, his sister pushed her nose out the rest of the way and emitted a plaintive peep. Bella purred and nuzzled her, wrapping all of us up into a tent of her wings outstretched overhead. I lost track of time, watching them, warm inside Bella's shelter. Our daughter's scales were black, like her grandfather's were. I glanced up and saw him, and Alger, in the corridor.

"Oh, come in." I told them softly. "It's not like a messy fairy birth or anything. Bella's quite decent. But Lavendar is asleep."

Bob loomed over Bella as she folded her wings back, his eyes reflecting the window light onto the babies. "So little."

"Like living jewels." Alger muttered. "Congratulations, Learoyd, on the most unusual family I believe I have ever seen."

"Golly, thanks." I grinned at him. He wasn't going to deflate me that easily. I could see the smile even through that beard he insisted on cultivating, like a hedge.

"Lavendar should see this." Bob shifted, and nudged her shoulder gently with his nose. She shifted, and I could see immediately that she was gone.

"Bob..."

"Damn." He closed his eyes. "Damn."

That was all he said. Bella looked blank. "Lom?"

"Lavendar..." I choked up. "Bella, your grandmother is dead."

A tear splashed onto our son's head, provoking a startled "Meep!" from the infant. "At least she saw them arriving." Bella nuzzled the little one. "Lom, take us home, please. Now..."

Chapter 25

Return

It wasn't that easy, of course. Provisions had to be made for Lavendar's body, and none of us wanted to bury her where the monsters would dig it up. Byrne pointed out he had access to her wards, and that he would have to come back to take care of the farm animals, anyway. Bella emphatically stated that she wanted her grandmother to remain here.

"She wasn't happy Underhill, Lom, and she was here." She said.

I nodded. "We will take care of it. You stay with the babies?"

"Yes, I know it's dangerous. And you don't need to be distracted by me." She nuzzled my cheek, unable to kiss me.

With magic, Alger had neatly carved a divot in the ground, and I laid her frail body to rest. Bob had shifted to human form, and he brought handfuls of flowers to lay over her.

"She always had a garden." He told me gruffly. "I used to tease her about her weeds, but it was pretty, and smelled good. I didn't mind it."

Alger replaced the sod, and looked at me. "She was a bright young thing. But an idealist, and never happy with the way things were. She wanted to be an iconoclast."

"She brought up a very wonderful girl."

We all turned away from the grave without speaking. The trip back to the Library was uneventful and silent. Beaker swam parallel to the wall, keeping us safely hidden and protected. Bella was waiting in the nest.

"I can only carry one." She sounded distressed.

"Don't worry, dear, I can manage." I scooped up my son. "Let's go home and surprise Ellie, eh?"

The little dragon was surprisingly heavy for his size, and quite warm. He wiggled around in my arms until his tail was curled around my forearm, and then closed his eyes with a little sigh. I held him close. Someone else was going to have to provide cover for us.

As it turned out, Beaker had that taken care of. The gates stood open, and he had formed a barrier with his body, a semicircular dragon wall. Bella walked over and showed him our daughter. He snuffled appreciatively, and I took my cue. The little boy yawned in Beaker's face, and I chuckled. "Most people would be impressed, you know."

He went back to sleep. I followed Bella to Alger and Byrne. "Bob went through." Alger told me as Byrne stepped into the shimmering portal.

"Want me to hold it open for you?" I asked. He shook his head.

"Get the kiddies home. I can manage."

I followed Bella into the between. My skin tingled, then burned. I swore out loud, and then stopped myself. The boy didn't need that example just yet. Must be the Library's changes shedding off. I stepped out on the other side, and immediately looked down.

In my arms I held a ruddy, naked newborn with a tuft of blackish hair. He squirmed, and erupted into an angry squall at the chill. I could hear Bella laughing and crying all at once. I looked at her. Byrne was wrapping his coat around her and the baby. Bella was as naked as her child.

"Here." Alger thrust his cloak at me. "Cover up before you both catch your deaths."

I wrapped it around me. I'd completely forgotten about the lost shirt at some point. It must still be in the nest. I had no intention of going back for it. My son stopped fussing once I had him skin to skin with me and covered warmly.

"Home." I said to Alger. I bubbled all of us, and took us there. I landed in the Library, just a tiny drop above the floor, with a huge sigh of relief. Having the bubble go astray in the library had been frightening, and it was good to have it go right.

Ellie ran out of the kitchen. We were a bedraggled bunch, and I didn't blame her at all for stopping with a little scream at the sight of us. Then she recovered, and ran straight for Bella.

"Look!" Bella pulled back the lapel of Byrne's coat. "See what we brought you?"

Ellie dissolved into tears.

The next few hours were a blur. I got myself and Bella and the babies upstairs into our room. Once in that refuge, where we could get into clean clothes after a bath... Bella was reluctant to let go of the babies, having taken both of them. Ellie held out her arms, and Bella passed them over with a kiss on each of their heads.

"I will call Ash, and have him bring someone to help." She told us. "There are so many things to tell you, but you both look filthy and half-starved. Go on with you."

We took turns bathing. As much as it had been a very long time, there were too many people in the house, and the children; Bella kissed me and growled, "tonight."

When we emerged clean and dressed again, Ellie was sitting on the loveseat, a baby in each arm. They were sleeping, and she had produced from somewhere little soft clothes, and I assumed, diapers. Baby dragons didn't need them, but baby fairies did. She smiled at us, her face crinkling into a million wrinkles.

"What are their names?" She asked. Bella and I looked at each other.

"We hadn't named them yet. There wasn't a chance, really. Oh, Ellie..."

Bella sat down beside Ellie and put her face on the elf's shoulder, crying. Ellie looked at me, her eyes wide.

"It's a long story. She's been through a lot. Ellie... how long have we been gone?"

Bella mumbled an apology, but Ellie shushed her. "You were gone for twenty-eight days. Corwin was beginning to talk about sending someone after you, but we weren't really sure where you had gone."

Bella sat bolt upright. "Corwin! I almost forgot..."

"I sent him a message. He's in the kitchen, and so is Joe, and Joe the younger. But before you go rushing off, there's someone I want you to meet." She raised her voice. "Come in, dear."

The door swung open, and a tiny wood elf with a mop of ringlets that were woven full of leaves and flowers looked in.

"All the way in." Ellie prompted. "Contrary to rumor, neither of them bite."

"Can't promise that for the babies, though." I smiled at her. She stepped in and bobbed a curtsey.

"Hello, I'm Bella." Bella got up and held out her hand. The little elf hesitated, then shook awkwardly. Ellie had to have been coaching her, that wasn't a Fae custom.

"I'm Luned, mum. Luned Aeron."

"I knew you would need a nursemaid for the babies. I just didn't know how soon." Ellie filled in the blanks for us.

"Did I take you away from anything?" Bella asked. "I know, we all thought we had months yet."

"Oh, no, mum. Just my little brothers, and well," Luned turned pink.

Bella laughed. "If they are anything like my cousins, this will be easier duty. Ellie, can we get the nursery ready?"

"Working on it now. You'll have it by tomorrow, and Luned can bring in bassinets for tonight, unless you'd rather they stay with her."

"Oh, no, they are going to stay with us." My wife said firmly. "For one thing, I don't know if I have milk, so..."

On cue, our daughter wailed. Bella made a face. "Never mind. That feels... ouch."

I was torn between feeling distinctly out of place as the three of them worked at arranging babies and Bella in optimum positions, while Ellie gave her a stream of low-voiced advice. It seemed that natural as it was, breastfeeding wasn't immediately obvious to any of the parties. I retreated. This was no place for a man.

As I came down the stairs, Corwin came out of the kitchen. He met me at the bottom with a warm grip on my shoulder.

"Lom." He looked me up and down. "Good grief, man, you look like you've been through the wringer."

I pulled a face. "Having babies will do that to you."

He laughed. "Come sit down, have a beer, and let's tell tales."

"We were gone longer than I anticipated."

The king and I sat at the table, along with Devon, Byrne, and Alger. I'd greeted my nephew with a clasp of his shoulder, and a searching look. He'd grown so much in the few months since his mother's death. Not physically, but his face was harder, more adult than boy. It grieved me to see this, and to know I had been gone far too much while he was thrown into the thick of running Elleria. The estate in human terms was like a mid-sized company, with employees, and problems that had no straight human translation.

"Devon, I am sorry about the delay in tracking down your mother's killer." I addressed him directly, after the first general comment. "And even now, the coronation is higher priority. After that, I will..."

He waved a hand in dismissal. "Uncle Lom, it's ok. I trust you, and

I know that you will not forget. Right now, I'm more worried with the living than the dead."

I raised my brow at him. "Specifically?"

Corwin cleared his throat, and Devon nodded at him to go ahead. "Well, the aftermath of the non-coronation was a lengthy Council meeting, which might still be going on, with contentions, if we hadn't been interrupted by an invasion."

My king has a small gift of storytelling. I leaned back and let him tell the tale.

"As soon as your party left, I ordered the Council into emergency session. Laenven objected, as I had expected her to. She was playing far too obvious a ploy, but that's precisely why I ordered the session. She'd been lying doggo right up until the coronation... there had to be a reason."

"Did you figure it out?" I knew better than to think she'd slipped and blurted it out. Confessions are a rare bird.

"I think she wants more power. She's clung to her position since the death of the Queen."

Even after all these years of close association, he couldn't bear to say her name. I chose never to think of it. She was dead and buried, let her stay that way.

"You think Dionaea has made promises." I filled in for him.

"Oh, absolutely." He responded almost cheerfully. "It's our job to make sure she reneges on them."

"The invasion?" The disorganized army had never been a big concern, but even a sloppy cricket pitch bowls a hit from time to time.

"Dean sent me daily reports. It was a party on legs. They would meander a mile or two, stop, raid the countryside, roast a few sheep or a cow, and drink around a bonfire."

"Sounds like fun." I cracked.

He laughed. "Maybe without the ogres and goblins, but then when I was ready to call in the troops, Dean said to wait."

He leaned back and smiled. "He raided the camp, after everyone fell asleep. Him, a passel of wood elves, and I don't want to know how many of my men. I didn't ask. That, and when he arrived in person to report that they had bagged a troll with a massive hangover, and two dead goblins, I didn't have the heart to tweak his nose. The goblins, I gathered, were dead when they found them. The troll didn't recover from his binge until the next night, and he didn't know anything clear. Somehow, she'd gotten the bulk of her little army out of there, and we don't know where to."

"Bubbled?"

He shrugged. "Had to have been. Outside the interdiction zone of Court, but that's a lot of power. I sent scouting parties out, but they found nothing. It's been quiet ever since you left."

I thought about this for a few minutes. "Maybe she's after me. And Bella, for revenge. So she aborted the raid when we dropped off the radar."

"Radar? Oh, that's right, you explained that.." He waved off my attempted explanation. "This could be, but why so sloppy? She has been very stealthy in her whole plan up until this point. An orgy in the countryside would have been more subtle."

I didn't laugh, he was absolutely right. "I said from the beginning it was a decoy."

"A decoy for what?" Devon asked. He'd been sitting and listening intently during the conversation.

"That's a very good question." Corwin answered him. "The trouble is, we don't know the answer. Lucia says there is nothing coming out of Low Court. It's gone dark, and silent, like night falling."

"That's a little scary." Devon looked troubled.

"It's frightening." Alger filled in. "I've been spying longer than any of you have been alive, and that kind of silence just doesn't happen. There is always some drunk fool in a pub. Or a spurned lover. Or..."

I cut him off. "What is the plan?"

I had been looking at Corwin when I asked this. "Special session of the Council, to begin with. As soon as they are all on the same page again, 48 hours to the coronation. I would do it immediately, but I don't want to sully the beginning of her reign."

"I don't think she cares." I pointed out.

"Lom, she's going to be doing this for longer than she has any concept of. She still thinks in human terms. A lifespan of three-score and ten years, and she's about a third of the way through that."

His eyes were dark, and I knew he was feeling guilty.

"She knows what she is committing to. She has doubts..."

He raised a hand in a signal to stop. "I'm glad of it. That, as much as anything, is why I lobbied for her. She didn't want this."

"Then why put it off?"

"Trust me?" He asked.

I subsided. "How long will the Council take?"

He and Alger exchanged glances, with a fierce look of glee. "Not long." Alger said. "I will need to take Bella along, however."

"I'll go see if she's feeling up to it." There were limits to what I would allow these two vultures to drag her into. She had been through things in the Library I knew we were going to have to deal with, but there was no time. No time to savor our children's arrival into the world. No time to heal. No time to mourn...

I opened the bedroom door and saw her sitting with a child in each arm. She looked up at me, smiling, and my heart constricted.

"They are asleep. Oh, Lom..."

I crossed the room to her. I'd never seen anything more beautiful than her, holding the babies. Her hair was falling down, and she was wearing a robe, with a blanket wrapped around the three of them.

"How are you feeling?"

She bit her lip and looked down at the babies. "Conflicted. I know I need to go finish what we started. But I don't want to leave them, and

I don't know that I'm ready to tell the Council I'm a monster. What if they turn me over to the Hunt?"

"What?" I didn't know where this was coming from. She was crying, silently, no sobs, just crystal tears rolling down her face.

"I'm a monster." She repeated in almost a whisper. "I can't possibly serve as queen, and what happens to the babies if I am thrown to the Hunt?"

Chapter 26

A Most Regal Monster

"You are not a monster." I tried to keep my voice even and low. "And you know I would never let you be thrown to the Hunt. Beloved..."

She shook her head. "The council would welcome any reason to be rid of me."

"No, only a few bad apples show that tendency." I was beginning to wonder where my serenely confident Bella had gone. "My dear sweet wife, we have a lot in common." I knelt in front of her, leaning over the babies, feeling their warmth. They smelled sweet and fresh. "I have been a monster, and you redeemed me. Ennobled me, even, and you know I'm not talking about a dukedom. You have been through so much."

I stroked the soft baby fuzz on my daughter's scalp, and listened to her breathe. She was so little. Bella looked down at me, and then bent forward to kiss my head, since she couldn't bend further. "You make me feel better."

"Can you stand a little more? Corwin would like to have you with him in Council while the Charter is read." I was fully prepared to defy my king if she said no, or even hesitated too long.

"I can. I must. It is my duty." She sighed. "I will have to leave the babies here."

"I'll get... Landon?" I couldn't remember the girl's name.

Bella giggled a little. It was good to hear. "Luned. And no..." she freed one hand from the sleeping baby, and flicked a message spell. "Help me with the little man."

"Are we going to name them?" I carefully scooped him up, blankie and all, and was pleased that I'd managed it without waking him.

"Of course we are." Bella got up with the little girl. "When we have two minutes to think..."

"In other words, about the time they take their first steps." I chuckled as I laid him down in the bassinet that had been set up by our bed. Bella cuddled his sister up next to him. Luned slipped through the door quietly.

"I have to go to Court," Bella told her. "I don't know how long I will be. But if they get hungry, I want you to send me a message, I will come."

"She could bring them to court." I suggested. Both women glared at me, and I raised my hands in surrender. "Or not. And it will be a much-needed break, I am sure."

Bella followed me down the stairs, and I reflected that had she gone the traditional route to motherhood, she would still be as big as a house. Or more time would have gone by, and she would be half-incapacitated by the trauma of birth. But she was physically unchanged to the eye, and if melancholy, had energy and strength. I hoped she didn't need it for the upcoming confrontation.

Corwin and Alger stood up as we entered the kitchen. Corwin asked, his voice unwontedly gentle, "Are you up to this?"

"I want to get it done." She told him. "But when the babies need me, I come back here."

He nodded. "Then we will hurry."

The four of us walked out into the library, and I opened the front door onto a gust of rain. Spring was coming, but it hadn't arrived yet. Alger, behind me, made an impatient noise and bubbled us. The trip to Court was made in silence.

The big room where long meetings were held was full of people. King Trytion simply walked up onto the dais, where now two thrones rather than the single one I'd seen there for so long, stood. He was making a statement. As the late Queen had fallen into her decline, he'd removed the throne, symbolically removing her from the Council's meetings. Now, it was back, if empty. Bella stood with me, facing into the U of tables and the Council, now taking their seats around it.

Trytion had put on his alter persona, and the jovial Corwin was not in evidence as he raised his hands to get their attention. He was frowning, and it was easy to imagine thunderclouds gathering around him. I suppressed a smile. He did theatrical very well.

"Be seated. We will review the Charter, and in two days, we will reconvene the coronation."

Lady Laenven looked up sharply from the stack of papers in front of her. "My liege, that is not a certain outcome."

He ignored her. "Duke Mulvaney, the Charter?"

I reached into the nospace and retrieved the two books I had taken from the Library. I placed them on the table in front of Lord Byrne with a slight flourish. Trytion wasn't the only one who could play at that game.

He looked down at them and touched the Charter reverently. The smaller book he set to one side. Then he looked up, directly at Lady Laenven. The quick movement surprised me. I had anticipated him losing himself in the old script right away.

"What, precisely, do you anticipate I will find in this document, Lady Laenven?" He put glasses on, and then gloves. Carefully, he opened the book, wincing a little at the broken cover.

When she didn't answer, he looked back up and crossed his hands gently on the open book.

"Unless you would like me to read the entire thing." He said. "It could take a considerable amount of time."

She looked at Bella and me, still standing before the council. I didn't plan to remain standing through the whole thing. I knew how hard it was to read that book. The ink was faded with time, and the scribe hadn't been the neatest writer. Which of course was why we had copies.

She opened her mouth, still looking at us. Then she closed it, and looked at Byrne. "The section regarding the ascension of a queen is sufficient, thank you."

Her tone was chilly enough, but I thought I detected a slight tremble in her voice. Fear, or anger? They could be very closely related.

"Mmm..."Byrne looked thoughtful, then began to carefully and rapidly flip through the book. He would, of course, know where that was located. The Charter was not a particularly thick book. Our fore-fathers had more brevity than some who had come after them. "Aha." He said. "The selection of a suitable candidate for a ruler is to be a lengthy process, enabling the accurate assessment of their suitability in situations diverse. The candidate should not be callow, but with suffi-cient experience to garner wisdom..."

He looked up. "Could I get a glass of water?"

Bella started to reach for the pitcher that was near her, and I put a hand on her arm, stopping her. I took Bryne his water.

"Thank you." He hissed under his breath, "What the devil is her problem?"

"Just read it." I told him quietly, and returned to Bella's side. This whole thing was beginning to feel not quite right, like there were undercurrents I wasn't aware of. I started to study faces. Trytion was behind me, and anyway, had a poker face I could rarely read. But

Alger looked bored, Laeven looked quietly triumphant, and my mother looked faintly smug. Buckingham looked sulky. Byrne's voice droned on. I scanned the rest of the group, and saw mostly boredom, some interest...

"The Queen shall be possessed of sufficient magic to activate the Crown, of sound mind and body, but no other considerations shall be allowed..." Byrne's voice broke into my consciousness. What was this about activating the Crown?

Laenven stood up, creating a stir in the room. "Read that again!" she demanded, her voice high and cracking. "No other considerations?" She didn't give him a chance to say anything.

Byrne looked up at her. "That is what it says, quite clearly. Would you like to take a look?"

I shifted, uncomfortable with allowing her so close to the old document, but held my peace. Lady Laenven marched around the table, her skirts rustling. She went the long way, to avoid passing by Bella and I. I was mildly amused.

My amusement fell away as she produced a pair of spectacles from her purse and leaned over Byrne's shoulder. I was watching her face, and this was not a happy woman. Had she really thought the founding Fae would discriminate? Those had been black times, when those who fought for civilization were huddled together in what little light could be found. Wood elf, fairy, even humans had all been in this enclave. The pixie clan had still been counted as part of fairy, back then.

"Why, that means even an, an *ogre* could sit on the throne!" She shrilled, standing up straight and flinging one arm out dramatically. She wasn't pointing straight at Bella, but the implication was there.

"Come now." My mother rapped out, standing. "The Duchess Mulvaney is hardly an ogre. Nor would the council select a monster to sit on the throne."

Bella flinched, just a hair, at that word. I resisted the urge to put an arm around her and draw her close. My wife was able to stand her own ground. For myself, I was raging inside. Bella had enough fear on that point without this evil bitch fueling the fire. I maintained my stoic face. Bella would not want a scene.

"On the contrary, dear Lucia." Laenven said sweetly, advancing toward my mother. "I am asserting this is exactly what you have facilitated."

Mother looked down at the other woman, a feat since Lady Laenven was a half-head taller than she was. "You claim that Belladonna Traycroft Mulvaney is a monster?"

I looked around. The whole room seemed to be riveted onto the unlikely combatants. As for me, I'd put my money on my mother. I looked at her.

"Pray, enlighten us." Lucia crossed her hands at her waist and smiled. "We are all waiting."

Laenven spluttered faintly, then recovered. "You are aware that her lineage is human and fairy, mingled."

"Certainly. As are most of us present. Your point?"

Laenven swelled up. Or just took a deep breath, which had the unfortunate effect of making her look like a frog about to croak. "Are you aware that she is also dragon?"

If she expected gasps of horror, and from her flickering glance round the room, I thought she had been, she was disappointed. Other than one murmured 'how interesting' from the far side of the table, there was no real reaction. I felt, more than saw, Bella relax, just a little. She had been standing very straight and still. I was having more trouble restraining myself from just bringing this whole charade to a sudden and violent end. Crashing through the doors with my sister's body in my arms was the least of the memories I could leave here.

Lucia smiled. "Certainly I am aware. However, she was herself not aware prior to coming Underhill. She was raised wholly human, and that, my dear, is the influence you perhaps should be more afraid of. Have you ever been Above?"

"What?" Laenven sounded confused at the change of subject. "No, of course not. How vulgar."

"Then you are unaware that the most successful polity is a democratic republic." Lucia was in full cry now, delivering her little lecture in crisp, clipped tones. "Where there is no aristocracy, and the reverence of the public is reserved for those who make good of their own volition. This is what Belladonna was raised to. As she is about to be crowned, you have attempted to make this about lineage, when perhaps you ought to be more concerned with a reluctant, egalitarian Queen."

Now I was beginning to wonder if Mother wanted Bella on the throne.

"Reluctant?" Laenven pounced on one word. She gave an affected sniff and turned to look straight at Bella. "Hardly. She has pushed herself forward from the very beginning, inveigling her way into our society and now, even to the highest honor we can offer. Far from reluctant, Lucia."

Belle looked at her, then spoke coolly, "Lady Laenven, I would gladly walk out of this room with no other commitments than to my husband and children. I cannot say that I would rather be back in my humble cabin in the woods, because I love my husband and I have made a new life here. Accepting the offer of the Crown was the last thing I ever intended to do."

"So you say. And what about your dragonish heritage?" the old woman moved toward us, and I felt my body stiffen. I forced myself to relax. No point in alarming her until it was too late. In my head, I was playing it all out. She would threaten Bella, and I would incinerate her. Tearing her limb from limb was a tempting thought, but messy, and Bella wouldn't like it.

"What about it? As you so evidently know, it is a mere fraction of my heritage. I am unable to take dragon form under normal circumstances." Bella was magnificent. She was calmer than I had seen her in... I wasn't sure I had ever seen her this cool and collected. I might be on the brink of explosion, but she wasn't.

"You are a monster..." Laenven hissed.

"Actually, no." Byrne cleared his throat and stood up, between Laenven and Bella. He faced the older woman, and slowly took off his glasses. "As a matter of fact, dragon kind predates the Fae, and may be the cause of our ascendancy on this plane."

Laenven's mouth was hanging slack, a most unbecoming look. I felt a certain glee as Bryne carried on in his most pedantic tone. "Dragons may even have excavated the Great Hall, before fairies took up residence. It is certain that their civilization sheltered ours, and after what I saw at the Library, I would go so far as to call dragons the mentors, the masters, and Fae the apprentice student at their feet."

The old woman spluttered wordlessly. She was turning a very interesting color, sort of a brick red. Her rouge created pale spots on her cheekbones. I wondered if her heart could take this sort of insult.

Byrne, ignoring the impending stroke victim, turned away to face Bella and Trytion. "In Bella's ascension to the throne, we see the culmination of thousands of years of partnership. It is most fitting that the last dragon should rise to join us in ruling Underhill."

Bella had a funny look on her face. I wondered if it was sheer astonishment, because that is what I was feeling. This was absolutely the last thing I had expected.

"Enough." Trytion stood up, his voice booming. "I ask you, is there any who can find true grounds to object to the coronation of the Duchess Mulvaney?"

No one spoke. I found the time to look at Buckingham, who was looking shattered. I made a mental note to have a man-to-man talk with him. It was long past time for that.

Trytion held them all with his gaze for a long moment. Still, there was silence. Finally, he nodded, and the whole room took a breath. He stepped off the dais, and reached out for Bella's hand. I stomped on the little jealousy critter that raised its head in my brain every time they did something like that. Bella gripped hands with him briefly, and he nodded at me.

"We will reconvene at morning on the second day for the coronation, then. You are dismissed... Lom, stay here a moment." He finished that in an undertone meant for Bella and I only as we stood close to him.

While everyone was filing out of the room, he spoke quickly and quietly. "Took the wind right out of that biddy's sails. Byrne surprised me, didn't know he'd made a study of that part of history."

"I think he's studied more of it than any of us know." Bella sighed. She leaned against me, as the last person left the room. The three of us were alone. "That was..."

"I really wanted her to give me a reason." I admitted. I knew they would understand what I meant.

A message spell appeared and zipped to Bella's quickly raised hand. "They need me." She looked at Trytion. "Will we see you?"

He shook his head. "Regretfully, I must remain at Court, to make arrangements."

"Bullshit, sir." The both of them looked at me with shock on their faces. "That's why you have Joe and a host of minions, to make arrangements. You need some time to get away from it. We will see you at dinner. Now, if I may, I'm taking my wife home."

Trytion looked at Bella. "This is going to be interesting, I can see. Very well..."

I made a rude gesture at him and bubbled us. I needed to get out of there before I exploded, and it wasn't his fault.

Chapter 27

The Crowning Moment

The morning of the coronation didn't dawn so much as gradually lighten under a heavy layer of clouds. This wasn't surprising, since it was the weather we'd been having since our return from the Library, and it was late winter almost spring Underhill. I found myself holding a baby, and listening to Ellie argue with Bella.

"I only wore it for a few hours." Bella was protesting. "And you must have cleaned it by now. Taking it in to compensate for baby belly isn't difficult."

"You are not going to reflect on him," Ellie pointed at me, and I looked down at my son.

"This is what you have to look forward to. Don't ever fool yourself, the ladies are in charge." I murmured, and he scrunched his face up.

Ellie hadn't been listening to me, and she kept going. "By wearing the same dress today. Would you wear the same dress to the second wedding?"

Bella opened her mouth, caught my eye, and closed it again. It wasn't that we could read one another's minds, it was the tiny headshake I had given her. This was Ellie's reputation. Everyone knew who took care of Bella.

Bella subsided and allowed herself to be dressed. She had, over the last day and a half, developed a strong tendency to ball up like a hedgehog with the prickles out over any resistance. Allowing the babies to be given bottles. The dress. I was sure there had been other little things I'd missed. She hadn't been in the mood to talk about it last night, had just curled up in my arms and cried herself to sleep quietly.

I was worried about her, and I didn't know when I would have time to get her away from all this, and have the time to do the grieving and processing she really needed. We had the momentum, and I knew how important the coronation was, even if she didn't. I was fairly sure she did, or she would have backed out after the Library.

All I could do was stand strong for her. She reappeared, pale, dressed in a royal purple gown with a long train. Ellie wasn't being subtle, this time. I handed my son to Luned, with a last kiss on his tiny forehead, and took Bella's arm.

This time, at Court, I was standing in the semi-circle of the Council around Bella. Trytion, not Corwin, had pulled me aside the day before and chewed me out royally for having shirked it the first time. I thought he was as angry for having missed it himself as he was at me. None of us were accustomed to me being on stage, as it were. I didn't like it, but for the two of them, I'd do it.

Laenven was pale, her lips pressed together so tightly they had almost vanished. Buckingham looked as though he'd aged overnight. But they both took oath to the Queen as the crown passed through their hands. I was at the far side, so I watched each of them as the crown passed toward me. Finally, it was in Mother's hands, and Lucia's tone was firm, even triumphant, as she spoke.

"I approve Belladonna Mulvaney as Queen!"

Then it was my turn, and my hands felt numb as I took the cool weight into my hands. The line about the activation crossed my mind, and I wondered again what it meant, and should I worry about Bella? But my lips formed the words, and I could hear a faint echo as they rang through the huge room.

"I approve."

I stepped forward, the crown in my hands, and Trytion took it from me. As I stepped backward into my place again, he turned to Bella, who dropped to one knee and lowered her head. I was viscerally reminded of the knighting ceremonies of the past. This was not an obeisance of Queen to King, when it came time, Bella would stand in Trytion's place, crowning his successor. The gleaming gold against her black hair, Bella looked up again, not at the King, but past him, to me.

I smiled at her. Inside I might be a mess of worry, but she needed me. Trytion reached for her hands, and helped her up. Together, smiling, they turned to the crowd, as court was already beginning to stand, applauding.

The thunderclap of sound caught us all by surprise.

In the aisle, a black bubble had appeared, and as I watched, it burst, sending a wave of dark smoke into the room. The smoke sank to the floor, oily and creeping. Where the bubble had been, Dionaea stood.

I recognized her instantly. She hadn't been much of a wife, but I had known her well. She was wearing a sleek black gown, and what was more interesting to me, holding a Heckler and Koch MP5 cradled in her arm. She sneered at the audience surrounding her.

"Take your seats, the show is only starting." She laughed, throwing her head back. "The Evil Fairy is here!"

She was mad. The old fashioned, bang them into Bedlam definition of mad. I considered my options. While she was that far away, I wasn't carrying anything on me effective at that range. The Colt 1911 strapped to my body was shorter range, and inconvenient to get in these robes. The family sword, belted to my waist... well, you never bring a sword to a gunfight.

Dionaea swayed forward, stroking the gun. Now I knew why Georgio had been targeted. The ghoul had been a reliable arms dealer for me. She hadn't been able to buy him...

"Well, well..." Dionaea crooned. "I wasn't good enough. And you think you can replace me." She stopped, and drew herself up. "But it's too late. I have the Queen's Crown, and you know what that means?"

She took a few more steps. I tensed, coiling like a spring. She was almost within range. I only regretted not having a chance to drill with the robes on. I'd never foreseen wearing them, and had never practiced drawing the gun through all the folds. Dammit...

The rest of the room seemed frozen, all eyes on her. Alger was in the niche, I knew, and I didn't understand why he hadn't made a move yet. Dionaea started to swing the gun toward Bella, with a throaty chuckle.

What she couldn't have known was how deadly Bella could be, and that I knew something no-one else in the room knew. Dionaea had no idea what she was doing with a gun.

I'd refused to teach her, even though she had pouted and made my life miserable over it. I never told her the truth. I didn't trust her. Not that she was incompetent, of that I had no idea. But that she would just spray and pray... she was holding the MP5 by the pistol grip alone, and I knew.

The world narrowed to just her, and the slender pale finger wrapping around the trigger. I broke the stillness that gripped us all, and ran toward her.

I didn't even try for my gun. In a Tueller Drill, you have 21 feet to reach the gunman before he can fire. She was a little further than that. I had two things in my favor. One, I knew that a bullet rarely stops an oncoming body, especially not a determined one. Hell, even several bullets didn't always stop them.

Two, I...

She pulled the trigger, and the second thing I knew happened.

She had it set on full auto, and I was close enough to see the look of surprise in her eyes, to see her mouth form a little moue of surprise as the gun muzzle climbed. The only thing she was endangering was the ceiling.

I hit her.

We went down in a tangle of limbs, black velvet, gun, and my sword. I hit her, once, blow to the temple and saw the dazed look as that sank in. I rolled off her and tried to untangle my sword so I could finish her, and she screamed in rage.

Before I could fully unsheathe it, she was gone. I stood there, panting, looking at the gun and a high-heeled shoe she had left behind her. I picked up the gun and put it on safe. Now that I could see it clearly, it was filthy. I wasn't going to try firing it, and why it hadn't jammed...

I turned to look at Bella. She was standing on the dais, holding a spell in her fingers.

"Sorry I got in your way, babe." I said before I thought about it.

She let out a little laugh, and put the spell away. "I..."

Something behind me got her attention, and as her voice stopped, I spun around, holding the gun and sword ready. The MP5 might not be fire ready, but it would make a club... I dropped them to my sides and started toward the figure that had just pushed through the great doors.

It clung to one of them as though the effort of gaining entrance was all it could manage. Filthy, furry, matted... it was Sean, the wolf.

He weaved away from the door, and I saw the muzzle. Oh, damn...

I looked over my shoulder. Bella was right there.

"Take this." I shoved the weapons at the person who was sitting by the aisle. Devon blinked up at me. "Hurry." I snapped at him. He took them.

I got to Sean in time to catch him. He flailed weakly, but I wrapped my arms around him. He was skin and fur and bones. The big wolf whimpered, and I felt his muzzle land on my shoulder.

"Here."

Byrne was there, now, he'd taken off his robe and was making it into a pillow. I lowered the wolf onto the floor, trying to make him comfortable. Bella knelt on the other side of him, and I could see the tears shimmering in her eyes.

I reached for the buckle on the muzzle, wincing at the matted fur under it, and the torn-off-claw stuck in it. I fumbled at it, and he reached up with surprising speed and grabbed my hand.

"No..." He whispered. "Don't..."

Chapter 28

The Wendigo

"What the hell happened to you?" Sean hadn't been a friend, exactly, but showing up, dying, at my wife's coronation couldn't be a coincidence.

The big wolf was wasted beyond belief. I could smell the sweetness on his breath. He was dying, fast. He closed his eyes, and gasped a little.

"Don't die on me." I growled at him.

"We..." His eyes opened slowly. They were crusted with yellowish matter. "Wendigo. I won't bite."

That was almost clear. "The wendigo got you?"

He nodded. Bella reached over my shoulder with a cup, and a straw in it. She'd brought a stock of those human inventions Underhill when I was ill to the point of death. I stuck it in his mouth, and he sucked greedily. Then he turned his head away, with another whimper.

"Don't got long." He spoke a little easier with the water in him. "Had to tell you... little fuzzy, here."

I realized he wasn't making a bad joke, his eyesight was going. His brown eyes were clouding over as I watched. He took a long, labored breath.

"Wendigo, bad news." I nodded. I'd let him deliver the news he'd suffered for. "Dionaea wants all... Underhill." He rasped. Bella cuddled up next to me, ignoring her train and dignity, and took his paw in her hand gently.

He smiled at her. "Pretty... crown. 'Grats."

"Sean..." she whispered. "Why did you risk it?"

"Had to. She's bugshi... Sorry the rug's mangy."

His voice was growing fainter. I leaned closer to hear it. He closed his eyes, as they turned pure white. "Baba Yaga. Gang..."

He was gone. His chest caved in, with a sickening wet crunch. The whole body twitched, and spasmed. I backed away as it writhed. The jaws inside the muzzle snapped weakly.

"Lom, what's happening?" Bella had scrambled back hastily, encumbered by her train.

"The wendigo. It's a hunger, you see. He's dead, and there's nothing holding it back. Damn..."

I threw a spell over the body, sealing it and the area around it. I wasn't going to risk that infection or whatever it was, spreading. The corpse took a long time to go still, and I looked around the room with a sigh. Joe and his men were shepherding people out the side doors.

"This casts a shade on your moment."

"So did Dionaea." She reminded me.

That had been a lot to happen in very little time. I shook myself out of the funk I could feel creeping over me. "We need to talk." I turned to look for Trytion.

"We need to call someone in, first." Alger walked up, Devon in tow behind him, awkwardly holding my weapons. I took the sword and resheathed it.

"Who isn't here already?" Bella looked around the room. Most of the people were gone, mother was sitting on the dais, Trytion was nowhere in sight. Lucia beckoned to us.

As we walked toward her, Alger answered Bella. "The Huntsman."

"What?" Bella stopped, and her voice rose an octave. "Why do..."

"Because with this," My mother held up the shoe Dionaea had dropped. "The Hunt can track her."

"And with the death of the wolf, we have the hard proof we needed to unleash the Hunt." Alger filled in.

Bella nodded, after a long moment of thought. "I don't like it. But I liked her showing up here even less. Lom..."

Delayed reaction, I knew. She wouldn't fully react – hell, I wouldn't either – until later. Then we'd have the shakes together. I'd run straight into a stream of fiery lead a few minutes ago, for her.

"I froze." She said. Bella wrung her hands together. "I couldn't move."

"No-one could." Alger gripped her shoulder. I was afraid to embrace her, because I knew that if I did, she would dissolve into tears and she didn't need that right now, nor did I. "Dionaea had something in that smoke of hers, a hypnotic agent, or a spell like it. She had us all in the palm of her hand, even Lom didn't react as quickly as he could have."

I nodded when she looked at me for confirmation. "She wouldn't have risked popping in like that unless she was very sure of herself. I'm actually not sure why she did it..."

She was a distraction." Bella had a faraway look on her face. I recognized it as thinking fast, and puzzle pieces dropping into place. I'd seen it before. "The wolf was the real threat. Only..."

"We knew what the Wendigo could do, so we didn't give him mercy." I finished. Had I undone that muzzle, he would have ripped through the crowd spreading famine and death in his wake. The infected would in turn have passed it on. I shivered.

"She meant to decimate us." Bella spoke softly. "It was a cruel ploy, to use that poor man like that."

"She thinks we're soft." Lucia stood up, gripping the shoe in one hand. She bared her teeth in a pseudo-smile. "She took my daughter's life, and we didn't immediately retaliate. She thinks we won't."

We all looked at her. She lifted a hand to her lips, her fingers bunched together. She blew across them and spread them wide at the same moment, and a flash of energy blinked out of existence.

"She thinks we won't call the Hunt to ride forth. Because we haven't in so long. But she is wrong, and we shall have vengeance."

Something about her face quenched any desire we had to talk.

"How long?" Bella asked.

The great doors swung open, and we all jumped. Bella gulped as she realized it was not the Hunstman, but Joe and Trytion. They walked toward us, carefully skirting the wolf's body.

"We need to talk." Trytion unconsciously echoed my earlier words.

"Lucia summoned the Hunt." Alger told him. He sagged against his staff. "We haven't much time."

Trytion inclined his head to my mother. "It was your right, Lady. Do not look so distressed."

Mother waved that away. "Lom needs to be gotten away." She said bluntly. "No point in rubbing him in the Hunt's nose."

"I have a mission for Lom." Trytion looked at me. "You understood what Dionaea said about the crown?"

"I didn't."

Bella pointed at her own head. "I'm wearing a counterfeit. Lavendar stole – or something stole – the real thing a long time ago. Not sure how long. Dionaea has managed to get it, and from the Charter..." She looked at Trytion and Alger.

"There is a magical link. Yes, and without it, you *are* Queen, let me stress that."

Alger picked up where Trytion had left off. "But you don't have the access to power you would with it."

"And you want me to go get it." I shrugged off the encumbering robes. Shirtsleeves and suspenders I could work with. All that cloth was damn annoying.

"I know it won't be easy. But with the hunt harrying Dionaea, and her pet monster..."

"That's another thing. The Hunt..."

The great doors crashed open. I don't think any of us even twitched. This was becoming quite the routine, and as I turned to look, I wondered if Joe ought to have bumpers installed to prevent damage.

The last person in three worlds I had expected to see walked in. I recognized him immediately, although he looked nothing like he ought to look. He took a few steps, and then stopped dead, staring down at the body on the floor. Dropping to one knee, he held both his hands out, over the body.

The small group of people in the room moved toward him of one accord. I was in the lead. We were all twitchy over the events of the last hour, and a stranger appearing in the room wasn't helping. I knew Bella hadn't recognized him. I'd only known him by the eyes.

The deep gray eyes that now met mine as he looked up from the wolf's body.

"Boy." He greeted me, standing. "The wendigo is here, then."

"Not here, here." I struggled for my composure. Raven always had this effect on me, and somehow he'd passed it on to his niece although there was no real blood relation between them. But she was of the tribe, and they were his People.

"Who are you?" Trytion demanded.

Just about then, it clicked for Bella. "Uncle?" She gasped.

I didn't blame her. He was a strapping man, looked to be about twenty, with smooth brown face and glossy black hair – black as a raven's wing. Dressed in a brown shirt, and battered jeans over work-boots, he looked normal. Which meant he stood out like a sore thumb, Underhill. She had grown up with an old man, white-haired, face a mass of wrinkles, and bent back. Now, he smiled down at me.

"I came, chick. You need me."

Trytion was looking back and forth between the two of them. Now, he bent slightly, in a formal bow-between-equals. "Raven."

"Yes." Raven returned the courtesy. "When Bob came home, he came straight to me, and he was right to. You do not know what you face."

"The wendigo. An evil spirit, used to rule the territory east of the Mississippi. Kills by starving the afflicted, even as they desperately gorge on everything and anything they can stuff in their mouths," Bella recited.

Raven shook his head. "There is more to it than that. I have never dealt with it..." He looked down at the wolf's body again. "Is this necessary?"

"What?" Trytion looked down solemnly. "This just happened, and we have not had time to deal with it. He will receive full honors, of course."

"Then perhaps a better place to talk would be the small chambers." Mother spoke up, firmly. A lifetime of social arrangements made her the obvious person to keep this meeting moving smoothly.

Delicately, she moved around Sean's corpse. "Follow me, please."

Bella slipped her hand into mine as we followed Trytion and Raven out the door.

"I feel like... like we fell down the rabbit hole." She whispered to me.

"More like the badger hole. The Hunt is coming." I raised my voice. "M'Lord, do you plan to allow the Hunt entrance to Court?"

He shook his head. "I will meet them at the gates. Damn." He stopped and looked back at us, then over my shoulder at Alger and

Devon, trailing behind us. "I had almost forgotten. So much keeps happening, I am..." he broke off and looked at Raven. "Do I need to know this?"

I broke in. "In my opinion, no. I'm the one who needs to deal with this. You have the Hunt, sir. I'll take this mission." I squeezed Bella's hand, then dropped it. "Bella..."

"Stay with Trytion." She put her hand up and touched the crown on her head. "I get it. I don't like it, but I get it." She took a deep breath, then put her hand into nothing. I had to admit it looked creepy, no wonder I got funny looks when I did it. She pulled out her pistol in a holster and strapped it on. "The hell with not being armed. I'd put the MGL over my shoulder if it were called for. Sir." She turned to Trytion, whose lips were twitching under his mustache.

"Bella..." I reached for her and kissed her soundly. "Be careful."

She nodded, and they walked down the hall toward the front gates. I looked at Raven. "There is..."

He laughed. "She is no delicate flower, boy. You know that."

I did. "Alger, Devon, might as well sit in on this." I looked at my mother. "Mother..."

"I need to hear this." She might have had a steel rod up her spine. Her eyes snapped as she pivoted. "Come." She commanded, and Raven followed her meekly.

When we were all in the smaller room, and seated, she looked at Raven. "Please tell us about this monster. I do not know how much you are aware of events here, but it took the life of my daughter. Others, how many we do not know, and I fear it endangers the very fabric of this world."

She paused as a girl carrying a tea tray entered the room. I wondered when she had ordered that. My mother never failed to astonish me. When the tea was on the table and the extraneous person gone, she continued. "The wendigo is not of our magic, and as such, is a destabilizing influence on a society that is, I am sad to say, stagnant."

Lucia poured tea. I hid my smirk at the sight of Raven seated in a silk-upholstered wingback with a delicate teacup balanced on his knee. He was gravely listening to my mother.

"Generations ago – we are long-lived, but not immortal, as I believe you are – the Courts split." Raven didn't even flinch when she said the word. I wondered... but this was not time to be nosy.

"High Court, this place we are allied with, was Chartered with the express purpose of maintaining peace with both Fae, and the upstart human communities that had begun to develop Above."

He nodded, took a sip of tea, and smirked at me. "I was aware of the Charter, Lom's Mother."

I cleared my throat. "Ah... Raven, this is Lucia Mulvaney. And Alger," I pointed. "My great-something uncle, and Devon, my sister's son."

Raven cocked his head. "You lost your mother. And you are connected to Dorothy?"

How he knew that I had no idea. Devon got a little pink. "Yes." He answered simply.

"My condolences on the one and congratulations on the other." Raven told him. He looked at Alger, and nodded.

I was stunned. They knew one another. Then I leaned back. That made sense, oddly enough. Raven turned back to my mother, who smiled a little. "I have no objections to being known as Lom's Mother. I am, no matter what he thinks, proud of him."

I was just as happy I was sitting down for that pronouncement.

She continued serenely. "If you know of the Charter, you know the relationship it has to travel between the planes. The limitations it was supposed to place on that, and the stresses the Low Court gave that treaty from the beginning."

He nodded. "The connection with my territory was not made until long, long after this, but when I became aware of who and what the Fae were, I made it my business to study you."

He looked directly at me. "I know you were unaware of me, boy, and what I was when you first arrived in my land. But I knew you. And Lavendar had sought refuge there, because it is so far from any passages to Underhill. Her blood mingled with my blood. I became entangled, despite all my efforts to avoid it through the centuries."

I shrugged. "If it hadn't been me," I began.

He waved irritably, making a face. "You are honorable, boy. Would I have kept you in my house were you not? Very uncomfortable guest. I have known something would upset the balance. Nothing lasts forever."

He leaned forward, setting the cup gently back on the table. "When the World was young, and the People few in number. Before the planes, as you say, touched as much as they do now... then, there were three of us."

He spread his hands. "I make the story simple. More than three, but... three. Here, on what humans call a continent."

I nodded. I knew what he meant. North America, more or less.

"Me, Coyote, and the Wendigo." He laid out one hand, palm up, to serve as the land, and marked it with his fingers. His lands, by this very crude symbolism, were the far North and West, Coyote from there to the Mississippi, and the Wendigo on the far side of that. A kingdom divided. Only it had never been a kingdom, from the myths and legends I knew.

"Coyote and I shared bread, told stories, got drunk." He shrugged, smiling. "Suppose you say, friends."

"Is he still around?" I asked, curiously.

"Maybe so, maybe not." Raven shrugged again. "This been long time, long ago."

Whatever that meant. I knew better than to press for an answer and subsided.

"One day, Coyote tells me a story. He has been to pay his People a visit, a little tribe, maybe four sets of hands, that live on the riverbank."

Forty people, give or take. This had been a long time ago. Raven leaned back and kept talking, his eyes hooded in recollection. "The People, they are all dead. Coyote wanders through the village, seeing them lay everywhere. There is no food, but the river is full of fish. The smoking-racks are torn down, and on the wreckage lay bodies with full bellies, and faces like skulls. Coyote howls, he is so sad. He sings to his lover, the Moon, and to his surprise, there is an answer."

"The other howl comes from across the river. Coyote jumps into the muddy water and begins to swim. He uses his tail to steer him in the current, a trick he learned from Beaver. Eventually, he reaches the other side. But he is very tired, cold, and wet. So he decides to wait until the next night to see who it was that howled in pain along with his lament."

"The next morning, Coyote wakes up. He had slept by the fire, and was dry, but now he was hungry, so he goes in search of food. He begins to walk down the river, and sees a village. No one is around, but it is early. Perhaps they all still sleep. He walks into the village, and finds all the People there, they are dead. Just like his People. Coyote is alarmed. What is this evil, that has killed all the People on both sides of the river?"

Raven paused, and Lucia silently refilled his teacup. He took it with a nod, his face solemn. I could see why. The hairs on the back of my neck were standing up. Something about the cadence of his story, and where I could see it going...

Raven drank, and spoke again, softly. "Coyote began to run. He ran to the next village, and the next, and the next. Coyote ran until his pads bled, and he had to hold a paw up and run on three legs, then rest another paw, but he could not stop running. And every village he could find, was dead. Still, Coyote ran."

"There came a day when Coyote could run no longer, and he lay down in the brush, panting, and he was horribly afraid that all the

People were dead. He felt he could move no more, and then he heard voices. So he crawled to the edge of the brush, and peeped out."

"He had run all the way to the sea. It stretched out before him, vast, and salty. Hot and tired, Coyote licked his nose. He knew the sea, and that he could not drink it. But this was not his sea. And the people on the beach were not his People."

"Coyote watched the people and saw they gathered clams, like his People did. He saw the children laugh and play. And finally he transformed himself into a man, and he limped out of the brush and asked for water."

"At first, all the people ran away. But Coyote sat down on the sand in the sun, and slowly, they came back. Coyote could not speak their language, but it is not hard to say I am thirsty..." Raven mimed the act of drinking. "So they brought him water. Coyote got a little boy to spit in the cup, and when he drank it, he could speak to them, and they to him. They told him the story of a monster who had appeared out of the ice fog that winter. When he was seen, then a madness fell on the people, and they ate until they died. The monster had passed by their little village, but all the others had gotten sick and died."

"Coyote thanked the people of the beach, and began to travel north. Once he was out of sight of the beach, he became his coyote self again, and he ran. He found many dead places, and a few that still lived. A little at a time, he was able to puzzle out what the meaning of it all was. Now, when he had started, it was spring. He had run all the way through summer, and fall was touching the trees with colors."

"Coyote ran home. He swam the river, and walked through the dead village, where the bodies had turned to bones. And he sat in the middle of the village, wrapped his tail around his toes, pointed his nose to the sky, and he howled. He sang of the dead, the rotting babies that would laugh no more, the sweethearts who no longer loved, and the grandmothers who gave no more wisdom. And then he fell silent."

"Across the river, there was an answering howl. But there was no song in it. It was hungry, and angry. Coyote felt the fur on his whole spine lift up, and his tail brushed, for there is a little cat in him, after all. He paced at the river bank, and he yapped across it, at the hungry thing in the dark."

"He never told me what they talked about." Raven shrugged. "Maybe they never talked. But he told me what to do if I saw signs of the Wendigo among my people."

He sighed, and sat up slowly. "I feel old as I usually look, Boy. Time we go."

"Wait!" Devon blurted. "What were you supposed to do? And a spirit killed all those people? When was this? I learned…"

Raven raised a hand and chuckled. "I know you are young, so many questions! Yes, child, the Wendigo killed them. Oh, sure, later, the rational men of science…" He snorted, making his opinion of them clear. "They say disease. But, child." Raven leaned forward, and fixed Devon with those eyes. Devon leaned forward, and I vividly remembered my first encounter with the ancient spirit, being kidnapped and taken for a ride. I wondered what Devon was seeing in his eyes now.

"This was before the white men, and their diseases. This was in the time of the People, who were numerous, and there was still magic in the land. But the Wendigo broke them, and the remnants were swept up when the men came from across the sea. Now, the Wendigo has turned his eyes on your plane, where the men of science are not. Here, he has power, and he means to use it."

Chapter 29

Immortal Death

Raven stood up. "I am afraid we must move quickly," He bowed slightly to my mother, and when she offered him her hand, he kissed it. I boggled, behind his back. The old bird put on a good act, but somewhere in that mind was more culture than I would have given him credit for. He headed for the door like he owned the place, and I had to hurry to stay on his heels. If he had given Alger a high sign, I hadn't seen it, but the old man stayed put, along with Devon and my mother. Devon seemed a little stunned from his close encounter with the birdlike eyes. I didn't blame him.

As the door closed behind us, he stopped, and I almost ran into him.

"So." He crossed his arms over his chest. "Where are we going?"

"I thought you knew that." I felt the old familiar exasperation rising up.

"Oh, away from here, sure. The Wendigo isn't here." He looked around. "Posh place."

"Drop the act, Raven." I growled at him. "My wife is facing the dark Hunt, you're telling tall tales, and the only way I know of to kill the Wendigo is to beard the lion in its den."

"No, no," He shook his head. "You can't kill the Wendigo."

"Why the hell not?" I grated out, controlling my anger with an effort.

"Like me, he is immortal. Cannot kill me, only..." He fluttered his fingers. "Disperse, then reassemble."

I blinked at him. "Then *what?*"

"Fight him. Warn him off, and deal with..." Raven sobered suddenly. "You know what Coyote told me?"

I shook my head. "I can guess."

"Any who are bitten by the Wendigo, you must kill. There is no cure."

I rubbed the back of my neck. "Do you know who Baba Yaga is?"

His reaction surprised me. He grabbed my arm. "Is she here?" He hissed, looking around.

"Um, no." I bubbled us. This conversation needed to be conducted elsewhere. He looked startled, and let go of my arm. Then he poked the bubble wall.

"Very nice. Yes, yes..." He peered closely at the bubble. I knew he wasn't looking at it, but the spell that allowed us to 'jump' through space. I popped the bubble and he grunted in disappointment.

"We'll do it again later, I promise. But we needed to plan, and I wanted to be away from any possible listening ears."

"Out here?" Raven looked around the sunny meadow. I looked, too, remembering with a pang the last time I'd been here, with Bella and Sean. "There could be birds..." He whistled, and a large raven pinwheeled out of the sky, squawking loudly. I wondered where Raven had called him from. Raven held out his hand, and the bird landed on his forearm, shaking to settle its ruffled feathers. Raven locked gazes with the bird, and then with a flick of his arm, sent it skyward again. It soared overhead, and he brought his eyes back to me.

"Now, we can talk." He settled onto the grass, his legs crossed.

I sat beside him, legs stretched out in front of me. "Bella and I encountered Baba Yaga when we went to Eastern Court – I'm surprised Dorothy hasn't told you about it, she was kidnapped by the Hut on Chicken Legs."

He shrugged. "Pixie girl is a little afraid of me, shy. I'm working on her."

I wondered what he'd done. "But you know who Baba Yaga is."

"Ayah." He looked up into the sky. The bird was a speck in the blue.

"How does this change things?" I asked him, trying for patience and achieving testy.

He shrugged. "Two immortals?"

"You're going to drive me crazy." I told him, letting my tone go as dry as I felt.

He laughed. "Maybe so. Lom," He had my full attention now. I didn't recall him ever using my name before. "This is going to be very dangerous, and I can't help you as much as I would like."

"I figured on that. It's never easy."

He laughed again, and got up. "Let's go beard the lion, as you say. It's a good day to die."

"No, it's not. I have a better idea." I scrambled to my feet. I hated having him loom over me. "For once in my life, I'm not wanting to die on a mission." I started to pace through the grass and flowers. The benefits of having a real office would be chairs, and a desk. I set that whimsical thought aside, and started to send messages.

Raven, a little smirk on his face, watched me muttering and waving my hands for a few minutes, and then wandered off. I ignored him, being busy planning a war. Sometimes the only way to eliminate a threat was to dig it out, and burn it with fire. I could feel the smile on my face at the memory of Bella and fire, those first few days. I sent her an extra message, knowing it would make her laugh.

When I had done all I could think of, I looked around. Raven had lain down in the grass and looked like he was fast asleep. I walked over to him and tapped his boot with my toe.

"Wake up, we're going to war."

He flowed to his feet in an elegant display of athleticism. I'd always known the bird had hidden depths... He was grinning. "Where are we going?"

I snapped a bubble around us. We'd be meeting up with others when we got there. Then I answered him, knowing he'd understand the spatial references weren't quite accurate, but it would do. "Chernobyl. Or Underhill, where the worlds touch there."

"And what are we going to do there?" His brow was furrowed, but at least he didn't ask stupid questions about radioactivity.

"Practice diplomacy. Which neither of us are qualified to do, but they say practice makes perfect."

He dissolved into cackling giggles. I didn't think it had been that funny, but he was ever fond of a joke.

"We will be meeting on neutral ground. I think." I hadn't been there in a long time, and things might have changed. The Underhill analogous to the Olde Worlde, to the Grimm tales humans were familiar with, even in their lighter versions, that part of our world had become a wilderness.

It had never been heavily populated, we simply weren't as fertile as humanity. One of the great fears of High Court was that the barriers between worlds would drop, and our world would be swept up in a flood of change. With the passage of time, the fluidity of the land, this area was now filled with ghostly castles of times gone by. It was to one of these I took us.

When our world had been smaller and more warlike, this place had been built at the peak of a hill overlooking a lush valley. Intended to house the inhabitants of said valley in a siege, it was roomy enough, but I wouldn't want to spend a winter in it. The gray stone walls were dripping with moisture in the cold spring haze, and I stepped around a clump of brilliantly colored mushrooms – toadstools, I corrected myself as one hopped into them for shelter – as I scouted the court-yard. I didn't go into the dark hallways. Shattered doors and scraps of wood, rotting slowly into earth on the lintels, spoke of a violent end to this place. Treachery, come to the impregnable fortress. I shivered.

"Unpleasant place." Raven watched me making my way around the open area, warding off doors as I came to them. I didn't know what was making the castle its home, and I didn't want to meet it. We'd leave soon enough, and disturb it no more.

I looked over my shoulder at him. "Have you ever been to her territory before?"

"Not this side of it."

I finished with the warding and picked my way back to him, avoiding the various piles of stuff. Bones would have long gone, but the earth was wet and muddy. Slimy in places. "That's right, you used to have people across the Bering Strait and even as far south as Korea."

He shrugged. "Wasn't Korea then, and Bering was an obnoxious little toad."

I laughed. Getting Raven to drop the local yokel act was worth it. "So has she always been a hagged old witch?"

"No, she can be beautiful when she wants." He sniffed. "Smells the same whatever face she's wearing, though."

I could smell it now, too. Rotted fish, soil, and decomp. I'd picked a place where she couldn't bring the Hut, or the disembodied hands Bella and I had fought off in our last encounter with her. They would come up through dirt, but not the solid stone we were standing on now.

She walked through the narrow gate alone, leaning on a crooked cane. Her head was covered by a colorful scarf, and she looked hideous. Her face a mass of wrinkles and warts, her long nose almost touching her chin. The very caricature of a Grimm fairy tale witch.

241

I snorted. "Really? Am I supposed to be Hansel, and this Gretel?" I jerked a thumb at Raven, who chuckled.

She stopped and fixed me with one beady eye in a piercing glare. Then she looked at Raven, frowning.

"Do I know you?" Her voice was in keeping with the guise she wore, cracked and trembling.

"You do." He crossed his arms over his chest. "Siberia lies between us."

She straightened and stepped back, almost stumbling. With a shrill cry, she flung up her cane and pointed it at us. "How... Dare!"

I thought she would fall, but instead she threw her cane, and flipped her apron over her face. The cane landed on the stones with a clatter. She grew, the form under the dress warping oddly, bulging and moving inhumanly. I raised an eyebrow at Raven, who gave me a quick wink. When I looked back, Baba Yaga was transformed.

There's a certain illustration I'd seen of a Russian fairytale, and evidently she had seen it as well, or the model for it, perhaps. Tall, slender, and blonde, the witch-queen was as tall as I – which was very tall, for Fae. She would stand head and shoulders over most human women. The dress was gone, or rather, altered to suit her newly regal guise. Unlike Dionaea's affectation of black, Baba Yaga wore scarlet and gold, embroidered with details so fine I didn't waste time admiring them.

"You came to my lands." She stalked toward us, ignoring her cane. Her voice was cultured, throaty. I had to admit that Raven was right, though. The smell was the same. As she got within a few paces of us, it was downright overwhelming.

"I did not. This is a neutral place, I am informed." Raven's face was blank, his arms still crossed. He looked almost bored. I was doing my best not to gag on the smell.

"It is not." She hissed, and whipped around to glare at me. "You!"

"None other." I kept my cool. I wasn't going to let the smell get to me. If Raven could take it, so could I.

"You bring my mortal enemy to my doorstep, and you were responsible for wounding the Hut almost unto death!" She waved a clenched fist in my face, and I suppressed a strong desire to laugh at the cheap theatrics.

"Damn. I was hoping we'd killed it dead."

She drew herself up and flushed brightly, a most unbecoming color above that fabric. She did much better with the pallor she'd had before I made her angry. "Why are you here?"

I decided from the near-howl she had delivered that with, we were close to our goal. Really, she was easy. "We're here to tell you to knock it off. What you do in your own territory..." I shrugged. "None of my business, although I hear the peasants are revolting. But you're not expanding. Dionaea only has the living death to back her, and she won't flinch from turning on you, which you well know. You aren't as stupid as you look."

She gobbled. I don't think I had ever heard anything quite like it. Had she been a mere mortal, the brick-red of her complexion would have had me worried for her heart. Sadly, I knew mere taunting would not kill this one. I kept going. "So back off. We're about to take out Low Court. If you pull off your dogs, then you get to keep what you have. Push onward, and well," I shrugged.

Raven spoke. "Well you remember the last time we met, witch. You nursed your wounds for a long time, Above. Underhill was barred to you. Could you survive that a second time?"

She sprang at us, arms outstretched and mouth wide. The beauty had fallen away, leaving the immortal unveiled. The twisted, gaunt limbs were tipped with talons, and the mouth was full of innumerable sharp teeth like a pike. Her hair whipped around her face in a sudden whirl of wind that filled the courtyard, stringy and greenish. She was shrieking, but if there were words, I could not hear them.

I was ready for this. She hadn't even looked at the pistol I wore on my hip, but I had my hand on it as soon as Raven started talking. She had been too wrapped up in her anger to catch on then, either. Now, I shot from the hip. There's a trick to it. If you lay your index finger along the barrel and point, the gun follows. That wasn't quite what I was doing now, but after long practice, I could put a bullet just where I wanted it. And she was almost on top of us, with her arms outstretched. I couldn't miss.

I didn't miss. I blew three holes in her chest, and then had to dive aside as she crumpled, momentum still carrying her past us. Raven had gone the other direction. I rolled right through the fall onto my feet again, pivoting to keep the gun on her, but she was lying in a tumbled heap.

"Is she dead?" I asked Raven, who like me was right back on his feet, muddy, but unhurt.

He shook his head. "It will take her a short time to recover, though. I would suggest..."

I nodded. "I agree."

Some space between us and the vengeful witch would be a very good idea when she came to. I had been ready for this attack, but the next might be quicker. Catching her off-guard would only work once.

Chapter 30

Beat the Drum Slowly

"So, that was fun. How did you get her to meet up with you?" Raven asked when we were safely away.

"She wasn't meeting me. I spoof my ex-wife pretty well, it turns out. If that's what she looks like for meeting the Low Queen, I wonder if Dionaea has any idea who she is dealing with." I shrugged. It would be easy to dismiss Dionaea as stupid and greedy, but I knew better. Greedy, sure, but not stupid. Not if she'd kept alive this long and risen this high in Low Court.

"Well, you did a pretty good job of inciting her into a killing rage." He looked at me assessingly. "What are you going to kick next? A wasp's nest?"

"Next, I talk to the Wild Hunt. Politely." I really wasn't looking forward to this one. I'd spent most of my life avoiding them.

"Them, I've heard of. You have interesting enemies, boy." He shrugged. "What do you want me to do?"

"Depends. If Bella is there, stick close. She's... volatile when it comes to me and the Hunt. If not, I may send you to her anyway. She and the King will be coordinating an army by this point if I know her."

"Big battle, eh?"

I smiled thinly. I wasn't going to show all my cards yet. "That's the plan."

The bubble dropped where I had asked him to meet me. The Huntsman was inhumanly tall, dressed in black armor from a forgotten age, and in an unexpected twist, not mounted. Instead he stood beside the black stag he usually rode, and as I appeared, he made a gesture that sent the beast trotting off into the mist.

"Mulvaney." He spoke, and the temperature seemed to drop.

"Huntsman." We were alone, and I nodded to Raven, who was standing to my right. "Go on to the Queen."

He looked between the black knight and I. To my surprise, the Huntsman let out a grating chuckle. "He is perfectly safe, as I have assured his wife. I will allow him to freely go when we have made our arrangements."

Raven nodded, and blinked out of sight. He was a quick learner. I looked at my old foe.

"I'm safe?" I echoed. "Since when?"

"Safe is a relative term." He turned his head to look at the ruined cottage. We stood in what had once been a garden. "You chose this place to taunt me, or perhaps..."

"It was the beginning." I felt a burst of impatience. "This is why you hunt me. Or rather, was. Since when am I safe?"

"Would you rather not be?" He sounded interested.

"I needed a favor, and that was my leverage." I laid my cards on the table.

"The Low Queen." He nodded. "She is the Hunt's quarry as we speak."

"Call them off." I growled at him.

"What?" He could show no emotion, but I could hear it clearly in his voice, surprise.

"Are they a match for an immortal spirit who causes famine and disease?" I asked him, not knowing the answer, but suspecting it.

"They are not themselves immortal." He admitted. "Nor am I. But she is not immortal. She is a fairy, as are you."

He didn't count the fairy/pixie clan split, being far older than it was. Like Alger, the Huntsman was beyond old, even if he claimed not immortal. "She's not immortal, but do you know what the Wendigo is?"

He cocked his head at me. "This is not a name I know."

"It came from Above." I explained, suddenly feeling very tired. "It's an ancient spirit, like Raven, who just went to Bella. It's not mortal, can't be killed, and I'm going to take it on with Raven's help. But she will sic it on the Hunt if you corner her, and I need you to do something else, instead."

"The Hunt does not do the bidding of the Court." The voice was implacable, blocks of granite grating together.

"I know, you are not a tame Hunt, you are the Wild Hunt." He wouldn't get that reference. "This isn't bidding, it's a suggestion. One you'll listen to unless you want to be decimated."

"I am listening." He sounded calm again.

"Besides, I'm not the Court. I'm the Hunt's meat." I bared my teeth at him. Safety, he'd promised, but he wouldn't have said for how long.

He snorted. I kept talking. "There's going to be a battle. We're forcing it to take place rather than letting her dictate to us. I'm asking you to fight beside the Court. Allies, not servants."

He nodded. "You mean to return to an earlier age."

"No. I mean to squash this insanity now, before it gets uglier." I looked at the cottage and wondered if her bones were still lying beside the fireplace, and if it were still a gate to another world. "Our world isn't always a kind one. But if Dionaea gets her way, she will destroy this one, and unleash an evil on another world she cannot control."

"That cannot be allowed." He followed my gaze. "She was breaking the laws."

"You know, in the human version of the tale, she married the king. Lived happily ever after. But then, their versions usually were kinder and gentler than reality."

"You defied the Hunt twice." He mused. "Once for kindness, yourself."

"Aye. The girl in the ashes deserved to dream."

I didn't give him a chance to reply to that. I hadn't had a chance to save my little playmate from them, but that hadn't kept me from being foolish and attempting to save her from their style of justice. Bringing it down on my own head with that defiance, while she lay broken and bleeding with the delicate slipper still clutched in her hand, only inches from her freedom in the world Above.

I knew he would do what I wanted. Without mercy, he might be. But he wasn't foolish. He would ride beside the army of the Court into battle, while I followed the forlorn hope in a different direction.

I found Bella. She was at Court, and seemed to understand when I whisked her into an empty room, then pulled her hungrily into my arms. She was warm, and I was chilled through after my conversation with the Huntsman.

"The Hunt will ride with Court into battle." I told her, when we could talk again. "I wanted to make sure you understood they are on our side, this time."

She nodded. "He said you were safe."

"He give you a time limit on that?" I felt my lips stretching into a feral grin.

She got a look of surprise on her face. "No... but Lom..."

"It's ok, honey, we have an understanding." I kissed her again. "I must go. I have a long trip to see old friends in front of me."

She let go of me. "I know what we're doing, and why, but I..."

I laid a finger on her lips gently. "Will be fine. More protected than anyone, and not on the battlefield, anyway. No more than I will be."

She nodded wordlessly.

"Dean is coming."

"He's here already. And that's where I was headed, to a council of war." She sighed. "When will you be home?"

"I may stay overnight at Eastern Court. I'll be tired." I didn't want to be away from her, but I recognized that I had limits. I didn't know how much talking I would have to do to persuade Yiu Jao to lend us support. Also, negotiations there were more delicately handled than I'd been doing so far. Involving plenty of saké and tea, which would leave me sleepy and wanting a bed and bathroom. The last time we had paid the old scoundrel a visit, those had been cut short. He would make up for that, I was afraid.

Bella kissed me lingeringly and stepped back, watching as I vanished. She would be out the door, I was sure, as soon as she had seen me gone. My woman was made of stern stuff.

I had sent a message ahead, but I never knew with Jao how the reception would be. In the past, we'd met in peculiar places. Only on the ceremonial mission with Bella had I met him at the palace in luxury.

The bubble popped and I realized that I was back in the Kyuden, the palace where we had initially encountered, and fought, Beaker. I was standing alone in a room with a low table. Jao knew I was comfortable with the lounging on mats style they kept here, and I shrugged and sprawled. Magically, food and drink appeared, and I didn't turn my nose up at it. He would come when he could. Yiu Jao was not the Emperor of the Eastern Court, but he held the strings figuratively. When we had been here before, we had foiled an attempt to wrest that power from him, and I was about to call in that favor.

Chong came into the room, with a low bow, and I stood to offer him a western-style handshake. Chong was educated in human ways, his uncle's way of making the boy a more rounded warrior. When we had met before, the teen had been kidnapped along with Dorothy, and had been ready for another round of excitement the last I had seen him.

"How goes the training?" I asked him now.

"Pretty good. Dean was here, showing me how to shoot a rifle, until last month. Hope he comes back to finish teaching me soon."

"He's busy right now, but I'll let him know you want more."

The kid had bulked up some, but he was always going to be a head shorter than I and whipcord slender. His uncle, on the other hand...

I bowed slightly, pressing my hands together, as Yiu Jao appeared in the doorway.

"Honorable Friend." I greeted him. He responded with a belly laugh.

"I know you want something when you lead off with the right foot." He teased me. "So how about we cut to the chase?"

I smiled at him. "But what about the saké? And the endless pots of tea, so you can consult with your advisors while I go to take a piss?"

He laughed harder, and sat down. With a wave of his hand, the table was replenished. "Am I so transparent, my friend?"

I sat across from him, and Chong sat at the foot of the table. The head was left empty, and I wondered who would be joining us. "No, but these walls are paper thin."

They were made of rice paper and bamboo, so he could hardly dispute that. "True, true. Not that I have ever worried about your honesty and forthrightness. How is your lovely wife?"

I took the seeming change of subject in stride. "She is Queen now."

"Ah, yes." He smiled so broadly that his eyes disappeared. I was forcibly reminded of a painting I had once seen of the Khan, and the blood connections between Genghis and this court. "The warrior

Queen. Do give her my deepest affection, and a wish to see her in action some day."

"I should hope not. We have children, you know."

"So soon?" He bellowed with laughter. "You work fast!"

"There was a temporal shift." I was beginning to wonder why he was killing time, when he had said he wouldn't.

The jolly laugh died, and his face was sober as he straightened up. "No doubt you are wondering why I delay."

I knew he couldn't read minds. He just knew me well. "Yeah."

"I was awaiting the arrival of the one whom you really desire speech with."

When old Jao went all formal, it was time to check your wallet and keys. "And who might..." My words died in my throat as she walked through the door.

I found myself on my feet without knowing quite how I had gotten there. With hands pressed together, I bowed to her, and was astonished when she sank into a low bow, revealing the many tails that swept behind her like the train of a gown. I thought I counted nine, and from the silver hair to the regal face, she carried herself like a queen. I knew she was a kitsune, and I knew what the tails meant, but I had no idea why she was here, or why she was the person I was to speak to.

I shot a look at Jao, who was rising from his own low bow – the bow to a superior – and he gave me a faint smirk. He was enjoying himself. She went to the head of the table and knelt, then clapped twice. Two little girls, each with a single tail, ran into the room. One wore a pink kimono, the other yellow. They bobbed bows, adorably, and I felt my lips quirk. They were perhaps six or seven years old, and tiny.

"I wanted you to meet the children of Matsuo." She had a soft voice, and wide dark eyes. The little girls swayed in unison.

"Hello and thank you." They chanted together. Someone had obviously been drilling them in the phrase.

"You are welcome." I answered them gravely.

They dissolved into giggles, and the nine-tail smiled a little. She spoke gently to them in a language I didn't recognize, and the girls dipped another little bow to me before running out of the room.

I looked at her. "That was very cute, but..."

"You returned Matsuo's soul to his family. They bear you a debt of gratitude." She sipped her tea, delicately, and I took a sip of mine. It was part of the ceremony.

I understood, now. Prior to our mission here, I had encountered a dying kitsune, and had taken his soul-pearl for safe keeping. I had delivered it to Jao, as proof of the suffering the kitsune had endured at the hands of Daniken. I'd never known the boy's name, much less that he'd had children.

"I am sorry for your loss," I told her now, convinced that she was connected in some way to Matsuo.

"I am grateful for the return of his essence." She placed her cup on the table, precisely aligning it with the pot before looking up at me again. "We kitsune made a grievous error in allying with Daniken, and I had turned a blind eye to certain of her activities. Without you, this could have led to disaster. We owe you a great debt."

So, this was why Jao had arranged the meeting. Not for the cute little girls. The nine-tail was being recklessly blunt. We hadn't even been introduced.

"Lady..." I started slowly, feeling for the right words. I had to handle this properly.

She flashed me a small smile. "I am Sakamoto Asuka. You may call me Asuka."

Jao's face was a study. He hadn't expected her to give me a name, much less a familiar name, I guessed.

"Lady Asuka. I came to beg a favor of my friend Yiu Jao. I had not known of the kitsune, aside from my short encounter with Matsuo. I am honored by your feelings, but I cannot ask of you what you know not."

She inclined her head a little. "Perhaps you should speak to your friend, and I shall listen. Then, we may speak again."

She picked up her cup and I imitated her action. She held her cup, pensively looking at the leaves in the bottom of it, and I looked at Jao. He made a subtle gesture with his chin that might have been a nod, so I started on my pitch.

"The Queen of Low Court has allied with a Wendigo, a spirit from the upper plane which cannot be killed, and which brings famine and death wherever it goes. The Low Queen has vowed to use this power to conquer all of Underhill, and then the human realms."

"You go to war against her." Jao nodded. "We have heard... rumors."

"I have seen it with my own eyes." I remembered the death and immediate aftermath of the wolf, and felt my skin crawl. "I came to you because this is a threat, even if it may seem distant as of yet, to your people."

He nodded. "It seems unwise of us to sit back and allow our friends and allies to soak up the punishment when we know it is our defense they are providing."

"We are setting the stage for a battle, of our own choosing." I put my teacup on the table, gently enough it made no sound. This motion was a signal that I had made my pitch. I awaited his next words.

"Ground on which we can only be saved from destruction by fighting without delay, is desperate ground." Lady Asuka murmured, quoting Sun Tzu.

I nodded. "Desperate ground, indeed, Lady. I would not have come to you for any less."

She nodded. "We will be at your side on the day."

Asuka picked up the teapot and poured a little into each of the three cups. We all picked ours up and drank together, and then she stood gracefully. Her evident age did not show in her motions.

"I have much to prepare. We will be ready in a day." Without waiting, she walked out of the room, her silver tails floating and flowing in her wake.

Jao slumped back to a sitting position, as we had both stood and bowed as she left.

"Whoo..." He blew out his breath in a great sigh. "I don't know about you, but I need saké after that."

I sat back down. "What the hells just happened?"

Chapter 31

Play the Fife Lowly

Jao threw back his drink. "You just met a goddess."

"I had a god as my wingman earlier today. What does this bring to the table?" I threw back mine. Then I refilled his cup. I hadn't a chance of getting him drunk, but it was the polite way to drink the lukewarm liquor.

Jao boggled at me a little, then grinned. "You tell the best jokes, Unpyou."

He'd nicknamed me 'cloud leopard' on my first mission here. I'd always been afraid to ask why. I decided I wouldn't try to explain Raven, who would be really offended to find out I'd called him a god. I waited for him to answer my question.

"She will bring the kitsune to the field. And we will bring warriors, as well. You are right, this is a matter that touches on us all."

I took a sip of the saké. I was beginning to feel it, with the fatigue building up. "This is bigger than I thought at the beginning. Then, it was one death. That was all that mattered."

I threw back the saké. Jao looked at me for a long moment, his face

255

losing the humor slowly. "One death is all that matters to each of us, in the end. Better to have those who will care, after."

I shrugged. "I wish I had known her better."

"Who of us truly knows another?" He stood up. "The guesthouse has been rebuilt since your last stay, and I would be honored."

I stood up slowly, feeling the heat of the alcohol. "Thank you, Jao."

I clasped forearms with him, and left for the peaceful sanctuary of the guesthouse.

I slept like a dead man. In the morning while the dew still lay heavy on the perfect gardens, and the sun only lent a lessening of the night, I went home. I'd slept enough to replenish me, and I needed more than that to make me ready for what I must do. Bella was asleep, still, even Underhill there is a difference in where the sun is to where you stand on the earth. I slid into bed, and she rolled over and casually draped an arm and a leg over me, murmuring in her sleep.

I chuckled and pulled her close, then fell back asleep myself. I hadn't meant to, but she was warm, and the essence of safety and comfort, even after our short time together. I was awakened by the sleepy cries of a baby. Bella rolled away from me, and I sat up to see her scoop an infant from the bassinet and crawl back into bed awkwardly. I pushed my pillow behind her to help her sit up for nursing, and then watched, fascinated, as she did so.

"Too dark to tell them apart..." I whispered, not wanting to waken the other one.

"Your son is always hungry." She smiled. I could see that, only inches away from her face, and with the dawn light seeping in the windows.

"He has a lot of growing to do. She will be petite like her mother." I cupped his warm little head. It was covered with a fine, silky fuzz that might become hair later.

"We need to name them." She sighed. "I had thought Lavendar, but..."

I shook my head. "If you must, but the tradition is to continue the mother's line by relation of names, not repetition."

"And him?" She looked down at the greedy little man who was making smacking noises.

"Up to you, dearheart." I kissed her.

"Not Lom." She stuck her tongue out at me, and I suppressed a laugh.

"Nor Learoyd. Please."

"David means beloved." Bella looked at me, smiling.

"You know he will think we named the baby for him." I pointed out.

"Maybe we are. I liked him, and he is... very fond of you."

My perceptive wife. I let out a deep breath. "David."

The newly named infant sighed, but that was because he'd fallen asleep, a drop of milk at the corner of his mouth. I got out of bed and came around to return him to his sleep spot.

"Linnea." Bella was sitting, her arms wrapped around her knees, and in the early morning light I could see her clearly now. "Will that work as a progression of flower names?"

"Linnea? What's a common name?"

"Twinflower, so it is doubly appropriate. They are these tiny little pink bells, just a few inches tall, and they carpet the northern forest floor in summer time. They have this pretty, sweet scent..."

I put a finger to her lips. "You've sold me. You'll have to show them to me sometime, and Linnea when she is old enough, since I doubt they will grow in our garden."

Bella bit my finger, gently, her eyes twinkling. I responded to that in the fashion it deserved, and as a result we were very late coming down to breakfast.

I was surprised to discover Alger and Mark in the kitchen. Ellie had left plates on the counter for Bella and I, but by the looks of their plates, they had been there a while.

"Have we kept you waiting?" I asked, pouring a cup of coffee.

Bella, walking in behind me and picking up her plate, laughed. "You are not going to apologize for that."

Mark clapped his hands over his ears. "Not listening! My baby cousin...la la la."

We all laughed, then. I put Bella's cup in front of her and got my own plate. "More seriously, what are you two up to?"

"Heading back to low places to make friends. Or at least try to talk to old ones." Mark looked into his cup, then got up to get more.

"Hang on a sec," I had just remembered something, and I looked at Bella, "Where is Raven?"

"He said he was going to do some scouting, and to tell you not to worry. He won't miss the fighting."

Alger spoke up. "Was the trip back East fruitful?"

I nodded, my mouth full. This might be the last hot meal I had in a while, and I was going to enjoy it. After swallowing, I assured him, "More than I had dreamed of. Evidently the kitsune think they owe us, so the fox people will be here tomorrow, along with Jao's warriors."

Bella frowned. "I have gathered from reading history that pitched battles were common at one time, but Lom, why?"

I shook my head. "This is as much a stylized dance move as anything else. We show up, present a united front, and they will know we are serious. That we won't lie down and let them waltz through the front gate."

"That seems rough on the guys dying on the field." She put her fork down.

"War always is. Underhill isn't the same as Above, though. There's a lot less messiness on the field."

Alger raised an eyebrow. "Which is not to say there won't be deaths. But the disease you associate with the wars of, say, your Medieval Europe, is missing. On those fronts, far more men were lost to disease before any set foot on the field of battle than were to die in battle."

Bella nodded. "I still don't like it."

"It's good you don't, my Queen." Alger told her, his face stern. "If you did like it, then Underhill would be justified in joining against High Court, as we do against Dionaea. She must be stopped, as she had begun to revel in her power, and the lives of her people mean less than nothing to her. You..."

He pointed at Bella, who was listening with a strange look on her face. I recognized that it was a little amazement at being called Alger's Queen. I figured she hadn't thought that through before.

"You rally people to you. The wood elves, the Eastern Court, even the Council here, they recognize that you care for the individual. You are not playing a game, with pawns that breathe until you are finished with them and crush them idly."

Bella leaned back. "I worry about that, you know."

He smiled, cracking the mood with a pointing finger and a cackle. "That's why you have him, m'dear."

I put a hand on my chest. "Me? I'm lazy, I'm just going to sit back and let her reform this whole damn place."

Bella snorted, a very unladylike sound from the Queen of Underhill. "Yeah, ok, I'll do it. But I'm not going to like it."

"Precisely the point." Alger looked upward. "I believe I hear the piping cries of one of your children, to prove my other point that you are not alone in this."

Bella got up hastily. As she walked out, I told them, "We named the babies, so you know. Linnea and David."

"Good names." Mark commented. "I can guess why Linnea?"

"Her favorite flower. When this is all over, do you think you can get me some starts? I'll see if I can get them started in the garden here."

He nodded. "Sure, I can have Min pull some things together for her. She's not going to be able to visit much, is she?"

I understood him to mean Bella, not Min. But then again, it applied to both of them. I shook my head. "I'm afraid not. She'll be busy, and..."

He nodded. "I understand. I wouldn't have, not too long ago, but that was before I started studying magic and what it can do. I'd rather keep it here, and not up there."

"Pretty much." I got up. "Keep me up to date with what you find out there?"

Alger stood, leaning on his staff. "I'm hoping we can hear something. All the quiet has concerned me."

I left them to head out on their mission, and I went back upstairs to say goodbye to my family. Bella was nursing Linnea. I kissed them both, and then went to David, who was sucking his fist and staring into midair with a quizzical expression. I picked him up carefully.

"How long will you be gone this time?" Bella asked quietly.

"I won't be here for the battle." I admitted to her. "That's not the plan."

"I don't want to hear all of it." She told me, looking around. Ever since Margot's body had landed on our doorstep, the only place we felt we could talk freely was the armory.

"I will not be going out to die." I sat next to her, David in the crook of my arm. Linnea popped off the breast and looked at me. "They are tracking already?"

"Yes, of course." Bella smiled. "I don't know how clearly they see, but they know our voices at least."

"Ah, hmmm... must watch my language." I was bemused by the newfound impact of fatherhood. I had never seen this day coming.

Bella chuckled. "Go, my love, and come back quickly."

I gave her David and went, my eyes a little misty, but in the bubble alone, no one would notice. That, and where I was going, it only really mattered how I smelled, because I wasn't sure he could see. He certainly didn't perceive the world like a humanoid did.

The bubble popped, and I shivered. It wasn't a fear response, it was really cold. The fear came a second later when the rock formation I was standing next to stood up. In my defense, I'd intended to go knock on his door. He had a house, I didn't expect him to be outdoors in the freezing mist. I was going to have icicles on my nose hairs if I was out here much longer.

The heap of rocks resolved into a smallish troll, bending over and sniffing loudly at me. I stood still and hoped I didn't smell too different since I'd last seen him. Trolls really can't see well, and I suspect they use some sort of sonar to navigate without tripping over obstacles, or falling off cliffs, which would likely be fatal even to a twelve-foot tall silicon based lifeform. He let out a deep sigh.

"Looommm...." His voice was as I remembered it, deep, husky, and lugubrious.

"Hey, Lug." His name was literally unpronounceable to a human mouth, and after a few tries that felt like gargling with pebbles, and hurt like it, too, I'd just called him as he was. Lugubrious.

He turned his head politely and coughed, sending a gob of sputum into the darkness. "Cooommeee onnnn..."

I followed him toward his home, grateful at the idea of some warmth. Lug was a relative genius among trolls. Most of them eat, sleep, and reproduce. Lug, for some mysterious reason, had built himself a house, and weapons. I had a surprise for him on that score.

He pushed open the door, which was a chunk of tree, and stood aside politely to let me walk in. Lug ducked, and then crawled, to get through the opening of the house he'd created by walling off a cave. I suspected he'd chosen this one for the other feature. It opened up a troll's body-length in, and he could stand up inside. The inside was dark, too, darker than the outside, with only a faint glow from the massive fireplace in the center of the cave.

Lug lit an oil lamp politely. I'd taught him that one. He didn't need the light, and too much hurt his eyes, but I did need a little light. So I'd showed him how to put a little oil in a hollow of the rock, and some sheep's wool for a wick. It was smoky as hell, but I could move around the cave with that on. I did so. He'd maneuvered huge slabs of rock near the fireplace, which was built of more slabs of rock, and didn't have a chimney. Far overhead, a crevice to the outside air mostly provided enough draft to keep the smoke heading out of the cave rather than lingering in it.

He'd also, somehow, I'd never asked but I suspected through mute demonstration of what a troll's fist could do, persuaded the bats to hang out on the far end of the cave. The only time they flew overhead was on their way in or out. The constant muttering and whispers as the colony moved was disconcerting at first, but became background noise if I concentrated on letting it flow through my brain and right back out again.

Not that talking to Lug was terribly challenging. It was more a matter of being patient. I waited for him to take a seat at the fireplace. It was his only furniture. He slept curled up like a pile of rocks – the same way I had found him earlier, only in one corner of the cave. I'd long ago determined that when he was a small troll, he had imprinted on humans. Only from the outside, largely, both of bodies and dwellings, so he didn't really get some things. Perhaps a human he'd encountered had had benches. A bed would have been out of sight, a secret from his quest for knowledge.

And this was my payment to him, always. Knowledge. I couldn't just offer him something, that didn't work for him. I had to wait until he asked a question. I'd met him when I was called in to deal with a nest of trolls. Similar to ogres, only slightly less nasty in their eating habits, trolls were often used by the Low Court as heavies. Ogres couldn't be trusted, but if you got through an idea to a troll, they stuck with it. Crush farmers in an area, eat their sheep and knock down houses? No problem, boss.

Only when I had showed up, expecting to be able to pull the usual trick with sunlight, there was Lug. Lug, and his crossbow, which was a trollish impossibility. He had intrigued me. So one night I'd waited by him until he woke up, and talked to him. It had taken most of the night, but to my astonishment, we had gotten to the point where I only needed to say something two or three times, and he got it. For a troll, this was savant-level intelligence. In the years since, he had assisted me a time or two, in exchange for an answered question.

I sat on the slab, my feet dangling above the cave floor, and let the warmth from the embers soak into me. Lug put a log on the fire, and sparks danced toward the opening in the ceiling, like fireflies on a summer night. If only the cave smelled as sweet. Lug dug around behind his slab and came up with the carcase of something, which had been re-wrapped in a slightly torn brown hide. I held up both my hands, palms out, and then rubbed my stomach, miming that I was full.

Even had I been hungry, there was no telling how old that kill was. Germs weren't really a thing for trolls. This one was likely fresh enough, but I vividly remembered one that had been greenish and added a sharp pong of its own to the cave smells. He simply nodded and pushed it back out of sight. We both sat and stared at the sparks for a while, rising into the night.

"Lom." He finally spoke, in his ponderous voice. I waited for the rest of it. "Are there... others like me?"

I considered this. I was sure he knew there were other trolls. What he was asking, then, was for trolls who were on his own intellectual level. Since my usual procedure with trolls was to kill first, ask questions later, I didn't really know. Then again, when a troll and I encountered one another, it was a dire case, where it had not been successfully driven off by an angry mob with torches, or tricked into falling off a cliff, say. I did know that would kill a troll. In fact, the only time I'd encountered a troll doing anything really peculiar was when the troll had attacked Bella, and in doing so, precipitated her into my arms. I looked from the sparks into Lug's eyes.

"Yes, I think so."

He smiled, a very odd expression on that stony face. I waited to see if he had more to say. We watched the fire some more. If it hadn't been for the smell, and my sense of urgency, this would have been a pleasant way to pass the time. What he'd asked me was a good way to broach what I'd come here for, but I wanted to be sure he was done.

"Lom."

"Yes?" I asked after a particularly long delay, even for him.

"Could I... meet them?" He picked up a massive stick and poked the fire, sending a spiral of sparks skyward.

This was the opening I had been hoping for. "Yes. I have something for you."

I stood up and used both hands to pull it out of nospace where I had put it before leaving home. That last trip to the armory had left me trying to figure out just how much I could carry this way. There was, I'd learned a limited amount of ways I could access, so an upper limit to the gear I'd have on this mission. Bringing this had been worth the loss of space, I could tell.

Lug's face broke into a big grin, exposing rows of gray teeth intended for chewing anything from sheep to rocks. "Bow!" He boomed. I staggered a little, and was grateful when he lifted the weight of the thing off me.

"Would you like to come with me? I need your help, and there are trolls where I need to go. You could try talking to them."

He had already strung the fearsome weapon, a crossbow made from steel and what I could have sworn was a railroad track. I hadn't brought any quarrels with me, I'd never had any. When I had taken this from him, he'd just used it to put a quarrel through a concrete wall, and negotiations were delicate. In the long run, he'd agreed to abide by some rules that involved not traveling Above, and I'd taken the crossbow for safekeeping.

Lug nodded. He couldn't stop smiling over the ugly weapon. He'd made it himself.

"Where we go?" He asked, cocking his head to one side. He'd picked up that this was serious, with the bow and my asking him to go with me.

"Have you ever been to Low Court?" I asked him.

He shook his head after a minute of thought.

"I need your help getting in." I told him. "I can't use magic, I need to be stealthy."

He scratched his head. "Lug not very quiet unless in woods."

He was right about that. Fortunately, that was where I needed him.

Chapter 32

Play the Death March

The last time I had attempted to enter Low Court in secret I had miscalculated. I had trusted a kelpie, and she had kidnapped me with malice, to father her children. This time, I wasn't alone, and I wasn't going near the river. The forest around the massive castle that held Low Court had been designed to keep unwanted visitors out of the fortress, and so far as I knew, it was impenetrable. I was going to test that with the help of a wily Alaskan spirit, and a super-intelligent (relatively) troll.

We'd met up with Raven, who hadn't been at all ruffled at being introduced to Lug. He knew the plan, and told us that he had over-flown the forest as much as he dared without venturing into the Low Court wards. He'd found a thin area, he told me, which looked like it was the result of a long-ago forest fire.

"Brush. That's what you get when a fire goes through."

He would know, being a person who preferred the wilderness.

"And how is brush good for us?" I looked sideways at Lug's chest. He was listening in silence. I wasn't sure how much he was catching of the conversation.

"We can travel without being seen in it. In the deep woods, it is very open." He spread out his arms in an exaggerated shrug. "And there are spider webs."

Somehow he'd never struck me as the kind to dance and squeal like a little girl when he got a web across the face.

"But open means faster travel," I pointed out. "And this needs to happen as close as possible to the first moments of battle."

He nodded. "There are game trails in the brush, no problem. And you don't understand about the spiders. I think I'll wait to see your face when you do."

Raven turned and looked at the faint light coming from the rising sun. "Right now, we should find Lug a place to sleep."

Lug spoke, startling me. "I sleep anywhere."

"Yes, but we need cover." I looked around. The dark forest loomed at the edge of the field we were standing in. The farmhouse it had belonged to was on the far side of it, the chimney an accusing finger pointing at the sky. The wood which remained was charred and scattered. The barn was sagging in the middle, and had holes in the side. I pointed. "That will do."

It had been a long time since people had been here. Something scurried out of the heap of rust and junk that had once been farm equipment. Magic was a limited tool, Underhill. Some things could be enhanced, but the procedures would have been familiar to a human farmer a mere century before, Above. Lug grunted and kicked the heap. Several more small brown things scurried out. I couldn't see them well enough to identify them. It was dark in the barn. Lug curled up and did his pile of rocks impression. He didn't snore. I contemplated his sleeping form. Snoring could be fatal to a troll, in this state they were vulnerable, as he could not waken until nightfall.

"Might as well rest, ourselves." Raven pointed out.

I nodded in agreement. I pulled a sleeping bag and groundcloth out of my stash. We would have two nights to get into place, for when

Trytion launched the attack and drew most of Low Court down on his head. All so I could sneak in the back door.

Raven transformed into bird-shape, and flew up into the loft. The beams creaked alarmingly under his weight, but nothing came crashing down on me. I found a pile of ancient hay, poked it until things stopped moving, and set up wards before lying down. I had no fancy to be nibbled on in my sleep.

Sleep came slowly. I resisted the urge to send Bella messages. She would be busy, and didn't need me jogging her elbow from a distance, not with Trytion, Joe, and Dean all running the war preparation. Joe and Dean were trained in this sort of thing, even if they hadn't needed it on a large scale. I tried to push memories of goblin raids out of my head, and finally, despite the light streaming in dusty beams through the broken walls, I slept.

Raven woke me at nightfall. He was back in human form, and had a tiny fire glowing in the earth floor of the barn. He'd dug a little pit, and had the dirt heaped nearby, so he could conceal the ashes when we left. I smelled the meat he had roasting on a spit. And the coffee he'd brewed in a battered enamel pot.

"Where did you find that?" I asked as I rolled up my bedding.

He grinned. "I never tell my secrets, boy."

The tin cup he handed me was scorching hot, but the coffee tasted... well, as bad as Raven's coffee ever tasted. He'd told me one time it was meant to be strong enough to float a mule shoe. With the mule still attached. For the moment, that was all that mattered. Hot and caffeinated. Food followed it, and I didn't ask where that had come from. Or what it was. It was tasty, although that might have been contrast with the coffee.

Lug was moving around by now, and Raven offered him some coffee. The troll sniffed it, and handed it back. I upped my estimate of his intelligence a notch. Raven used the rejected cup to put the fire out. Lug helped bury the remains of it, with a quick scoop of the dirt, and a stomp of his foot.

We left the barn as the last streaks of red and purple faded from the sky. The sunset had probably been pretty. Raven pulled something from his pocket and put it on his head. As we walked across the field, he beckoned to me.

"You need to see something."

I followed him toward the hedgerow that divided this field from the next one over. In the corner of the field, where it merged into the forest, he pointed upward into a tall tree. I had noticed before that unlike a normal forest, this one didn't really have a softening line of brush and smaller trees. The huge black trunks simply loomed up at the end of the field like a wall. I followed the direction of the point. The light was going fast, and I squinted at the shimmering of something up there.

A movement made the shimmer move along cords, and it resolved into the biggest damn spider web I had ever laid eyes on. The movement was a spider about the length of my forearm, with a roughly rectangular abdomen. It had shifted, and now was disappearing back into the night, long legs stretched out fore and aft on the web. It looked like nothing more than a tree limb.

I looked at Raven, who chuckled softly. "Look on your face was worth it. But that's the male."

It took me a minute to remember enough about spiders to cue in on what he was saying. Then, I scanned the trunks of the two trees the web was mostly anchored to. When I finally managed to pick her out, in the dim light, I took an involuntary step backward. Other than one impossibly long, slender leg, she was lined up on the trunk nearest me, so well camouflaged it just looked like that tree was heavy-trunked. The leg, though, was resting possessively on a silk-wrapped bundle, from which protruded...

"Antlers?" I hissed at Raven, deciding that retreat was indeed the better part of valor in this case. I'd missed the silk cocoon when we first walked up, as it was behind her, and the tree trunk she was hiding on. She was, just in body, as long as I was tall. The legs tripled that, easily.

We walked back to where Lug was waiting. He hadn't followed us, but had stayed by the game trail we would use to enter the forest. I saw now why Raven had recommended this. The brush and young trees were too small to support a behemoth like he'd just showed me. I shook my head. Only magic could allow that monstrous growth of a creature with no real skeleton. But this explained much of why those who ventured into the forest rarely came back out.

And the howls that sounded, faintly, as the moon rose. Those were another good reason. I had no illusions about Sean the wolf's wild cousins. They would have no witty quips, sartorial taste would be limited to tearing off our clothing to better reach our flesh, and they were agile enough to follow us on these paths.

I looked at Raven. "Are you taking point?"

He usually did, an instinct left over from long ago, I suspected. Raven shook his head, and pulled the thing down that he'd put on, adjusting it. I blinked in surprise at the sight.

"Why are you wearing an eye patch?" I asked him. He looked less like a pirate of human lore, and more like a certain irascible... he held out his arm, and two lesser ravens landed on it.

"I will be with them, and with you. You will be the eyes on the ground. I will be in middle, with him," Raven shook the birds off his arm and pointed at Lug. "Bringing up the rear."

I bit my tongue on the question of his raven's names – I really didn't want to know – and walked into the game trail. I was very grateful there weren't any spider webs to brush my face just here, I was afraid I'd lose my cool if I encountered them just now.

By the time I did discover a spiderweb, I was able to limit my reaction to a slight jump. It was an eerily silent walk in the woods. Raven wasn't talking, distracted by having to split his attention between his eyes in the sky and the path his physical body was walking on. I was glad he could do it - I'd be throwing up and passing out by now. Lug, in some mysterious fashion, could walk through heavy brush without making much noise at all beyond the occasional rustle. I couldn't watch him, as he was behind me in the single file we were walking in, but one of these days I wanted to see how he did it.

The biggest problem, I quickly discovered once we were in the cool darkness of the woods, was the smallest things. I was swarmed by tiny biting gnats. Swatting didn't bother them, ten more would take the place of the bloody mess I'd left on my skin. I couldn't put up a magical shield, we were minimizing our magical use so we couldn't be tracked if there were watchers at Low Court. Sure, they couldn't see out this far, but...

The bugs were making my life hellish. I broke off a small bundle of twigs and used them like a horse uses a tail, to keep them away from my mouth and nose, at least. Perhaps because of the distraction, it took me far longer than it ought to have to realize what was going on. I stopped dead in my tracks. Raven stopped, putting a hand on my shoulder to steady himself.

"What is wrong?" He asked.

"These flies are attacking us because we're intruders." I said, turning around to face him. Lug loomed over his shoulders, looking vaguely concerned. The bugs wouldn't bother him. "The whole place is against us."

Raven nodded. "Yes, of course. Very clever, the person who designed this. But not clever enough. Stand still."

He bent and pulled away some of the loose dead leaves and twigs from the soil beside the trail, and then scooped up a double handful of it. With this, he advanced toward me, and I started to step back, wondering what he was up to.

"Hold still, I said," he sounded irritable. I obediently let him pour the stuff over my head, closing my eyes as it flew everywhere. He rubbed it in energetically, through my hair and onto the back of my neck.

"Now, you smell like the forest." He stepped back and surveyed his handiwork with a little smirk. Damn his sense of humor. I could have done that myself had he told me what he was up to. I knew I could, because now he was kneeling and scooping more dirt onto his own head. I rubbed loose earth into my hands and rolled my sleeves up again, making myself filthy and muddy with dirt and sweat. The bugs, on the other hand, were already going away, with only a lone straggler whining in my ear. I swatted it, and looked at Raven, who was as muddy as I.

"Are you ready now?"

He nodded, and waved me on. We were not making quick progress, which I had anticipated. I had also planned for a quick, cold lunch, eaten on the go. Building a fire, or even the smell of cooking food, could attract unwanted attention. I was also expecting an ambush, but that hadn't come yet. When you are constantly on alert, it begins to hurt after a while. Your muscles, drawn tightly and ready to sprint into action, ache and your brain wants to wander. Wary as I am, through long training and the experiences I'd had, I couldn't maintain that level forever.

Adding to that was the travel in darkness. My eyes adjust further than a human's eyes can, more equivalent to a cat. But this was wearying. I was very glad when the faint light of dawn finally penetrated the thick brush and leaves to put an end to our 'day' although I did keep pushing on until we found a small stream Raven's eyes had located. Here, we could get off the trail and be out of sight while we waited for the return of darkness.

Lug promptly made like a pile of rocks. I splashed my face with water, then dried it roughly before dirtying again. It seemed counterproductive, but I felt a little better without the sweat mixed in there too. Raven propped himself up against a tree. I had been keeping a wary eye out for massive webs, and hadn't seen any. Although I suppose even an enchanted forest could only support so many predators. We'd heard the wolf pack a couple more times, without being able to tell if it was closer to us than before.

Raven pulled a lump of pemmican out of his shirt pocket and munched it.

"How much further?" I asked him. Without his birds, and the density of the undergrowth, we could walk right into Low Court before we knew we'd arrived.

"We're more than halfway. There is a lot of movement in the city."

I didn't know he was scouting that far. "Not surprising, the army at High Court will have gotten their attention by now. Seems like it's going to plan. I just wish I could be there, too."

He chuckled. "Being in two places at once, that would be quite a trick. Let me know if you manage it, I want to learn."

I shook my head at him. Ruefully, I gave up on wishes, and turned my mind back to reality. I was soft – we all were – through reliance on magic. This trip in a bubble would have been over almost before it began. The grueling trek through the forest was taking a toll on me already, and I'd gotten far too used to home cooked meals every day. I patted my complaining stomach, and drank more water. Not out of the stream, which had Mother Titania only knew what floating in it. The human microbiome hadn't translated entirely to our world, but still I drank the water I'd packed with me.

Then I tried to sleep.

Chapter 33

Carry Me Along

I awakened feeling like my sleeping bag had shrunk. Opening my eyes, I discovered that it wasn't the sleeping bag, I was trussed neatly into it. Raven was bound, as well, and the one visible eye I could see was remarkably calm. He winked at me. Or blinked, hard to tell with the other eye behind an eyepatch.

I wasn't as calm about it. If Raven was going to pull one of his moves where he infiltrated from the inside out, I wish he would have at least given me some warning. Waking up like this was bad for the digestion. We were lying on the bank of the stream, and the three people I could see... a fairy man, and two goblins, were obviously Low Court. The fairy walked over and kicked the sleeping troll.

"Get up!" He shouted. Lug sat up slowly. It was still light enough outside that he was slow-moving and apparently groggy.

"Whu?" He grunted.

The rough fairy kicked him again. I doubted that affected Lug at all, but the fairy would have sore toes in the morning.

"Up, troll." Lug lumbered to his feet, blinking down at me, then at

Raven. I didn't say anything. I'd be hurt by being kicked with cloddish boots, and I was waiting to see what happened.

The fairy jabbed at him with his finger. "Listen up, you. I'm in charge now, you understand? I'm the one giving orders. You hear me?"

At the end he was shouting, and I winced. Trolls are slow, but they aren't deaf, and Lug isn't even slow, just... contemplative. He was contemplating the fairy now, with a deadpan face.

"Ya." He said slowly.

I hid a smile. Lug was taking his cue from me. If I wanted to be a prisoner, he was going to play along.

The fairy pointed at Raven and I. "Pick them up and carry them. Pick them up. Carefully!"

Lug stooped and gathered up the pair of us, tucking one under each arm. Then he just stood there, looking at the fairy. The goblins, not being stupid, were keeping the fairy between them and the troll. The fairy pointed. "You follow me."

He started walking toward the trail. I wiggled into a slightly less painful position and resigned myself to some discomfort. Arrival at Low Court in this way wasn't dignified, but it did solve a few problems, like how to find Dionaea. I imagined we were about to be presented to her like presents without the proverbial bow on them.

I could get out of this cocoon at any time I wanted to. Raven could as well, and I was a little surprised he'd consented to be captured at all. However, the trickster stories often had his schemes involving being eaten, so he could attack from the belly of the beast. It suited me just fine. I craned my neck and looked up at Lug. Keeping my voice low, I asked him, "Are you all right?"

He nodded.

"Thanks for playing along." I murmured, hoping he could hear me.

He smiled, and I relaxed. This was going to be entertaining. They hadn't even taken Lug's bow, which was slung across his back. As the darkness gathered, I got to see the troll's stealth in action. He sort of slid through the forest. I suspected there was a deep magic in action here, as we never seemed to get a branch across the face. It was like they moved out of his way. But when I closed my eyes to See with the second Sight, I couldn't tell that he was using magic, other than the glow of his life. I expanded the Sight, encompassing our captors and confirming that one muddy-auraed fairy, and two ghastly green goblins were all there was. She had a sort of ranger service patrolling the forest, which we had theorized, but with the disruption and us not using magic... I opened my eyes.

"Hey, chump." I called out to the fairy.

He turned around and glared at me. Lug didn't stop walking, so the fairy wound up walking backwards, which struck me as hilarious. I struggled to keep the laughter out of my voice. "How'd you find us, anyway?"

He stumbled, and gave up walking backwards. "We patrol here."

"So what's your name?" I was going to be bored hanging in Lug's arm, anyway, might as well make conversation.

"Tommy. And yours?"

I was starting to feel my laughter morph into insane giggles. He didn't know who I was.

"I'm, ah, Leroy. So this is your beat, huh. How about them spiders?"

His shoulders tensed. "They have learned to leave the path alone."

Which explained why one or more hadn't set up an ambush across the game trail. And it implied that the spiders were semi-intelligent, which was enough to knock the silly out of me. Those things scared me like few other things I'd encountered in a long life hunting down monsters.

"Just you and two goblins, that's an accomplishment." I kept the conversational ball rolling. Tommy seemed to be a normal person in that he was answering me when prompted. Most people like to talk, and being encouraged to brag almost always worked. Tommy was no different.

"We keep the spiders in their place, and the wolves know better than to get too close. My crew keeps this path clear." I could hear the simple pride in his voice.

"So this isn't where the deer pass through the forest?" Never hurt to put a little doubt into our motivations. Sure, sure, we were only poaching.

"No, this path is..." He broke off and looked over his shoulder suspiciously. "Deer?"

I tried for goofy grin, but the effect was rather spoiled by bouncing along slung under a troll's arm. Or possibly the piratical looking Raven, who had been practicing his poker face while I was talking.

"So where are you taking us?" I wondered just how much I could get out of Tommy.

"To th' Castle." He sounded disgruntled.

"Your boss there?" I didn't give him a chance to answer, sliding into his dialect as I went on. "Bosses, a necessary evil. You can allus say you were just followin' orders when it comes down to it."

"Aye. Better'n havin' to take m'chances alone." Tommy sighed audibly. "T'forest ain't so bad, not when..." he bit that off quickly, and I could see his head turn from side to side like he was checking that no one had heard him.

Very interesting. Not all her people liked and trusted her. Dionaea was about to learn that a rule of fear was ineffective, and sometimes terminal to the ruler, if I had anything to do with it. I lapsed into silence. For one thing, my side where I was draped over Lug's arm ached abominably. We were making good progress, it felt like. Raven would know for sure, but I couldn't chat with him about it, and he had his eyes closed, at the moment.

If he was sleeping, I'd eat my hat. The old bird was up to something. I was willing to keep playing along. Although I was going to be half the man I'd been not too long ago, unless we took a break soon. I was just opening my mouth to call out to Tommy when I saw the light.

The path ended in an open area, and the light was moon-shine, not sunshine. But after the dark of the forest, I was left blinking my eyes to adjust to the brightness. I craned my neck to see what I could.

Low Court, in an ironic twist, was mostly above ground, unlike High Court, which was dug into the vast hill as it had been since the Court was established. In that time, warmth, security, and perhaps even the human legend of under-hill origins had dictated the digging of the Great Hall, then the sprawling tunnels that came after. It was only in relatively recent history that the above-ground buildings of High Court had come into being, and they are blocky, warm stone, and to my eye, welcoming. Even on days I hated the Council and the power they held.

Low Court, on the other hand, was built by powerful magic users who had reason to convince outsiders of that power and influence. It was a mad dreamer's conception of a fantasy castle, soaring above the small city that had grown up around it. Towers, turrets, and enough spires to keep any number of evil wizards holed up and working without ever interacting with one another. Once built of white stone, it was now marred with streaks of black. From the distance we were at, I couldn't tell why.

The moon glowed bright and full overhead, turning the landscape into a chiaroscuro of shadows and reflections. I could see the river, a silver thread in the distance. At least we hadn't come out on the bank of that. In my current position, that could have been interesting.

"Hey, Tommy." I called. Lug was still standing on the verge of the forest. "Can we take a break for a bit? I'm about to break in half, and I gotta piss."

Our earlier rapport building paid off, and he hesitated, looking toward the castle, then back at us. "Sure, sure. Only no funny business, and one of you at a time, ok?"

I waited for him to untie me, noting with interest that he didn't use magic, as he hadn't used it in the bindings. I wondered why, but I really did have urgent needs to care for.

I went first, and then Raven stalked into the brush when I returned to the small group gathered by Lug. I held out my hands to Tommy. "S'pose I could have 'em tied in front and walk?" I put a little whine in my tone. He seemed to appreciate that.

Raven reappeared out of the darkness, and imitated my action without speaking. Tommy tied our wrists, looking back at me while he was working on Raven's.

"Does he, y'know, talk? Or is he a deaf n'dumb?"

This was a brilliant idea. I wished I'd come up with it. "Nah, he c'n hear all right. Just can't talk none."

"Oh." Tommy grunted, and spoke a bit louder, seeming not to have heard me say Raven could hear. "Follow me. That aways." He pointed toward the castle.

As he turned away to take the lead again, I rolled my eyes at Raven, who broke into a brief, broad grin, then wiped his face clean of expression again. I could take lessons from him in not showing my thoughts, and I thought I had been pretty good before. We followed, but slowly. It was harder to walk out in the open than it had been in the woods. In the woods your eyes could adjust to the low, diffuse light. Here? It was bright, and the rutted sheep path Tommy led us to was in shadows, and rocky. I nearly fell a couple of times before losing my patience at the situation.

"Hey. Look..." I stopped dead on the path, and Tommy looked back at me, frowning.

"We're coming peaceable." I pointed out, hoping he would hear the rational tone and not think through the rest of it. "Maybe you could untie us, so we don't fall and get all busted up? Your boss won't like blood on his clean floors..."

"I dunno." But he was thinking about it, I could see it on his face. "Mebbe. Blood isn't a problem, see."

I did see, and it felt like a chill in the cold moonlight. "Well, is there going to be blood? With us?"

He shrugged. "Dunno. But guess I could untie you. Or have the troll carry you again."

I put as much whine as I could muster in my voice. "Aw, man, that hurts!"

He walked back to me and pulled out a knife. I chose to play dumb, and thrust my hands toward him. He could easily have cut me... but he didn't. He cut the cords binding me, and then looked over my shoulder.

"How about you? Gonna behave?"

Raven thrust his bound wrists past me and Tommy let him loose. "Now behave, or I'll turn the troll loose on you."

This made me blink. You can't assume your enemy is stupid. That will get you dead. But Tommy was quite sincere in threatening us with our own troll. As he turned and walked away, I looked over at my shoulder at Lug, who shrugged and smirked. He was in no danger. I thumbed my nose at him and started in Tommy's footsteps. The castle was looking very near, now.

I was feeling it in my gut, that knot of tension building and growing more complex as we got nearer. This wasn't quite what I had planned, but it would get us in without alarm. What happened after that, we would wait and see. With the armies assembling near High Court, the Low Court ought to be low on personnel. We had a very slim window and I meant to exploit it.

My theory was not challenged as we walked through Low Town toward the ever-more impressive spires of the unnaturally tall castle. In fact, we weren't challenged at all. We were passing through empty streets, footsteps echoing off the cobblestones. Lug was silent as ever, but Tommy clattered, the goblins pattered, and Raven was unusually loud behind me. There wasn't even as much as a curtain twitched in a window. The place was deserted. I walked a little faster and drew up next to Tommy.

"This place is spooky," I said, my voice low.

He glanced around, like he was afraid someone would hear us. "Yuh."

I thought he might say more, but instead he pointed. "Through that gate."

We all followed him, Lug with a very low bow, through the gate into a courtyard of nightmares. Tommy seemed not to notice the landscaping. I skipped sideways as an overgrown Venus Flytrap nipped at my ankles. Above us, a Dryad dangled brokenly from her tree, trapped half in and half out of the trunk. The trunk wept blood, but the human half was pale and limp. Dead, perhaps.

If she was decaying, I couldn't have smelled her over the cacophony of rank odors that assailed us. Tommy brushed past a thick stand of purplish-black grass, and a wave of sulfur roiled up in his wake, making me cough and my eyes water.

He didn't seem to even notice it. Even if I worked here and this was my daily routine, I'd notice. Maybe his sense of smell had been removed. Mercifully, we were walking through a small side-door before I lost my stomach contents on the noxious foliage that surrounded us.

The interior was almost a relief after that. It was dark in here, the only light cast through an open doorway at the end of a short hall. Tommy headed for the light. I followed slowly, looking into the dark. There were other doorways here, three, I thought, but with no light it was very difficult to see what might be through them. Halls, rooms, there was no way to tell. Tommy stopped in the lit doorway, his body dark against the warm yellow of the light.

He cleared his throat. "Brung in some trespassers." He ducked his head, like he was embarrassed. "Couple 'o guys."

"You brought them here?" The voice from the inner room was gravelly. I heard a scrape, and an odd thump. "Why the hells did you..."

He pushed Tommy out of the way and peered into the darkness, then recoiled. "Thass a troll!"

"Well, yuh, he was with 'em."

"They had a troll and they surrendered?"

Now that I could see Tommy's boss, I was busy making assumptions. "Not exactly. Tommy invited himself into our camp, and asked nicely."

I stepped forward into the light, and was gratified when the sodden mass of what had once been a fairy recoiled. He was hugely fat, missing one leg well above the knee, and between the nose and the eyes in matching reds with broken blood vessels, I knew about the drinking before I could smell it. Behind him, the room was empty. The filthy floor was the backdrop for a battered wood table and a single chair in front of it. Behind it, an overstuffed leather chair with splitting seams was obviously his.

I heard nothing else, other than his labored breathing. We were alone. I stepped forward again, into his face. "You recognize me?" I kept my voice low, knowing I had his full attention. "You know who I am, at least."

He nodded, his eyes riveted on mine. He had light brown eyes, currently slightly dilated in his fear. He licked his lips and moved them like he was trying to talk.

"Yes?" I prompted when he made no noise.

"Y-you... why are you here?" He managed. "Why aren't you out there?"

He was pointing in the general direction of High Court and the coming battleground. I shrugged. "Felt like paying her an informal visit."

He gobbled slightly. His words seemed to either flood out or get stuck like a cork in a bottle. I took a slow step forward, and he broke, backing rapidly into the room. I followed him in. Behind me, I heard a suspiciously wet crunch. I had to think that was one of the goblins. Probably Lug, as Raven had likely taken care of the other in complete silence. Tommy had vanished. I knew he hadn't gotten far. I could trust Raven.

Tommy's Boss, though.

"So, you have a name?" I asked casually. I waved at the leather chair. "Why don't you sit and take a load off?"

He looked frantically around. There were no windows in this room. No art hung on the walls. A tapestry on the end wall, the one I was facing as I came through the door, was the only thing that broke up the dingy white walls. It was as dingy as the walls, the scene it had once portrayed long gone into the dull smoke and gray and yellow of long abuse.

"Now what are you thinking?" I asked him casually, swinging the straight-back wooden chair around and straddling it casually. I could feel the weight of the pistol on my hip. Tommy hadn't even looked twice at it, and I'd been wearing it when I slept the evening before, the holster. The gun had been tucked under my pillow, and I'd holstered it when Lug picked me up and Tommy wasn't looking. It had been easy enough to do. The fairy, like most, had likely never seen a gun, or knew what it could do.

I was still waiting. The big Boss had collapsed into the other chair, and was looking fixedly at the doorway. I followed his gaze.

"They aren't coming." I told him without turning my head back toward him. I could see him well enough to know that he wasn't making any sudden moves. I wasn't using magic, didn't need to use any. This was old hat, soft, comfortable, and lethal.

"In fact, no one is coming. So you have some time to answer a few questions."

He shook his head. I nodded. "You're going to tell me how many men are in the castle right now."

He shot a glance at the doorway, still dark and empty. We both sat in silence for a moment. There was nothing out there. He swallowed hard.

"Maybe fifty men at arms." He suggested.

"Try again." I leaned forward, crossing my arms on the back of the chair. "Try again, or I will call my troll friend in here. You can talk without either leg."

He collapsed, burying his face in his hands. "Buh... buh... 'Bout ten of us, I think."

That took a minute between sobs. I stood up. He looked up at me, his face a ruin of tears, snot, and scars. "Are... are you going to kill me?"

"Where are the Queen's Quarters?" I asked, keeping my voice even. His eyes got wide and his lips quivered.

"Sh-she's no-not here."

I waited. He sobbed once, an ugly sound. "She has the south tower. The servants are on the first floor, her rooms are above that. No one goes up there. No one."

I looked down at him and shook my head silently before walking out the door. Behind me, I could hear him hiccupping.

Chapter 34

Queen's Lair

In the dark hall I paused for a moment to let my eyes adjust, and then saw Raven waiting for me.

"All clear?" I asked him.

He nodded. "There were the three we came in with, and two more. Want me...?" He jerked a thumb toward the room I'd just left. I shook my head.

"Waste of effort. We are looking for the South Tower now. Lug?"

He loomed out of the darkness. "I left my bow in the Forest." His voice sounded the way I'd named him. "This game is good, though."

That explained where the bow had gone, I'd been wondering, but there had not been a chance to talk until now.

"The plan is in place. Find the Crown, get it to Bella. If we find the Wendigo..."

"He's mine." Raven interrupted me. I could hear the anger in his voice, his face too shadowed to read. This was an unusual amount of emotion from the old bird.

"Got that. Not sure what I could do about him, to be honest."

The Wendigo on the battlefield was a shiversome idea. We'd lose men to it, and then to one another as his infection spread. I headed in the general direction of the center of the tower, looking carefully as I went. It was all dark. The only light was far behind us now, in the room with the broken fairy.

I've never been a nice man, no matter what my wife thinks. When we found the next light, it was the kitchen, and the little drab sleeping with her head on the table received a rude awakening.

Lug picked her up by the back of her dress at my gestured command. Her eyes wide, she squeaked once on an indrawn breath, and then her bladder let go.

"Ohpleasedonthurtme." She ran all the words together into one long wail.

"Take us to the South Tower, to the Queen's lair."

I gestured, and Lug set her down. She collapsed into a heap on the floor next to her puddle.

"Get up. I'm not going to kill you, and I don't have a lot of time. Who else is here?"

She pushed herself up, shaking. I was beginning to wonder about the reactions I was getting here in the Castle. Normally it took a little more effort to get results like these.

"Just Cook, and she's sleeping." The drab, of a species I couldn't determine beyond humanoid, hugged herself.

"Get on, then, take us to the Tower." I prompted. She scuttled for the door.

We followed her. She led us through more dark, disorienting halls, and finally stopped at the foot of some stairs. She pointed up the ornate, sweeping staircase. I peered around into the gloom. It was as ornately decorated as a rococo brothel. This was Dionaea's style, all right.

"I – I can't go – go any more." She panted.

I pointed back toward the kitchen. "Are you going to warn

anyone? Clean up your mess, and no-one needs to ever know you even saw us."

Her eyes huge in the dark, she nodded rapidly.

"Go." I said.

She scuttled away down the hall, tripping and nearly falling in her haste. I looked at Raven.

"Soft, boy."

"Not really. There will come a time when we will rebuild Margot's contacts, and now I have one in the belly of the beast."

We started up the stairs in silence, Lug taking the rear as always. I stopped at the top of the staircase, facing three doors and another staircase, this one a tight spiral. I held up a hand in a sign for them to stop, and listened. There was nothing. The dead silence was unnerving. This place ought to have at least something stirring, but there wasn't even a mouse.

"It will be up there." I pointed to the stairs. "Lug..."

"I stay here. Watch your back." He knew as well as I did that stair would never hold him.

"Good man."

I started up the stairs. There was a faintly silvery light at the top of them, but it seemed to take forever to get there. I hadn't thought to count steps when we started, and I wasn't going to bother with retreating just to estimate the distance. I knew from the exterior that there were some very tall spires. Added to that, the main staircase to her quarters had been a double-height, starting us at the equivalent of three stories. I stopped thinking about it and looked out the narrow window we had just reached.

The town was visible in the bright moonlight, and the river was a broad stretch of silver, broken only by a bridge. No boats were visible. I didn't have the angle to see much of the castle itself from here. We were pretty high up, though.

Raven nudged me. "Can you open that thing?"

"I don't think so. Hang on a minute." With magic, breaking the window silently would be effortless. I was not using magic, though. From the nospace I pulled a small bag, which contained a nice set of burglar's tools. There had been more than one occasion I'd used them, and practice meant that with a suction cup and a cutter, I quickly had the pane of glass out of the window. I held it while watching Raven close his eye. He'd been wearing the eyepatch long enough I'd almost forgotten why, but now, as he opened the visible eye and gave me a wolfish grin, I remembered.

The lesser raven landing on the windowsill didn't come as much of a surprise, then. Raven held out his arm, and the small bird hopped on. They slipped past me, and I laid the glass carefully on the steps. I'd have to remember it on the way back, but at least no one was going to sneak up behind us. Even if they made it past Lug, which I doubted. But no sense wasting a chance to prepare.

Raven seemed to be talking to his bird minion. I had fallen far enough behind I could only hear a low murmur. Then the bird took off and flew up the stairs.

"Looking for trouble?" I asked him, keeping my voice low.

"I keep expecting booby traps." He paused and I caught up with him. "I would..."

"She obviously feels like she has everyone terrified." I thought about what we had seen that night.

"To the point of being brittle, and shattering like glass at any pressure?" He shook his head. "The bird is at a door, above. Still, I hear nothing moving."

"Lead on."

I was feeling the tension, my shoulders were knotting and my back stiff with anticipation of a knife, even as I knew it wasn't a rational fear. My legs were feeling the seemingly unending stairs, too. I'd gotten back into shape after my illness, but this was enough to tax anyone but the seemingly indefatigable Raven. Not knowing what was behind that door, but certain that opening it would bring her down on us... I flexed my shoulders and took a deep breath as we reached the tiny landing. Raven waved me toward the door, and I closed my eyes before I reached out to the handle.

There was something there. Not much. The door itself was not magicked. But beyond it, in the space I presumed to be Dionaea's working room, there was a flicker. Something was alive in there. I opened my eyes and took a deep breath. Then I reached out and pushed the door open.

The bird darted in over my head and surprised me into ducking a little. This saved my life. The crossbow bolt, which was aimed rather too high, sailed over my head and a moment later, we heard it clattering down the steps. But by then, I was facing the very frightened wood elf nose to nose. I'd dropped to one knee when I'd heard the snap of the weapon. She still clutched it, but it was unloaded and she was shaking like a leaf in the wind as I stared into her eyes.

"You shot at me. Shall I kill you?" I kept my voice conversational.

The crossbow dropped to the floor with a clatter, and she whimpered. I got up quickly to avoid the splatter of urine.

"This seems to be a habit people have around here. I would have thought Low Court was more housebroken."

Raven wrinkled his nose and stepped around the elf. "Brittle and dissolving."

The elf fell to her knees. She still hadn't spoken.

"I'm about done with this place." I walked around her, toward the crown. "Gives me the creeps."

Raven held up a hand. "It is warded."

I nodded. I'd expected that, just as I had expected it to be on display as it was, in the center of the room with elfglobes illuminating it. The room glittered, and the crown seemed to emit a soft golden light of its own. Dionaea had indulged herself here, in her lair. Even the floor was gilded wood, with ivory inlay. I hoped it was ivory, at any rate. Bone was just one other possibility.

"I think it's possible that as soon as I take it, she will appear like a silent fart."

He chuckled.

"The Wendigo may well be along."

At this, the elf began to wail, a high pitched ululation that told me, finally, why the whole castle was paralyzed with fear. They'd seen what it could do, and knew their own fates should they not comply.

I bent and took her shoulder, feeling the tiny bones so close to the skin. Her leaves, the token woven into her hair to indicate her time away from her tree, were skeletonized as though they had been under the snow for a winter. "Child. Let us take you home. At the foot of the stairs there is a troll. Go to him, and tell him Lom said to protect you."

She stared up at me, her eyes so wide I could see the whites entirely. Raven came to the other side of her. "There is a way to break a soul. Simply put, you say... 'there is a spot you must not stand on. There.' Then, you punish them if they come too close to it. And they learn to stay away from it. Now, if it is the fireplace, a babe learns not to touch, and it is good. But not this person. Now, they change their mind."

She turned her face a little toward him. He went on softly, his voice almost melodic.

"The breaker then changes the spot the child must not touch. It is not marked, it is invisible, and the child is no longer certain, after a few times, where they can, or cannot, be. So they stand still, afraid to move at all. Because to move is pain. And so they are broken."

She sobbed, silently. Raven held out a hand to her. "Come, child. You may go down the stairs, may you not?"

She nodded, a tiny motion.

"Go down, and stand with Lug. We will be along shortly." Raven lifted her to her feet. He led her to the door, and she started down the stairs like an automaton wound up and let go.

"Bad business, this." I got up and returned to the crown. He came to stand on the other side of the pedestal it rested on.

His face was grim and his voice harsh. "Time to clean out this hell hole. There's no reason to not use your soap-bubbles any longer, is there?"

"I don't fancy seeing her here, no. But Lug, and the elf?" I reached out for the crown.

"Pick them up and skip." He nodded, and I clasped the crown firmly.

It was like grabbing a live electrical wire. Fairyland has no need of such things, but Above... I'd felt this kind of pain before. I swore out loud, and snapped a bubble around both of us as Raven grabbed my shoulder. I fell to my knees and felt the bubble sway.

I was still on my knees when the bubble popped. We were only downstairs, next to a startled Lug, and an elf who wasn't paying attention to anything any longer. I didn't have time to assess her, though.

"Lug, pick her up." I ordered. The crown felt like it was burning my hands.

Once she was safely cradled in his arms, and I could hear the pounding of feet in the hall, I knew it was time to go. Using the spell had set off alarms, as I had suspected it would. It was time to get out, if we could.

The entire area, not just the castle was strongly warded and wrapped in an interdiction spell. High Court was, as well, and I knew Bella had broken that. So, I would get us as far as I could. The bubble walls trembled around us, and I sent it for the coordinates I'd planned beforehand with Bella.

What happens when you lose the integrity of a bubble can range from not much, to catastrophic. It's not really like flying a balloon across the landscape, and as a matter of fact, I wasn't entirely sure of the physics of it. But I could feel the spell attenuating as we broke through the interdiction, and I channeled more energy into it. Since Bella had stripped the elfshot poison from me, and freed my ability to do magic, I had reveled in it, but I had not tested myself for any limits. I knew I ought. After a lifetime of being punished for every attempt, I was like that broken child Raven had described.

Now, I was pouring it out, and I felt the snap when I broke the interdiction spell. Not that I broke through it. I broke it. I'd only needed to get out of it, away from the castle, but... I was angry. The condition of the elf I was looking at, the burning sensation of the stolen crown in my hands, the indignities of the Wendigo. I felt the spell go down.

Perhaps others would feel it, and they could run away, now. That, I'd leave for another day. Now, we were rushing toward another confrontation. Bella would be on the verge of a battle, one I hoped to put a stop to before it began.

Chapter 35

Battlefield Meeting

W e popped out atop the grassy knoll I had staked out for Bella. It had a lovely view of the battlefield we were funneling the armies toward, and as I had told her, she wasn't supposed to be in the thick of battle. Her presence was an encouragement, literally to be an inspiration. The dawn was breaking with a splash of color and light on the mountains that loomed in front of us. Bella was nowhere in sight.

"Lug. Sending you to someone who can help the elf girl." I barked at him, throwing a bubble around him as soon as he nodded. Ellie was the only person besides Melcar who might be able to do anything, and Melcar...

I looked down into the valley. Melcar was down there, and likely so was my wife. Raven pulled off the eyepatch and rubbed his face.

"They attacked early." I looked at him, feeling the weight of the crown I still held. "I have to get to her."

He nodded. "Ready for this?"

"No." I hated this form of transport for so many reasons. "Let's do it."

He transformed into a giant raven, towering over me, and stretched out a wing. I stepped back, and then ran lightly up it and onto his back. He leaped off the ground, and I clung to a feather for dear life, the crown clutched in my other hand. We soared into the air, and my eyes watered in the wind. It was cold up here, always was. How many times now had I traveled with him? Too many.

He circled upward, wings flapping, and then soared out over the valley, balancing on a wind I could not see. I leaned forward and tried to look over his shoulder without off-balancing him. I knew very well there was magic in what he was doing, but it seemed the courteous thing to do.

Far below us, the fields stretched out. It was late spring, and the river was no longer in flood. One side was ours, the other theirs. Vast camps sprawled within sight of it, and there was a line of troops drawn up on either side. Raven swooped toward them in a move that left me swallowing hard. I hate flying. I don't mind airplanes, but I hate flying. My stomach was trying to crawl up through my mouth.

The reality of battle is not what most people think it is. Part of what was going on down there was posturing. Trytion would be talking with Dionaea, trying to convince her to give up her plans. She would be reveling in this acknowledgement of her power. Above, in the age of guns, all this stylized gamesmanship was gone. But here, in a land full of virtual immortals, the days of blood and thunder still reigned. Raven banked, and I could see them.

There was a pavilion set up, flags flying, the sides pulled back until it was almost a mere canopy. Ranks of men with torches stood around it. One side held the black silks of the Low Court, the other the sky-blue of the High. They would have been talking through the night, wearing on one another, while the flanks tried to jockey for position in the dark.

That would be where she was. Raven circled, and the men looked up in alarm. I could see the pale ovals of faces in the torchlight, the dawn did not reach here yet. We were too high to recognize anyone. I didn't see the monstrosity that was the Wendigo, and shivered to think he was inside the tent with Bella.

Raven screamed hoarsely, the crowing war-cry grating across my nerves like a file. Then he stooped like a warbird, and I held on for my life. I could feel the feathers slipping through my hand, and then he spread his wings and almost stopped in midair. I sensed through my grip the flexion of his body as he landed with talons outstretched. I slid off onto the solid ground, panting a little.

Raven launched himself back into the sky with another hoarse cry. I'd been well announced. I walked toward the tent, seeing the two women facing me. Trytion was not in sight, they were alone in the pavilion, each standing on opposite sides of a long table.

There were chairs that made me think others had been there. I'd missed something. But at this moment, I had eyes only for Bella. The crown in my hand, hanging at my side, I strode to her, ignoring Dionaea, although I heard the hiss of her indrawn breath as she saw what I held.

"You thief!" She looked like she might come right over the table at me. I still didn't look at her. Bella held out her hands to me. She looked magnificent.

Dressed in leather and armor, her hair pulled back off her face in an intricate braid, little tendrils falling out to frame her cheeks, she was amazing, and mine. I wrapped my free arm around her and kissed her quickly. No time for more.

Dionaea made an inarticulate, angry noise, and I flicked an amused glance at her, still holding Bella.

"I used to think marriage was like being in jail." I lifted the crown. "And then I learned that with the right woman, it is like serving a Queen." I put the crown on Bella's head as Dionaea let out a howl of rage and really did try to leap over the table.

I turned to meet her, catching a look of surprise on Bella's face, her hands going upward to feel what I'd just put on her... Dionaea sprawled on the table, tugging at the sword she was wearing. Like Bella, she was wearing leathers, but hers were red, blood red. The sword was far too long for her, and she gave up as she rolled across the table and launched herself at me, shrieking. I straight-armed her in the chest, watching her bounce backward into the table off me.

She came up with rage in her arms, and a ball of fire in each hand. They were in the air before I had time to do more than throw up a warding spell, and they bounced off it. Her face twisted.

"You are a cripple!" She spat. "How can you possibly...?"

"He isn't any more." Bella was at my shoulder. Above me, the tent caught fire from the deflected energy blast. Bella pulled her pistol and leveled it at Dionaea. "It's time for you to go."

She fired, and Dionaea vanished. I knew it was a bubble spell, but perhaps...

I looked upward at the flames. "I think we need to go, too."

Bella nodded, holstering her gun. "Lom..."

I caught her hand and ran as the silks seemed to explode. "What the hell?"

Between us and the men with torches, who were mostly running away now, there was a familiar ugly shape.

"A salamander!" Bella gasped. She reached for her gun. "You distract it!"

We had done this before, well, not as a team that time. At least there wasn't a dragon chasing me at the moment. I threw a bolt of energy at it, putting my weight behind it, so to speak. It squalled loudly and scuttled toward my wife. She leveled the gun and shouted. "Again!"

I threw something else this time, having had time to think. A lance of elemental cold, not ice, but beyond that, and the creature screamed in mortal fear. This time, when it opened its mouth, she fired twice, and it pawed frantically at its throat, rolling over and thrashing. As the salamander died, it burst into flame, and I could feel the heat of it. Bella skipped backward quickly, still holding her gun and scanning the gray dawn for more opponents.

Now that Dionaea had seen what I had done, I knew she would throw the full might of her forces against us. We were smack in the middle of the battlefield here, with the ford of the river right behind us. Most creatures Underhill hadn't the power or the skill to travel via bubble. We did, at least.

"Where's Trytion?" I caught her free hand and she bubbled us.

"Um." Bella put her hand to her head. No, to touch the crown. I remembered how it had shocked me, and hoped that it hadn't her. "He's... she pointed. "I seem to be linked somehow to him."

"To his mind?" Maybe I ought to have left that magical symbol where it lay.

She looked shocked. "No, just... like a compass."

The bubble changed direction. "Are you... why were you?" I wasn't even sure what to ask her first.

"Trytion had an emergency." She sounded tired. "They sneaked a platoon... a unit? Anyway, a bunch of Trolls around behind our position in the night. So he called me to negotiate, while he led the troops in a defense."

"What was she looking for?"

"Unconditional surrender." Her face looked severe, and all the young, playful girl I'd fallen so hard for, was stripped away. This was the Queen, the core of steel Trytion had seen when he elected her Consort. "Surrender, or suffer the loosing of the Wendigo."

"That cannot happen." I took her hand. "The crown..."

"Is a channel." She clasped hands with me and I felt the bubble land and drop. "I can tap into the accumulated power of the High Fae, Lom."

"Oh." Here, and I'd been thinking it was just a symbol. No wonder it had been stolen so long ago. But there was no time.

"Bella!" Ash was there, his face smeared with mud and blood. Not his, as he was moving easy, even missing an arm. "We need you right away."

I followed them at a trot to a big tent. Inside, elfglobes bobbed against the canvas ceiling, illuminating a scene from hells unimaginable below the floating lights. It was the hospital tent. Ash led us to a bed, where Trytion lay, his armor in a heap next to him, and his face twisted with pain. He reached out for Bella's hand.

"Sorry, m'dear. But..."

"His hip was slashed open to the bone." Melcar broke in, appearing on the other side of the bed. He laid a hand on Trytion's forehead. "He wouldn't let me operate until you arrived."

"Sent a messenger..." The king groaned. "You must take the banner."

He didn't seem to see me, behind her.

Bella bent over him and kissed his forehead. "I shall lead them, my king, and you must let them give you surcease."

He closed his eyes, and Melcar beckoned to another elf, who pushed past us and began to work on the king. I backed out, Bella with me, and headed for the outside, where the peachy light of dawn was beginning to give enough light to see. It had been a very long night. I took a deep breath, purging the foul odors of the tent. It wasn't dirty, but blood, vomit, and shit accompanied violence everywhere.

"Bella."

She put a hand on my arm and looked me in the eye. "I must, Lom."

"This isn't what you signed up for."

"No. But it is what I must do." She looked over my shoulder. "Ash. I need a mount."

I could hear him trotting off. "What can I do?"

"Be my general. Rally the troops. They respect you deeply, husband, and would follow you into the fires."

"And you?"

"I will take the banner to war." She turned away from me, and I saw that Joe had come up while we were talking, a long silk-wrapped pole in his arms. I'd seen it before, hanging over the thrones at High Court. She took it and set the butt in the ground by her feet. "I need my helm, and a horse."

"Not a horse." The deep voice of the Huntsman made me startle and my hand go to the butt of my gun without conscious thought.

Behind him, a black shape loomed. As it walked closer, I could make out details. It was being led by one of the Hunt, a faceless knight in matte black armor. How they could walk noiselessly wearing that heavy plate was beyond me, magic was the only conceivable way. But the beast he led... was also armored. I could hear a clank as it swung its head from side to side, glaring with red eyes. It snorted and lowered the horned head at the Huntsman, who gave it an affectionate buffet on the nose.

"Your rider. Take care of her." He ordered it.

I choked. "You... you..."

Bella laughed. "It's magnificent." She walked forward and patted it on the nose as well, and it dipped the massive horn which grew from its forehead and nudged her with its nose, gently enough to not even move her. I spluttered. "I shall call him Brutus."

I found my voice. "You will not!"

She looked at me. "Can you think of a better name?"

"You are not riding a rhinoceros into battle!" I didn't like the way the black beast was looking at me. Or at her. Only... She patted its nose and walked to one side of it, and it awkwardly buckled a knee. She looked at the harness for a moment, then grabbed straps and swarmed up the side of it with the device that looked like a rope ladder hanging from the saddle. Setting into the high-cantled seat, she looked down at me.

"I love you, but I must." Her voice was soft, and almost sad.

I stepped back and she picked up the reins. Be damned if it wasn't a good idea. Who the hell was going to stand before a charging armored rhino? She looked at the Huntsman and nodded.

He looked at me. Or so I assume, since he turned his helmeted face in my direction. "We ride with her. I cannot promise no harm will come, but it must pass through the hunt first."

I sighed. "I suppose I owe you thanks."

He laughed, a gravelly sound. "I shall collect after it is done."

"Where is Raven?" I wasn't really asking her, just letting her know what I was doing when I tipped my head back and looked skyward. High above us, I could make out the dark silhouette of the spirit. He would be looking for the Wendigo now that we'd delivered the crown to Bella.

"Bella, where is Beaker?" This time I really did need to know.

"I set him to guard the children. He is wrapped around the garden along with what I think must be all of the wood elf women." I could see her smile. Ash trotted up with a simple silver helm.

"Here." He stepped back quickly as the rhino bared a mouthful of seriously carnivorous-looking teeth at him. "Um..."

I took it from him, thwacked Brutus on the snout, and stepped up onto the ladder thing. Bella took the helmet. "Pull this thing up, so attackers can't board you." I told her, and pulled one hand to me. "Come back to me, princess." I kissed her hand and jumped down, turning my back on her and feeling my throat contract painfully.

"Ash. I need a horse."

"Got one already, boss." He was smiling at me, and I suppressed a growl. Everyone thought it was cute I'd gone all mushy.

"Which direction to the kitsune?" I asked, stepping up into the saddle of the solidly built chestnut he'd beckoned forward. The groom handed me the reins.

Ash pointed down the hill and toward the field of battle. "I sent them to left flank."

I'd start with them, then, and work my way across the field. I could hear the drums, now, and the light was more golden than pink as the sun rose. Across the valley, a sudden howl of raw voices screaming and skirl of trumpets told me that action was imminent.

"Let's get to it, then." I kicked the horse and he broke into a startled trot, and as I got out of camp, a canter.

Chapter 36

The Fog of War

Even with magic, there is no way one mere mortal can see the whole field of battle at once. Magical messages might fly faster than any messenger from one end to another, but the ability to micro-manage was something that had been strongly discouraged from before I could remember in High Court army doctrine. That led to defeat in detail, I'd been taught, and from what I had seen in two centuries of human combat Above, no truer words had ever been spoken.

I didn't know about Low, but the High army was given directions, and initiative. The commanders of each part of the field further delegated downward, until each unit was not a rigid gear existing only as part of a machine, but an autonomous tool that could be wielded by itself.

I realized that my nerves were coming out in absurd metaphors, and dragged my focus back to the other side of the river, which I could see across the clear field. The kitsune were supposed to be in this area, but I didn't see them yet. There was a thick patch of willows that stretched all the way up to the river bank.

My horse shied as a big red fox popped out of the willow thicket. With four magnificent plumy tails, he was likely one of the men in charge. I pulled the horse to a halt.

"Hai." I greeted him. "How goes it?"

"Well, milord." I decided not to correct him. Duke or no dukedom, I was woefully unqualified to be in charge of anything, much less appointed a general on the field. But this much I did know. That would wait until later, right now they needed to have a figurehead. If she wanted me to play mascot, I'd take it to the hilt.

He was wearing samurai armor, sans the helmet at the moment, although I suspected it was in that tangle of brush. "Your plan?" I asked. Not much I could do about it now, but I was curious.

He bowed slightly. "The plan is to draw the enemy as they ford the river, in what will look like a rout, and then..." He bared his long teeth. "We hamstring them."

Guerilla warfare, use the countryside against the enemy. I don't know why I had worried, the people of the islands had been perfecting that for some time now. I bowed slightly in return from my horse-borne vantage point. "May your knives always find tendon."

He laughed, and I turned the horse away, wondering if I would see him again. I'd known, in the past, men who had died under my command. But that was the key. I had known them. I had known they were warriors, who met the end with valor and purpose. But today, I didn't even know the big kitsune's name, much less that of his men. I was sending them to die wholesale, and it hurt.

Across the river, I could see a force of mounted men riding toward the ford. I watched them come, feeling the force of their charge even though I was too far away to hear them. I reached into the nospace and pulled out a pair of binoculars. Now, I could see them more clearly, from the armored fairy man in the lead, with his sword held out in a classic charge! Gesture, to the men behind him with open mouths, screaming something as they leaned into their horse's necks and hit the river in a spray of foam and hooves.

I felt detached, analyzing the charge as being an act of sheer foolhardiness. Unless... even if they had scouted the ford, hitting it at a gallop was a good way to get someone killed even before contact with the enemy. I scanned the group, and saw that, yes, one was down. The horse he'd been riding was kicking wildly, straining to get up again, but the man was gone, out of sight entirely. I let out a huff of breath, and slung the binoculars. The charge was already losing steam, and from a tightly grouped force, it was down to a line of straggling horses that could easily be flanked.

As I rode in their general direction, I could see that indeed, they were being attacked by my men. Bella's men. Whoever they were, they rode smaller, lighter horses, and nimbly swung out of a creekbed where they had been lying in wait, with short bows firing almost as soon as they crested the bank.

I couldn't tell from here how well they were aiming, and likely it didn't matter. It wasn't about hitting the men, after all, but the horses. One screamed so loudly I could actually hear it, and I saw one rear wildly, throwing and trampling his rider. Might have been the same horse, but I doubted it. The arrows had the effect of a thrown wasp's nest as horses bolted in all directions to escape the stings.

The last battle of this magnitude Underhill had taken place when I was a child. Armies were not kept standing, here, unlike the human realms where I had taken part in battles from India to America and in jungles and deserts few had heard of down here in my home. Here, armies were raised by lords who ruled over fiefdoms which owed allegiance to a king. The king's responsibility, as Trytion seemed to see it, was to avoid war at all costs, but to pressure those lords and ladies to keep their musters ready for when the call came.

I'd never trained with a muster. Magic was used in place of guns, Underhill, and I was pretty useless with magic. I was, however, good with a gun due to my human training. I lacked the patience to become a sniper. I had, however, practiced with a rifle... I dismounted on the hill overlooking the ford. I'd practiced daily until recently, but firearm handling is a friable skill. It goes away if you don't use it.

I pulled the rifle out of nospace. I'd left the Sharps .50 cal out of the way and got the hunting rifle. I was hunting officers with the Lee-Enfield 303 Snoxall had taught me to shoot. The Sergeant Instructor had been a machine, and I couldn't possibly reach his rate of 38 rounds downrange in a minute. I really ought to get a Barrett, but a century of practice made this the most comfortable choice for me at the moment. As I lay on the grass, feeling the prickle of briars through my shirt, and the smooth wood of the stock on my cheek, I took a slow breath, let it out, and squeezed.

Far below, the idiot with the sword fell out of his saddle. His horse squealed and bucked, I could hear the sounds faintly. Fae can shield magically against bullets, sure, but they need to know what's coming, and it takes too much energy to run a shield all the time, as my wife had discovered trying to protect her whole team from ogres. Which reminded me, as I took another shot, this one missing, to keep an eye out for ogres. They were why I'd packed the Sharps.

I fired again. Two shots more, and I would scoot to a different place. A strong magic user could possibly reach me with fireballs up here, but when they shielded and got scared, I would have achieved my goal. Draining their energy would leave them vulnerable. I missed again, and forced myself to take slow breaths and focus. The fourth and fifth shots both hit, but I didn't pay too much attention. It was time to go.

The chestnut looked peevish about being taken from his chance to graze a little, but let me get back onboard and urge him down the hill toward the light cavalry that was regrouping after their successful attack. I rode up and sketched a salute to the man in charge, who I recognized.

"Waters." I greeted him. "Looked good down there. I didn't realize we had mounted bowmen."

He pulled off his helmet, revealing a red, sweating face and smiling blue eyes over a thick brown beard. "Aren't they just the thing? And where did you come from?"

I jerked a thumb over my shoulder at the hill I'd just left. "Had a vantage point, decided I'd wait until you had them on the run before coming down."

We both looked toward the river, where the last of the enemy heavy cavalry was riding through the water, harried along by a unit of his riders. He grunted. "You were doing a little covering fire, weren't you?"

"Richard, would I do such a thing?" I grinned at him and he flashed me a smile, before his brows drew together.

"Dammit! That boy is a bit too enthusiastic. Jonny!" He bellowed at the rider who'd just gone into the river. "LaForce, you get your tail back here before I come pull your ears off!"

The last part of that was muffled by his shoving the helmet back on and reining his horse in the general direction of his errant troop. Shaking my head, I rode on.

A double troop of heavy cavalry was coming toward me, the ground shaking as they rode in well-drilled unison. They weren't even at a full speed and I was intimidated. I turned the chestnut and rode to the side, letting them pass. I tossed a salute at Lord Roberts, who peeled off and rode up alongside me.

He boomed in his resonant voice that had earned him the nickname of Speaker, and which I'd always thought he enhanced with more than a touch of magic. "Mulvaney, m'boy, didn't expect to see you. Last I heard you were off doing secret squirrel things."

"Got back just in time for this, the Queen asked me to rally the troops. But it looks like your boys are champing at the bit, don't need me."

He guffawed. "Been an age since I rode into battle." He squinted at me. His helmet hung from the other side of his saddle, and he'd put it on at the last minute. It was not designed for optimal visibility. "Matter of fact, last time your Da rode with me."

I didn't want to detour down memory lane. "I take it your men are the drawing force?"

He nodded and pointed. "I have Taylor and Saults riding point for me. 'Fraid I'm too old for that any longer."

I shook my head. "You're not old, Speaker, just canny enough to let the young'uns get blooded first."

He laughed again. A happy warrior. I sketched a final salute and watched him ride back into formation. Behind the cavalry, I glimpsed a head pop up over the creek bank and back down again, like a gopher. Hand on my pistol, I walked the chestnut over toward the brush-lined creek, and looked down on a unit of infantry.

"Hello, boys." I dismounted and made like I was checking the chestnut's hoof for a stone, so I wouldn't give their position away. "You must be backup to the kitsune."

"Yep." The nut-brown face of a pixie split into a broad smile. "Pleased to see you so careful an'all, my Lord."

"Your name, man?" I didn't recognize him, although he seemed to know me. The horse decided that leaning on me was restful, and I grunted, shoving his weight back and dropping the hoof. This would be a short conversation.

He tugged his forelock. "I'm Harlan, sir. Thankee."

"Happy Hunting." I remounted the horse, and he vanished back into the brush. They'd set a clever ambush, but time would tell if the enemy would rise to the bait. I looked across the river at the gathering crowd. It looked like they would. There was no rhyme or reason I could see from here to the mob that was grouping on the river bank. Then it split, and Dionaea rode through them to the water's edge, mounted on a solid black horse. It didn't want to step into the water, dancing sideways a few steps while the flagbearer almost came to grief getting out of her way.

I kept going. I knew that behind the creek, I would find the archers, and this would be where Ash and Olive were. Ash could no longer pull a bow, but his brother could, and Ash would have been assigned to shout orders, I was sure. The wood elves were not a wasteful race, and there were few enough of them. Which is why I'd sent the broken child to Ellie. Unlike the fairy drab in the kitchen, the wood elf girl was not born in that stone castle. I just hoped her tree could be found and some healing come to her in time. I bore no illusions about her ever returning to anything resembling normalcy. Scars linger.

I splashed across the creek, letting the chestnut take a drink. Behind me, I could hear a shrill shouting, which I presumed was Dionaea addressing her troops. I still hadn't glimpsed the Wendigo, not that I wanted to, and Raven... I tipped my head back, shielding my eyes from the sun. It was getting to be late morning. I hadn't realized how long I'd been working across the field. Raven wasn't in sight.

Beyond the creek, where the slow rise of land toward the mountains began, Ash was waiting for me.

"Lom."

"All's well?" I asked him, looking around. The archers were arrayed both on the ground and in tree stands. I'd only seen them a few times before, and looked curiously up at them. The forest swept up the side of the mountain, and we wouldn't be fighting in it, today, not all these men. But the elves had simple rigs which gave them a nice advantage over the field below. As I watched, one swarmed up a tree with a climbing belt, a small hatchet quickly removing any little limbs, and then with another broad belt, he got the stand set up, spikes sinking into the bark below the support, and keeping it stable.

"Doesn't that make them a target?" I asked Ash. I knew that the other side would have at the very least, mages capable of tossing fireballs.

"We keep a reserve of shield-maidens," He pointed. "Jonna, Vanessa, and Cyn." He'd raised his voice a little, and the three elves all raised a hand in what looked like a sort of salute. I saluted them gravely in return. Fairy women almost never go to battle. Children are too rare and precious among us to risk their mothers or potential mothers. Bella and Dionaea might be the only females of fairy on the field today.

"They protect the tree, and the archer in it."

I nodded. "You ok? You didn't answer me."

He pulled a face. "Nervous. You know how it is."

I did. My stomach felt like lead. Behind me, the noise of the gathering army was muted, but I never stopped listening to it. It seemed to be building to a crescendo. Ash looked toward it. I could see the look on his face, so I twisted around in the saddle.

Chapter 37

Queen's Gambit

B ehind me, they were coming across the river. Not charging, this time, but in a relatively quiet and slow fashion. The storm of screaming and shouting was dying down, and Dionaea stood her horse at water's edge, the silk of her flag snapping in the breeze above her head. It was the calm before the storm, and the fighting would come in a few moments. Time for me to move on and finish my task.

I rode slowly along the treeline, greeting elves as I went. I knew many of them, having spent much time with the shy people over the years. I reined the horse in as the treeline followed the curve of the creek upward. There was someone I recognized walking across the creek on a rough-split log bridge.

"John?" I called out. He looked up and nodded.

"John Farmer, why are you here?"

He got up the bank in three easy steps, no mean feat as it was steep, and he had both his arms spread out and draped casually over the thick oaken staff he carried across his shoulders. Now he unlimbered it and stuck the butt into the soft ground, leaning on it. Everything the big pixie did was lazy, deceptively so.

"Wa-all..." He began slowly, squinting off toward the river. "They tole me t'ere was a fight."

"You haven't got a sword, or armor?" I felt the familiar exasperation in dealing with him. I'd seen him kill an ox with that stick, and I had reason to believe that like Alger's staff, it wasn't just wood. Still, this was a battle. I was sending enough trained men into die, no need to do it recklessly.

"No more have you." He pointed out, a little twinkle in his eye.

"I'm not going to the front lines." I said, turning to look over my shoulder.

The heavy cavalry was beginning their charge. Dionaea was still on the other side of the river, but her troops had created a beachhead and were bracing long polearms, or pikes, hard to tell from here, against the onrush of horses and men.

"No. You aren't. Better get on, lad."

He continued to walk toward the wood elves, and I kicked the reluctant gelding forward and down the bank. He seemed to want to try the bridge, which wasn't going to hold him, and I had to argue with him to get him into the water and up the other side. I could hear the fighting behind me, and it wasn't easy to keep heading in this direction.

On the other side, I saw Bella and the Hunt in a column, riding toward the river. I kicked the chestnut into a canter, and we intercepted them. The chestnut really didn't like Brutus, but I kept my movements firm and confident. The nervous horse settled down as he took his cue from me. I only wished I could do that to myself.

"Bella," I said, then stopped. I didn't know what to say.

She leaned over and took my hand in hers. "I will see you tonight."

I nodded, and reined the horse back out of the column. The Hunt would protect her. I watched them riding, wondering who they had been, before they became the creatures in armor, mute, seemingly senseless.

I trusted them not to be human, but to be inhumanly violent on her behalf. And I still had another stop to make. There was another ridge here, like the one the hospital tent was atop. Only this one was rocky, with jagged boulders and no cover from the sun high overhead.

I had already figured out there was a waterskin and food in the saddlebags the horse had come to me with. Which was appreciated even if I did have the supplies in nospace. It was going to be a warm day. I knew where the unit was, even hidden as they were, because I could feel them.

Not any weirdness there, just the vibrations of rounds going out over my head. It wasn't artillery in any way a human could have set up, but still, he might have recognized the cannons for what they were. Simply put, we'd discovered that two or three spells, packaged together like a mad Roman candle, made an effective delivery system. One for propellant, another for explosive, and sometimes, one for effect. I swung down off the horse and slapped Guptill on the shoulder. The crusty artilleryman was one of the rare fairy who had ventured Above, and when he returned, brought this concept with him.

"Hitting what you aim at?" I asked.

He grunted, squinting through a long spyglass. I'd offer him my binoculars, but I knew better. He liked it his way. I squatted next to him and used the modern glasses myself, following his vector to see the next target.

"Ogres. How charming of her." I said.

He chuckled at this, shutting his long glass. "They do make a nice splat, though. Wait and see."

I kept watching the milling group, counting four still on their feet, and what looked like two more on the ground. There were enough pieces it was hard to tell. Maybe three. Over my head, I felt the concussion of the shockwave as the spell arced over the battlefield.

There was a long moment of nothing, during which the ogres got themselves oriented and headed toward the river, since they were still on the wrong side of it. Guptill had adjusted for that, though. I'd only seen him in action a few times, but as always, it was impressive. Through the glass, I could see the ogres suddenly flinch in unison and look up.

"Put a whistler in. Doesn't..."

The ogres disappeared in a puff of dirt and blood. He kept murmuring in my ear. "Give 'em time to run. But by god, they know they've been hit."

One ogre emerged from the smoking crater, running in the wrong direction. I turned my glasses toward the beachhead the Low army had established, and saw that the heavy cavalry had hit it, caving in one side, but the bulge was extending toward the kitsune's hide, now, and a troop of the cav was trotting slowly in that direction with a horde on their tail.

"Seen Dean?" I dropped the glasses, not wanting to start looking too closely at the dead, dying, and wounded on the field. Speaker was either still roaring, or not. Nothing I could do about it right now.

"His rangers are all in the woods. Herself was worried about goblins."

He rolled his shoulders and neck. Nerves. I felt them myself. We might not be anywhere near the field, but there were still ways magic could reach out and hammer us.

"She should be. Nasty little bastards."

He'd been with me on a mission to cleanse a village of them, when they invaded and started eating children for snacks, the local cats and dogs having been their appetizers. That was one of the times I'd seen him in action. He might be a sadistic sick bastard, but he was my sadist.

"Keep an eye out for the Wendigo." I told him. "You won't be able to kill it, but might disorient it."

He nodded and took a long pull of his waterskin. Another spell soared overhead, his men were firing for effect now. I walked back to the horse.

I'd about run out of people to talk to, I figured. Time to see if I could wreak a little havoc on the field. The chestnut was reluctant to go back down there. Not a warhorse, him, just somebody's riding hack, and not a dumb one at that.

There was a lot more noise than there had been in the morning. Screaming, explosions as spells were detonated en masse, and the clash of metal on metal when the armies closed to hitting distance. I had scouted a fold in the land earlier that gave me a vantage point, and I headed there now. A copse of trees gave the horse some shelter and kept my location less visible, and then I climbed up the side of the bluff to see what I could see.

Bella and Brutus were easy to spot. It was like a tank in the middle of the field, with the Hunt forming a long black lance in front of them. With the glasses, I could see that she was holding the flag aloft, the butt of its pole securely in the socket that was built into her saddle. With her free hand, she held her pistol, and every so often would extend her arm and fire. I wondered how she would reload, until I saw her do it. The magazine went into her lap, there was a strap to hold the flag to her for a split moment, and a fresh one in... when she ran out of ammo, she'd go to magic, I knew. She wasn't being swarmed with the enemy, because the Hunt was fighting like a machine, and a windrow of bodies lay in their wake.

I could see what she was doing. Driving across the field toward Dionaea not only let her confront the Blood Queen, it split the enemy forces. The bulk was effectively being driven toward the kitsune, who I couldn't see. The land wasn't entirely flat, and the willows were good cover. I refocused on Bella.

She was being good, not outpacing her escort, and still moving slowly toward the river. Dionaea, on the other side, was spurring her horse, I could see it tossing its head and balking at the water. She'd picked it for looks, not training, I guessed. Finally, the horse splashed into the water and bolted for the other side. I had a flash of amusement at the thought of it snapping a leg and dumping Dionaea ignominiously into the water. It didn't happen, though, and she reached the other side, her escorts right behind her.

Bella reached her a moment later, and I could see her throw a spell. Dionaea's shields sparkled, momentarily visible to the naked eye. She threw a ball of fire at Bella, but it splashed and arced around the shield Bella was holding around not only herself, but Brutus. Then the two women, having gauged their enemy's defenses, began to throw everything at one another. I closed my eyes. A mage battle isn't much to see, not with the eyeballs. But with the Sight, I could see both of them, the spells, and most importantly... the thick cords of energy both women were drawing on to fuel their battle. I opened my eyes. The Hunt had pulled back and formed a pocket around Bella and Dionaea, excluding minor fighters from the Queen's own battle.

I bubbled and traveled as close as I could to Brutus, who swung his head irritably and snapped at me. I punched him in the snout, hard, splitting my knuckles, and he snorted, settling down. I added power to Bella's shields.

She didn't look at me, focused on Dionaea, but she shouted. "Why the hell are you here? You don't have armor!"

"I don't need it. Bell, she's connected to the Wendigo."

I gauged the distance and with a micro-bubble spell, managed a leap up onto Brutus' back. I stood on the saddle pad, over Bella, and added my power to hers. We threw a lance of pure energy, crackling purple in the light of the sun, at Dionaea, who leaped off her horse as the bolt hit it. The big black stallion died with a scream. I hated to do it to a poor dumb brute, but I needed her dismounted and off balance.

I knew from prior encounters that we could anger her past the point of reason. Right now, her face was twisted into a silent scream as she brought both her hands together, coalescing a ball of... something. I couldn't make it out yet. I braced, one hand on Bella's shoulder. Under us, Brutus stood like a rock.

Dionaea lifted her hands, slowly, like she was handling a great weight. I could see the roil of iridescent energy between her palms, and her head tipped back, looking at the spell. The cords of her neck muscles stood out, and Bella threw a familiar spell, the excavation spell she'd caused so much havoc with, before.

Her spell hit and dirt sprayed everywhere. Dionaea looked full at us, her teeth bared, her hair flying out as energy infused her, and I could see the forward motion beginning as she hurled her spell.

It spun off her hands and high into the air, in an arc that would not come near us. Below it, her body slumped to the ground, her head a bloody ruin. Overhead, the spell detonated. The shockwave almost knocked me off Brutus, and I dropped to my knees, holding Bella and the saddle while the waves rolled over us. She'd intended to breach our shield, and she might have, if someone hadn't shot her.

The man with the gun was standing in the middle of the river. I squinted, and saw through his glamour.

"Devon!"

I'd had no idea my nephew was on the field, much less how he'd sneaked behind enemy lines with one of my rifles. He waded toward us, his glamour fading as the Hunt opened ranks to let him through. I jumped off Brutus and went to greet him. Bella waved me on, looking pale and exhausted. She'd taken the brunt of Dionaea's attack.

Devon paused as he reached the Blood Queen's body. He looked down at it, his face a mask of pain. Then he viciously kicked it. "That's for screwing with a Mulvaney, you bitch."

"Devon," I started to say, but Bella's voice cut through the air and got both of us looking at her. She was standing in her stirrups, pointing.

"Lom!" She sat back down and kicked Brutus into forward motion. "She loosed the Wendigo!"

I took a flying leap, assisted a little with Magic, and got back on the tank-like rhino, who was beginning to charge. I hung on to Bella's waist again, looking over her shoulder.

"Call Raven!" I shouted in her ear, over the heavy thudding of Brutus's tough feet. Then there was a mighty splash as he hit the river. "He's our only hope to stop that thing."

Behind me, I heard the crack of Devon's rifle. The boy was attempting it, and he was a pretty good shot, as I saw the impact of the bullet against the thing's chest. It... rippled. There was a neat hole, but no blood, and although it swung its skull-like face from side to side, it didn't even stagger. The rack of antlers it carried spanned probably ten feet, and it was tall enough to tower over the troll it casually knocked down with a backhanded blow as it tried to pass the Wendigo.

I was peripherally aware that Dionaea's army was fleeing like water thrown on a hot griddle. Evaporating was an apt metaphor for what was happening in the wake of her death. They all knew, it seemed, what the consequences of the Wendigo's unleashing meant for them.

The Wendigo shambled forward in the sunlight, casually walking toward us. Great, liquid black eyes deep set into the animal-skull face weren't looking at us, as we reached the other side of the river, but downward at a trio of goblins that was trying to run past it on the beaten grass road the army had been using all morning. One impossibly long arm tipped in three talons reached out and took one of the goblins, screaming wildly, off the ground.

With a vicious jab, the Wendigo either bit it, or pecked it. Hard to tell from here. Then it set the goblin back down, almost gently. The wendigo kept walking, and behind it, I saw the rest of the tragedy play out. The other goblins had frozen in place when their comrade was snatched, but now one blurred into action, slashing the bitten one's throat. Then he fell to his knees, clutching the body and keening. They knew what would happen, and had given him grace. I swallowed, hard.

If Bella were infected...

Chapter 38

Ripped Asunder

There's a peculiar feeling in focusing on one thing, one moment, so hard the rest of the world falls into silence around you. I found myself gripping Bella's shoulder hard enough it had to have hurt her, but she didn't say anything. Brutus, under us, shifted his weight nervously, as the three of us stood our ground in the middle of the freshly-beaten road to the river ford.

The Wendigo made no noise as he paced forward, his head lowered slightly, arms dangling. Under us, Brutus shuffled sideways a couple of steps.

"Easy, easy boy." Bella leaned forward and patted his neck, sticking her fingers through a joint in his armor to scratch his hide. He settled.

"What's next?" She asked me, not turning her head.

I looked up. Far above was a bot in the clear blue that might be Raven.

"We delay it. Ever played at jousting?"

The two of our lives, versus a world, and most importantly, our babes. We'd spend ours, if necessary. I knew this without having to ask her.

"With the flagpole?"

"And some magic." I told her my plan.

"What about Brutus?" She had already pulled the pole out of the socket and lowered it so I could reach the top, which I was now modifying.

I snorted at her, swaying as Brutus pawed the ground and dipped his head. "Let him have free rein and see what happens. They don't call them the world's angriest animals for no reason."

"I have no prior experience with them, and Brutus has been a lamb." I could hear the smile in her voice as she scratched him again. My heart skipped a beat. This was my woman, making a joke in the face of death. I was a lucky man, even if it hadn't been enough.

"Ready." I slipped the flagpole back into the socket and helped steady it as she tilted the whole thing forward. The gilded sky-blue banner now hung almost to the ground, flapping slightly away from Brutus in the light breeze.

Bella dropped the reins, and kicked Brutus hard in his ribs. I held onto the saddle with one hand and the pole with the other.

"Gittem!" Bella shrieked.

Brutus snorted, pawed, and lunged. I reflected in the microsecond as the propulsion hit me that I was trusting whoever had designed the saddle, and whoever had strapped it on that day, an awful lot. But I didn't have time to think about more than that, as the Wendigo looked at us in astonishment, and then crouched with outstretched arms and open mouth.

The flagpole hit it first, in the side of its chest, below the ribcage, and threw it to one side as both Bella and I lost our grips on the pole. It was heavier than the gaunt appearance would suggest. The pole had hit the bloated belly that protruded below the prominent ribs, and even though it wasn't sharp, it pushed through and out the back, the blue silk spoiled forever with black blood and guts that gushed out of the hole. I turned my head to see the monster lying on the side of the road, thrashing.

Brutus's charge carried him quite a ways before he spun in a surprisingly agile move to face back toward the prone Wendigo. I was hanging on with both hands, and pondering using a bubble to keep on-board at this point.

Brutus did a little dance, like he was thinking about going back and trampling the downed enemy. Having seen a rhino in action, I could easily picture that, and was not at all opposed to the idea. But as we watched, the Wendigo stopped flailing arms and legs, and slowly stood up again, one arm pressed to its side where the pole still jutted from his side.

Bella made an exasperated noise. "What is it..."

The spell I'd stuck to the pole went off, finally. I'd begun to wonder if Wendigo gore had disabled it. In a whoosh of flame and sparks, the whole monster was engulfed in an inferno. Above, I'd watched enough modern entertainment to learn that the idea was an explosive was always exothermic and kinetic. That is, a big baddaboom.

The reality I'd learned working with modern explosives, was a lot quieter but far more targeted. On the Wendigo, what I'd done was pair a plastic explosive with a conflagration spell. I had not secured it to the tip, foreseeing the results of a through-and-through. However, I wasn't sure if it had gone off in the monster, or just near it. Wasn't sure it really mattered.

The fireball contracted, and the monster, blackened and smoking, staggered out of it. Shedding charred bits and sparks, he headed straight for us.

"Oh, crap." My lovely bride said as Brutus lowered his head for another charge.

Riding a charging rhino doesn't get any easier after the first time. I clung onto the saddle like a demented monkey again, and this time Bella screamed as we seemed to be on a collision course with a demon soaked in hellfire.

I had forgotten about Raven, in the rush of trying to hit the Wendigo and knock it down. So when he arrived in a screaming dive-bomb and explosion of black feathers as he hit the Wendigo, I lost my grip and fell off the rhino.

I hit the ground hard and rolled, wrapped in a shield I'd managed in midair, but it still knocked the breath out of me. I lay there gasping for a second before I realized the thudding was Brutus thundering down on the fighting spirits rather than my heartbeat.

As I looked up, pushing myself off the ground, I saw him hit them. Raven had his talons sunk into the Wendigo's face, or what was left of it, and Brutus knocked them both apart. Bella was shouting something, probably trying to get him to stop, but the rhino had his mad on, and he wasn't a quitter.

Armored as he was, the big animal had to weigh over three tons. Even an immortal like the Wendigo must feel that when it hits them. Raven had just turned in midair on a wingtip and joined Brutus in the assault on the staggering, flaming spirit. With a terrible scream, it slashed out at them with hooked talons, and as I was running toward the fight – never said I was smart, did I? – I saw it begin to grow in size.

From cracks in the blackened carcase, fire erupted like lava oozing from the mountainside of a volcano, and Bella suddenly vanished from Brutus's back. Smart girl. The Wendigo's arm raked through the air where she had been a split second before. Raven spiraled up into the air, while Brutus hooked his horn into the Wendigo's thigh and ripped it open in a gout of fire.

Bella appeared next to me, pistol in hand.

"That won't work." I skidded to a stop, reaching into nospace for the Sharps.

"I know! But..."

Raven hit the Wendigo from above with all the force of a crashing jetliner. Both of them smashed to the ground, and the sparks from the demonic transformation flew upward.

"I don't know." I couldn't get a clean shot. Brutus was circling the combatants warily, eyeing the fire.

"Lom!" Bella squeaked.

I dropped the gun and started reaching for magic.

The Wendigo had torn Raven into shreds.

Feathers filled the air, and I could hear my wife screaming in rage and shooting her pistols dry. The sun seemed to have gone behind a cloud; it was abruptly very dark.

I had my hands full of coruscating fire, and was trying to see where the Wendigo had gone, so I could burn it from the face of the earth, when I heard the little voice.

"A gate." It rasped in my ear. "I need a gate."

I glanced sideways, and saw the tiny black bird clinging to my sleeve. It had bright gray eyes.

"Bella!" I roared. "I need you!"

It took me taking the three steps to her side and taking her arm to break through.

"We need to open a gate!" I pointed. "Look..."

The air was full of little black birds, then bigger ones. As we watched, they were coalescing back into ravens. Enough of them to block out the sunlight.

"A gate to..."

"Earth. Home..." The bird on my sleeve cawed. He was getting bigger, too.

"Uncle." Bella stroked his back with a finger.

"Quickly, girl. Get it done." The bird launched itself toward the mass of others that were gathering around something. I was sure it was the Wendigo, and I knew we only had a moment.

Building a gate is not an easy feat. Matching the fabric of the worlds is normally only possible in thin, or overlapping, places, depending on which theory you ascribe to. I grasped Bella's hands in mine, and felt our wills match. I'm not into woo-woo crap. Our minds didn't touch. But the magic... She's damn powerful. And she'd poured some of that through me, and made me bigger in the process, when it came to ability.

I lost track of the outside world again. We were creating something... it started as a ball drifting in the air between us, arcing energy through us, and as it slowly grew, I could have sworn we were floating. I held onto her hands, and felt her clinging in return.

All I could do was channel the energy through, to her. She was whispering under her breath, like she was reading aloud. Her hair floated around her face as I stared through the shimmering ball of energy at her eyes. She wasn't focused on me, but the unseen Library book, I was certain. The ball, sphere, whatever it was, grew beyond us. Encompassed us, and the tension was intolerable now. We couldn't hold onto it much longer, it was going... the energy started to shift, to wobble off-center.

"Raven!" I was shouting. Bella wasn't paying attention. "Raven, now! Now!

The world exploded. Pain rippled through me, followed by cold, and then there was nothing.

Nothing. Just my thoughts, and did I remember a ball of black birds flying through a rift in the sky? Had I seen that, or only wished for it? Where was I? What was I?

Bella.

Bella...

Fingers. So cold...

Chapter 39

At the End of All Things

In the rift between worlds there is nospace. When we pass through gates it's not a long distance. Between established gates, where the world's touch. I had no idea where Above was, from the point we started out Underhill. So in essence, what we had done was open two gates.

One was Underhill, which we saw at first as a ball of energy. It had snapped closed behind us. Or detonated, I really wasn't clear. One, the other, both? And then, we were locked into nospace. Sensory deprivation is the complete lack of any external stimulus, and in nospace, you can't even feel yourself. Nothing...

I don't know how long it took. Passing through a normal gate takes perhaps a few steps. It's relative, anyway, not real, although to be honest I'd never thought about it that much. People climb into planes every day without knowing what holds them up in the air, beyond a vague notion about Bernoulli.

You can lose your mind after extended exposure to sensory deprivation.

I woke up in a dark alley, with rain falling on my cheek. Or was that tears?

Sitting up was a process, I was dizzy, and not entirely sure I was sitting *up*. Felt like I was trying to dive deeper into the air. Fortunately, there was nothing left in my stomach. I wondered how long I had been vomiting. Maybe I should lie down again, at least until the head stopped spinning.

Bella.

I opened my eyes again. Oh. I'd had them closed.

That sucked. There was light out there and it hurt. I closed them again.

Bella was lying a few feet away, I could see her magic with the inner sight. It was burning brightly, and that was all I needed.

I crawled over and put a hand on her. Warm, breathing.

"Bella." I think I said it out loud. Speaking seemed to turn my hearing back on, and I could hear traffic somewhere nearby, and voices. "Bella!" I put urgency into my voice. We were in an alley Mother Titania only knew where, and Above is a very big world, and not a nice one.

She moaned. I shook her, and heard her gagging.

Bella sat up slowly, and I put my arms around her.

"Where are we?" She whispered.

"Above... Earth. I think."

The voices got closer, and I opened my eyes to look around. One standard alley flanked with concrete walls, check. Rain, not tears, falling on us out of a narrow slice of gray sky. A dull orange dumpster with Budget Dumpster stenciled on the side of it.

"Honey, I don't think we're in Oz anymore." I muttered.

She hiccupped and chuckled. "Ow."

"Can you stand?" I asked, trying myself. The dizziness seemed to be wearing off, at last. "There are people coming..."

"And lying on the ground is a bad idea." She agreed, making it to a kneeling position. Then her mouth made an 'o' and her hands flew to her head. "Lom!"

I picked up on what she was thinking. The crown was conspicuously, well, a crown. Not that fighting leathers and partial armor were any better. I might, sort of, be able to pass for normal, but she was going to stick out like a sore thumb.

So when they walked around the corner I was standing in front of her. She'd made it to her knees and was swaying, her face a greenish-pale. I whipped around to face them, and found myself staring up, up... up into a thick murder-hobo beard.

"Hey." He said, looking down at the two of us, the streetlight reflecting off his scalp. "Did you guys get mugged?"

His shorter companion pushed up his glasses. "Great cosplay. But are you ok?"

I weaved a little on my feet, confused at their reaction. I opened my mouth, but not a lot came out. It certainly wasn't words, but at least it wasn't bile.

"Better come with us." The big guy leaned down and offered Bella a hand. She was still wearing the crown, and he didn't even bat an eye. He lifted her to her feet, and led her toward the mouth of the alley.

"The hotel's not even a block away. What happened to you two? My name's Mike, and this isn't a good place to LARP, you know."

I didn't know what he was talking about, and the world was going 'round and round again. But the big guy was walking with my wife, and I wasn't going to lose sight of her, so I followed. He was saying something, and I only caught the tail of it.

"... ought to be armed, for defense."

Bella shifted her mail shirt and showed him the holster. Black kydex looked funny with the leathers, but he just nodded approvingly. "Don't show it off too easy, though."

She just shook her head, then staggered. He caught her elbow. "Hey! Easy there."

Mike caught up with them and took her other arm. "Seriously, you ok, Ma'am?" He looked doubtfully back at me. "This guy drug you or something?"

I blinked. Now, there was a thought.

"Both of us." I croaked. "that must have been it."

Bella looked over her shoulder, and then nodded, catching on. "We were in a bar and the muggles were teasing..."

"Ugh. Some people." Mike swiped a card against the door, and it beeped. He pushed it open. "Let's get you into your room."

"Don't have one yet..." I said, trying to play along and buy some time. "We just got in..."

Yeah, from another world. This was hi-freakin-larious.

"The hotel's probably full." The big guy helpfully pointed out. "We're only up because Mike here couldn't sleep, woke me up, and we went out for a scone."

"Wha?" Bella sounded as confused as I felt, but at least she was walking on her own.

"Did they take your wallets?" Mike asked, looking perky.

For a man who hasn't slept, he had way too much brain power. I pretended to put a hand in my pocket, and not make it look like I was up to my elbow in nospace. I brought it back out with the slim leather fold I carried for emergencies Above.

"I have mine."

"Let's see what the front desk has, then."

What they had was a cancellation, and they were more than happy to take my plastic, in the name of Jim McCoy. I had ID, too. They didn't ask Bella for any. She leaned on the counter after thanking our rescuers, looking like she might slide off onto the floor.

"We need food." I told the guy behind the counter, who didn't seem phased at our appearance, either. I was beginning to wonder just what dimension we'd slid into.

"Oh, sure, the pizza delivery 'round here works 24 hours when the comic con is in town." He assured me.

I looked at my watch. "I have no idea what time it is."

He laughed. "About 4 am. Fly in from another time zone?"

"Yeah." I took the card keys. "Thanks."

Supporting Bella now that I was a head shorter than she was took a bit of effort. It would almost have been easier to do a fireman's carry, but first of all, that might have gotten more than funny looks, given I'd already been accused of drugging her, and secondly, I didn't have the energy for it.

We were drained to a scary level. I was beyond caring by the time I picked up the phone in the room and asked the boy on the other end of the line to send up three of his largest pies. Bella had collapsed onto the bed, and I started tugging on her boots. We'd gotten both our foot-gear off when the knock on the door came. My hand on the butt of my gun, I slid the door open a crack.

"Pizza."

I opened it the rest of the way, offering him folded bills. He recoiled. "Don't you gamers ever wash? Damn, that's realistic gore you got there."

I bared my teeth at him and took the boxes. He split. I'd probably tipped him far too much, but again, didn't care. I turned around to see Bella sitting up on the bed, her hands cupped together.

"Look..." She held out her hands to me.

I looked down to see a wren-sized bird, glossy black, looking at me with gray eyes. "Raven?"

It cocked its head at me, but didn't say anything. I opened the pizza box, and it hopped into it.

"Hey!" I swatted, but it was pecking busily at the pepperoni and ignored me. "Oh, hell."

I lifted the piece it was standing on away from the rest of the pie, to the lid. "You keep that one. Don't eat it all, you'll pop."

Bella giggled around her mouthful. I shoved food in my mouth and chewed, eyes closed. Bliss. Warm, greasy heaven. I might try to eat until I popped, too. We did eat until we passed out in a pile of boxes. Not sure where the bird ended up.

We'd both been awake and under great stress for far too long. For some reason, my brain had ticked into 'hotel Above: safe' mode. Maybe it was the guys in the alley. I don't know. I do know we slept for hours. I woke up to Bella shaking me.

"What?" I sat up, then grabbed my head. I had such a headache. "Ow. Ow... Are you ok?"

She was looking clear-eyed, but pale. "Lom, where are we?"

"Um." I blinked. "Above? At a convention for comics?"

"I know that. But the gate... where did it open?"

"Er. Not sure. I mean, I think this is an American city. But otherwise?" I shrugged. "Is there coffee?"

She nodded. "It's horrible."

"I don't care. Ichor of the gods."

I stood up, and blinked in surprise as she collapsed into the chair with a wail. "Oh, Lom! Raven... and the babies!"

The little bird fluttered from its perch on the curtains into her hair.

"There's Raven." I pointed. "And we're going to go home as soon as I've had coffee."

She reached up and touched the tiny bird. Well, not so tiny. It seemed to have expanded with pizza. "Uncle?"

I got my coffee. She was right, it was really bad. Burnt. Still, it had caffeine, and together with motrin from my survival kit pulled from nospace, restored me to something more human.

"Most of Raven stayed in nospace." She looked up at me, her eyes brimming with tears. "That's what happened, isn't it?"

"I think so." I held out my hand, and the bird hopped over amiably. "At least, I think I saw that. Hard to tell, there at the end."

"Is.. is this enough?" She wiped her eyes and made a face. "I'm crusty."

"There is a bath." I pointed out. "And my darling, this will have to be enough. The Wendigo... couldn't be allowed to run loose."

She nodded. "I know, it's just..."

"You just lost your grandmother, too."

She nodded again, her chin wobbling.

"If you want to cry?" I offered. I was holding a bird in one hand, and a cup of hot coffee in the other, or I would already be holding her.

She shook her head again. "No, it's ok. I'm going to wash. I have clothes stashed, at least."

"Good. I'll go after you, then we can start figuring out how to get home."

She went into the bathroom and closed the door behind her. I lifted up the bird on my finger and looked into the gray eyes. "Women. Did you ever figure them out?"

The bird shook his head, and I sighed.

Figuring out just where we were wasn't difficult. I picked up the restaurant guide from next to the television. Which was handy, as I was hungry again. The room clock said the time was 05:00 which wasn't terribly helpful, as that could mean we'd slept for 12 hours, or for 24. I doubted that it had only been an hour. A phone call later, I knew it was early evening in Salt Lake City, and another large meal, with beverages, was on its way to us. I knew Bella was anxious for home and the children, but I knew we needed to eat and recuperate. I was still getting a spinny sensation when I walked around much at all.

I knocked on the bathroom door, which was oozing steam. "You ok in there?"

"Yeah..." She opened the door. In all her glory, the towel wrapped around her head. "Your turn." She was wearing an impish smile and nothing else.

"Um. There's more food coming. Plastic is on the table... but..."

Her eyes lit up. "Food!"

"Clothes." I said firmly. "Then food."

She was munching when I got out of the shower myself. "Sorry I didn't wait." Bella apologized through a mouthful. "And champagne?"

"Well, we never did have a traditional honeymoon."

She giggled. "We had a dragon, instead."

I sat down and snagged a plate. "And don't worry so much about the babies. Beaker and Ellie can hold off the apocalypse, if need be."

She nodded. "I know. And my milk is... uncomfortable, but I expressed in the shower, so I feel better now."

"Can you manage that magically?" I was curious. She shrugged.

"Am I going to need to? How long until we're home, anyway?"

"Well, the good news is, you can aim. We're in the US of A. The bad news is, it's Salt Lake City."

The bird, who'd been given his own saucer, bounced up and down with a faint chirp.

"Raven may have aimed, then." I frowned. "How are we going to travel with a bird? He's too little to fly on his own."

A tiny gray eye glared at me indignantly.

"Well, you are," I told him. "I feel responsible for you, so shuddup."

Bella giggled, sipping champagne. "He can pretend to be a hair ornament."

Now she got the dirty bird eye.

"We'll rent a car and drive. The Oregon coast gate is closest to here, I think, there's one in Cali but it's all the way down south."

"Sounds plausible." She sighed. "I never did learn enough about gates. I was doing that literally by the book, you know?"

I nodded. "I thought that's what you were doing. I was just trying to feed you enough power. Which is why we're both eating like we've been on a week's fast."

Her face sobered. "Who knows how long we were in transit, too. Lom..."

"We will get home. Do you want to try a bubble to the gate?"

She held out a hand, palm-up. A tiny flicker appeared, and then went out as she winced. "Ouch. No... No, there's not much left, and I don't want to wait to see how long it takes to recover."

"Done, then, I'll get a car." I stood up and stretched, feeling the various aches and pains the fight had left me with. I'd found some scratches and a cut on my temple while washing, nothing major. The magic shielding had kept me from the brunt of it, and I didn't see anything wrong with Bella other than the deep purple shadows under her eyes.

"After you eat." She pointed at my plate. I obeyed.

It took the better part of three days for us to drive to the familiar pull-out in Oregon. It wouldn't have taken more than two, except we were forced to stop and sleep for another full day to recover. The winding road was obscured with fog, but I knew right where I was going. Bella was already out of the car when I'd barely come to a stop, holding the backpack with the crown hidden in it. I looked at the keys, then tossed them onto the front seat. I'd picked up a burn phone and told the rental company where they could pick it up. They'd blustered at me, but I was in no mood to make long detours or walk for hours.

"Ready?" It was foggy, but we knew the way. Bella held my hand and smiled as we took the short hike up the hill. When we reached the gate, I closed my eyes and saw the familiar shimmer of magic in the arch of the doorway.

"Let's go home." We stepped into the gate, hand in hand.

Epilogue

We stepped out into the meadow where Bella had been horrified at her wings. It seemed like that had been a very long time ago. I let out a deep breath I didn't even know I'd been holding. The black bird, who'd doubled in size as we passed through to Underhill, flew up into the air, and we stood there for a moment, the sun on our faces, watching him.

"He'll recover." I told her. Perhaps myself. Losing Raven to the Wendigo would have seemed an uneven trade, if it hadn't saved two worlds.

"In time." She sighed and squeezed my hand. "Home."

I bubbled us, feeling the twinge at the magic use. It was going to take us some time to recover, too. We landed in the library. No one was in sight, but as usual, there were voices in the kitchen. Bella headed to the kitchen door, and as she got there, an unfamiliar young woman walked out with a baby in her arms, laughing as she bounced it.

Bella held out her hands. "Linnea!"

The young woman froze, her mouth open. "Ellie!" She shouted a second later. "David!"

People came running out of the kitchen, and someone down the stairs. Ellie was about the third person out of the kitchen, and my heart fell as I realized what had happened.

"Ellie?" Bella whispered, her hands falling to her sides. "Linnea? David?"

The young woman who was clutching the baby to her chest gasped. "I'm Linnea."

"No..." Bella looked at the silver hair crowning Ellie's head. "What? Lom..." I had her by then, and looked at the young man who was walking up. He looked so familiar, like a glimpse into a mirror, or perhaps a portal back in time.

"Father," He said, then held out his hand to Bella. "And you must be mother. Your pictures..."

Bella sagged into my arms. I caught her as she fainted, forewarned by her weakening knees. I looked up at my tall son, feeling like death warmed over.

"How long?" I asked. I lifted Bella and carried her toward the couch, with him hurrying alongside. "She'll be all right," I said, trying to reassure my son as much as myself. Linnea appeared with a blanket in her hands and covered her mother as I arranged her comfortably on the couch. "She's had a rough few days, and the fight damaged both of us..."

"The fight? Days?" Linnea echoed, a look of confusion on her face. She looked so much like her mother...

"It's been twenty-two years..." Ellie said, taking my shoulder in a gentle grip. "We thought you were dead."

The door opened, and I looked up to see Devon, his face a little more mature. It hadn't been that long, in Underhill time. He looked confused for a second, and then leaped forward with a joyful shout. "Uncle!"

Dorothy was right behind him. "Lom! Bella... Oh, how wonderful." She knelt next to the couch with me as Bella's eyes opened. "Bella..."

"Dorothy dear." Bella took her hand. "How..."

"I got here just about the time you two ripped a hole in the world." The pixie was still sweet-faced and happy, but there was something... She went on. "The stories say there was a mighty blast, and everyone in the valley was knocked to their feet. Some are deaf to this day. But when they got up, and started to look, there was no more trace of you two than a unicorn and a few feathers."

Unicorn? That would be Brutus, and the stories had no doubt put a little polish on the poor old fellow. Dorothy looked up at Devon.

"So we looked for you." He shrugged. "But I had been right there, and, well, it didn't look good."

I nodded. "What about Trytion?"

Devon nodded, "That's right, he was wounded right before the last bit, wasn't he? He's got a cane, but he's never been willing to declare her..."he looked down at Bella, who was listening intently, "Or you dead. So you are still the Queen."

Dorothy reached up and Linnea handed her the baby. "This is Bella."

The older Bella took the baby and cuddled it. Devon beamed proudly. "She's ours, and well..."

I blinked at them. Well, of course. Twenty-two years.

Bella was crying. "I missed you growing up..." She whispered. "I wasn't here for you..."

Linnea swooped over the arm of the couch and kissed her mother's hair. "You were doing what you needed to do. We have always known that you were saving the world when you died, and... and you didn't die!"

I took Bella's hand. "It is so a happy ending. Even if it's not the one we expected. We're home."

She sniffed. "Yes, we're home."

Read the rest of the series...

The East Witch

Also by Cedar Sanderson

Other Works by Cedar Sanderson

The Case of the Perambulating Hatrack

The Tanager Series:

Jade Star (a novella)

Tanager's Fledglings

WitchWard Series:

Snow In Her Eyes

Possum Creek Massacre

Children of Myth Duology:

Vulcan's Kittens

The God's Wolfling

Short Fiction:

Crow Moon: A Fantasy Collection

The Groundskeeper Tales

Raking Up the Dead

The Hoodoo that You Do

My Ghoul

Warp Resonance: A Science Fiction Collection

About the Author

Cedar Sanderson is an author, artist, and citizen scientist who makes her living as a technical writer. She is also the house designer for Raconteur Press, as well as running her own business, Sanderley Studios, which publishes her books. She has authored ten novels, countless shorter works, and edited several anthologies. She lives in a small town in Texas along with her long-suffering husband and a flame-point cat named Lightly Toasted Marshmallow.

You might also like...

Witchfinder by Sarah A. Hoyt

In Avalon, where the world runs on magic, the king of Britannia appoints a witchfinder to rescue unfortunates with magical power from lands where magic is a capital crime. Or he did. But after the royal princess was kidnapped from her cradle twenty years ago, all travel to other universes has been forbidden, and the position of witchfinder abolished. Seraphim Ainsling, Duke of Darkwater, son of the last witchfinder, breaks the edict. He can't simply let people die for lack of rescue. His stubborn compassion will bring him trouble and disgrace, turmoil and danger -- and maybe, just maybe, the greatest reward of all.

Nocturnal Origins by Amanda S. Green

Some things can never be forgotten, no matter how hard you try.
     Detective Sergeant Mackenzie Santos knows that bitter lesson all too well. The day she died changed her life and her perception of the

world forever. It doesn't matter that everyone, even her doctors, believe a miracle occurred when she awoke in the hospital morgue. Mac knows better. It hadn't been a miracle, at least not a holy one. As far as she's concerned, that's the day the dogs of Hell came for her.

Investigating one of the most horrendous murders in recent Dallas history, Mac also has to break in a new partner and deal with nosy reporters who follow her every move and who publish confidential details of the investigation without a qualm.

Complicating matters even more, Mac learns the truth about her family and herself, a truth that forces her to deal with the monster within, as well as those on the outside. But none of this matters as much as discovering the identity of the murderer before he can kill again.

www.ingramcontent.com/pod-product-compliance
Lightning Source LLC
Chambersburg PA
CBHW030636260626
47157CB00007B/2353